LINEAR SHIFT

Global Endeavor
PUBLISHING

LINEAR SHIFT

PAUL B KOHLER

Part 1 edited by Kyle Hooper and David Gatewood
Parts 2 & 3 edited by Kyle Hooper and Amy Maddox
Part 4 edited by Allison Krupp and Carol Davis
Interior & Cover design by Paul B. Kohler

Give feedback on the book at:
www.Paul-Kohler.net
Twitter: @PaulBKohler
Facebook: facebook.com/Paul.B.Kohler.Author

Printed in the United States of America

First Edition

Publisher's Cataloging-in-Publication Data

Kohler, Paul B.
   Linear shift / Paul B. Kohler.
      pages cm
   ISBN: 978-1-940740-06-5 (pbk.)
   1. Time travel—Fiction. 2. Espionage—Fiction. 3. World
War, 1939-1945—France—Fiction. 4. Man-woman
relationships—Fiction.   I. Title.
PS3611.O3674 L56 2015
813`.6—dc23
                                                    2015903060

For Cheryl

PART 1

CHAPTER 0

February 11th, 1942

Dr. Bernard Epson sat triumphantly in his studio laboratory, applying the final touches to his theory of time travel. It had been twelve grueling years since he'd first begun his groundbreaking project. Completion was near, and his tongue could taste the finality, like the tang of history itself. He leaned back in his worn leather chair, basking in his accomplishment, his eyes surveying the notes and scribblings placed on virtually every surface in his modest workshop.

Bernard dreaded his next exercise. With the majority of his progressive research documented in his journals, this final stage was troublesome but necessary. The creak of the front door redirected his attention to the man entering his lab.

"Professor? Good morning. Have you been here long?" asked his assistant as he closed the oil-starved door behind him.

"Wha? Oh yes. I, um... I haven't been home yet. Is it really morning?" he replied drearily, longing someday for a workspace with a window. He'd lost count of how many sleepless nights he had spent in his lab alone.

"Yes, Professor. It's just after seven." he paused as he crossed to his diminutive desk in the corner of the room. "You promised me that you wouldn't work yourself so hard. Have you eaten?"

"Um, yes. I had Miss Stewart bring me a *croque-monsieur*

before she left last night," lied the doctor. As the words escaped his mouth, he realized he was famished.

"Well, that's good, sir. Did you make any progress on the final equations?" he inquired with abundant interest.

"As a matter of fact, I resolved the final hurdle not fifteen minutes ago." Dr. Epson sprang from his chair, ignoring the protests from his fatigued muscles. "You see, if we replace this algorithm with..."

As Dr. Epson continued with his explanation, his assistant listened intently, masking his concerns. As a member of the Society, he, like his associates, prayed the professor would never unlock the secrets to time travel. The professor's successes were a complication that required subtle interference. Only half-listening to the doctor's commentary, his mind began to devise a way to sidetrack the man's progress. He needed to get the doctor out of the lab for a while, so that he could alter a few of the minute, yet critical calculations before they could be recorded.

"That's fantastic, Professor! You must be extremely proud of this monumental achievement." His compliment was genuine, but not entirely sincere. "I think what we need is a celebration. You've been here all night and must be exhausted. Why don't you go home and catch a quick nap? After you're rested, we can go out for a celebratory lunch. It'll be my treat—and afterward, we can begin the process of recording all of your data into the journals."

Bernard was tired and knew that if he began the tedious task of documenting the observations now, he would make mistakes. What his trusted assistant suggested was wise.

"All right. I accept your offer of celebration. Let's make it three and invite Miss Stewart." Dr. Epson hoped his affection for the attractive Miss Stewart would not canvas his face. She had been in his employ from the very beginning, and although they had worked together for years, he had never yet found the courage to act upon his feelings.

"I think that is a wonderful idea, Professor. I'll set everything up. You go and get some rest." He nearly shoved the doctor towards his coat.

"Yes, yes. I'll get some rest, but as soon as we're back from lunch, we'll get this recorded and begin staging the build. I want to test this device by mid-year!"

His assistant was staggered. "You want to what?" he stammered.

"I want to start testing the device within the next four months."

'But—but how can we do that without funding?"

"Oh come now, my boy. Do you think I haven't been dreaming of this day for years? I have more than enough money to build the first device, and I know that once it's complete, I'll be able to persuade someone to invest in the future. Or the past, as it were." He chuckled.

Dr. Bernard Epson's devious assistant was speechless. He'd have to act more swiftly than he'd anticipated in order to keep the doctor from moving the project to the next stage. With subterfuge on his mind, he smiled brightly. "Fantastic, sir! I can't wait to assist you in this historical undertaking!"

The doctor donned his topcoat and hat and bid his assistant a brief farewell. As he walked out the door, he began to eagerly ponder what his first time travel destination would be.

CHAPTER 1
Present day

The sign on the door read "NOTICE OF EVICTION"—it was unmistakable. Peter was at a loss for words, despite having known it was coming. He stood there, staring at the notice as if waiting for the words to mysteriously change before his eyes. They did not. Peter pulled the attached document from his entry door and read it thoroughly.

Disgusted, he folded the notice in half and unlocked the door before going inside, just like he had done thousands of times before. *This is my house, dammit! You'd think unemployed folks could get a break!* These thoughts flooded his mind as he mindlessly dropped his keys on the table in the foyer and walked into his study, ignoring the pile of mail on the floor.

The lights were out and the wooden shutters were closed tight. It was dark, just the way Peter liked it in his study. He crossed the room, clicked on his Tiffany-styled desk lamp and fell into his tufted leather chair. He was still holding the eviction notice and he read it once more for clarity. He *was* going to lose the house. He felt like he was losing everything. First his wife, two years ago, then his job a year ago, and now the house. Pretty shitty three-year run. It wasn't even the house itself that Peter felt so attached to, so much as the fact that it was the first purchase he'd made with Minnie after getting married. He believed they would grow old and die in this house. Peter closed his eyes, and wondered where it had all gone wrong. He thought he was a good husband. Hell, he *was* a good husband, but that didn't matter to the drunk driver that stole his wife. He thought he was a good employee. He was, but that didn't matter when the economy hit the skids and he was laid off. He knew he was responsible with his finances, but without a job, and without a secondary income, his savings could only go so far.

He leaned forward, scanned the papers strewn across his desk, and placed the eviction notice in the appropriate pile: delinquent. The unfortunate thing about the piles on his desk was that they were *all* delinquent bills, and the house payment being ninety days behind trumped them all. He was screwed, and he knew it.

Leaning back with his eyes closed, he thought back to the first time he'd walked into the 1940's-era French Eclectic, hand-in-hand with Minnie. It had been such an exciting time for them. Having married earlier that year, and then finding out that she was expecting their first child, they both realized that starting a family in a small, two-bedroom brownstone wasn't ideal. They made the decision to move out of the city and into the suburbs. Their broker found an old provincial in desperate need of repair. With a fixer-upper, there was a deal to be had, and Peter was right for the job. He had recently completed his first internship with a well-known architecture firm and was applying for his registration. His strong knack for design and construction made the remodel a perfect fit. He and Minnie had walked from room to room, imagining the potential each possessed. Every nook and cranny of the house seemed to have a story of its own, and they talked about all the future memories they could create.

The house was old and had a lot of character. The floorboards squeaked. The doors stuck. Several light switches did nothing that they knew of. It was perfect. They closed on the house some forty days later, and immediately started remodel work. Floor by floor, room by room, they stripped paint and sanded floors. Their plan was to get the baby's room done first, and then work from the far side of the house inward, so the noise would be far enough from Tori's room that they could work during nap times. Within eighteen months, they had finished the remodel. And with timing bordering on perfection, Minnie was then pregnant with their second child.

Peter forced the memories from his mind. He knew that dwelling on the past would make moving so much harder. Where did he go wrong? What karma had caused him to have such bad luck? He'd asked himself those questions every day since Minnie was killed by that drunken bastard. If she could have been just a few minutes early or late, she would still be there with him, and everything would be all right. But she wasn't. She was always on time, and time was not kind to Minnie.

Peter straightened himself in his chair and glanced at the clock. It was 2:45 on a Wednesday. He wiped the tears from his eyes and walked out of his study. He didn't want the kids to see him like that and they would be coming home from school shortly.

CHAPTER 2

Peter sat in the cluttered living room, patiently listening to his fifteen-year-old daughter explain the multitude of reasons why she should have her nose pierced.

"Please, Dad?" Tori begged. "All my friends have theirs pierced... Becca even got her tongue pierced!"

"Tori, I don't care how many of your friends have piercings, or what parts of their bodies are pierced. You're not getting it done. When you turn eighteen, you can put as many holes in your body as you want." Peter sighed. "Until then, no holes."

"What about my ears, Dad? *They* have holes!" Tori pulled the long black hair away from her face and thrust one ear toward her dad.

Peter looked up and winced ever so slightly. He could never get used to the idea that Tori had chosen to dye her beautiful, naturally blond hair a solid jet black.

"Ears are different, Tori, and you know it. We've talked about this before, and you know where I stand on all the 'body art' that goes on these days." Peter used his fingers to make air quotes when he said 'body art.' He had an affinity for air quotes. "I will not have a child of mine, who lives under my roof, have any of that crap."

Tori sat in silence and glared at her father. She knew now that she should have listened to Becca. Becca had told her that her dad would never agree to it, and that she should just get it done. "It's better to ask for forgiveness than permission," she'd said. "The worst that could happen is you get grounded. And after that, you'll have your nose pierced!" Becca's words had rattled inside her head all afternoon.

"Mom would have let me get it done," Tori blurted out after several moments of silence. The words were out of her mouth before she could pull them back. The look on her dad's face was indescribable. He still found it hard to even hear her name without breaking down.

"Well, mom is not here, and I'm done talking about this."

"Well, I'm not!" shouted Tori. She said it loudly enough that her brother Brett opened his bedroom door and peeked out, but nobody noticed. "I'm fifteen years old, Dad. I get my license in eight months. You keep telling me that I'll have so much responsibility then. Why not let this happen now?"

Peter glared at his daughter with that look that only a single father can muster, then walked into the kitchen. Tori didn't follow.

As Peter started making dinner, his mind replayed their argument. He wondered if he had been right to be so firm with Tori. He seemed to be asking that question of himself more and more lately. Ever since his Minnie had died, both of the kids had pulled away. And to a certain extent, he felt they resented him—simply because it wasn't him that had died in the car crash. Neither of them had come out and said it, but Peter could feel the truth by the way they both looked and reacted toward him.

After standing in front of an open fridge for far too long, he pushed the thoughts from his mind and returned to making dinner.

Conversation at the dinner table was practically nonexistent. Tori barely touched the spaghetti. She just sat in her chair, sulking and pushing her food from one side of her plate to the other.

Brett, on the other hand, had no problems eating. He

scarfed in silence, and as he neared the bottom of his plate, he just as silently stood to clear his place. Not a single word by either of them.

Peter was okay with the silence. As tense as he and Tori had been an hour earlier, he knew it was best for everyone to simmer down a bit.

CHAPTER 3

Peter guided his newly acquired minivan into the parent parking lot of Willow Canyon High School and found a vacant space in the second row. Turning off the engine, he reached over to the passenger seat and picked up the manila folder filled with the dealership documents. With teary eyes, he opened the folder and flipped through the sales forms for his trade-in. His Mercedes had been a conduit to his old life. It had been an anniversary gift. He knew that trading down to the 1995 Chevy Astro was the logical thing to do; it seemed to be the cheapest yet most reliable ride on the lot. And the residual cash would aid in finding a new home. The mortgage payments and late fees were far beyond this meager sum, but it should at least be enough for a security deposit on an economy apartment across town.

Tossing the folder and contracts onto the console, Peter glanced at his watch. He was early. He had expected the negotiation at the dealer to take much longer than it did, but arriving at the school early gave him time to assess how he would tell the kids that they would be moving.

Over the past few weeks, he'd rehearsed the conversation in his mind. He'd ultimately known this day was coming, and he loathed himself for not having been able to avoid it. He knew that Tori would be devastated by the news, but also knew that

Brett would go with the flow. He wished Tori could be more like Brett. Why did she have to be so much like her mother? Damn, he missed Minnie.

Moments later, teenagers began to pour out of the school exits. Peter had decided that today was the day for "the talk." Brett would probably be out first, and Tori would amble out a few minutes later. Knowing they wouldn't recognize the turquoise POS, instead of the crimson S-class, he climbed out and walked over to the sidewalk. He leaned against a light pole to wait.

It wasn't long before Brett walked up with a confused look on his face.

"How was your day, buddy?"

"Okay, I guess. Whatta ya doing here?" he replied, looking around for the car.

Peter noticed, smiled as best he could, and said, "I've got some news. We should wait until Tori comes out and we'll talk about it."

Brett nodded and stood uncomfortably to Peter's side. Tori came out a few minutes later with a few friends, and when they got closer, she whispered to them and they redirected without breaking stride. She looked up to her dad nervously. "What's going on, Dad?"

He loved and hated how smart she was. She knew something was coming... "I've got some news. Let's go somewhere where we can sit and chat."

Peter grabbed Tori's backpack and led the way. As they approached the van, Peter exclaimed—in his most chipper tone— "I traded in the Mercedes today. What do you think?"

Brett was silent, as always, but Tori was never one to hold her tongue. "I think it sucks! I can't believe you're picking us up in this. Where's the car?"

Inside, Peter hurt. Outside, he clowned. "Oh, come on, Tori. Don't you like the color? It's kind of funky, don't you think? This *is* the car!"

"Barf, whatever..." is all she muttered as she climbed into

the passenger seat.

"How about we go for some ice cream? It's a warm day, and two scoops would hit the spot," Peter said, trying to make the best of the situation. Neither kid answered. "Okay. Ice cream it is."

Peter pulled the minivan out of the parking lot and headed toward the nearest ice cream shop. Thankfully, Geno's Gelatos was not three blocks from the school. He pulled off the street and into a parking spot near the entrance. Just as he turned off the engine, Tori looked over at her dad and asked, "What's going on, Dad? This is all too weird."

Before Peter answered, he glanced back in the mirror to see if Brett was paying attention. He was staring idly out the side window, but looked up a moment later.

"Well... I've got some bad news. Because I've been unemployed for so long, the house payments have gotten behind. There's no way for me to get caught up, and the bank has exhausted their patience. We're going to have to move."

As he said it, he looked at each of the kids. Brett was looking outside again, while Tori stared straight ahead. Neither of them said anything. Peter continued to watch them in silence, and it wasn't long before Tori began to cry. He couldn't tell how Brett was handling what he'd just said, because Brett's attention appeared to be focused elsewhere. Peter followed Brett's gaze and his eyes landed on a couple passing the van. It was obvious why his son was so enthralled with the couple. The woman gave him goosebumps. She was stunning, around five-foot-six, with long, vibrant brunette hair. She was very athletic and had a regal bearing. That's when Peter noticed the man she was with. He seemed ridiculously mismatched to the woman: he was six-six, thick without being portly, with a receding hairline and a pockmarked face.

While watching the two walk into the ice cream shop, he momentarily forgot about the bad news. His heart ached. Snapping back to the moment, he once again glanced at Tori. She had wiped the tears away from her cheeks as the rage built in her face. *Here it comes*, Peter thought.

"Can't you get a loan or something? I'm a sophomore in high school, Dad! It's hard enough making friends here! I cannot start over at another school!"

Peter tried to keep his voice calm and positive. "I'm not so sure we would have to change schools. If I can find a place we can afford for a while, we might be able to keep you both here." Peter wished that what he was saying *could* be true—but in reality, he knew they would have to change schools. Their current neighborhood was fairly upscale, and there was no economy housing in the area.

"When are we going to have to leave?"

"I don't know, Tori. The notice came yesterday. They usually give three to four days on something like this. First off, we can put most of our stuff in storage until we can find a place. We'll probably need to stay at a motel for a week or so."

"A motel?! Seriously?! Dad!"

"Listen, Tori." Peter didn't mean to snap, but he did. "It's not like I planned for this to happen. I want to stay in the house as much as you do. But, this is how it is. I sold the Mercedes to help with money for now. I'm really trying to do my best here."

Tori began to sob. Looking back at Brett, Peter saw that now he was crying too. Seeing both of his children in tears, Peter began to cry, too. He wanted to be strong—*needed* to be strong for the kids, but it was so damn hard. He hurt deeply for letting them down and there was nothing he could do to make things right.

"Let's go in and get some ice cream," Peter said finally, wiping his own tears away. Brett was already out of the car heading for the door before Tori unlatched her seat belt. "Listen, kiddo. Please believe me when I say this. I love you both and I want only the best for you. If I could make things right, you know I would."

She relented. "I know, Dad. But what will all my friends think?"

"Well, they shouldn't give it a second thought if they're real friends. I promise you, Tori. I will do everything possible not to interrupt your high school experience. If I have to drive you back and forth to school forty-five minutes each way, then that's what I'll do."

Tori sat in silence a few moments longer. Brett still stood just outside the shop, staring inside at the couple that had walked in moments earlier.

"Okay, Dad. I'll do my best to stay positive."

"Thanks, kiddo." Peter hugged her warmly. "Let's go, before Brett adopts that other couple as his parents." Tori chuckled lightly, and that was the first time in ages he had seen her smile.

CHAPTER 4

The knock on the door was loud enough to be heard in the basement, where Peter was going through some old boxes. He was trying to make some headway before they had to move. Another knock, more insistent this time.

"Dammit," he exclaimed aloud, even though only the dust heard him. Ascending the stairs two at a time, he swiftly made his way to the front door. Just as he reached for the door handle, the loud knock came again. Peter yanked the door open and, without thinking, blurted out, "Enough already!"

"Hello. I'm looking for Mr. Peter Cooper?" said the man at the door. To Peter's surprise, the man was wearing a U.S. Army brigadier general's uniform. Peter recognized it right away, from his days in the service.

"I'm Peter," he said, looking around the general to see if he had any more company.

"Not to worry, Mr. Cooper. There is nothing wrong. I'm here on somewhat of a private matter. May I have a few moments of your time?"

Peter stood there for a moment, wondering what a general from the army would want with him. His mind flashed back to the days prior to his enlisting, his forced enlisting, and he felt the same sour feeling in his gut that he'd felt back then.

"Will this take long? I'm rather busy."

"Not at all, Mr. Cooper. I'll only take a few minutes of your time. May I come in?"

Peter opened the door fully for the general and stepped aside. "Please don't call me Mr. Cooper. Peter's fine."

"Very well, Peter. What a lovely house you have here."

"Thanks," replied Peter insincerely, as he led the general into the living room.

They chose opposite chairs and sat in silence for a long moment before Peter said, "Uh, can I get you a glass of something?"

"No thank you, Peter. Hopefully, this will not take long."

"Well then, what can I do for you?" asked Peter.

"Do you remember me at all, Peter? We met many years ago."

As soon as the general mentioned it, Peter noticed a slight tic in the general's demeanor that triggered a small bit of recognition... But he lied, "Sorry. You don't look familiar."

"Well, that doesn't surprise me," said the general with a smile. "It was back when you enlisted. I was a staff sergeant stationed at the admin office. I administered your ASVAB."

"Okay. I *might* remember seeing you there," Peter admitted.

"Well, as you can see from the shiny star here," the general pointed to the brigadier general star on his uniform, "I've had a few promotions since then. I'm now Brigadier General Harrison Applegate."

Applegate. That was the name that was on the tip of his lying brain.

"And in a strange sort of way, I'm actually here to talk to you about that day twenty-two years ago."

"How so?" asked Peter, his interest reluctantly piqued.

"The ASVAB exam tests ten separate categories, as you may recall. The scores you had in each of those categories are combined to get an overall score. Your score was a 94, where the minimum to enter the army at the time was 31. In short, Peter, you were far above the norm. And by all accounts you were very successful at your job. Yet you only stayed in the army for four years. Why is that?"

"I'm not real sure, to tell you the truth. I enjoyed my tour in Germany, and I made a few friends while enlisted. I guess... military life was just not my style."

"And life after the military, how has that been for you?"

Peter sat and contemplated that for a moment. Life had been great after the military. He'd met the love of his life. He'd had two great children, and a rewarding career. But then came the three-year decline into hell, and he was not about to discuss that.

"Life has had its ups and downs." Peter didn't offer any more than that.

"To be honest, Peter, I already know a considerable amount about you and your life since the military. I've been keeping tabs on you."

The army had been keeping tabs on him? "Why?"

"Because, Peter. You are a bright, intelligent man; far more intelligent than you give yourself credit for. Your entrance exams were exceptional, to say the least, but you scored particularly high in one area. Off the charts, as a matter of fact."

There were several moments of silence as this information penetrated Peter's mind. The general sat across from Peter, arms to his side, and not once did he take his eyes off him.

"Why are you telling me this now?" Peter demanded. "Why didn't you tell me this back then, if it's so important to you? I'm no longer in the army and I'm not going back. What does it matter anymore?"

"Would it have made a difference if I'd told you this twenty-two years ago when you enlisted? Would you have stayed in the army longer with this information? Would you have still married? Would you still have become an architect? Would Mary still have died in an auto accident?"

All these questions floated through the air, but Peter flinched at the mention of Mary. Mary was his wife's given name, and anyone that knew her called her Minnie. Hearing her name spoken out loud felt like an ice pick in the heart.

Peter was confused and irritated. "What's the point of all

this?" he asked, angrily.

"Peter, I clearly have more knowledge about you than just the basics. I know you are about to lose this house. I know your kids are barely passing their classes. I know you were laid off, and are currently looking for work. What if I told you that I could drastically change your circumstances, almost instantly?"

Peter was a proud man. To hear a stranger plainly spell out everything that he was struggling with almost brought him to tears. He had failed, and he was embarrassed. He was far too ashamed to ask for help from anyone.

"Are you sure I can't get you something to drink? I'm going to get myself a scotch." Peter stood without waiting for the general to reply and walked to the bar cabinet. He pulled out the bottle of Glenfiddich and two glasses. He returned to his seat and poured out two fingers each.

"Peter, this is not the answer to your problems," said the general as he took the glass from Peter.

"It might not be the answer, but it might help ease the process."

Peter brought the glass to his lips and tilted it back until the glass was again empty. The general sipped at his glass and returned it to the table. Peter poured himself another and leaned back, glass in hand.

"So, what do I have to do to get this 'help' that you're offering?"

"Before I can really tell you more about that, I have to have your word that you will not divulge any of the information that we are to discuss to anyone. Not even your children—although I don't think they would believe any of it. I have to be clear here: no one. No one at all."

Peter held up his hand, his pinky finger pressed against his thumb and said with mock solemnity, "Scout's honor."

"I'm sorry Peter, but I'll need more than that. I have a confidentiality agreement that you would need to sign. What I am about to tell you is beyond top-secret-level clearance." The general opened his attaché case and removed a file folder with the words "EYES ONLY" on the cover. From it, he slid out two sheets of finely typed paper. He handed one of them to Peter, then sat back in his chair and again sipped his scotch. As Peter read over the forms, the general finally took his eyes off of Peter and scanned the living room. He was quite surprised to find the house in good order, considering all of Peter's troubles, including raising two teenage children alone.

After several minutes of silent reading, Peter looked up at the general and said, "This must be seriously top secret if the army would go to these extremes, were I to talk. Do you have a pen?"

The general produced a blue-marbled Mont Blanc pen and Peter signed the document before returning it to the general.

"Actually, Peter, this isn't an army operation. It's an unclassified branch of the government that only a very select few even know exists. It's so clandestine that I'm currently not at liberty to inform you of its call sign. The document that you just signed will only afford you just enough information to make a rational decision whether or not to assist us; no more than that. If you agree, there will be several more documents that will need to be signed along the way. Do you understand?"

Peter nodded.

"Good. Now that we have an understanding, and your signature, we are inviting you to join a small team of exclusively selected civilians, others such as yourself, to travel back in time. Back to 1942, France to be precise."

CHAPTER 5

Visibly stunned, Peter sat in silence. Not sure if what General Applegate was saying was a joke, he said, "Come again?"

Applegate smiled. "You heard me correctly, Peter. We want to send you back in time. Back to 1942. Without disclosing too many overly complicated details, we have found—hypothetically, that is—a way to time travel, and there is something that we would like the team to accomplish back in 1942. Something so simplistic, yet so monumental, that life as we know it could possibly be changed forever."

Peter slumped back into his chair, his mind reeling from the words escaping the general's mouth. He looked down at the empty scotch glass and wondered if the alcohol had anything to do with how outrageous this whole scenario was. He mentally shrugged off the thought and focused on General Applegate. Was he telling him the truth, or was this all some kind of ruse? Then the words started to hit him, as if on a time delay. "Wait— hypothetically?" scoffed Peter.

"Well, yes. The technology allowing us to travel in time is limited. Meaning, we are confident that we can send our team to 1942 and retrieve them back to the present; but only once. Obviously, once put into motion, we are committing to a certain number of events that will begin to unfold. You, Peter, are the last team member necessary to complete this operation. If you agree to participate, you will be one of four in total that will be going on the mission. You, an associate with similar ties to the military, and two scientists. The two scientists were chosen to ensure you have passage back to the present. You and your associate will focus on the mission. It's simple, really."

"Simple? You call going back in time and changing some event simple? How safe is this 'hypothetical' device? If you can't test it, how are you sure that it will work? And more importantly, how are we guaranteed that it'll be able to bring us back?"

General Applegate merely nodded at each of the questions. When he was sure Peter was finished, he replied. "Again, without divulging classified information, we are very confident that the mission will be successful. Once you commit, everything that is pertinent will be disclosed to you."

Peter shook his head. "I just don't know. Why are you asking *me*? I am sure there are a hundred other candidates currently in the military that can handle this mission much better than I can. As you said, I've got many personal issues to deal with already, and I'm not sure that adding one more to the list will make my life any better."

"First off, the reason we selected you for this mission relates to your ASVAB scores. Your scores from twenty-two years ago have been flagged for many potential missions over the years. With many of those missions, I have proposed adding you to the team, and each time, my superiors have rejected it. This is your chance, Peter."

"Rejected? Why?"

General Applegate's eyes darted to the side and then back to Peter. "Because of your legal issues prior to enlisting. Nothing more."

"What?! Those were supposed to have been removed from my record if I enlisted. You mean they're still there?"

"I'm afraid so, Peter. They're not on your civilian records, but they will always be in your government file. No getting around that."

Again, Peter sat in silence, attempting to comprehend

everything the general was telling him. Peter had long ago believed that his juvenile escapades of stealing cars and dabbling with drugs were no more than a bad memory. He was assured at the time by his father's attorney that the whole mess would be "cleansed" from his record if he joined the army. To hear that it still existed worried him. It was all quite overwhelming.

"Peter, you don't need to decide today. Take some time to think it over. This is a big decision. Just remember, you cannot discuss this with anyone, but you do need to think it through completely."

"How long is this mission expected to take? As you so astutely pointed out, I have personal issues that need immediate attention. More importantly, why should I trust you?"

"The mission should be completed in less than three months, from start to finish. You will need training and be completely *read-in* on the entire mission, and that is expected to take six weeks. The overall time you will be away will be four months. In that time, I am prepared to take care of all of your financial obligations, including stopping all foreclosure actions against you. I will also arrange for proper care for your children while you are away. As to why you should trust me, I'm offering a solution to a majority of your problems, beginning with the financial. I believe you have found no other avenues to provide solutions to these issues. Not to mention, this will be the greatest adventure on which any human being has ever embarked."

"God, my children. What'll they think is happening? Where will they go?"

"We are aware of your situation. We know, as I've said, that your wife died in an automobile accident twenty-one months ago. In that time, you have not contacted Mary's parents once. I would imagine that they would love to see their grandchildren. And perhaps that would help the children to let go of some of their anger toward you. I understand that they are both quite rebellious right now?"

"That's an understatement," replied Peter. "How is it you

know so much about me?"

"As I said earlier, I've been keeping tabs on you. Since the first time I met you, I believed there was a spark of brilliance inside you. Your test scores supported my hypothesis. Unfortunately, my direct superior back then is still my direct superior now. He still feels I am wasting my time with you, but I have lobbied hard for you, and he finally conceded.

"In fact, you and I both have a lot riding on this operation. I am taking leave from the army because of this mission. This is an unsanctioned mission, and there cannot be any paper trail whatsoever that could lead back to the government."

"If not backed by the government, who'll be taking care of my financial commitments?"

"That would be me."

"You? Why would you do that?"

"Because, Peter. I feel that strongly about this mission. The lives that it could positively affect are worldwide. The entire global economy could be profoundly affected in a positive way. By how much, nobody knows."

"Two weeks? You need to know within two weeks?" asked Peter.

"We would like to know much sooner than that. The training begins in about a month. Should you choose to decline, I will still need to fill your spot on the mission."

"Understandable," agreed Peter. "What about pay? Will you also be paying for my time on the mission?"

"There will be no pay, Peter. I will be personally paying all your bills, along with getting the mortgage payments caught up. That alone should be plenty of compensation for your time and effort. Besides, you will be doing this for your country. That should be reward enough."

"To hell with your 'for my country' crap. If my country gave a shit about me, they would have told me about my skill set when I enlisted and given me a better job than a cook's assistant, and not held it in some general's pocket until they needed my help," shot back Peter, surprising both himself and General Applegate.

"I can understand your anger, Peter. I'm sorry that it had to be done this way. But if not for your country, consider this: the changes you make on this mission may very well affect your life in ways that neither of us can comprehend. We don't know for sure what will happen after the changes on the mission transpire. It could be nothing, or it could be amazing. I would ask that you consider it."

Peter took in these last words, and agreed that if what the general was saying came to fruition, his life could be better all around. If this mission could improve the global economy, maybe he wouldn't be in the financial crisis that had developed over the last few years. "All right, General. I'll think about it. I'll let you know by the end of the week, one way or the other."

They both stood up, and Peter led the general to the door. But before Peter had the door open, the general opened his attaché case once more, this time producing an envelope and handing it to Peter.

"Here's a little something for your time and consideration. I understand your unemployment has run out. This should help you out until you come to a decision." He left before Peter had a chance to open the envelope.

CHAPTER 6

Peter stepped back into the house, pondering the absurdity of the last thirty minutes of his life. Time travel, he wondered. Was it even possible? If it was, could he actually change the future? These questions would have to remain unanswered, for the moment at least. He dropped the unopened envelope onto the coffee table next to the bottle of scotch. Seeing the bottle, he decided another drink would help calm his mind.

With a refreshed drink in hand, he paced around the house. Peter often paced when his mind was working. Minnie use to tease him about "wearing a path in the carpet." What would she do? She was the adventurous type, and Peter thought she would most definitely go for it. But he was not his wife. Regardless of his failures since her death, he had to remain somewhat responsible for his kids.

The kids. What would they think? He knew he couldn't tell them about it, so how would he answer their questions? Questions about why he would be leaving for four months, maybe longer. On the bright side, Minnie's parents could be a part of their lives again. He had tried many times to get his in-laws involved with the kids' lives, but every time he picked up the phone to call them, he'd stopped halfway through dialing their number. He just couldn't swallow his pride long enough to ask for their help, let alone help from anyone else.

As he paced around the house, sipping his scotch, he heard the familiar click of the front door. He walked into the foyer and was surprised to see Brett.

"Brett? Everything okay? Why are you home early?" Peter glanced down at his wristwatch; it was just after one o'clock.

"The nurse sent me home. The school tried to call, but they said the phone had been disconnected. I'm having another migraine." Brett dropped his backpack next to the sofa and tossed the day's mail on the coffee table. "Can we call the doctor now? This is the third time this month that I've been sent home with a migraine. I think something's wrong."

"Sure thing, kiddo. I'll call and see if I can get an appointment for later this week. Why don't you head up and get in bed. I'll bring up some aspirin."

Brett just nodded and sluggishly climbed the stairs to his room.

Peter stood in the hall, staring up the stairs, wondering where he could get the money for another doctor visit. He finished his scotch in one swallow and headed to the bathroom to get Brett some aspirin.

Once Brett was seen to, Peter returned to the living room to tidy up a bit. He returned the bottle of scotch to the liquor cabinet and picked up the mail that Brett had brought in when he got home. It was the usual: bills and ads. He tossed them back onto the coffee table and opened the envelope from Applegate. Inside was a stack of hundred-dollar bills. Peter sank into a chair as he began to count them. He counted out twenty crisp hundred-dollar bills. Peter smiled and thought his week was taking a turn for the better.

CHAPTER 7

With Tori at a sleepover, and Brett quietly moping in his room, Peter decided to go out to the bar. After changing clothes, he stopped in his study and pulled a few hundred-dollar bills from the general's envelope. It had been a while since he had gone out, and he felt that his recent windfall was as good a reason as any to celebrate.

He was pretty upbeat considering everything that had been happening lately, especially that day. He decided that this monetary bonus would not go to waste. So, with pep in his step he moved vigorously through the house and out the front door. The nine-block walk did his mind good. As he headed down the sidewalk, he thought about what life would be like in 1942. Could he fit in enough to not draw suspicion? What if someone caught him and found out he was from the future? He giggled. He realized that if the police picked up some guy today that claimed he was from the future, they'd think he was from the loony bin.

As he crossed the street, he glanced down and noticed a penny lying next to the curb. He leaned over and picked it up. He inspected it with the idea of adding it to Brett's coin collection, if it was worth anything. He flipped it over and noticed that it was a wheat penny. Flipping it back over, he looked at the front more closely: 1947. He chuckled, and thought how ironic it would have been if the penny were from the same year as the mission. That's when Peter paused. He smiled as he slid the penny into his pocket. A plan was starting to form in his mind. A plan, *his* plan, which could change *his* future.

Even though it had been four months since he had last been there, Peter sauntered into Herb's Corner Pub like it was yesterday. Joe, the evening bartender, looked up and smiled at Peter as he approached the bar.

"Howdy, stranger! It's been some time since we've seen hide or hair of you. Pull up a chair."

Peter smiled as he slid onto the only available bar stool. "Hey, Joe."

"What brings you in this fine evening?" asked Joe as he started to pour Peter a drink. "Still scotch and water?"

Peter nodded. "Oh, nothing too much. Just thought it would be good to get out. It *has* been a while."

"Well, you've been missed, that's for certain. Benny's been asking about you. So has Stella." Joe slid Peter's drink across the bar, eyeing his expression. "How are the kids?"

"You know. Teenage know-it-alls. Nothing I can't handle." Peter paused to sip his drink, then continued. "Can you believe Tori wants to get her nose pierced? Seriously? Everyone wants to get perforated these days."

"My kid got her nose done first, then it was her tongue, and just a month ago she got her eyebrow done. I thought about putting my foot down, but I could tell in her eyes that if I said no, she'd go ahead and just do it anyway. Granted, she's seventeen, but I still hate seein' it."

"Tell me about it, Joe. Tell me about it."

"Are you working yet? I imagine unemployment won't last much longer."

Peter winced at the topic. Being unemployed for the last eighteen months had been rough, and his mood on the topic had not been great. But Peter pushed away the negative thoughts in his mind and said, "I haven't found anything yet, but I have a promising lead. That's why I came here tonight, to sort of celebrate." Once the words were out of his mouth, he realized that he had already decided to take the mission. He smiled to himself and took a long sip of his scotch.

"Well, that's great news, Peter. First one's on the house, then!" Joe smiled at him and moved to the other end of the bar to fill a drink order.

Peter sat in silence, briefly scanning the room to see if he recognized anyone. To his surprise, the atmosphere hadn't changed at all. The same tacky vinyl booths lined the outside wall, and that tear in the pool table felt still hadn't been fixed. He felt comfortable in his local dive bar. He turned back to his drink and noticed a reflection, in the mirror behind the bar of a woman staring back at him. Peter smiled, lifted his drink toward her reflection, and then took a sip. She returned his smile then looked away, her eyes darting to something across the bar. Peter continued to look in her direction as he tried to place her familiar face, but she didn't return his gaze. He supposed it was her pleasant, but remarkable profile. She reminded him of... His recollection was interrupted as a man walked up and sat across from her. They whispered briefly, before he nonchalantly glanced up to the bar. Without focusing on anyone in particular, his eyes landed on Peter momentarily as he scanned the place. Peter noticed the not-so-obvious glance from the stranger. The two sitting in the booth were obviously discussing him. He began to wonder if the general had had him followed. But before he could give it another thought, he was tapped on the shoulder.

Peter turned his bar stool to see Stella Fryer standing behind him. Stella stood a gracious five feet, two inches tall, and wore a jean miniskirt. She wore three-inch black pumps, which greatly improved her height. Her top was slightly sheer, and he could see the outline of her black bra beneath. Her ruby red painted lips smiled ear to ear, and parted to say, "Long time, no see, handsome."

"Hello, Stella. It has been a while." Stella was a few years older than Peter, and was the only woman that he had considered romantically since Minnie died. But something always delayed Peter from acting on his visual attraction. He wasn't sure if it was her over-flirtatious personality that stopped him, or if it was the fact that she was the local "bar ornament" with a moderately slutty disposition. After many nights spent drowning his sorrows there, he never saw her leave with another man. Still, Peter found it difficult to make a move. "I'd offer you a seat, but as you can see, all full."

"Don't worry about it, baby. Grab your drink and come back to my booth. I've got someone I want you to meet anyway."

Stella was the one person Peter didn't want to see tonight. The last time he was there, he and Stella had a few too many drinks, and things moved a bit too far, too fast. She knew he was still suffering the loss of his wife, and he told her he wasn't ready, but Stella pushed and pushed and had her hands down his pants most of that late night. Stella was a good part of the reason why he'd stopped going into Herb's—that, plus his lack of discretionary income. That had been four months ago.

"I would love to come back to your booth, Stella, but..." Peter paused to think of the right words to communicate the messages "not interested" and "no chance in hell" without hurting her feelings. "It's just that I need to talk with Benny, and Joe thinks he'll be here any moment," lied Peter. "Maybe later?"

Stella turned on a heel and ambled back to her table. Peter felt bad for being so blunt with her, but he was still not in a place where he felt comfortable, romantically, with another woman. Deep inside, he still felt devoted to Minnie, even though enough time had passed. Benny would tell him "Just sleep with her, already" anytime Stella would hang around them. Benny's thought on the matter was "It's just sex." Maybe Benny was right, thought Peter. Maybe he should just sleep with another woman—maybe he would feel better for it. Maybe with another woman not named Stella.

Peter chuckled to himself about the thought as he downed the last of his scotch. He flagged Joe down for another. Joe nodded and held up his finger indicating it would be a minute. While he waited, Peter began to review the conversation with the general again in his mind. Could it all be possible? Could time travel actually work? Peter recalled reading many science fiction stories where time travel was possible, but only if you didn't change the past. But that was exactly what the general was proposing. What if he went back to make this small change, and it ended up making a much bigger transformation than anyone ever considered? He surmised that the think tank behind the mission had to have already given that a lot of thought if they were moving forward with the program.

Completely lost in his thoughts, Peter didn't see Joe slide his drink in front of him. Peter picked up the drink and toasted him. Joe returned the nod and continued about his business. Peter raised the glass to his nose to smell the woody notes he was so fond of. He took a long drink, savoring the burn as it went down. Peter was not a lush, but the day demanded drinking. This was now his fifth or sixth drink for the day, and he was feeling a bit fuzzy. Granted, they were spread out through the day, but it was a nice buzz nonetheless. It was a good feeling after so many months of self-control.

The longer Peter sat alone, the more the loneliness started to creep in. He was really hoping that Benny would have been there by now. What were his options to kill the boredom? He could strike up a conversation with one of the strangers to his left or to his right—both of whom were deep in conversation with others. He could venture back and talk with Stella. He knew where that would lead: having Stella play footsie with him beneath the table, and possibly getting blown in the parking lot. Or he could sit and wait until Benny or somebody else he knew arrived. He tossed back the remaining few swallows of his drink and flagged Joe for another. He would wait. It had been a long time since he and Benny had talked, and he had things on his mind that he could only share with Benny.

As Peter waited, he peered into the reflection in the mirror to see if the couple was still in the booth across the bar. The booth was now empty, and once he noticed it, he turned and looked around the bar to see if they had moved or just left. He found them sitting in the corner booth with Stella. From what Peter could see, they were in a deep conversation and Stella did not look comfortable.

Peter looked over at Joe and waved him over. "Hey Joe, you see those two talking with Stella?" Peter tilted his head in their direction. "Have you seen them here before?"

Joe, not the most discreet person, flipped his head in their direction. "Nope. First time I've seen them was tonight. They came in right about the same time as you. Why do you ask?"

"I noticed them earlier and they seemed to be watching my every move. Kind of creeps me out." As he told this to Joe, he began to develop a plan—an alcohol-induced plan at that. He leaned closer to Joe and whispered into his ear. As Peter continued to talk, Joe's solemn expression turned into a devious smile. He nodded and said he'd play along.

CHAPTER 8

"What do you mean I can't have another drink?" Peter exclaimed loudly, while standing up so quickly his bar stool tipped back and crashed to the floor, grabbing the attention of everyone in the bar.

"I'm cutting you off, Pete. You've had enough. I can get you a cup of coffee or you can find another place to get a drink." Joe winked ever so slightly.

"No, no. It's fine. I was losing my fondness for thish plashe anyway. I think I'll take my hard-earned money to Charlie's over on Seventeenth. He never turns away my money." Peter grabbed his glass and took the last swallow and tossed the glass to the floor, breaking it into dozens of pieces. "Now, I'll leave."

Peter peripherally glanced around the bar, ensuring he had the appropriate eyes on him before he turned for the door and stumbled out. Once the door closed, he ran straight for the alley and ducked out of sight. Standing in the shadows of the dark alley, he leaned around the corner to get a good view of the front of the bar. Moments later, the couple burst out of the double doors in pursuit of Peter. He held back until they crossed the street and got into a nondescript black sedan before he turned and walked down the alley. Peter entered the back door of Herb's, completely unnoticed.

Through the back door, he found himself face to face with

Stella.

"Oh Peter, what have you gotten yourself into?" cried Stella, with an overly concerned look on her face.

"Gotten myself into? What are you talking about?"

"Those two! They cornered me in my booth and they really gave me the willies. They kept asking me questions about you and how well I knew you. What's going on, Peter?"

"I've never seen those guys before in my life. I caught them watching me earlier, and then when Joe and I noticed that they were talking with you, we devised a plan to get them out of the pub. I'm not sure who they were, or what they wanted, but I'm glad they're gone."

"Oh, Peter!" exclaimed Stella as she thrust herself into his open arms, hugging him. "I was so scared."

Not knowing exactly how to react to Stella hugging him, he lightly patted her on the back and said, "There, there. It'll be all right."

She continued the hug for a few moments, but when it became a little too awkward, Peter began to pull away. "Not yet, baby." Stella said. "I like feeling your warmth."

"I should at least go check with Joe. Make sure he's not pissed at me for breaking his glass."

"Okay, baby. Come back to my booth soon," replied Stella, and then walked into the ladies' room. Peter realized he also had to pee, so before heading back up front, he stopped in the men's room to take care of business.

When Peter emerged from the back hallway, he was met with a round of applause from the entire bar, and Joe was grinning ear to ear. He must not have been too bent about the broken glass. Peter gave an embarrassed wave to everyone, and the applause began to die down. With everyone returning to their own devices, he made his way back to his bar stool and sat back down. Joe made his way over to him, then pointed to the booth where the two strangers were seated earlier. Peter's eyes followed Joe's pointed finger and found Benny sitting alone, staring back at him.

"Benny!" Peter called out across the crowded bar.

"The one and only. I hear I missed quite the performance from you."

"Joe, another scotch for myself and whatever Benny is drinking. Oh, and a couple shots of whatever you got handy. Can you send the drinks over to the booth?"

"Sure thing, Pete." Joe started mixing fresh drinks.

Peter walked over and slid into the empty seat across from Benny. "How the hell are you, buddy? It's been way too long."

"I can't complain. The powers-that-be at work have been keeping me busy. Just when I think I'm getting ahead of things, I get a new load of crap dumped on my plate."

Benny hadn't changed. It had only been four months, but Peter thought everyone was going to be different when he came in tonight. Everyone was exactly the same. Maybe it was just him that was changing.

"Well, at least you've got a job, you schmuck," Peter teased.

"Yeah, sorry 'bout that. Any luck on the job front?" Benny's look became a bit too somber for Peter's liking.

"I've got some things in the works. Great things, Benny. That's kind of why I came in tonight. I wanted to talk to you about some things. Where the hell have you been?"

"Long story, buddy. Short version, I was having a few drinks at, uh... hold on." Benny paused as Joe brought drinks.

"Hey Joe, could you bring us a few more shots? Tequila this time, and no training wheels either," asked Peter.

Joe nodded and returned to the bar.

"Shots? Peter, I'm already a bit too liquored up to have shots."

"Trust me, with what I've got to say, you'll need these, plus a few more. So, you were telling me where you were before?"

"No, no. No changing the subject like that. What's this big news you've got to share?"

Peter leaned back, looking at Benny, wondering how much he should share about the mission. He had to talk to somebody about it, and Benny was his go-to guy. He'd been there for Peter through all his troubles the last few years. Benny was his best friend and had a good head on his shoulders. He couldn't tell his kids. Stella wasn't bright enough to understand what the offer meant. Yes, it had to be Benny.

"Tell me, Benny. What do you know about 1942?" asked Peter, before he tossed back a shot.

CHAPTER 9

It was the third succession of heavy knocks that finally woke Peter from the dead. He had been dreaming about rare coins, Stella's ruby red lips and shots of tequila.

A loud knock-knock-knock was heard throughout the house.

"Brett!" Peter yelled. "Can you go see who that is?"

Not hearing an acknowledgment, he wondered if his son had heard him. He pushed the sheets off himself and swung his legs to the floor as he sat up. He stretched, then leaned over, resting his face in the palms of his hands, reliving the night before. He felt like crap, and once again, he mentally swore off drinking heavily ever again. It was an all-too-familiar agreement that he'd made with himself over the last few years. And each time, the self-imposed deal was broken for one reason or another.

Peter sat on the side of his bed for several more minutes before Brett came into his room.

"Dad? There's some guy here to see you. He says you know him? General Applesomething."

"Thanks, kiddo. Tell him I'll be down in a few minutes."

"Do you really know him? He's got a couple people with him, and Dad, they look kind of familiar."

"Familiar how?"

"I don't know. Almost like I've seen 'em before, but I can't remember where."

"Okay, well, I'll tell you and your sister all about it later. Can you make some coffee and offer them some? I'll be down in a minute."

Brett nodded and closed the door as he left. Peter glanced at the clock: 11:35. He was surprised by how late it was, but not as surprised as he was about the general's visit. He thought he had a full week to decide whether to accept the mission or not.

Not wanting to fall back asleep, he forced himself to get up. He grabbed the pile of clothes from the night before and went into the bathroom to clean himself up.

As he washed and brushed his teeth quickly, his mind replayed the events from the night before. Most of the night was pretty clear. He remembered talking with Joe. He remembered avoiding Stella's advances far too many times. He remembered making some kind of scene and breaking a glass. *Why did I do that?*, he wondered. He remembered talking to Benny, but couldn't remember everything they talked about. He sort of recalled talking about old pennies for some reason, but he couldn't be sure.

Peter rinsed the toothpaste from his mouth and spat. He looked at himself in the mirror and felt like he was missing something important from last night. He again tried to retrace his steps from the night before. There was something about Stella... but he couldn't pull the memory into view. He remembered her hugging him and thanking him for something. What was it?

He turned from the mirror and grabbed his clothes. He pulled on his jeans and slid his arms into the button-up shirt, all the while thinking about Stella and the hug. He turned back to the mirror to run his fingers through his hair, and that's when it hit him. Everything began to rush into his mind at the same time. The couple that was at the bar. The image of their faces in his mind was so much clearer now, and he strangely felt a familiarity with them—like he had seen them before. But where?

Back in his bedroom, he slid his feet into his loafers and

walked toward his bedroom door. As he reached for the handle, he paused a moment, still thinking about the couple. Could they have been the two walking into the ice cream shop the day before? As he recalled the memory of them walking in, he was positive that they were the same couple from the bar. He wasn't completely positive, but he also felt like he may have seen them other places throughout the week. He was being followed. He was sure of it now. He pulled open the door and walked down the stairs, determined to get some answers from Applegate.

CHAPTER 10

Peter was dumbfounded at what he saw when he walked into the living room. He was expecting to see the general and two other people, as Brett had mentioned. Just not the general and... the same couple that had been following him around over the last week.

"Peter. Sorry to drop in unannounced, but we need to talk," the general said as he stood up to greet Peter.

"That's fine, General, but I thought I had a bit of time to think the offer through," Peter replied, not looking at him, but at the two others in the room.

"That's why I'm here, Peter. I'm afraid the decision now needs to be made immediately—because of your indiscretions last night."

"What do you mean? I don't think my discretions from last night are of any of your business."

"Oh, but they are, Peter. You made them my concern when you talked about the mission to your friends. Benny and Stella, was it?"

Peter flinched noticeably upon hearing his friends' names. Clearly, the two others in the room did in fact work for the general, and had been there to keep tabs on his movements. This sudden realization pissed him off.

"First off, I've not told anyone about the mission. Second,

what gives you the right to have me followed around?" he snapped, while gesturing towards the general's companions.

"Calm down, Peter. There's no need to get upset." Applegate smiled while waving him toward a seat.

"Peter, I would like you to meet a couple of people. They are not the bad guys. This is Julie. She has recently signed onto the mission." Applegate turned from the woman to the man next to her. "And this here is Mark. He's part of the security detail that everyone on the mission is assigned. If you accept, security personnel will be assigned to you as well."

Peter finally took his eyes off of the couple and looked directly at General Applegate. "Is all this security really necessary? If nobody knows about the mission, why would they matter?"

"To be blunt, Peter, it is because of actions like the ones you undertook last night. We have to be absolutely sure not one word gets out regarding the mission."

"I understand that, but a heads-up would have been nice. And for what it's worth, I didn't say a word to anyone about anything," Peter exclaimed, hoping his actions from last night would not betray his spotty memory.

"That was a pretty crafty scheme that you and the bartender pulled last night," Julie said, speaking for the first time, a slight smile attempting to cross her face. "It wasn't until we tracked down Charlie's clear across town that we realized you'd given us the slip.

"Yeah, about that. I wasn't sure what to think about you two. I would have bought you a drink if I had known you were only there to babysit me." As Peter said this, Julie broke his eye contact and looked away, obviously embarrassed. Mark, on the other hand, stared directly into Peter's eyes, his gaze unwavering.

Peter watched the body language of his visitors, and realized that all three were relaxed. It was only him that was uptight. Just the night before, he was nearly positive he was going to take the mission. Now, he wasn't so sure. The whole mess was a bit too cloak-and-dagger for his liking. There was silence in the room as these thoughts crossed Peter's mind.

"Peter, how can we really know for sure you haven't mentioned anything to your friends?"

"Is my word not good enough for you?"

"Honestly, Peter, no it's not. Mark feels that you may have compromised the mission by talking with your friend Benedict Welsh, and—"

Peter stopped the general. "You can forget that right now. Benny knows nothing. I'll give you that it may have looked suspicious last night. To tell the truth, I'd just about decided to accept your offer before I went to the bar. It had been several months since I'd been out, and I knew that if I did in fact go on your mission, it would be a while before I would be seeing my friends again. I just wanted to see them one last time before..."

Peter trailed off. As he spoke, he realized that he could potentially lose everything he had—his family, his friends—if the mission failed. And for all he knew, he could possibly lose everything if the mission was actually a success as well. Up to that point he had thought only of how the mission could help him. Digging out of the financial hole he'd been in for the last two years had been his main motivation. He'd never really thought about how this decision would affect so many other people. What he'd earlier thought of as being a simple decision, he now saw was a life-altering resolution.

Peter stood and began to pace about the room. The eyes of the general and his companions followed his every step. He was, again, re-evaluating everything the general had to offer. He just wished he knew more about what kind of effect time travel would have on him and his life. He thought about pouring himself a drink, but ruled out the idea just as quickly.

"Peter? Everything okay?" asked Applegate.

At the sound of the general's voice, Peter felt like he was being overly scrutinized, everyone watching him. "Can we speak privately, General? Do they need to be here?" Peter said, pointing to Julie and Mark.

"Not a problem, Peter," he replied. He turned to the couple. "Why don't you two go grab a coffee around the corner. I'll call you when we're finished."

Julie and Mark stood and silently walked toward the door. As they did so, Julie paused near Peter and gave him a reassuring smile. Moments later, the door clicked shut, and Peter and the general were alone.

"Now, is this better, Peter?"

"Much." He sat down across from the general and tried to recall everything that he had planned on asking. "I have some more questions, if you don't mind."

"By all means, Peter. If I can answer them, I certainly will."

"First off, if I go back in time, and happen to die, what will happen to my kids in the present?"

"As I understand it, Peter, your children will only know that you died in your training cover story. They will know nothing about your time travel mission."

"Okay, about that. If I accept, I want a college trust in place for both of them. I also want my house paid off. If I'm going back in time, risking my life on a hypothetical mission, I want some assurances that my family will be taken care of."

"Don't get me wrong, Peter. I completely understand where you're coming from on this matter. I will certainly agree to those requirements for you, but I have to tell you: they will not matter."

Peter was stunned. "Not matter? How can it not matter? They're my children, for Christ's sake. They absolutely matter!"

"I'm sorry, Peter. You misunderstood me. It won't matter if I pay off the house, or pay for their college today, because once you go back in time, you will instantly alter how history will advance from the moment you make a single change in 1942. You see, once you change something in the past, the future might not be the same as you remember. Your memories—as well as the memories of everyone else going on the mission—will remain in place, as they will be *linear* to you and only you. But for any of us staying in this present, well, we will have no recollection of the events happening up to that point. Our memories will shift at the point when you and your team come back."

The general paused a moment to let Peter absorb what he was telling him. "The dynamic of you and the team going on the mission will allow you to maintain your memories, as if they actually happened. But in reality… they never did. You could come back to a world where you are single, or married to another person entirely."

"Why didn't you tell me any of this before?" Peter demanded.

"Because if I did, you may not have considered the mission in the first place. Listen, Peter. According to our calculations, the mission has nothing but upside potential for all of civilization. If you go back and complete your mission successfully, our analysts assure me that your life will be very similar to, if not better than, the way it currently is. The algorithms that have been run on the success of the mission—run hundreds of times, I assure you—mostly result in you marrying Mary, and having two children."

"How can you know exactly who I would marry again if the mission is successful? Who is to say I don't find French women irresistible after the mission?"

"Just because you're going to France on the mission does not necessarily dictate that you will have a fondness for their women. You see, you're going back to 1942 from the present day. You will return to the *shifted* now. Your mission will have no influence on whom you will marry in-between. You will have not have been born in 1942, so, you will have no contact with yourself."

Peter's head ached from trying to wrap his mind around the whole theory of time travel. He closed his eyes and rubbed his temples.

"Peter, the odds are with you on this. You have to trust me."

"What exactly are the odds? Or are you not allowed to tell me that either?"

"No, unfortunately, I am not at liberty to discuss the exact odds with you, but believe me when I tell you, they are outstanding."

Peter broke down and crossed the room to the liquor cabinet and poured himself a scotch, despite the hangover. He wasn't sure of the exact cause of his headache anymore. He twirled the glass around in his hand, thinking about everything the general had just told him. He had been prepared to accept the mission, with all the promised benefits, yet without any concessions on the general's part. That was, until now.

"I'm sorry, General. I need more information. You tell me that I will have full access *if* I accept and sign the mission accord. I am not going to sign anything unless you give me the exact odds of success."

Now, it was the general that was silent. He sat for a long moment before speaking.

"The probability that you will have the same life and family upon your return..." the general paused momentarily before continuing, "...is fifty-five percent."

"Fifty-five percent?! How the hell is that an outstanding figure?"

"That is a fifty-five percent chance that you return to the same life as you have now. There are many other variables that directly affect those odds, and most of them are only positive. Your life when you return may very well be significantly better. Those odds are incalculable. Peter, you asked for the odds that your life will remain relatively the same. That is what I gave you."

Peter listened, and although he was working through a puzzle far beyond his understanding, he did realize one thing. During the entire conversation with the general, Peter had been gradually recalling more of the discussion from the night before, the one with Benny. He remembered the 1943 copper pennies, and he knew that they were *his* way of making the situation right for *him*, and him only. He would accept the mission and make sure he had some alone time back in 1942.

After several minutes of exaggerated reflection, Peter finally spoke.

"Okay, General. I know you say it won't matter, but I would like the college trust and the house paid for. Once those are taken care of, I'm in."

Peter looked Brigadier General Harrison Applegate in the eyes and smiled.

"When do we leave?"

PART 2

CHAPTER 0

May 8th, 1942

Michael Gallagher slid the final Thyratron into the empty slot then began retracing his path back out from inside the monstrous device. As he ducked and crawled beneath several crossbeams, he contemplated just how much longer Dr. Bernard Epson would chase his dream. This was his third trip into the belly of the Atanasoff–Berry Computer-styled processor that the doctor had designed and built to control the hundreds of calculations for his partially-completed time machine. He wondered just how many more blown tubes and melted wires would have to be replaced before the doctor surrendered. Michael knew what the problem was, and had known for quite some time, but he wasn't about to aid the doctor in his dangerous enterprise. Michael smirked as he pulled himself out the final five feet.

"All fixed!" Michael announced as he brushed himself off for what felt like the hundredth time over the last month.

"Good. Good. How many was it this time?" asked Dr. Epson.

"Thirteen in all, Doctor, but . . ." Michael intentionally paused before continuing, knowing the reaction he would receive from his longtime employer.

"But what, Michael?" asked the doctor.

"Well, those were the last of our Thyratrons." Michael waited optimistically for the explosion of Dr. Epson's verbal fury. But, to his surprise, there was no outburst.

Dr. Epson looked perplexed. "Then I suppose we should double- and triple-check everything before we try another computation," he stated while studiously examining various settings across the vast control board.

"Shall I order another batch before we proceed, Doctor?" inquired Michael.

The doctor stood unresponsive in front of the control panel in silent contemplation. Several moments passed before Michael cleared his throat. "Doctor?"

"Hmm? Yes. What was that, Michael?"

"I asked if I should order more Thyratron tubes before we proceed."

"Well that would be quite a merry chase, indeed," replied Dr. Epson, pausing briefly to adjust a few settings. "You see, we are out of money. I was hoping that I wouldn't have to bring it up at this particular moment, but . . . ."

Michael could feel the goose bumps dance across his skin like spiders attending a masquerade ball. He longed to hear those words. He needed to hear more. "But what?"

"But until this morning I still had hope that one of the bevy of financial suitors I've made contact with would come forth. Unfortunately, I received a wire from the last of them today; no one will help. Unless I can prove that this confounded device can do what it is supposed to do, nobody will lend us a red penny." Dr. Epson exhaled loudly and went on adjusting knobs and levers on the control panel.

Michael remained silent, unsure of which way to guide the conversation. He stood just behind and to the left of the doctor. His eyes sparkled with glee as he glanced at the panel which housed his subtle rearrangement. Having worked shoulder to shoulder with the doctor from the beginning, it hadn't been difficult to steer him away from the simple crossed circuit during the construction two months previously. The circuit board seemed the obvious location for sabotage. It was in plain sight, and the doctor would have never thought twice about it being faulty, because he was the one who initially installed all the delicate circuits.

After several minutes, Michael broke the silence. "Is there anything I can do?" he asked, feigning sincerity. His mind and commitment were clear, but his heart remained divided. Even though his main dedication was to the Society, he remained indebted to the doctor. It was Dr. Epson who nurtured him right out of college and gave him this amazing opportunity so early in his career. Michael hated seeing the man brought to his knees so publicly, but he was faithful to the cause, and it dictated that this path of research needed to be culled at all costs.

"Unless you can pull together a few thousand dollars by next week, I am afraid we are going to have to shut down."

"A few thousand dollars?" Michael gasped "That's a lot of money, Doctor."

"Yes, I am aware. You see, I put my house up as collateral to the bank a few months back. I was so confident that my algorithms were precise that I had no hesitation in doing so. Now the note is due, and I haven't paid rent on the lab since March. Everything I had has gone into this blessed machine." Dr. Epson tapped the base of the large computer lovingly with the toe of his shoe.

"If it's any consolation, Doctor, you can forgo paying me this month. If it helps," offered Michael.

Dr. Epson turned to face Michael. "What a gracious offer, Mr. Gallagher, but we are both professional men here, and I do not intend to short your stipend one cent. We've worked together for many years, and I value your mind and your service far more than I do my money. You will have your weekly pay on Monday."

The two men stood in silence a moment longer before Dr. Epson wandered into his office and shut the door.

Michael stood alone in the quiet, dusty lab, wondering if he should start checking the processor now or wait for the doctor to return. He sat at his desk, and after a quick glance to the doctor's office to reassure himself that he was, in fact, alone, he pulled out a telegram from beneath the leather ink blotter. It was neatly scribed in his own handwriting. He skimmed the lines:

Mr. Cypress
Box 42
San Francisco

Start: Objective nearly complete. Project funding depleted. Society success imminent. Awaiting further direction.

Stop.

Michael read the telegram once more before folding it and sliding it into his breast pocket. He had known this moment was inevitable and had written the telegram weeks ago. All that was left was to excuse himself for lunch and have it sent immediately. He stood and took off his lab coat. As he was exchanging it with his overcoat from the rack, the creak of the front door startled him.

"Good morning, Michael," said Miss Stewart, Dr. Epson's secretary. "Is the Doctor in his office?" she asked excitedly.

"Yes, he is. Is everything all right?"

"I'm not quite sure. There is a gentleman from the military here to see him."

"Do you know what he wants?" asked Michael.

"I'm pretty sure it has something to do with his research. The doctor had me send a cable last week looking for backing. This man may very well be our savior," she replied as she knocked and then disappeared into the doctor's office.

Speechless, Michael slumped into his chair, pulled the telegram from his pocket, and tore it to pieces.

CHAPTER 1

The penetrating briskness of the thin night air chilled Peter to the bone. His eyes had adjusted to the darkness of a moonless sky. The few scattered streetlights shone harsh in contrast to the gloom throughout the village, their hardened light causing mysterious, foreboding shadows. The cobblestone streets were vacant, just as they had been all night, and the sound of silence was louder than the thoughts in his own mind.

Peter glanced at his night-glow watch, only to find ten minutes had passed since his last inspection. What, he wondered, are they waiting for? He shifted nervously in his crouch and decided it was time to move.

He crept stealthily along the stone wall that bordered the winding road. As he neared the edge of the shadows, he slowed his pace and briefly leaned into the glaring light to see if the street around the corner was vacant. He noticed the silhouette of another person slinking along the face of the building across the street. At first he could not clearly identify the individual, although a moment later the shadowy figure slipped into the light and it became clear to Peter that the silhouette was that of a woman. He exhaled softly. He quickly recognized the high cheekbones and silky brunette ponytail. It was his partner, Julie Frey.

Peter pursed his lips together and made a short bird chirp to attract her attention. Julie glanced around and, a moment later, returned the call. Peter once again checked his watch. Their time limit was critical; this mission needed to be complete inside of two hours. It was now 1:37 a.m., and it had been ninety-seven minutes since they entered the small French village. They had begun their incursion from separate ends, headed as discreetly as possible toward the same destination: the small café near the center of town. They were currently on opposite sides of the narrow street, just a few hundred feet away from their target, and Peter felt confident they would have no problem completing the mission with time to spare.

Cautiously, he stepped into the deserted street and began to amble in Julie's direction, his leisurely pace belying his extreme nervousness about being exposed.

As Peter reached the halfway point, Julie also stepped onto the cobbled road and proceeded toward him. They met in a shadow at the edge of the light cast from the nearest light pole.

"Any problems on your end?" whispered Peter.

"I came across a few drunks stumbling out of a bar a few blocks over, but it was nothing I couldn't handle. You?"

"I haven't seen a soul all night. It's a little too perfect for comfort. Let's move before we're noticed."

With Julie at his side, Peter stepped from the shadows and walked confidently toward their destination. Despite the darkness, he could begin to make out the word *café* painted on the brick above the glass storefront. Seeing the familiar word, he instinctively relaxed; this was the closest they'd gotten all week.

With renewed energy Peter continued closer, but he stopped instantly when he heard the noise. Julie heard it too. It was the unmistakable sound of footfalls on the pavement. He could not tell which direction they were coming from, but he knew they were close. Their options were limited. They were out of cover and near the middle of the street. He intuitively reached out and took Julie's hand and began to walk in the opposite direction. As the two made it to the end of the block, they began to veer down a side street. But before they got around the corner, a loud voice startled them both.

"Arrêter!"

Peter's French was improving, and he recognized the word *stop*. He gripped Julie's hand tighter and halted. In unison, they turned to face the person behind the startling voice.

The man moving toward them towered higher than six feet tall. His face was pockmarked and sported a wiry mustache. He was pointing a rifle in their general direction, and his uniform was clearly that of the Vichy France Army. "*Où vas-tu à cette heure de la nuit?*"

Peter understood the soldier's question–*Where are you going?*—but had been instructed to let Julie do all the talking.

"*Nous sommes tout simplement pour une balade. Belle nuit, n'est-ce pas?*" she replied perfectly. "We're just out for a stroll. Beautiful night, isn't it?"

"*à 1h40 du matin?*" The soldier directed the question at Peter. "At 1:40 in the morning?"

Peter simply nodded.

"*Que, chat a obtenu votre langue?*" The soldier asked if the cat had Peter's tongue.

Both Peter and Julie laughed out loud before Julie answered that Peter had a sore throat and the doctor had instructed him not to speak for several days. Peter nodded his head as Julie recited the scripted answer.

The soldier stood a few feet from them, still holding his rifle steady. He examined Peter before moving his eyes to Julie. As he raked his eyes over her feminine form, meticulously scrutinizing every luscious curve far longer than appropriate, Peter noticed how uncomfortable she had become. Unfortunately, there wasn't anything he could do about it.

After visually molesting Julie, the soldier grinned slightly, and said, "*vous êtes plutôt sexuelle.*" Peter clinched his fists and stepped between Julie and the armed man.

The man raised his rifle to Peter's chest and demanded he get back: "*récupérer!*"

Julie placed her hand on Peter's shoulder and whispered,

"It's not worth it."

Peter was about to step aside when the soldier suddenly elbowed him in the face.

Peter dropped to his knees yelling, "Fuck! What did you do that for?" The words, in English, were out of his mouth before he could pull them back.

"*Américain soja?*" accused the soldier. Peter thought he was half right. He was American, but he was no spy. At least he didn't think he was.

Peter stood back up and turned toward the soldier to explain, but the soldier jumped back and re-leveled his rifle at Peter's chest.

"Wait!" is all Peter could say before the soldier opened fire on him, shooting him three times in the torso. Julie screamed as Peter fell back, hitting the cobblestone street.

Lying on his back, Peter blinked his eyes. His head throbbed where he cracked it against the pavement. He brought his hand to his chest and the pool of wetness he felt was not reassuring. When he lifted his hand, it was covered in red. He was shot. He tried to sit up, but Julie, kneeling next to him told him in English to wait a moment.

"Shh!" Peter whispered to her. "He'll hear you!"

"It's okay, Peter. The training is over. We failed again."

Training? Peter tried to sit up, but his head was spinning. Julie pushed on his shoulders in an effort to make him lie still, but he still managed to push up from the cobblestone street into a sitting position. He wobbled, then steadied himself and looked around. The scene—which had been dark just moments before—was now in full light from the mercury-vapor lights above. He reached back and felt the growing knot on his head.

"What? But we were so close," Peter said.

"Yes, Peter. You were closer to your goal than you've been all week. But do you understand your error?" General Applegate asked as he stepped out of a doorway in the mock village.

Peter rolled to his side and got a leg underneath him. He

stood up and looked menacingly over at Mark. The ogre was dressed in the Vichy uniform. "It's because that asshole crossed the line."

"There will be no lines in 1942. You have to expect anything and everything. Heaven forbid that you two encounter a soldier such as the one Mark was portraying." Applegate nodded to Mark, who returned the nod before turning to walk away. As he passed by Peter, he flashed a petulant smirk that grated on Peter's nerves.

Peter forced himself to look at General Applegate. "Okay then. What would have been the correct reaction to Mark's sexual advances? Do we sacrifice Julie for the sake of the mission?"

"Don't be absurd, Peter. Julie has been through several levels of advanced combat training. The soldier would have suffered greater injury if he were to make that advance than he would from your efforts to play protector. Isn't that right, Julie?"

"Let's just say he would have to sit to pee for at least a week," replied Julie, now standing next to Peter. "But that was a very noble gesture," she said as she patted his shoulder.

"Right. Why don't you two get changed and wrap up for the day," suggested the general. "We'll discuss your results tomorrow."

Peter and Julie stood in silence as Applegate walked through the village and stepped into a dark alley.

"Are you going to be OK, Peter?" asked Julie, the patting of his sholder turning to a gently rub. "You hit your head pretty hard."

"Yeah, I'll be fine. My pride is what's really injured right now. I can't believe I let Mark get to me like that. Seriously, did he have to hit me *and* shoot me?" asked Peter, not really looking for Julie to answer.

"Let's get this paintball goo cleaned off you and get out of here before Applegate changes his mind on more training."

CHAPTER 2

Peter was mentally and physically exhausted when he got home. Trevor, the security detail that General Applegate assigned to him two weeks ago, had just dropped him off. Although he hated having an adult babysitter, he was much happier with Trevor as his watcher than Julie was with Mark.

The past two weeks had flown by in a blur. After accepting the general's mission and signing a number of nondisclosure forms, Peter was whisked off to "the warehouse" for training. Peter managed to persuade the general to let him stay in his home during the four weeks of training. The general begrudgingly agreed but insisted that Trevor stay with him for the majority of his time away from the warehouse. Meaning any time that he spent away from his home, Trevor would be close by.

As these thoughts revolved through Peter's mind, he slid his key into the lock on the front door and turned it over. Upon stepping into the foyer, he could hear both kids in the kitchen. He dropped his keys on the table and was off to hear about their day.

Tori was sitting at the kitchen table, earbuds in, singing along with her music. The nubs did little to limit the range of the *thump* of her latest hip-hop obsession permeating the room. Brett was standing over the kitchen sink, still wearing his soccer cleats, shoving nearly an entire piece of pizza into his mouth.

"Slow down there, slugger!" Peter exclaimed. "We're going to have dinner soon."

Brett nearly choked when he heard his dad come into the kitchen. "Thorry, dhad," Brett spat, trying to retain every soggy morsel of his afternoon snack. He chewed hastily and swallowed. Brett smiled sheepishly and said, "I was hungry. Coach really worked us hard today."

Peter smiled and winked at his son. "It's alright, bub. I just don't want you to ruin your appetite. I'm making Texas Tacos tonight." Brett's smirk turned into a full-blown grin. Texas Tacos were Brett's favorite, and Peter knew that no matter how much his son ate before dinner, he would still clean his plate.

Tori was so engrossed in her music and homework she didn't hear them talking. Peter had to move into her peripheral vision before she took notice. She instinctively pulled the buds from her ears and looked up. "Hey, Dad."

"Hey, kiddo. How's the homework going?" he asked as he pulled up a chair and sat down.

"Almost done. Biology sucks."

"Tori?"

"Sorry, Dad. Biology blows," Tori said with a devious grin. "Better?"

"Yes, thank you. 'Blows' is *so* much better than 'sucks,'" Peter replied sarcastically. "Want to help with dinner tonight?"

"Sure," exhaled Tori, as she rolled her eyes and tucked her hair behind her ears. As she did, Peter could see the shiny new ring in her nose. It had been a little more than a week since he let her get it done, even though he had sternly forbade it earlier. He hated to see it, but his heart smiled. He knew that he only had to live with it for a month at most, since when he returned from his mission, the offending nasal hoop would never have perforated his child.

"Thanks, kiddo. I'll cook, I just need help cutting things up."

Tori looked relieved and smiled. "Cool. You know how much I hate that stove."

"Yes, Tori. I know you hate the stove," Peter chuckled.

Brett sat down across from Tori, pulled out his history textbook, flipped it open to a marked page, and began to read.

Peter watched his son, reflecting. It had been years since they all sat at the kitchen table when a meal was not being eaten. It was nice. He almost felt content at how things had changed so dramatically since General Applegate reemerged into his life. Peter knew it was a false sense of contentment, because nobody knew what life would be like after the *shift*. Peter hoped that if he could just get through the mission cleanly, he could return to a normal existence. No more debt. No more misery. He could have a brand new life and a fresh start. If only he knew what changes would happen because of his mission.

Peter was anxious to hear what Applegate was going to say tomorrow in the operations briefing. He had believed that once he agreed to and signed all the confidentiality documents, he would know the extent of the plan immediately. But the general still had not gone into detail about what that mission was. He had only given them enough information to begin their training. Damn, Peter hated being in the dark!

Peter mentally shrugged and stood up. "I'll let you two finish your homework. Tori, come get me from the study when you're ready to flaunt your culinary prowess." He grinned.

"OK, Dad," she replied, not taking her eyes off her biology worksheets. She replaced the earbuds before Peter left the kitchen.

CHAPTER 3

The drive into the warehouse passed in silence, and that suited Peter perfectly. After two weeks of training, and having been told only a few minor points of the mission, he was still unaware of the ultimate goal. This irritated him incessantly, and he hoped the briefing that morning would bring answers to the mysteries surrounding the operation.

Trevor maneuvered the black Crown Victoria through the twists and turns on the hillside before he slowed to the guard shack. As he pulled up to the gate, he lowered his window and held out his credentials for inspection. After a cursory review, the guard nodded to his partner sitting inside to open the gate.

Peter decided there was something peculiar about this particular morning. Besides not being able to sleep through to his alarm, the fog was extra thick and there was an eerie silence surrounding the area. He realized that he could not hear any birds singing or the rustle of the wind. Odd indeed. The apprehension didn't ease with the grinding hum of Trevor's window rising back up.

They crossed the deserted campus and parked in the small parking lot outside of Warehouse 41. As Peter released his seat belt, Trevor asked "Same time this afternoon, Mr. Cooper?"

"Trevor, please. It's Peter. Hell, call me Pete if you want. Just drop the Mr. Cooper business." For most of his adult life, Peter despised being referred to as "Mr." He was far more casual and felt more comfortable when those around him were equally informal.

"Uh, yes, sir. Same time . . . Pete, um Peter?"

"Sure thing, Trevor." Peter chuckled and shut the car door. Trevor was a strange fellow. He was polite but quiet. At least he was better company than Mark. Poor Julie. Still, Peter felt it odd that when Trevor picked him up and drove him in every morning, he would sit motionless in the car instead of accompanying Peter inside the building. Peter knew that Trevor had access to the facility, because he would see him inside not thirty minutes later. Odd indeed.

Peter walked through the oversized entry door that led directly into the cavernous warehouse. Inside, the scene was like something lost in time. It reminded Peter of what a Hollywood movie set would look like. Several city blocks of some historic French city were built inside. When Peter arrived at the warehouse for the first time, he didn't think it was possible to enclose such an enormous facsimile. However, upon inspection, it became apparent that the buildings were all facades—simply framed walls, supported by guy-wires and temporary bracing. They were set up like this so that he and Julie could familiarize themselves with the area he assumed would encompass their mission goal. The goal that he hoped to finally learn the full details of today.

Peter continued through the dimly-lit scene and ducked into one of the alleyways that led to the stairway up to the second-floor mezzanine. This was where a small break room, a number of unmarked offices, and the operations center were located. The placard on the door read "Conference Room #2," but everyone referred to it as Ops. Aside from Ops and the break room, Peter had no access.

When Peter approached the open door to Ops, he hesitated briefly before entering, as he noticed Applegate and Mark in a heated conversation. He felt uncomfortable gawking, and although he would have loved to hear what was being said, he walked past the open door and stepped into the break room. Julie was standing at the coffee machine waiting for the brew cycle to end and didn't notice Peter come in.

"Good morning, Jules," Peter said. Startled, Julie swung around and gave Peter a brief smile that quickly dissolved into a frown.

"Hey, are you OK?" Peter asked.

She shrugged. "Yeah, I'm fine. Just had a misunderstanding with that crap-weasel Mark last night."

"About what?" He pulled a cup from the dispenser and set it on the counter next to Julie's.

"Nothing really. I went to visit my stepfather, and because I didn't tell Mark first, he was beyond pissed that he had to track me down."

"Hate to say it Jules, but Applegate was pretty adamant about not talking to other people before the mission. How did he find you?"

"That's the thing. I don't know exactly. I have not been to my stepfather's house in months, and I didn't think they knew we were in touch. But sure enough, I wasn't in the house for fifteen minutes before Mark nearly burst through the door. I was so embarrassed. I was just there for dinner, and it hurt that I couldn't even tell my stepfather why I was being taken away."

"Did Mark say anything?"

"Yeah, he mumbled something about me being needed in the office, or something like that. Luckily, Frank, my stepfather, knew that I had a security background and didn't ask any questions as I was practically being dragged from his house."

The brew cycle was complete, and Peter poured two cups as they stood in silence.

"Wait a minute. Was your mother home?"

"That's not the point, Peter. It's just that I'm tired of all the secrecy. Why do we have to be so secretive when everything is supposed to be *shifting* anyway?" Julie had begun to mimic Peter's penchant for fingered air quotes.

"Hey, you're preaching to the choir. I'm just as irritated by all this covert bullshit as you. Don't you remember when we first met? You and your friend Mark were tailing me all over San Francisco for weeks."

"First off, Mark is NOT my friend." She paused to stir the clumpy dry creamer into her coffee. "And second, Applegate forced me to ride along with Mark. I wanted no part of it, but it wasn't my choice."

Silence again filled the room as they both moved their plastic stir sticks about their coffee cups. Peter thought about their situation and something seemed off. He understood that the general needed to keep tabs on everyone to ensure nobody talked, but how did the dim-witted guards know where they were at all times? He was about to ask Julie that very question when Applegate walked in.

"Good morning, troops!" General Applegate exclaimed as he approached the pair. "We're about to begin the presentation in Ops. Peter, could you give Julie and me a moment? We'll be in shortly."

"Sure thing," Peter replied, stepping past him on the way out. Peter knew what Julie was in for, and he felt sorry for her.

Peter walked into the ops center, which was now bustling with activity. Across the room, Dr. Brett Lamb was sitting at the computer console with his sidekick, Dr. Griff Larsson. They were chatting between themselves as they both stared at the computer screen in front of them. Several assistants were scurrying about the room collecting papers and filling water glasses. Peter glanced up to the SMART Board and saw a spreadsheet with the heading "1942 Statistical Information." It was filled with various numbers and data. As he skimmed through the information, Peter slid into a chair at the enormous conference table. A moment later one of the administrative assistants passed by, dropping fire-engine red binders in front of each chair around the table. Emblazoned across the top were the words "Operation Swallowtail."

Before Peter could start to peruse the information, Julie and the general walked in. Julie's eyes were teary, but when she made eye contact with Peter, she smiled. She walked around the table and sat next to him.

"So?" he whispered.

"I'll tell you later."

General Applegate sat at the head of the table and glanced over at the two scientists. "Boys? Are we ready to go?"

"Yes, sir. We just finished updating the files. You have control," replied Dr. Lamb.

Both he and Dr. Larsson moved to the conference table and found chairs. The assistants milling about exited the room, closing the door behind them.

"Good morning, everyone. Before we get started, I just want to say how great of a job you all are doing with your training. We are halfway through training and just two weeks away from mission departure. Or, *To Linear Shift* as the Drs. prefer to call it."

Hearing the reality of just how close they were to actual time travel left Peter anxious. He wondered if the others felt the same way.

"So far you've been introduced to a bevy of 1942 factoids and received a half dozen generalized espionage training sessions. Today we will be talking about a few new and specific details regarding the mission. In general, they deal with time travel idiosyncrasies. For the most part, these are common sense matters, but they do need mentioning. First off, don't go kill any notorious historical figures or unpopular distant relatives. That should be obvious. It will cause certain paradoxes which we will not discuss."

Peter let out a deep breath. At least he wouldn't have to kill anyone. One new thing learned today.

As General Applegate paused momentarily, Peter asked, "Should we be concerned with conversing with someone from our family, supposing we happen to meet them in 1942?"

"Please, could we hold all questions until after my initial briefing? I am positive that most everything that you might ask will be answered shortly. Right then, where was I? Oh yes—time travel. As I am not the specialist in the field, I am going to turn the presentation over to your mission companions, Drs. Lamb and Larsson."

Peter glanced at Julie, who was oblivious. She was intently reviewing the contents of the binder in front of her. Peter had forgotten about it when the general walked in.

"Good morning," began Dr. Lamb. "Inside each of your packets, you will find some information that we feel might be beneficial to our mission. The information is statistical in nature and largely relates to cost of living, both in the United States and France in 1942. You are also provided with cultural and lifestyle habits in each region. As Dr. Larsson and I will not be accompanying the two of you to France, that information is provided for your benefit only."

Dr. Larsson cycled through a few images, swiping his fingers across the SMART Board display, as Dr. Lamb recited some of the various data points of ordinary product values. Peter was amazed at the amount of information they were being provided about all things 1942. He was particularly surprised at the percentage increases on a few common place items. A postage stamp sold for three cents in 1942 and has increased more than 1500%. Not to mention that snail mail was hardly ever used anymore, except for spam and mortgage late notices. Milk has only increased 600% in the same time. Minimum wage was thirty cents per hour, and has increased 2600%. While interesting, what bothered Peter was the relevance to their mission.

"Why are you showing us this? Does any of this information pertain to the actions of our mission?" he asked.

"Not directly. This information is provided so that you will not offer to pay more than necessary for something that you may require. How peculiar would it be if you provided a five-dollar bill for purchasing a gallon of milk valued at sixty cents?"

"Honestly, I don't plan on buying milk while on our mission. Unless, that is, our mission is stopping world hunger. How about we get to the pertinent information on the mission instead of this irrelevant garbage?" Peter replied sarcastically.

Both doctors looked flustered at Peter's comment. Dr. Lamb looked at General Applegate for guidance.

"Peter. Please allow the doctors to conclude their presentation. We will be reviewing more elements of the mission shortly. This information is critical for the success of the mission, regardless of whether you see it clearly now or not," Applegate said sternly.

Peter nodded, but his patience was wearing thin. The doctors continued, and Peter's mind drifted as they droned on about various facts like who was president or prime minister or whatever the leaders of the other countries were called. He leaned back in his chair for the next 30-plus minutes. Toward the end of the presentation, Dr. Lamb arrived at the topic of money. Peter snapped to attention and leaned forward slightly.

"Regarding currency in 1942, you will each be provided with an amount of date-specific bills to use while on the mission. This money was not easy to come by, and the value in today's market is far greater than the face value. As an example, an uncirculated one-dollar bill from 1942 has a current value of well over $30 dollars."

"Why does it need to be uncirculated?" Julie inquired.

"The money does not necessarily need to be uncirculated. There will be a mix of circulated and uncirculated cash, in dates ranging from the mid-20s through 1940. Everything you bring with you, from money and clothes to documentation and paperwork, needs to be as authentic as possible in the time to which we are traveling. We have gone to great lengths to make this mission to 1942 as authentic as possible to ensure a high chance of success."

As Dr. Lamb continued, Peter thought back to the conversation that he and Benny had at Herb's. Over the past few weeks, he had recalled nearly every detail of that drunken conversation. Benny had suggested that Peter research currency values and somehow bring back something of value from 1942.

The first thing Benny had in mind was rare coins. Small, portable. Peter initially thought about the penny well before Benny brought up coins, but it was their collective thought process that brought the plan together. Peter had begun to think of the idea as Operation Abraham.

Since that night, Peter had contemplated whether or not to act upon their alcohol-induced flight of fancy. When the idea first germinated, Peter's life was in a much different place. He was about to lose everything and his kids hated him. Now, two short weeks later, he thought he was really on track with repairing things with his kids. His bills were brought current, thanks to General Applegate, and he was working. Peter had no compelling reason to actually follow through with his plan. There was always the *shift*. Would the shift have an unforeseen effect that he had yet to realize? Might he come back to a completely different career? What about family; he might have married a different woman, or never had children. The possibilities were endless, and Peter preferred not to think about the consequences too much.

Peter's attention was returned to the meeting when General Applegate cleared his throat. He glanced up and everyone in the room was staring at him. "I'm sorry. Did I miss something?"

"I'm not sure, Peter. Did you?" asked Applegate. "Your mind appears to be someplace else. Would you like to take a break before we continue on with the discussion of the Butterfly Effect?"

"Um, no. I'm fine. I was just thinking . . ." Peter paused ". . . thinking about the French leg of the trip. Most everything you are discussing now is dealing with the US side of the mission."

"Oh, yes. The French information is there, but it's toward the back of your binder. We will be reviewing France another day. Because it only affects you and Julie, that briefing will be only for the two of you. Please read through the information provided beforehand."

Applegate again looked at Dr. Lamb and nodded.

"The Butterfly Effect. I assume that each of you are

relatively familiar with the theory." Dr. Lamb paused and looked about the faces in the room for acknowledgment. He found a steady stream of nods throughout the room until he came to Julie, who looked confused.

"Would you mind giving us the *Readers Digest* version, Dr," asked General Applegate, also noticing Julie's obvious look of incomprehension.

"Certainly. In essence, The Butterfly Effect is this: The flap of a butterfly's wings changed the air around it so much that a tornado broke out two continents away. That is to say that however minute your actions may be, they will have a certain domino effect. One thing will affect another, and so on. Chaos Theory states that: A man traveled back in time to prehistoric ages and stepped on a butterfly, and the universe was entirely different when he got back."

"So, no killing butterflies in 1942. . ." Peter said, sarcastically.

"The butterfly is merely a metaphor. I will point out that while on the mission, it is imperative that you leave little trace of your presence while there. Dr. Larsson, do you have anything to add?" asked Dr. Lamb

"Yes. Unless it is absolutely necessary, try not to converse with the natives. Your mission, once it is presented to you, will include precise instructions which require no personal contact with anyone in France. We have run through the computer simulations multiple times, and with each occurrence of contact with French citizens, the results are slightly different. You should know that the purpose of this mission is to change circumstances minutely, so let's not get carried away with making friends."

"Thank you both for the great presentation. Unless there are any questions, I think we are done here. Peter and Julie, you two can report to Hugh for today's training." General Applegate began to stand up.

"I've got a couple questions."

Applegate sat back down "Alright, Peter. Go ahead."

"I was just wondering when you were actually going to tell us what our mission is. We've been here a few weeks now and have only been given snippets of information. I know we are going to France. I know we will be on a covert mission, but beyond that I am completely clueless as to what is supposed to happen. Hell, we're leaving in two weeks, and I would think that Julie and I need more information on what we're supposed to be doing."

Peter glanced at Julie as he said this and she silently nodded her head in agreement. Peter's eyes returned to Applegate as he waited for a response.

"I completely understand your concerns, Peter. We are limiting the information given to you for a reason. Because there is so much to be absorbed prior to departure, we are feeding you both just enough intel so it can be retained in a reasonable fashion. You will both be brought up to speed prior to leaving for 1942. You'll have to trust me on this. We need you to focus on the training at hand as opposed to focusing on the end game."

Peter again glanced at Julie, and he could see she was equally frustrated with the evasive answer they got from the general. But he knew that regardless of how much he pressed for answers, General Applegate was not going to budge.

"Well, as long as we'll be brought up to speed in time . . ." Peter said, drifting off in disappointment.

"If there is nothing else?" Applegate said as he again stood up to leave.

Peter sat for a moment before standing himself. He waited for most everyone to exit. As Applegate was about to leave, Peter said, "General? A word please?"

When they were alone, Peter moved to close the door, and turned to the general.

"I am not sure what is going on here, but why are you holding back information? You've admitted as much and if you want this mission to be a success, you need to be more forthcoming with us. You picked Julie and me for a reason. We can handle it."

"Peter, what I said in front of the team is true. We are feeding you information slowly to promote thorough absorption. Could we be providing you the full mission specs? Yes. Yes, we could. But let's not forget what happened with you, Benny, and Stella just a few short weeks ago."

"I told you General. Nothing happened. I didn't say a word," Peter lied.

"I know what you said Peter, but in the event you get a little too inebriated again, we would feel more comfortable with limiting the information prior to departure. Peter, you will have to trust me. I am doing this for your own good."

Peter stared into the general's eyes. They were not the friendly eyes that had greeted him prior to learning of or accepting the mission. He felt deceived.

"I can tell you this. Once back in 1942, you will have a week to review the complete mission briefing prior to your departure to France. We built extra time into the schedule specifically for that purpose. We want you all to arrive and remain concealed while you get acclimated to the new timeline. We will not need to rush the mission once you leave the present."

Peter remained stoic and upon hearing that nugget of information his frustration abated, slightly. "OK, General. I'll play along. It's just that I feel like I could be planning more effectively if I knew what was supposed to be accomplished. That's all."

"I completely understand. That is one of your strengths, Peter. You are always thinking two steps ahead. Why do you think you are on this mission in the first place? We want to utilize that skill to its fullest potential. However, since you have plenty of time to acclimate in 1942, we are limiting any potential damage that could occur in the present." Applegate slapped him on the back as he walked to the door and left.

Peter paused a moment before following him out of the room. Heading to the training area to meet up with Julie, Peter began to reflect on what wasn't said during that conversation. He had to find out what Benny remembered from Herb's. The success of both missions could very well depend on it.

CHAPTER 4

Twelve days to Linear Shift

After dinner, the kids retreated to their rooms. Peter finished cleaning up the kitchen and decided it was time to head to Herb's to touch base with Benny. Peter had tried to call Benny several times over the last few days. He needed to know just what Benny remembered from their discussion and warn him about the general and his cronies. But Benny's answering machine always picked up on the first ring. The man seriously needed to move into the twenty-first century and subscribe to voicemail.

He knew he would have to be careful to circumvent Trevor, so now was a good time to practice the tradecraft instilled in him over the last couple weeks. He changed into dark clothing and stepped out the back door.

The evening was cool and a light mist was hanging in the air. The moon remained hidden behind the clouds, giving Peter's covert expedition a beneficial head start. Carrying a half-full trash bag to toss into the alley dumpster, he crossed through his backyard to the gate at the alley. Without hesitation, he slipped into the alley and tossed the trash into the large green bin. The thud caused a few barks from neighboring dogs but nothing more. Peter paused in front of the dumpster, glancing up and down the alley. He sensed no movement in either direction. He noticed a burgundy sedan with tinted windows under the street lamp at the north entrance to the alley. He began to move down the alley, staying out of the sedan's sight line and in the shadows as much as possible.

After a half dozen houses, he reached the end and ducked behind a parked car, waiting. He listened intently but heard nothing except the occasional chirping of crickets. Satisfied, Peter crossed the alley and swiftly jumped the three-foot-tall fence, praying that the yard he was invading had no dogs. He ran toward the rear of the house and slipped along its side, ducking below the windows as he crept by. The occupants were home, and as he slid by the nearest front window, he could hear the nine o'clock news being broadcast.

Having made his way to the front of the yard, he discreetly lifted the gate latch and walked out onto the sidewalk. He resisted closing the gate, not wanting to make any more noise than necessary.

Peter could feel his heart pounding from the excitement of his stealthy prowess. He loved the feeling of adrenalin pumping through his veins, and he reveled in this new adventure. The previous year of complete inactivity paled in comparison, and he was grateful for having been guided into his new profession.

Without incident, Peter repeated the 'duck and weave' through the next five blocks before he was sure he was not being followed. He casually strolled the last few blocks to Herb's in plain sight, still checking for a tail as they had taught him in training. He was not followed, and he felt great.

Standing in front of Herb's, Peter suddenly realized he had not had a drop to drink since accepting the mission. It was a conscious decision because he wanted to have complete focus for the mission training. He contemplated whether to have a drink or not before he went in. He had hoped that Benny wouldn't entice him into a rowdy night of debauchery and mayhem. Deciding not to heed his own concerns, Peter swung the door open and walked inside.

A sense of déjà vu came over him. He walked up to the bar and had a seat. He glanced around, hoping to see Benny in his usual booth, but no such luck. The crowd was thin, but then again it was a work night. Joe noticed him and sauntered over.

"Hi there, Pete," he said, leaning on the edge of the wood rail. "What brings you in on a Wednesday?"

Acting casual, Peter said, "Nothing too crazy. Just want to clear my head a bit. How 'bout a beer?"

"What, no scotch tonight?" asked Joe as he reached back for a pint glass.

"Nah, trying to lay off the heavy sauce for a while. Actually, make it a light beer. I'm trying to lose this gut." He patted the much-less-ample belly. An additional benefit of military training.

"Whatever you say, Boss."

A moment later, Joe slid a pint of some nondescript, wheat-colored lager toward Peter. He turned to retreat across the bar, but Peter called after him.

"Hey, Joe. Seen Benny around lately?"

"Nope. Haven't seen hide nor hair of him," Joe replied, glancing up to the ceiling in contemplation. "Now that you mention it, Benny hasn't been around since that night you two closed this place down. I figured he and Stella finally hooked up, 'cause she's not been in since that night neither."

Peter was shocked at the news, but he kept his poker face. "Heh, yeah. Benny is just crazy enough to actually take Stella out for a spin," he chuckled. He picked up his beer and downed a few swallows as he thought through this new dilemma. Hesitant to raise suspicion, but wanting more information, he pressed on "How 'bout that pretty brunette and the goon that were in here that night? Have they been back?"

Needing to attend to other customers, Joe replied shortly, "Nope. Not seen them neither since that night."

Joe moved to the other side of the bar, and Peter nursed the remainder of his beer over the next fifteen minutes. While he sat, he wondered what might have happened to Benny and Stella. He knew it was not Benny's style to just disappear like that. He knew even more so that Stella would not miss her regular watering session. Herb's was her home away from home, if there ever was one. He was certain of one thing. Ever since General Applegate came into his life, it seemed that the present had already *shifted*.

Peter finished his beer, tossed a five near the empty glass, and silently exited the bar.

As he walked through the gloom back to his house, forgone was the stealth training approach because his mind was lost in thought. What the hell happened to Benny and Stella? Subconsciously he knew, but he was afraid to admit it to himself. He wanted to give the general the benefit of the doubt, but deep-down he knew it was a wasted effort.

His walk home from Herb's was much quicker than his trip there. When he neared his front yard, he noticed the familiar burgundy sedan parked across the street. Just then, both the driver and passenger side doors opened. Trevor and Mark stepped out. "Shit," exclaimed Peter under his breath. He slowed his pace and met them at the sidewalk leading to his front door.

"Good evening, gentlemen," Peter said.

"Where've you been, Mr. Cooper?" asked Trevor.

"Oh, just out for a stroll on this beautiful night," stated Peter. The night wasn't particularly beautiful; it could have started raining at any moment.

"Cut the crap, Peter!" exclaimed Mark. "We know you were up at Herb's."

Dumbfounded, Peter recalled his clandestine trip to the bar, and was absolutely confident he was not followed. How did they know?

"Come on guys. I just needed to get out. You know, clear my head? We've been training pretty hard lately. Can't you guys lighten up a bit?" Peter said, more as a statement than a question.

"Sorry, Mr. Cooper. We can't do that. You know how critical your discretion is. General Applegate will need to hear about this," said Trevor matter-of-factly.

"Yeah, sure. Fine," Peter barked. "Whatever you two need to do. I'm going inside now." He proceeded to the front door.

Once inside, he locked the door and peeked out the side window to see if his babysitters had returned to their car. They both were still standing on his sidewalk, and Mark was on his cell phone. Peter was certain he was tattling to General Applegate. He didn't care. He was reaching his threshold for tolerance with all this distrust. He decided that to make this worth his effort, he would make certain Operation Abraham succeeded. After everything he had learned that night, it reinforced that he needed to look out for himself.

CHAPTER 5

Ten days to Linear Shift

The next few days of schlepping back and forth to the warehouse were uneventful at best. Peter was certain that Mark had talked to the general about his late night escapade at Herb's, but strangely enough, Applegate hadn't said a word about it.

With the arrival of the weekend, Peter was looking forward to a little R&R —and some time away from the general and the warehouse. Most importantly though, he had two full days to spend with his kids, which was something that he hadn't done a whole lot of since taking the mission. He knew his time with them was limited, so he wanted to make the best of what little time was left. The only problem was that Tori had screwed up family time by having a sleepover at a friend's house. At first Peter was upset at her self-centered attitude. But in the end, he couldn't be too angry; she was a teenage girl living in a house with two guys and no mother figure. She got a pass.

Peter hoped Brett was ok with it as well, because it gave them some guy time.

"Well, bub. Looks like it's just you and me this weekend. Anything you want to do?"

Peter and Brett sat at the kitchen table finishing up breakfast. Brett had just swallowed an enormous bite of syrup-laden pancakes. He shrugged. "I don't know. I was kind of hoping to rearrange my room."

Peter remembered how in his teenage years he had also liked to change his layout every few months, just to keep the monotony to a minimum. "All right. How's about I give you a hand and later we can go see a matinee or something?"

Brett's eyes lit up at the thought of going to the movies. "Could we see that new alien abduction one in 3-D?"

"Sure thing, sport. Let's finish breakfast and get cleaned up. Why don't you clear the table and I'll go check the movie times? Meet in your room in 10 minutes?" Brett was already starting to stack the dishes before Peter's words were out of his mouth.

After forty-five minutes of moving practically every piece of Brett's furniture to a different spot in his room at least three times, Brett conceded that where everything had begun made the most sense. As they finished moving everything back to its original locale, Peter noticed a book on Brett's shelf titled *The Expert's Guide to Collecting & Investing in Rare Coins*. He pulled the book out and began to flip through the pages.

"That's the book you bought me last year for my birthday," Brett offered when he noticed his dad looking at it.

"Any good information in here?" Peter asked.

"Eh, not really. I mean it has a ton of information, but it was all kind of basic to me. I like the *Red Book* or the *Blue Book* better for values."

"Um, what? You lost me. What's the *Red Book* and the *Blue Book*?"

"They're books on US coins that come out every year, and they are way better at identifying and rating coins in your collection." Brett reached up and pulled the 2012 version of the *Red Book*. "See, it shows values of coins by their year." Brett flipped through a number of pages to show his dad.

Intrigued, Peter returned the book he was holding back onto the shelf before taking Brett's *Red Book* from him. He flipped to 1942.

"What do you know about coins from World War II?" he

asked his son.

"Not much. I think there is something about a mercury dime . . ." Brett answered, but Peter was already scanning the values of all the coins from 1942. The mercury dime was in fact valued the highest of all, but not as high as he had hoped.

"If you want to see a high-priced coin, Dad, look at the 1943 bronze penny."

"Bronze? Was that new in 1943?"

Brett chuckled at his dad's ignorance. "Uh, no. The penny is actually not copper, dad. They're made of bronze, which does include copper, but not 100%."

Peter, feeling foolish that his thirteen year old son was schooling him on what a penny was actually made of could only say, "Oh."

"Actually, in 1943 the US Mint ordered all pennies to be made of steel, in order to save copper for the war efforts." Brett paused, as he flipped the *Red Book* to the appendix. "See, the bronze pennies that actually made it into circulation were made from planchets that were not removed from the presses from the 1942 run."

"What exactly is a planchet?"

"It's the metal disc before they do the imprinting."

"Right."

Peter skimmed the appendix while Brett continued on "It's unknown just how many made it into circulation, but there was at least one from each of the three US mints. The rarest of all came from the San Francisco Mint—"

"What's that? The San Francisco Mint?" Peter asked, now ignoring the book.

"Yeah, the one and only 1943 penny from San Francisco known to exist sold a few years ago for a million dollars."

Peter felt chills run through his body. "A million dollars? For a penny?"

"I know, right?"

"What year was it again?"

"1943," Brett replied, deflating the optimism he'd just built.

Peter's mission wasn't going back to 1943; he'd be a year early.

Peter flipped back to the section for 1942 and again scanned the coin values for that year.

Looking over his dad's shoulder, Brett asked, "What's so important about 1942?"

"Nothing particular. Just a conversation on World War II coins Benny and I were having. And you're right. The mercury dime looks to be the best." He began to flip back through the book year by year, looking at various values within ten years of his mission target. Nothing was jumping out at him.

Feeling defeated, he wondered what else of value he could use. It had to be cheap and compact to fit his plan. Something that, at the time, would not be missed and that could increase in value over seventy-odd years.

His mind returned to the 1943 penny, and he cursed the unlucky timing of his mission. "If that 1943 penny were only made in 1942 . . ." He mumbled allowed.

"Well, actually, it was. But we can't afford it, so it doesn't matter anyway," Brett explained.

"Huh? What did you just say?"

"We can't afford it. Besides, it's in some permanent collection now. I don't even think it's for sale."

"No, not that. What about it being made in '42?"

"Oh. Yeah, I think it was actually made in the latter part of 1942, to be released in 1943. I'm not exactly sure though."

His enthusiasm reignited, Peter asked, "What about the other pennies from that year? You said something about having at least one copper penny from each mint."

"You mean bronze . . ."

"Yeah, I meant bronze. Are they equally valuable?"

"Not even close. The other mints also let out bronze pennies, but their values are much, much lower because of the number of them circulated."

"How much lower?" Peter asked quickly.

"Something like $60,000 or so. It's such a price difference because there are ten or more from the other mints known to exist."

Peter whistled in amazement. "Sixty grand is still pretty nice."

The two sat there for a few moments in silence as Peter continued to turn the pages of Brett's *Red Book*. Peter's mind was now racing, trying to figure out how he could get a hold of a few of those 1943 pennies while on the mission. If he could just get three or four of them and stash them away, when he returned from his mission, he could recover the hidden coins and sell them to a collector in the *shifted* present.

Peter's plan was interrupted when Brett cleared his throat and asked, "What time does the movie start? Are we going to eat lunch before?"

"What? Oh yeah. Lunch sounds good." Peter closed the book and handed it back to Brett. "Let's get changed and head out.

CHAPTER 6

Eight days to Linear Shift

Peter was the first one to arrive for language training on Monday morning. He chuckled at the irony. He hated this aspect of the training sessions most of all, and his desire to learn French was close to nil. He preferred the tradecraft and espionage lessons because he felt like he excelled at them, even though he still needed lots of work.

When Julie and Hugh walked in, they were in a deep conversation in French. Peter shook his head in bemusement at the ease with which the two could carry on. Julie happened to notice Peter's irritation and quickly added, "*On dirait que quelqu'un se sent exclu.*"

"Oh, ha ha. I can understand you just fine, and no, I am not feeling left out." Peter turned away so they couldn't see him roll his eyes. One of the drawbacks of spending too much time with his teenage daughter.

"It's OK, Peter, we understand you are not as fluent in French as your partner here," Hugh began, "but these lessons are here to provide you with the basics of speech ."

"I can understand it just fine. I'm not sure why I need to speak it fluently. As long as Julie is around, I'll be okay."

"Yes, it's a real benefit that Julie speaks fluently. However, what if something happens to her? Hugh moved to the sit next to Peter and handed him another training pamphlet. "You don't have to be exact. You have grasped understanding quick enough. You just need to practice speaking French."

Over the next three and a half hours, Hugh and Julie took turns quizzing Peter on various common French phrases and correcting him with proper pronunciations. This was the fourth or fifth lesson since training began; Peter felt he was making great strides toward the end of the session. When he had enough, he proudly asked "*Quelle heure est-il?*"

Hugh and Julie both glanced up to the clock on the wall.

"Very clever, Peter," Hugh chided. "Looks like our time is about up."

Hugh began to shuffle his training materials back into a pile before sliding them back into his manila folder. "Might I suggest that you two continue with your training outside of the warehouse? You will be going on this mission as a couple, and frankly, you two don't talk or act like it."

Peter was well aware of this fact. Even though he found himself attracted to Julie, it was still difficult to treat her like she was his wife. He knew he needed to work on that.

"How about dinner tonight?" he asked nervously.

"Aw, gee, Peter. Are you asking me out on a date? I'd love to have dinner with you," Julie teased, batting her eyelashes.

"Great. Um, I don't think we should eat at my house. I haven't told the kids anything. It's probably best that they don't see me having dinner with a strange woman. They might start asking questions. How about I pick you up around 7:30?"

"So, you think I'm strange?" she scoffed while raising one eyebrow.

"No, that's not what I meant!"

"I'm kidding. That's fine. How about we go to that new French place downtown? That way we can practice ordering dinner."

"Great. And by 'we,' you mean me."

Julie batted her eyelashes again, and tilted her head innocently. "It would be the gentlemanly thing to do."

Peter smiled, and he would have been lying to himself if he

thought he wasn't looking forward to it. "Whose goon do you want to escort us? Yours or mine?"

"Oh, God. Yours, please!"

"Works for me. I'll go have a chat with him before lunch."

———————⌒———————

Peter left the room, and although he had seen Trevor in the warehouse many times, he was not exactly sure where he spent his time during the day. He descended the stairs to the ground floor and walked through the fake French village looking for the rear of the warehouse. He turned down an alley off one of the side streets and found a door marked "Stairs." He recalled seeing both Trevor and Mark coming and going out of this area a few times. Peter twisted the handle and entered.

The door opened into a stairwell to a basement level. He scurried down, and at the bottom there was a newly installed door. The door was steel and contained a small wired-glass opening centered at eye level. Peter tried the handle, but it was locked. He leaned close to the glass to see who or what was on the other side. A cement wall. He angled his view, but all he could see was a narrow corridor perpendicular to the door. He instinctively tried the handle again, as people tend to do, but its condition was unchanged. Just as he was about to knock on the door, a voice from behind startled him.

"What are you doing down here?" snapped Mark.

Great, Peter thought. Captain Commando.

"I'm looking for Trevor. Have you seen him?"

"He's not down here. Go back upstairs and I'll let him know you're looking for him." Mark circled around and placed himself between Peter and the door.

Peter didn't argue and left without saying another word. He found it peculiar and annoying that Mark was protecting the basement. What was down there?

CHAPTER 7

Eight days to Linear Shift

Peter stood motionless in his closet for close to five minutes as he scanned each of his dress slacks and button-down combinations. It had been more than fifteen years since he'd been on a date, and he was nervous. He wondered if he was overthinking it. Was it really a date? he questioned. No, it was just an extended training session on communication, he answered himself. Then why did it feel so much like a date? He had no answer.

Finally deciding on the charcoal-colored slacks, he pulled them on before grabbing a matching shirt and moving back into the bedroom. Peter was startled to find Brett silently sitting on the end of the bed.

"Hey, champ. How long you been there?" asked Peter.

"Not long. About as long as it took you to pick out your clothes," Brett answered with a grin.

"Hey. No comments from the peanut gallery," Peter teased. "What're you doing in here anyway?"

"Just thought I'd help you get ready. It's your first date in, like, forever."

"It's not a date, Brett. It's just a work thing."

"Are other people going to be there?"

"No, it's just going to be Julie and me."

"Yep, it is *so* a date," kidded Brett.

Peter acknowledged his son's jibe. It was a date, and he found himself excited.

"So, who is she dad? Is she pretty?"

"She's just a coworker. And yeah, I think she's attractive," Peter said as he slid into his shirt.

"Can I meet her? I mean, will Tori and I meet her?"

"Not today, kiddo. Maybe next time."

With shaky hands, Peter struggled buttoning his shirt. Tucking and slipping his belt through the loops also proved a challenge, as his thoughts were on calming his nervousness. As Peter finished dressing, Brett sat quietly, his gaze roaming.

"Dad?"

"Yeah?"

"Do you still miss Mom?"

Peter stopped knotting his tie and turned to face Brett. The question took him by surprise, and he suddenly realized that he had not thought about Minnie since asking to take Julie on this French communication date.

"Sure I do, buddy. I loved your mother. Don't ever forget that."

"I know. It's just that I've been thinking about her a lot lately."

"How so?"

"They're good thoughts. Remembering her making my lunch before school or reading to me before bed. Just things like that."

Peter sat next to his son.

"Do you remember when we were up camping? After we got unpacked and put the tent up, we started to make dinner and mom had forgotten to pack the meat from the fridge. You were so pissed."

"At first . . . . But we made a great Cooper team effort, remember?"

"Yeah, we made s'mores for dinner. That was my favorite camping trip."

"Mine too, kiddo. Mine too."

Peter and Brett sat in silence on the foot of the bed for a few more minutes. "Look at the time. I've got to get going. The driver is going to be here in five minutes. Want to talk more when I get home? I don't think dinner will go too late."

"Nah. You have my permission to stay out late tonight. You deserve it, Dad. It's about time, you know?" Brett grinned.

"Well, thanks for your blessing, kiddo. Means a lot."

───────────⌒───────────

The black town car arrived at La Merise ten minutes before their dinner reservation. Trevor, dressed in a black suit and tie, stepped out and quickly moved to the rear passenger side to open the door for Julie. He held his gloved hand, palm up, in front of the door for her. Julie accepted the hand as she pulled herself out of the backseat. She was wearing a black sleeveless dress that ended just below her knees. She had open-toed, strappy heels to match, which made it difficult to steady herself without assistance.

"*Merci*, Trevor," Julie said as she stepped away from the car. Peter popped out the rear driver's side.

"Are you sure you don't want to come in and wait in the lounge?"

"No, sir. I'll be fine. Just send me a text when you're finished. I'll be a few minutes away," he replied before climbing back behind the wheel.

"OK then. Shall we?" Peter offered his arm to Julie and began to escort her toward the restaurant.

Julie slid her arm into his and fell into stride. "Thank you, sir."

As they approached, the door opened with assistance from the doorman. "Good evening."

"Good evening," Peter offered in return.

"Peter, this is supposed to be a French lesson. You should try," suggested Julie.

Stepping through the door and away from the doorman, Peter said, "But he's just a kid. Do you think he understands French?"

"I think you'd be surprised, that's all."

They walked through the vestibule and approached a gentleman in a black tuxedo and white gloves.

"Hello. We have a dinner reservation under Cooper," Peter said to the man behind the podium.

The maître d' looked down and scanned the list in front of him. After a few moments of reading names and comments, he looked up and said, "*réservations pour les deux?*"

Stymied, Peter replied, "Uh, yes, reservations for two."

Julie nudged him slightly. Peter was quick to the hint and responded in French this time.

The maître d' nodded, told them that it would be just a moment, and asked them to wait there. He stepped away from the podium and disappeared into the bowels of the restaurant.

Peter leaned over slightly and said to Julie "That was weird. This must be a pretty authentic restaurant to require their staff to speak French."

Julie didn't reply but just smiled knowingly.

A few moments later, the maître d' returned and asked them to follow.

"*Merci!*" Peter replied confidently.

Their table was situated in a private alcove near the rear of the restaurant. The maître d' pulled a chair away for Julie as Peter sat across from her. Before leaving, he informed them that their waiter would be with them shortly.

Peter looked across the table at Julie, who was beaming with pride. "I don't suppose you had anything to do with this?"

"Whatever do you mean, Peter?" Julie replied, with a lovely, devious look in her eye.

Peter smiled at her. "I thought so. French lesson indeed."

Julie nodded her head in admission of her chicanery.

"By the way, have I mentioned just how wonderful you look tonight?" Peter said.

"Yes, you have. I think that was three times now. But keep it up; a girl loves to hear compliments."

Peter was about to expound on her choice of outfit but was interrupted by the waiter. "*Bonsoir. Puis-je vous offrir un verre au bar?"*

"Seriously?" Peter asked Julie sarcastically.

Julie nodded.

Peter replied in the best French he could muster, ordering a French 75 for Julie and a scotch and water for himself.

After their waiter retreated, Julie said, "Not bad. Your enunciation is improving."

"I do my best."

"How'd you know what I wanted to drink, by the way?" Julie asked.

"I took a shot. If it's not good, we'll get you something else."

"It will be fine. I've had one before, and besides being a bit strong, it's pretty good. Are you trying to get me drunk?" Julie winked.

Peter could feel his face redden, and hoped that it would not surpass the hue of Julies lips.

"What looks good?" she asked, opening her menu.

Peter opened his, too, and was relieved that it was in English. He smiled and looked up at Julie. They both laughed at the irony.

———————————⌒———————————

After ordering dinner for them both, Peter tried his best to make small talk.

"So, Jules, where are you from?" he asked.

"Well, I am native to California. I grew up in Sacramento and moved to the Bay area about six years ago."

Peter studied Julie's facial expression as she spoke and decided right then that he might very well be smitten. Her face was quite exquisite. She had beautiful hazel eyes and high cheekbones. Not wanting to gawk too long, he nervously glanced down at the table.

"How about you, Peter? You're a native right?" Julie asked, never withdrawing eye contact.

"Yeah, for the most part. I was actually born in Chicago, but we moved west before I started grade school. My grandparents came over from England in the early 50s."

"Oh, how interesting. Have you been to England to explore your heritage?"

"I have. I was in the army many years ago and traveled there for a few weeks on leave. I would love to go back and visit more of the countryside. Have you been?"

"England? Sure, a few times. But France is my passion. My ancestors are French and came from a small town called Oradour-sur-Glane. Have you heard of it?"

"It sounds sorta' familiar, but I've never been to France. Do you go back often?"

"Not as much as I'd like. Besides, I no longer have family there. The town was destroyed in '44, toward the end of World War II."

There was a moment of uncomfortable silence, which was broken by the waiter dropping off their entrees.

"Your mother and stepfather are here, right?" Peter asked after the waiter left. "Any other family local?"

"Yes and no. My stepfather lives near Berkley. My mother passed away a few years ago. I was an only child, so it's just me."

"Oh, I'm sorry."

"Don't be silly. She passed away a while ago. I've moved on," replied Julie, as she took the first bite of her Osso Bucco.

"Hey speaking of that night, the general must have come down on you pretty hard. You looked pretty shaken up when you came to the briefing." Peter probed, before diving into his own meal.

Between bites, Julie replied "Yeah, a little. He basically told me he owns me, and that I have to do whatever he says."

"He said that? Why does he think that?"

"He didn't say it in those exact words. He thinks he owns me because of something he is holding over my head. Something that happened a long time ago and I'd rather not talk about." Julie said, looking away from Peter.

"No pressure, Jules." Peter said assuringly. "How did they know you were there in the first place?"

"You see, that's what has me stumped. I was very careful not to be followed. I didn't want any of this to come down on Frank, but they still found me there."

"I totally get what you are saying. It seems Trevor and Mark know where I am all the time, regardless of whether they follow me or not."

"Do you think they bugged us with some kind of tracking device ?" Julie asked.

"I wouldn't put it past them. I'm not sure what to think anymore."

The conversation paused briefly, and they both idly played with their food.

Feeling full, Julie pushed her plate away and said "You have . . . two kids, right? Any other family?"

"Nope. Just the kids. I think of my friend Benny as a brother though." Peter furrowed his brow and frowned.

"Is there something wrong?"

"It's probably nothing. It's Benny. He's disappeared."

"Disappeared? From where?"

"Do you remember that night at Herb's when you and Mark were asking Stella questions? It was just before Applegate convinced me to sign up."

"Sure."

"Well, ever since that night, Benny and Stella have vanished. Gone. Nobody has seen either of them since."

Julie looked concerned.

"Do you know something?"

"Well, I'm not sure. After you conned us, Mark dropped me off and sped away in a hurry. The next day when he picked me up to head to your house, he was wearing the same clothes as the night before. It looked like he hadn't slept. I asked him if he had a good night, but he was rude and told me to mind my own business."

"Do you think the two are related?" asked Peter.

"I don't know. Maybe. I know the general was pretty upset with you for talking to your friends about the mission."

"Again, I didn't say anything!"

"Well, the general thinks you did."

"Do you think he kidnapped them?"

"Possibly. I wouldn't put anything past him, if you know what I mean."

Peter knew, and he wasn't comfortable with the thought.

Seeing his eyes intensify, Julie asked, "What are you thinking, Peter?"

"I don't know. The thought of them being taken makes my blood boil. I didn't sign up for this expecting my friends to be hurt." He paused to catch his breath "I'm gonna march right over there and . . ."

"Peter, be careful. Whatever you're thinking, please be careful with the general. He is not the man you think he is."

Peter contemplated Julie's warning. He leaned back, wine glass in hand, and thought. General Applegate was not the man he once thought he was. That was obvious.

"What do you think?" Peter asked sincerely.

"I don't know what to think. If he lured you into this mission like he did with me, we don't have a lot of options. Part of me wants to be right there with you, and march right into his office and junk-punch him until he gives us our lives back . . ."

Peter raised his eyebrows slightly when he heard Julie's choice of torture. "Junk-punch?" asked Peter, with a smile.

Julie shyly smiled back "Well yeah. What were you thinking of doing to him?"

"I want to get to the bottom of this, but punching another man in the twig and berries seems a little over the edge." Peter winked. "Perhaps a more diplomatic approach is in order. I think I'll have a talk with our fearless leader tomorrow."

He was having a fantastic evening with a beautiful woman. A rarity, for sure. Unfortunately, now all he could focus on was Applegate. Peter wanted the truth, no matter how he had to get it.

CHAPTER 8

Seven days to Linear Shift

Peter sat in the kitchen thinking about last night with Julie. He couldn't shake their conversation about how Applegate was probably responsible for Benny and Stella's disappearance. As he waited for Trevor to pick him up, he ran through a number of scenarios about what might have happened, and each result pointed at Applegate. He stressed about the inevitable confrontation with the general and jeopardizing his place on the team. Then he wondered if Trevor knew anything about their sudden vanishing. He made a point of asking him on the drive in.

Lost in thought, he didn't hear the car pull up or the first rap on the door. It was the second knock that got his attention. Peter sprang from his chair and answered the door.

Trevor was standing patiently on the edge of the porch when Peter opened the door. "Morning, Trevor."

"Good morning, Mr. Cooper. Ready to go?"

"Just about. Come on in while I grab a jacket and my keys," Peter said, hoping to have a moment with him before they left for the warehouse.

"That's all right. I'll just wait in the car. You won't be long I trust?" replied Trevor.

Peter retraced his steps to the kitchen to grab his jacket off the back of his chair. He turned off the lights and made his way back to the foyer. He scooped his keys from the table and locked the door on his way out.

Trevor was still driving the town car from the night before. Peter fastened the seatbelt as Trevor pulled away from the curb.

"I wanted to thank you again for last night. You really went beyond the call of duty dressing up in that chauffeur outfit. Julie was quite impressed as well," Peter said, hoping to soften Trevor's usually rigid demeanor with flattery.

"It was my pleasure, Mr. Coop . . . Peter," Trevor replied.

"You seemed to handle the role of chauffeur quite well. Did you used to drive limos or something?"

"No, sir. I've been in security for the last four years after spending twenty years in the marines."

"Wow. Twenty years as a jarhead?"

Trevor took his eyes of the road momentarily and glared at Peter. Oops.

"Sorry, Trevor. Nothing meant by it. Old habits, I guess. I was an army guy myself." Peter felt relieved when Trevor's expression returned to its usual passive state. Trevor was a guy that stood six two and was clearly pushing 275 pounds. Peter did not want to piss him off.

"It's all right, Peter. Army guys and marines have never really seen eye to eye."

You speak no lies, Peter thought to himself. He then pounced on the opportunity to shift the conversation.

"Security for four years? All with General Applegate?"

"Nope. I've been independent for most of that time, contracting occasionally with the secret service. I've only been with the general for a few months."

Holy shit, thought Peter. This guy worked for the secret service? Applegate didn't fuck around.

"So, you were probably involved with that whole situation at Herb's a few weeks ago?" Peter asked, hoping that his frankness wasn't out of line.

Trevor continued to focus on the road for a few moments before replying, "I'm not at liberty to discuss details of my position without General Applegate's approval."

"Oh, I didn't mean to pry," Peter interjected. "It's just that I remember seeing Mark and Julie there, and I was just curious if you were part of my recruitment."

"I'm sorry, Peter. I can't talk about the mission," Trevor said with such finality that Peter knew the door just slammed shut. The rest of the ride passed in silence. Peter decided that Applegate was the only person who could answer his questions. Lucy's got some splainin' to do, he thought.

After Trevor dropped him off, he made his way up to the ops center. He hoped that he was early enough to have some time alone with the general before the morning briefing.

When Peter walked in, the room was vacant. The computers were humming, probably processing some mission scenarios.

Returning to the mezzanine gangway, he walked down to the break room. It was also devoid of any personnel. Strange, Peter thought. There is usually at least one of the doctors around.

He continued down the walkway and decided to try the unmarked offices. The first door was locked, and after a series of unanswered knocks, he moved on. The second door was unlocked, but the office was empty. Peter moved to the third door, also unlocked. He popped his head in and found Applegate and the two doctors. Applegate looked up at the sound of the door opening.

"Peter. Is there something you need? Briefing is still twenty minutes from now."

Stepping fully into the office, Peter said "I was hoping to have a few words with you, General. Before the briefing."

"Can't it wait? We're really quite busy," Applegate said.

"No, I think we should talk now," Peter pressed, as he moved over to the general's desk.

"All right then." Applegate looked at Drs. Lamb and Larsson. "Can you two finish this report and have it ready for the briefing?"

They nodded in unison and extricated themselves from the

two chairs in front of Applegate's desk. They walked out, closing the door behind them.

"OK, Peter. You have my full attention. What is so important?"

Peter sat across from General Applegate and paused. He had stressed about how he was going to confront the general on the drive into the warehouse. Now that he was there, he froze.

"Peter?" prompted the general.

"Uh, yeah. I wanted to talk to you about something that's been bothering me."

General Applegate sat silent, waiting.

"Well, it has to do with my friend Benny; actually, it has to do with my friends Benny and Stella. I cannot seem to find either one of them."

"Why would you concern yourself with either of them?" inquired Applegate.

"Well, they're my friends. That's what friends do—they talk to each other from time to time," Peter replied. As the words left his mouth, he began to get upset again. He had hoped to maintain a cool demeanor, but he quickly realized that it was going to be difficult.

"Talking to them put us all in an uncomfortable position in the first place. I understand your desire to maintain your friendships, but after the *shift*, they may or may not even be an acquaintance."

"What the hell kind of answer is that?" demanded Peter. "You can train me and send me on this mission, but to hell with you for telling me who I can or cannot have as friends."

"That's not what I said. I merely suggested that you forget about maintaining friendships that might not be the same after you return from your mission," Applegate said.

Peter sat a moment while the general's words sank in. When he spoke, he tried his hardest to not snap. "I know for a fact that both Benny and Stella are missing. I think you have something to do with it. I ask," Peter raised his voice, "no, I demand that you tell me what happened to them!" Peter pounded his fist on the edge of the desk.

Barely flinching at the outburst, Applegate maintained his composure. He stared Peter directly in the eye as he said, "Yes, they are missing, but not lost. I have them here in the warehouse."

Peter was speechless.

"Trust me Peter, they are unharmed. Actually, they are being well cared for."

"You took them? That's kidnapping! What gives you the right to take people against their will?" Peter snapped.

"You gave us that right when you talked about the mission, Peter." Applegate snapped back. "You gave us no other choice. Besides, they were not kidnapped. They are just our extended guests." General Applegate leaned back in his chair and clasped his hands across his ample belly.

Peter, in turn, leaned back in his chair. He supposed he always knew the general was involved, but it was still shocking to hear him admit it.

"Call it what you will. You took them without their consent. What are you going to do with them? People will start asking questions sooner or later."

"Oh, that will never happen. They are our guests until the mission launches. At that point, they will be released," Applegate stated.

"So until then, they are just rotting in some cell here?"

"They're not in a cell, Peter. They are in two small apartments in the basement. The apartments are fully furnished and I assure you, they are quite comfortable."

"Do they know what is going on? I am sure they must be confused or scared, or both for that matter."

"They have been told that it was for their own safety that they remain here and that it was a security precaution linked to your new job."

Calming minutely, Peter asked "So, they're OK with everything?"

"They are coping with the changes as expected. Would they

be happier in their own homes? Certainly, but that's not an option."

Peter paused in contemplation. General Applegate didn't offer anything further. The room was silent; the tension thick. Peter pressed on with his next round of questions.

"I'm curious, general. Why is it so important that we not talk about the mission? Why all the hush-hush? If we're going back to make this big *shift*, why would it matter if people know?"

"It's not that simple. There are organizations in the world that don't take time travel lightly. These people will stop at nothing to prevent our success. Once the team has departed, the threat will disappear."

The reasons from the general seemed valid enough, but Peter was still not satisfied with the situation with his friends. "Do I have your word that they will be released when we leave for 1942?"

"Yes, Peter. They will be released unharmed. If I did not plan on releasing them, why would I keep them alive?"

Peter's blood ran cold. Keep them alive? He was afraid to push the subject any further.

"All right then. If they are aware of the situation, can I see them? A friendly face might go a long way."

Now it was Applegate's turn to contemplate. He sat motionless for a moment before replying, "I don't see a problem with that. However, we will be listening to insure that you do not divulge anything about the mission."

He thought about arguing that it wouldn't matter because of the *shift* but recanted. "Fine. It will be just a friendly visit, and I'll tell them that it's all top secret and I can't say anything. Deal?"

"That is acceptable. I'll set something up at the end of today. I need your focus on training. Also, I ask that you please keep this between us. No need to involve the rest of the team."

"Agreed." Peter stood up and strode out of Applegate's office without another word.

CHAPTER 9

Seven days to Linear Shift

After another arduous day of training, Applegate led Peter through the mock village. They arrived at the basement door within minutes—the same door where the confrontation with Mark had occurred just a few days before. Peter wondered if Mark had talked to Applegate about the incident. He decided to not ask.

Applegate opened the door and motioned Peter to lead the way down the steps. At the bottom, he stepped up and swiped his RFID badge across a reader hidden behind a wall panel. A metallic whine and click sounded as the door popped open.

"Well. This is as far as I go. I have far too much going on at the moment to accompany you down to sublevel 10," Applegate said as his left eye blinked rapidly, and his neck tensed up causing his head to tilt to the side.

Making a mental note of Applegates bizarre reaction, he asked "Should I be concerned?"

"Oh, no. Not at all. It's just that this facility is a decommissioned military bunker, and where you are headed is several stories down. This warehouse was built over the bunker entrance, where we are standing right now. You will understand my hesitation once you've arrived."

"If you're not coming, how will I find my way?"

Just as Peter asked the question, Trevor stepped through

the security door. "I'll be taking you down, Mr. Cooper."

Peter looked up at the behemoth and felt a little more at ease. Despite Trevor being a bit odd, he actually liked the guy.

"Great. We're back to Mr. Cooper again," Peter teased. Before Trevor could reply, Peter stepped through the door and nodded to General Applegate as he disappeared out of sight.

Trevor closed the door behind them and took the lead down the corridor. Peter could smell the scent of fresh paint and new vinyl flooring.

"So. We're going to see Benny and Stella," Peter said pointedly. Trevor was quiet but not stupid.

"Yeah, sorry about this morning, Mr. uh . . . Peter. I wanted to talk to you about it, but you know. I was just doin' my job."

"Don't sweat it, big guy. Where are we going anyway?"

"We're going pretty deep. Ten floors down. I don't enjoy going down there myself, but it's part of the job, you know."

Trevor stopped at the end of the corridor and swiped his own RFID card across a reader and the door opened. Trevor pressed on, barely waiting for Peter to keep up. On the other side of the steel door, their environment changed. It was like the door itself was the time machine. They walked into something out of an old military movie: a long, semi-circular shaped tunnel with pipes and conduit running along the apex of the curve and old jelly jar light fixtures hung every fifty feet or so. From what Peter could tell, the tunnel went on for several hundred feet.

They continued down the tunnel until they came to an older steel door that looked like a blast door. It was more than a foot thick and was wide open. Peter imagined it probably hadn't been closed in many years due to rust. Trevor turned into the wide opening and followed a new passage another thirty feet before coming to a stairway heading down.

"You ready?" Trevor asked, pausing only a moment for Peter to reply.

"Really? Stairs? Isn't there an elevator or something? You said ten floors down, right?"

"Yes, sir. Ten floors down—no elevator. This place is a relic from the cold war. It's pretty much essentials only down here. You're not concerned, are you?"

"Me? No. I'm not worried about the trip down. Just the trip back up."

Trevor laughed, and Peter couldn't recall the big man laughing at any other point since meeting him.

Trevor started the descent, and, fortunately, took the stairs at a relatively leisurely pace. The stair treads were diamond embossed steel. The original army green paint was mostly worn away from years of use, and even the diamond pattern had significant wear near the center of the stairs.

The stairwell consisted of three tiers per floor, with a landing on the fourth side. In the center of the tiers was a large shaft that Peter assumed was meant for a lift during construction. But try as he might, he could not see through the wire metal screen, most likely installed to prevent a fall.

As they passed each landing, Peter mentally noted the approximate floor height. Based on the number of risers per floor, he estimated that each level was about twenty-four feet tall. A door at each landing had the associated level stenciled in black paint. They started at SUB-1, and as they descended, the number increased consecutively.

Some fifteen minutes later, they arrived at SUB-10, and from what Peter could see, the stairway continued to drop down farther. He also felt the temperature drop. Ten degrees, he guessed.

Breaking the silence, Peter asked, "You have to make this trip every day?"

"Nope. Mark and I alternate every other day. It's not too bad. Great exercise, if you ask me."

Trevor walked up to the door, slid a large steel shaft to the side, and pulled the heavy door open. The door squeaked in protest, but the offending noise was short lived. Peter could instantly smell something baking. The aroma of cookies or maybe a cake permeated his nostrils. Trevor stepped through the door and then to the side. Peter followed, and as he did so,

Trevor pointed toward a light at the end of yet another corridor.

"That's where your friends are. They have this entire level, and I think they will be happy to see you."

"Thanks, Trevor. How long do I have with them?" Peter asked.

"The general didn't give me a time limit. Seeing as I'm your ride home, you can take your time."

Trevor stepped back into the stairwell and began climbing the stairs two at a time. Peter was surprised at being left alone with his buddies.

———————

Peter walked down the corridor, and as he got nearer the light at the end of the tunnel, he began to hear music playing. Then, like an old warm blanket on winter's day, he heard Benny and Stella's voices. They were arguing, naturally, and Peter smiled as he stepped into a large, well-lit gathering room. The room had a large plasma television on one end surrounded by a sofa sectional. On the other end was a large, open-ended kitchen with a dining table for eight. He stood there, smiling for a moment listening to the two bicker about whether Stella should put nuts in the brownies again.

Peter cleared his throat. Stella was the first to notice him.

"Oh my God, oh my God, oh my God!" yelled Stella, as she shuffled her way around the kitchen island and over to Peter. With each step closer, her arms widened. When she reached him, she wrapped them around Peter and squeezed for all she was worth. "Oh, baby. What have they done to you? They won't tell us nothin'."

As Stella held Peter in her bear hug, Benny moved his way around the island and strolled up to Peter as if nothing were out of the ordinary. Peter reached out a free hand and shook Benny's in firm greeting. Peter freed himself from Stella before he spoke.

"How are you guys?" grimaced Peter.

Benny opened his mouth to speak, but Stella took over. "How are we? How the hell are we? I'll tell you how we are. We're—"

"Stella, shut up already," Benny interrupted her. "Let the man breathe, for Christ's sake."

"It's OK, Benny," Peter smiled at Stella reassuringly. "I understand how she feels. I'd feel the same way if it were me down here."

Stella smirked in disdain towards Benny but did as he suggested and remained quiet.

"Really, how are you two?" Peter asked again.

"We've been better, Pete," replied Benny. "What the hell is going on? Why are we being held down here?"

Peter didn't answer right away. Knowing the General was listening, his hands were tied to certain extent. "Well, I'm working on this top secret thing. I can't go into too much detail about it, because it's, well, top secret."

"That's what that pompous ass said when they brought us down here."

"That would have been General Applegate. He's sort of my boss."

"Yeah, that is one messed up dude, my friend," added Benny.

"Why do you say that?"

"He was all right when we first met him upstairs in that movie set. But when he came down here to show us around, well . . . let's just say he was acting pretty erratic. I mean he was really buggin' out. His eyes were dartin' from side to side, and I honestly thought he was gonna jump right out of his skin."

Peter frowned slightly. "Yeah, that Applegate can be a loose cannon sometimes." He said, satisfied at the verbal jab he just delivered to the man upstairs listening.

"If you say so. Still no excuse for locking us up down here." Benny reiterated.

"To that statement, Benny my friend, I whole-heartedly agree. But . . ."

"But what, honey?" asked Stella, hanging on Peter's every word.

"Well, I'm involved in some pretty deep shit. Until I am

through with this 'project,'" Peter laid out his famous air quotes, "anyone that I have talked with might be in danger. The general actually brought you here as a precaution because of me. Because of that night at Herb's. They thought I was being followed by . . ." Peter was actually having fun with the ruse, pausing again, and fictitiously looked around to see if anyone else was there to overhear him. "followed by spies," Peter ended the statement in a near whisper.

Stella gasped and Benny looked confused. Peter had hoped that Benny would understand and not reveal any of what they talked about that night. To help ensure that Benny didn't say anything, Peter gave him a slight wink when Stella was looking dumbfounded at the floor. Benny caught the wink and nodded slightly.

"Well, I for one feel a hundred percent better knowing we are safe down here." Benny exclaimed, aiding in Peter's ploy.

Stella on the other hand looked a bit fearful. She was speechless.

"Stella? Are you going to be OK?" Peter asked.

"Oh, honey. What have you got yourself into? I'm fine, but I'm worried about you to death."

"I'm safe, Stella. I actually have my own security detail. You've probably seen him around. He's the big oaf-looking guy. Trevor's his name. He's a good guy."

"Oh, I like Trevor. He's so polite when he comes down here. That other guy though. He's a real you-know-what," Stella said dramatically.

"You ain't whistlin' Dixie, kid. He's a real pain topside as well," explained Peter. "For what it's worth, the general has informed me that you'll both be compensated for your troubles," Peter added, knowing that if the general were listening, he was about to have an aneurysm.

"How much are we talkin', darlin'?" asked Stella.

"Well, if all goes well, you will both be allowed to leave in a little less than two weeks, and—"

"Two more weeks?" gasped Benny.

"—and if all goes well you will both be reimbursed for any loss in wages, past and future. Sorry buddy, but all this is for your safety."

"I doubt I'll have a job after another two weeks down here," Benny said with a frown.

"I'm not so sure about that. But if you are let go, the general has guaranteed that you'll get paid up until you get a new job," Peter said, satisfied that Applegate was probably bouncing off the walls of his office about now.

"Hell, they can fire me!" drawled Stella. Benny just grinned at the thought of not having to work for his current employer again.

Peter felt pretty satisfied with the handling of his friends' situation. So what if the general has to pay a bit more to make things right, he thought. It's the right thing to do.

"I, for one, think we need to celebrate," Stella proclaimed as she stood up. "Can you stick around for a drink, for old time's sake?"

"Yeah, sure. Just one though. I am in some pretty intense training every day."

"Cool. Stella, why don't you mix up some of those wonderful margaritas, and I'll give Peter the dime tour of our humble abode," said Benny.

Stella smiled and gave Peter a quick peck on the cheek before moving toward the kitchen.

———————

Benny took Peter room by room, bragging about the fine amenities his new residence had to offer. The sleeping quarters were to be expected, but the fully equipped gymnasium was quite impressive.

"And this here is our little spa," Benny boasted as he walked into a fully-tiled hexagonal room. The "spa" had four separate saunas and a large hot tub in the center.

"What's in here?" Peter asked as he walked around the corner from the saunas and into a large showering area.

"This here is where the biggest mistake of my life happened," cried Benny.

"Come again?" asked Peter.

"Well, we had been down here a few days, and I had a moment of weakness," Benny explained, hanging his head low. "You see, Stella and me were just coming out of our separate saunas and I felt like a dip in the hot tub would finish off the day nicely. One thing led to another, and, well . . ." Benny's words drifted off.

"No. You didn't," insisted Peter.

"Yeah. I did. Stella was on me quick and there was nothing I could do about it." Benny looked up and continued. "And I didn't know how long we were gonna be down here, so I thought, what the hell, and dipped my toes in the ocean."

"And?" pressed Peter.

"And what? We screwed. What else do you think happened?"

Peter, not wanting to further embarrass Benny, quickly changed the subject. "So, uh . . . these are the showers?" His voice echoed off the floor-to-ceiling tiles. As Peter reviewed the room, he thought there was no place to hide a camera or microphone, so he moved quick. He ran to two of the shower handles and cranked them as fast as he could to the right. Cold water spluttered and violently sprayed from the nozzles.

"Benny. Listen quick," Peter whispered. "I don't think we are being watched in here, so I need to know; did the general ask you about that night at Herb's?"

"Yeah, he asked both Stella and me about it. He wanted to know what you told us about some mission." His voice was low.

"Did you say anything? Did you mention what we talked about that night?"

"Nope. That conversation's between you and me. Nobody else needs to know. What's goin' on?"

"I AM going on the mission that you and I discussed that night. Do you remember?"

"Yeah, you're going through some time machine, right?"

"That's right. And you haven't told anyone, have you? Nobody knows about it, right?"

"You have my word, Peter. You're like a brother. I'd never betray you."

Peter paused a moment and basked in Benny's proclamation. "I love you too, man." He slapped Benny on the back, and they fell into a momentary man hug before pulling apart.

"One more thing, Ben. Be careful with these people. 'Specially that Mark guy. I think he's the real loose cannon. Don't trust him."

"What about that general guy?" asked Benny.

"He assured me that you two would be treated well and be released as soon as I leave. I hope that's the case, but just stay sharp anyway."

Benny nodded in agreement.

"Good. Let's get back to Stella before she comes after us and corners us both." They both shuddered . . . then chuckled. Peter turned off the water and they retraced their steps hoping for some killer margaritas.

CHAPTER 10
Five days to Linear Shift

With only five days left before the time jump, Peter needed to do some research on Operation Abraham. He also knew he would need some cash back in 1942 in case he ran into obstacles securing necessities for his personal operation. He figured a grand should do. Based on Dr. Lamb's dollar value comparison, that would be equal to around $15,000 today. He needed to find $1,000 in pre-war bills to take on the trip.

With the advance money that the general gave him prior to joining the mission in his pocket, he was off. Well, he and Trevor were off.

"I want to thank you for being my chauffeur today," Peter said as Trevor maneuvered his car through the evening rush hour traffic.

"Not a problem, Peter. Isn't it your son's birthday? How old's he gonna be?" asked Trevor.

"He's going to be fourteen. He's a big coin collector, so I thought I would surprise him with something from the antique coin shop over on Valencia."

"I collected coins once. My granddaddy left me a shoebox full of 'em."

"You don't say?" Peter asked, trying to sound interested, while really deciding what questions he should be asking the shop owner.

Thirty minutes later they pulled off the 101 and navigated the dozen blocks to the coin shop. The closest parking spot Trevor could find was around the corner.

"This will be fine, Trevor. It shouldn't take me but thirty to forty minutes to find something," Peter said, hoping to coax him to stay in the car.

"I'm supposed to have eyes on you at all times. The general was very specific about keeping you in view." Trevor paused.

"That's fine, Trevor. Let's just drive around until we can get a closer spot. Shouldn't take more than fifteen minutes or so," Peter exaggerated.

"No, no. It'll be fine. I've got an errand to run for the general anyway. I have to have your word that you will not pull any shit like sneaking out to Herb's."

"Scout's honor."

"Ok. I'll swing by and pick you up after, and not a word gets back to the general, or he'll have my ass," Trevor said nervously.

"Mum's the word, Trevor. I'll meet you out front when I'm done."

When Peter walked into Yesterday's Change, he was greeted by a wiry old man sitting alone behind a glass display case at the back of the small shop.

"What can ah do fer ya'?" asked the store keeper.

"Um, hi. I'm looking for a bit of information and possibly some old bills," Peter explained.

"I think you're in the right spot," replied the man. "What kind of information you looking for?"

Peter began his recitation. "I'm throwing a themed dinner party in a few weeks, and I am trying to make it as authentic as possible. I'm also looking for information about bronze pennies from 1943."

The old man whistled loudly. "I ain't got any of them here. That's one rare find if you can get one."

"I'm not actually looking for that specific penny, just information about it. I am, however, looking for a fair bit of cash with dates around 1940."

"That, my new friend, I can do. How much you lookin' for?"

Peter paused, hoping not to shock the old man into a cardiac event. "Say, around a thousand?"

"Holy criminy!" exclaimed the man. "Whaddya need that much cash for?"

"Well, I'm a time traveler and I am here from 1941. We ran out of money and I'm here to replenish the supply," Peter joked, hoping to lighten the shock.

"Ha! Good one. But, seriously. Seems like a lot of moola for just a dinner party."

"Actually, I want to use the cash for the casino part of the event. It's a big charity thing. And honestly, I only need to borrow the cash for a week. I'd like to sell it back to you after the event," Peter said, embellishing.

Nodding in acceptance, the man behind the counter said, "The name's Chet. It'll be a pleasure doin' business with ya'. So what's the deal about the bronze penny?"

"Oh, that," Peter said. "It's all part of the charity event. I am doing some trivia about the wrongfully released and circulated bronze penny. I've done a bit of research already but just need a few things cleared up."

"I'm your man," said Chet. "Just so happens I'm a bit of an expert on that fabled gem."

"Expert? How so?"

"You, sir, are lookin' at one of the original employees of the mint when they reopened and started minting again in '68."

Peter could barely contain his excitement. He had hit the mother lode with Chet. Over the next thirty-five minutes, Chet explained that the bronze penny from the San Francisco Mint was in fact released on purpose by a disgruntled employee. Chet went on to explain that in '42, when the 1943 pennies were minted, there was a backlash from the employees because of the order to mint them in steel rather than bronze. They felt the population had grown comfortable with the distinct color of pennies and if they were silver, there'd be issues with the dime. Each of the three mints in existence pressed some fifty to sixty pennies from the bronze planchets. However, most of them were confiscated by mint officials before they were released into circulation. The San Francisco Mint was the only one that severely curtailed the release of those erroneous pennies. All because of Bartholomew Canter. Chet continued his history lesson about Bartholomew being recognized as a hero in US Treasury circles because of his ability to stop the release.

"Obviously, none of this information was ever made public," Chet added as he was wrapping up the historical cash for Peter.

"Why not?" Peter asked, hoping to extract every drop of information out of Chet as possible.

"Because. If word got out that there were a handful of bronze pennies in circulation when they weren't supposed to be, the army would have had some kind of hissy about how incompetent the US Mint was. Remember, we needed the copper for the war. I was at the mint many years after it all took place. I was one of the guides after it reopened and was privy to a lot of concealed facts about the facility and its inner workings."

"You said earlier that the mint was reopened in '68. Why was it closed?" asked Peter.

"That's another good story," replied Chet. "You see, the mint was built in '37 or '38, if memory serves. After it was opened, operations were moved from the old facility to the new building. What wasn't noticed was the gaps in design. The original architect left out a few minor security walls in the basement. It wasn't caught until routine maintenance of the sewers found the hole in the security. They had to close her down in '50-something for repairs. It was '53, I think. They covered it up with some story, never publicizing the potential security problem. The government took fifteen years searchin' out new architects and fixin' all the holes before they could reopen."

Chet clearly enjoyed sharing his intimate knowledge of the controversial situation.

"Now, is there anything else I can do for you?"

"Actually, there is. I need a birthday gift for my son."

Ten minutes later, Peter stepped out of the coin shop

carrying a bag with his son's gift inside. To his surprise, the burgundy sedan was parked right in front of the coin shop, and Trevor was leaning against the front fender with his arms crossed.

"Trevor. I'm sorry for the delay. The old guy in there talked my ear off."

"It's fine. I just pulled up ten or fifteen minutes ago. Did they have a gift for your boy?"

"They did. I picked up one of those books with slots for coins from each year they were minted. I filled up half the slots from the coins in the shop. Brett should be pretty happy," Peter replied. "Are we ready to head home?"

"Yes, sir. Let's make like a tree . . ." Trevor said.

As Trevor drove toward the Cooper residence, Peter thought about his conversation with Chet. Operation Abraham may have taken a positive turn, given this new security issue. He had to try to get some private time on the computers at the warehouse over the next few days. There was information to be verified and addresses to find.

CHAPTER 11

Three days to Linear Shift

Benny Welsh had wandered anxiously about sublevel ten's living quarters for the better part of the day. Since the surprise visit by Peter earlier in the week, he could not get some of the things Peter said out of his head. "Keep your options open" and "Don't trust anyone" continued to reverberate.

As he made his thirtieth lap around the large gathering room, Stella finally said, "Would you please sit down, Benny? You are going to wear a path in the floor."

"Aren't you worried, Stella?" asked Benny.

"You heard what Peter said. It's all going to be over shortly. I take that as good news. You should do the same thing. Now sit!"

Benny swatted his hand toward her.

"Back off!"

He continued pacing and walked down the long corridor leading to the entry door of the living quarters. He slowed toward the end of the corridor and noticed that the large steel door was slightly ajar. Cautiously, Benny stepped closer to see if any guards were outside in the stairwell. Inching the door open farther revealed nothing. He pulled on the door and stepped fully into the shaft. He stood at the junction of stairs and waited momentarily, listening to silence.

Certain nobody was using the stairs, Benny rushed back down the corridor.

"Stella! Grab your stuff. We're gettin' out of here," Benny blurted out as he ran by into his sleeping room. Stella was stretched out like a cat on the sofa reading *Cosmo*. A moment later he returned to the gathering room hauling his possessions in a duffel bag. "Well? Didn't you hear me? Let's go."

"What are you talking about? We're not going anywhere," said Stella sitting up.

"But the front door is open, and there are no guards out there. Let's go while we've got time," repeated Benny.

"I'm not going anywhere and neither should you. It's Saturday, you fool. Obviously there's no guard at the door. They're probably up top, guarding the front of the building or some secret thingamajig," Stella replied.

"Fine, you can stay, but I'm outta here," Benny said as he moved toward the corridor.

"Why are you in such a hurry to leave? Don't you want the money they promised? It's only going to be a few more days and we will be free. Just stay with me, honey," Stella begged.

"Listen, Stella. I didn't tell you this earlier, but when Pete and I were back in the showers, he told me some things about these guys. He's scared and told us to look for a way out," Benny said, fabricating the facts to entice Stella to leave.

"I don't know, sugar," Stella said, pausing momentarily to grasp what Benny was saying. "I really think things are going to be fine. Maybe the door is a test. You know, to see if we are trustworthy enough to be let go."

Benny shook his head. "Not gonna bank on that one, baby. Are you with me or not?"

Stella looked around the gathering room, contemplating her decision.

"Well, woman?" demanded Benny.

"Well, if you're gonna talk to me like that, no, I'm not. I'll stay right here," Stella stated obstinately and leaned back on to the cushions.

Benny turned and raced down the corridor. With no hesitation he burst through the door at a full sprint. He began the climb bounding two steps at a time. After just two banks of one flight, he slowed and continued at a normal pace.

Back in the living quarters, Stella sat alone, agitated at being left by herself. She really thought that staying put was the right choice, but she didn't want to be alone. She stood and walked down the corridor. As she neared the opening, she could here Benny's feet stomping up the steel treads.

"Oh, hell," Stella said aloud and returned to her room to gather her things. She hated being left alone, so she decided to catch up to Benny and make a run for it.

Passing SUB-6, Benny's breath was hard and heavy. He didn't think escaping out of the bowels of the bunker was going to be so exhausting. Slowing to conserve energy, he trudged onward. A moment later, he passed SUB-5.

Stella left the lights on in the gathering room as she slung her duffel bag over her left shoulder and walked down the corridor. Not rushing, she started at a slower pace climbing upward. There were so many stairs! She knew that Benny was going to be darn near spent when she caught up to him, so there was no rush.

Benny's determination to make it out of captivity revved his adrenalin. So much so that he didn't feel the leg cramps until it was too late. Feeling the weight of panic, he collapsed to one knee and nearly lost his balance. He moaned in pain, trying to rub the knots free in his calves. Several minutes passed and he began climbing again. His speed was reduced, but he was continually moving toward the exit. The *womp-womp-womp* of his heart was pounding is his ears, otherwise he would have heard Stella coming and waited. She was just a few flights below him now.

Passing SUB-2, he knew he was close. Benny drove on and he reached the landing for SUB-1. He walked down the corridor to the tunnel he had passed through weeks before. Once in the frigid tunnel, Benny leaned against the wall to catch his breath.

As he rested, he looked up and down the tunnel wondering which direction to go. There were no signs illuminating EXIT anywhere in sight. He tried to think back to his capture but came up with nothing. He made a choice and went left, hoping against hope that it was the right way.

Just as Benny began his trek down the tunnel, Stella reached SUB-1 and paused for a breather. Still tired from the tremendous climb, she moved slowly toward the tunnel. When she reached the intersection, she looked both directions. In the distance, she thought she could see a man moving away from her, but she couldn't be sure. She called out "Benny!" but the man did not stop his movement.

As Benny steadily moved down the tunnel, the lights cast ominous shadows. He instinctively slid from shadow to shadow, staying out of the brightened areas as much as possible. As he neared the end of the tunnel, he recognized the newer framed door and knew he had chosen wisely. When placed with a directional choice, always go left, someone once told him. You'll be right at least half the time. He reached for the door handle and gave it a twist. The latch moved minutely, but the door remained locked. He tried twisting the other way but the door remained sealed. Frustrated, Benny shook the handle fiercely, to no avail. The only thing it managed to do was draw Mark's attention, who was sitting in a chair on the other side of the door.

Stella walked slowly down the tunnel after Benny. When she watched him try the door handle unsuccessfully, she giggled to herself. "Damn fool," she whispered. She stopped and decided to wait for Benny to come to her, confirming that his escape plan was futile. As she watched, the door opened suddenly and a large man stepped through. When he appeared, she could see Benny try to jump past him. The large man grabbed Benny and pushed him to the floor. Stella almost screamed but remained quiet to avoid the guard's attention. Subconsciously, she began to quietly step backward as she watched the fracas unfold.

Benny lay on the ground looking up. Mark was sneering down at him. Quickly analyzing his options, Benny figured he could either fight the man or cowardly retreat back down the ten flights of stairs. Benny was no coward, so that left one option.

"OK, you win," Benny conceded. "Care to help me up?" He extended his hand out for Mark to tug him up.

Mark paused momentarily before stepping forward to pull Benny to his feet. As soon as he took Benny's hand, the full force of Benny's foot connected with his groin. Mark yelled out and crumpled to the ground, one hand grabbing his crotch and the other reaching for his gun.

Benny recoiled his extended leg and rolled to his knees. Pushing himself up, he lurched for the door. The door closed right as he grasped the handle. He tried turning it once again. Locked. He spun quickly just as Mark was pulling his pistol from its holster. Benny threw his bag at Mark's head and ran back down the tunnel.

Stella, horrified, could only watch silently. Before she knew it, Benny was sprinting as fast as he could toward her. There was a look of recognition on his face and she heard him yell, "Run, Stella! RUN!" as the first bullet pierced his back. He didn't fall immediately but staggered forward grasping for anything to stop his momentum. The second bullet split the air, and as it punctured his shoulder, Benny fell to the ground, gasping.

"NO!" Stella screamed and ran back toward the stairs.

Mark shivered in pain, climbed to his feet, and walked down the tunnel after her. As he passed Benny's now-lifeless body, he re-holstered his gun. He turned down the corridor to the stairway. That bitch wasn't going anywhere.

CHAPTER 12

Three days to Linear Shift

It was the final weekend to spend with his family before the trip, and Peter had a lot planned for the Cooper clan. He had cleared it with Applegate earlier in the week and Trevor would be just a phone call away. It struck Peter as strange that in all the years they lived in and around the San Francisco area, they had never been to Alcatraz. They'd been to Ghirardelli Square and ridden the street cars to Fisherman's Wharf, but had never taken the boat across the bay. They talked about hitting several attractions all week and although Alcatraz was discussed, it got bumped because the tour alone was around three hours long. That gave each of them time to choose a destination.

Trevor was punctual as usual. He again donned the black-tie chauffeur garb to dazzle the kids. It had the greatest impact on Tori, who was impressed with the ride and the presidential treatment. Trevor opened the door for her and assisted her in and out of the luxury town car. Brett found it entertaining, but his highlight was going to be the tour of the San Francisco Mint.

"Trevor, are you sure you don't want to come to Chinatown with us? You could park the car and spend the day having a little fun," Peter urged.

"Thank you, Mr. Cooper, but I will be fine dropping you off. Do you have a preference on where you would like to disembark?" Trevor asked.

"Uh, yeah. How about on the north end of Grant street. That way, we can head south and end up at California," Peter replied.

"Is that where you would like me to pick you up?" Trevor inquired.

"No, we're going to jump on a cable car and ride up to Grace Cathedral. You can pick us up there, but I'll give you a call when we get close. It'll be at least four hours. You sure you don't want to come with us? I'm going to introduce the kids to dim sum. It's good stuff . . ."

"I'll be quite alright, Mr. Cooper. But thank you for the invitation," Trevor replied as he maneuvered through the streets of the financial district.

Trevor pulled up to the curb near the intersection of Broadway and Grant and got out to open the doors for the kids. Peter stepped out and met them on the sidewalk in front of the New Sun Hong Kong restaurant.

"Thanks again, Trevor. Last chance if you want to change your mind. I'll even buy you a pair of Baoding balls."

"No need, it's my pleasure, Mr. Cooper. I'll see you later this afternoon," Trevor replied politely. Then he quickly slid behind the wheel of the shiny black car and pulled off into the congested street.

"Wow, Dad. Your boss must really like you. You've had a personal driver ever since you started," Tori said.

"I wouldn't get too used to it, Tori. I think budget cuts will eliminate the driver next month," Peter replied, repeating a rehearsed line from Applegate.

They crossed the street and began their stroll down Grant Street. As soon as they were on the sidewalk, Peter asked "Well? What do you guys think?"

Both Tori and Brett were in awe at the bustle of the patrons along Grant. It was Saturday and they would see the full ambiance of Chinatown. The streets were packed with tourists.

"Oh. My. God! I love it, dad." Tori exclaimed as her eyes began to take in the gaudy scenery of Chinatown. She neared the first of what were probably hundreds of Chinese vendors along the street. Brett and Peter followed.

Once in the shop, Tori and Brett perused the packed shelves of mostly handcrafted Chinese products. Most of the displays were in the recognizable, yet unreadable Chinese characters.

"Dad," Brett whispered. "What do the signs say? Can you read them?"

"You can ask, bub." Peter replied, certain that the vendors get asked the same question several times a day. He was sure they appreciated the social interaction of running a tourist trap.

"I don't wanna ask. Will you do it for me?"

Peter chuckled, "Sorry, dude. You're on your own for this one. It'll be good for you to talk to them."

Brett remained silent and hoped that Tori would ask. It wasn't long before she obliged when she asked the price for a particular hand painted doll. Brett sighed and walked away.

After a few minutes more in the shop, they stepped back onto the sidewalk and continued their southerly trek down the street. They walked into a few shops packed with shelves of similar handcrafted Chinese items. After seeing the same items in nearly every shop, Brett finally noticed the Chinese lanterns that were strung from light pole to light pole up and down the street.

"Wow. Check that out Tori," Brett said pointing to the paper lanterns.

Tori looked up and smiled. "Cool."

The next forty minutes were spent popping in and out of various shops through Chinatown. Brett successfully negotiated his purchase of a hand-carved wooden snake, while Tori filled her tote bag with random trinkets for her friends. As he watched his smiling kids working their way through the shop, Peter began to realize that this might be one of the last days he would spend with them. He swallowed back tears and tried to focus on the day.

As Tori haggled, Peter walked to the back of the shop and picked up a pair of the Chinese meditation balls he had tried to use to lure Trevor. He paid the owner and slid the box into Tori's tote bag to carry.

Upon leaving the shop, Tori asked, "What about lunch, dad? I'm starved!"

Peter looked at Brett and he just nodded in agreement. "OK then. Let's eat. It's time you two tried dim sum."

Brett, unsure, asked, "What's dim sum?"

"It's nothing scary, I promise. It's just bite-sized portions of food, usually served in steamed baskets. You'll like it, I promise."

They continued their walk until they came upon a Cantonese restaurant and went in. They were promptly seated near the front window and brought a kettle of hot tea. Tori poured herself a cup, as did Peter. Brett, still unsure, watched Tori's expression after tasting the hot liquid. She smiled in satisfaction, so Brett caved and poured himself a cup. Bringing the cup to his lips, he sipped and smiled. He proceeded to gulp his tea despite the temperature.

The menus were in both English and Cantonese, so no assistance was needed when they ordered. Each of the Cooper family chose a few selections, and fifteen minutes later their food was on the table. They ate family style, sampling from each of the six baskets until there was nothing left.

Once the dishes were cleared, Peter looked at Tori, then to Brett. They were still elated, amazed at the colorful decorations. Chinatown was such a different culture from what they knew, yet it had been only thirty to forty minutes away all their lives. Peter reflected on his life since Minnie had passed. He had lived so much of the past two years in self-pity and regret that he had lost focus of what was still important, what was always important: family. They should've been his number one priority. His only regret was that it took him so long to get back on track.

Moments later, their bill came. Peter promptly paid the check and they set off once again. Their walk down Grant passed in comfortable silence.

Thirty minutes later, when they arrived at Old St. Mary's Center, Tori said, "OK, I think I'm about done with Chinatown. How much more is there?"

"This is where we head up California to Grace Cathedral," replied Peter, noticing the looks of relief.

Serendipitously, the ringing of the cable car caught the kids' attention. "Are we going to ride the trolley, dad?" asked Brett.

"I'm certainly not going to hike up that hill. It's only four blocks, but it's all uphill. These are long blocks. Mom and I walked this hill many times before you two were born."

Brett smiled. Peter was unsure if it was because of hearing they were going to ride up or hearing mention of his mom. It didn't matter to Peter, he was just happy that his kids were having a good time.

They walked across the street to where the loading and unloading of passengers took place. Because the last car had passed just moments before, Peter knew they'd have to wait ten minutes for the next one to arrive. As they waited, Tori asked, "Dad, why are we going to this cathedral again?"

Peter paused to compose his response. "Before mom and I married, I was finishing up my degree in architecture. One of my final classes was on architectural history—a class that I should have completed in my freshman or sophomore year. Well, seeing as I held off on taking the class until my last year, it gave me a bit of an edge. I had to write my final report on a specific style of architecture or a historical building. I chose Grace Cathedral because of its beauty and my love of Gothic Revival architecture. My last semester in college, I made dozens of trips to the cathedral, and that is when I met your mother."

Tori and Brett were captivated by Peter's story, so he continued.

"When we met, I was sitting out front on the steps. It was a cool March morning, and the sun was just so high." Peter held his hand up to a level just above the apex of the buildings. "The light was shining from behind and highlighted the face of the building. I was sitting alone, sketching the façade, when Mom sat down next to me. She didn't say anything for a few minutes; she just watched me draw the cathedral freehand."

The bell of the trolley broke his train of thought. As the

cable car came to a stop, they climbed on board, but there were only two seats in the outfacing row. Peter let the kids sit, and he stood on the outer foot rail after paying the man at the controls. A moment later, they were teetering up the hill.

Tori and Brett, still looking up at Peter, waited for him to continue the story. He held up a finger, indicating "in a minute." Street by street, the car climbed. It slowed and dinged at each stop, people climbing on or departing. Five minutes later, they pulled to a stop at Taylor Street, and they all got off. As Peter began to cross the street toward the cathedral, both kids slid a hand into his. He was delighted beyond words and could barely contain his emotions.

They approached the steps in front of the stone edifice, and a moment later, Peter came to a stop.

"This is where I was sitting," he said, indicating the granite steps. He sat down, and the kids sat on each side of him in silence. "When Mom sat next to me while I sketched, I was unsure of what to say. I was shy back then, and women didn't really go out of their way to talk to me. We sat in silence for ten or fifteen minutes before either of us spoke."

———————⌒———————

"You have a beautiful hand," Mary said, breaking the uncomfortable silence.

"You really think so?" asked Peter, embarrassed by the compliment. "They're my own, you know."

Mary giggled. "No, I mean your sketching is beautiful. You are very talented."

Peter was now embarrassed at his obtuse response. He supposed he should have appreciated her compliment and just shut the hell up. "Well, thank you. Very nice of you to say. I'm Peter."

"Hi, Peter. I'm Mary. Do you mind if I sit and watch for a while? I love architecture, and this is one of my favorite buildings in San Francisco."

"Sure. I don't mind." Peter turned back to his drawing and continued to accentuate the details around the twin spires.

The memory was painstakingly vivid as he described it to Tori and Brett.

"How long did you two sit there?" asked Tori.

"Oh, I don't know. Maybe an hour or so. After sitting for a while, we began to talk about ourselves and asked each other questions. At the time, it seemed quite magical. We were so comfortable talking, it was like we had known each other for years. After I finished that sketch, we went to lunch together." Peter paused to wipe the teardrop escaping down his cheek.

"Over the next month, Mom would meet me here on the steps and I would draw. We would go to lunch when I was done and talk for hours. I was nearing the end of my last semester and had finished my cathedral studies, but I continued to come to the church to draw. It was more to see her than anything else. We had yet to go on an actual date yet, but I knew I loved her. I think she knew too, but neither of us said anything."

Peter pulled his moistened eyes away from the front of the church and looked at Tori and Brett. They were huddled next to him, crying as they listened to their father tell the story of their mother and Grace Cathedral. Instinctively, he pulled each of them close in a big family hug. They sat on the steps for several moments in the loving embrace, appreciating each other, none of them wanting the moment to end.

Finally, Peter let go and wiped his eyes. "You guys want to go inside? The church is handsome outside, but the inside is absolutely stunning."

Both the kids nodded in unison, and they stood and climbed the rest of the way to the entry. As they walked through the side doors, the smell of incense permeated their noses. Once inside, they rarely spoke; they just moved about the cavernous beauty. Peter led them through the nave, the sanctuary, and the choir aisle. After reading a number of placards and viewing several priceless sculptures, they returned to the front of the church, near the base of two towers.

Peter pointed out that one tower housed the stairway up. In

the base of the other, called the Singing Tower, there was a bank of votive candles, and the ceiling was open all the way to the pinnacle of the spire. It was believed to provide a private area for angels to gather and celebrate. Peter walked over and dropped a twenty in the donation slot and proceeded to light three candles, one for each of them as they thought of Minnie. No tears were shed, but they were somber as they stood close to each other in the glow of the flames.

Some fifteen minutes later, they went out the north exit into the large courtyard. Just to the east was a labyrinth, and they each took turns walking their way to the center. Tori and Peter struggled, but Brett succeeded on his first try.

Peter happened to glance at his watch and noticed that it was nearly 2:00 pm. Since they still planned to visit the mint, he thought they should be on their way. He called Trevor to pick them up from Grace Cathedral, and within minutes they were on their way to the mint.

The fifteen minute drive to the mint passed in complete silence. Peter remained deep in the memory of Minnie after the emotional visit to where they first met. He wondered how the kids felt. But the silence was comforting, so he didn't broach the subject.

When Trevor pulled up in front of the mint, Peter's heart sank. The entire block was surrounded by a tall, chain-link fence with razor wire across the top. Trevor parked the car next to the curb on Herman as they all looked up at the barricaded building.

"Well, kiddo," Peter said to Brett, "it looks like the tour of the mint might be out. It doesn't look like they're open to the public."

In a deflated voice from the backseat, Brett said, "Oh, it's OK, dad." He paused momentarily "Maybe the tours are by appointment only?"

Peter never imagined security being an issue for public tours. He made it a point to do some heavy digging on the mint's procedures over the next few days to solidify his plans for Operation Abraham.

"Yeah, maybe so. I'll look into it next week. Sound like a

plan?" Peter replied, feeling heartbroken. It was all Brett had been able to talk about after hearing about the family outing a few days ago.

"Yeah, OK."

"Well, Trevor, I guess the Cooper family outing is done for the day. Care to drive us home?" Peter requested.

"Not a problem, Mr. Cooper. Are there any other stops you would like me to make on the way?" Trevor asked.

"Well, now that you mention it . . . kids, how about a stop for ice cream before we get home? Geno's Gelatos sound good to you guys?"

There was a unanimous 'Yes!' from the backseat, and they left to cap off their day. Although he was happy to have spent the day with the kids, he was extremely sad. He didn't know what his *shifted* future would hold and prayed that today wouldn't be his final goodbye.

CHAPTER 13

Twenty-seven hours to Linear Shift

General Applegate stood at the head of the conference table, ready to address the team. "Good morning, everyone. This time tomorrow, you will all be suiting up for your trip. I want to complement each and every one of you for a spectacular effort throughout training. Minus a few missteps along the way, I could have not asked for more dedication. Your commitment to the mission has been exemplary."

The general moved around the table, pulled out his usual high-backed leather chair, and sat. "Now that we are close to departure, it's time to complete your mission briefing. I have a lot of information to disseminate, so please, hold all questions until after my initial presentation." General Applegate paused and looked at each of the four team members for acknowledgement. "Thank you. As you know, you are all going back to 1942. The precise date of arrival is July 24, 1942. The time will be 10:42 a.m. The location is our current position, where you have been training, but down several levels."

Peter had figured as much once he visited Benny and Stella. The general had to have the time travel device somewhere, and so far neither he nor Julie had seen it. But there were many levels to this place.

Peter glanced toward Julie to see her reaction, but he could not read her. The general continued.

"Before I get too far ahead of myself, I should explain how you will be traveling." General Applegate paused to take a drink of water. "In early '42, a theoretical physicist named Dr. Bernard Epson mathematically calculated equations that would allow the theory of time travel to become a reality. He also constructed the hardware to test his theories. These equations and equipment are the foundation of your trip tomorrow. At the project's inception, the doctor was a privately-funded individual who was conducting his research alone, save for a few assistants. His research advanced to the experimentation phase later in the year, and when he began construction of the two devices, he quickly ran out of money. By mid-year he was forced to make a monumental decision: halt his project until he found additional grantors, or accept the gracious offer from the United States government. Fortunately, he chose to accept the government's assistance, and his experiments continued. The devices reside here, on sublevel six beneath this building. Unfortunately for the doctor, he had a momentary lapse in judgment, and the testing resulted in his death in the fall of that year. His research and experiments were largely abandoned and classified at the time, and the level was sealed off for nearly seventy years. In early 2012, we unlocked level six, digitized all his research, and analyzed the hardware. We've determined the doctor's miscalculation and have rectified his error.

"His theory of time travel primarily relies upon known locations of miniature black holes. The process, in layman's terms, reduces you to a stream of digital data and transports you through the nearest opening using ultra-high-frequency radio waves. A device needs to be present for you to rematerialize. Dr. Epson's fatal flaw was that he assumed the device would be functional when he sent himself forward in time. Theoretically, he would have been successful had he taken the appropriate actions before sending himself forward."

"If the device he built has been here since 1942, could it have served as the receiving device as well?" Peter asked. The general paused, clearly annoyed at the interruption.

"Theoretically, it might have. The doctor built two separate machines—one as the transmitter and one as the receiver—and his experiments were largely successful. He was able to send himself back in time, but only by a few hours. Once he switched the polarity and tried to move forward, the doctor met his demise."

"If the receiver was built and here, why did he fail?" Julie jumped in this time.

"It's quite simple. He forgot to tell someone to turn the receiver on. He assumed that by simply conducting the experiments, all parties would be privy to the process in the future. Obviously, that was not the case. What he should've done was mail a letter to someone with authority in the future. It needn't have been an actual person, but could have been more generic in terms of position, such as Senior Scientific Adviser, with a delivery date sometime in the decade prior to his arrival."

Peter and Julie smirked collectively at the ridiculous brain fart of a supposed genius. Two words: Darwin award.

"I know it sounds ludicrous, but I assure you it's true. He was mostly considered a foolish old man, wasting his talent chasing down an unachievable dream. But Dr. Epson was brilliant, with ideas generations ahead of any other scientist at the time—including Einstein. We have verified his research and are now capable of sending the team back to his receiving device at precisely 10:42 a.m. on July 24, 1942.

"If there are no further questions on the time travel portion of the mission, let's continue on to your objective." General Applegate paused momentarily to field any questions. "Good. Your mission in 1942 is to travel to a small village in France and destroy a memorandum. Then, simply return to San Francisco and travel back."

"That's it? That's our whole mission? To go back and destroy a memo?" Peter asked, flabbergasted.

"In essence, yes. That is the entire mission. You see, the document you are eliminating has great implications regarding the success or failure of many military operations in World War

II."

"Such as?" Peter asked.

"The specific operations are not important. The memo is your objective. Succeed, and there is a high probability that the *shifted* present will be a much better place than it is today."

Peter sat there feeling a little silly. Seriously, all this training and subterfuge for one memo! He was trying to assemble an even-tempered response to the general for once again withholding information. Julie broke the silence.

"General, I think your lack of willingness to share this information will inevitably jeopardize the success of this mission. Would it hurt you to finally share all pertinent information with those of us that are risking everything—our lives, present and future? We have the right to know everything if you want us to proceed. I, for one, am willing to walk away unless we are fully briefed," Julie said, glancing at Peter for reassurance.

"I agree," Peter said, as he nodded at Julie.

General Applegate stared at Julie for a solid minute, and then glared at Peter. "OK then." Applegate paused for another drink of water, clearly annoyed. He began rifling through the bottom of his stack of file folders. Finding the one he was looking for, he continued.

"Operation Sledgehammer was devised by the United States and Russia in the spring of 1942. Sledgehammer was a plan to capture French seaports in the fall of that year. Both the US and the Soviets lobbied hard for the operation. However, the operation was designed to be mainly carried out by British troops because of their geographical position at the time. Churchill resisted. Because of Churchill's reluctance to support Sledgehammer, it was ultimately labeled as not feasible and forgotten about. Churchill decided Sledgehammer's fate solely on that memo in France. It must be destroyed so that Operation Sledgehammer can be implemented."

"Why is it so important for Sledgehammer to succeed?" asked Peter. "We won!"

"For a number of reasons. First, the small village that you

will infiltrate might not be completely destroyed. If successful, France will become a much stronger ally throughout the war."

Julie leaned forward and asked, "What is the name of the village?"

Applegate looked down at his notes. "It's called Oradour-sur-Glane. It's about five hundred kilometers south of Paris."

Peter was dumbfounded. He recalled his dinner conversation with Julie and was certain that the general had her full attention. Julie, to her credit, remained stoic.

"Our simulations indicate that World War II could possibly end a full year sooner than it did in our current timeline. Also, since Oradour-sur-Glane might never be destroyed, the German frontline may relocate to another part of the country by 1944. Beyond the war, our simulations vary quite substantially. The key is intercepting that memo and destroying it."

The ops center radiated silence. Peter continued to look at Julie for signs of a reaction. There were none. He panned to the rest of the personnel in the room and realized that neither Dr. Lamb nor Dr. Larsson had said a word throughout the entire briefing.

"What about our two doctors?" Peter asked, indicating his two remaining companions. "What is their part of the mission?"

"They will be staying in San Francisco to correct any anomalies with the devices so that you all have a safe trip back to the present. They will have no contact outside of Dr. Epson and his assistants," replied the general.

"What about Epson? Do we expect any resistance? Are we just going to show up through his time machine and say 'Surprise!'"

Applegate smiled for the first time all morning. "Well, that is the sum of it. He should be elated that his devices are successful. He will be surprised at first, but we feel that he will accept the situation relatively easily. We believe he will be anxious to assist."

"What about our mission to France? Will Epson be told?" asked Peter.

"He will be told nothing. His knowledge of your mission could disrupt the entire outcome. We have devised a cover story for why the team is traveling back to 1942 and why the two of you will be leaving for more than a month's time." Applegate produced two new folders from the bottom of the pile and handed them to Peter and Julie. "Everything you need to know is in there. After our briefing, go home. Read through the intel, and get some rest. Your training is complete, and all you need to do is wait until tomorrow. If you need any final information on 1942, the lab's computers are at your disposal before you go home."

Peter felt overwhelmed. He wanted to use the computers for a few hours of research on Operation Abraham, but he also wanted to review everything he had just received.

Julie stood suddenly and silently walked from the room.

"Are we done here, General?" asked Peter, wanting to follow.

"Yes, I think so. It's imperative that you are all here by 7:30 sharp. We'll need to get you completely outfitted and stripped of anything modern."

Peter stood and quickly walked out. He caught Julie before she got to the stairs.

"Jules. You OK?" asked Peter.

"I can't believe it. I might be able to change my family's history," Julie said, nearly in tears.

Peter was unsure of what to say, but he knew that nothing was simply by chance on this operation. "Do you suppose the general knew about your family history and that is why he wanted you on the team?"

"I don't follow, Peter. He knows that I have French heritage."

"Suppose the general knew your family originated from Oradour-sur-Glane when he recruited you. Your devotion to our success would be that much stronger if you have something personal at stake."

"If that's the case, the general is absolutely right. If I can do anything to prevent the annihilation of that village, I will."

Peter accepted her genuine dedication but felt at odds with

how the general continued to control everyone like marionettes.

"Peter, I need to go. I want to read through this and take care of a few things before we leave tomorrow. Can I call you at home later if anything comes up?" Julie asked.

"Yeah, sure thing, Jules. I'm going to hit the computers for a while, but I'll be home all night."

Julie leaned in and hugged Peter tightly. "Thank you. We are going to make a great team."

Julie pulled away and walked down the steps. Peter's eyes followed as she walked through the village. This quaint little fictitious hamlet held more meaning than either of them ever imagined.

CHAPTER 14

Fifteen hours to Linear Shift

The knock on the door came just minutes after Peter had sat down for dinner with his family.

"Want me to get it, dad?" asked Tori eagerly.

"No, you two eat. I'll go see who it is," Peter said as he stood and walked from the kitchen.

Peter opened the front door, expecting to be accosted by some ill-timed missionaries. Or . . . maybe it was Jules! To his disappointment, it was General Applegate.

"General. Everything OK?" Peter asked as he stepped out onto the porch, closing the door behind him.

"Did I catch you at a bad time?" inquired the general.

"We just sat down for dinner," Peter said, irritated that his last meal with the kids was interrupted. "What can I help you with?"

"I won't take too much of your time, Peter. I just wanted to give you this." Applegate pulled a large, sealed manila envelope and handed it to Peter.

Peter inspected the envelope; it was blank. "It's sealed up pretty good. Do I open it now or later?"

"I want you to open this when you reach 1942. No sooner. After you open it, I need you to follow the instructions to the letter. No hesitation, no questions. Do you understand?"

"Uh, sure. Anything I need to know about the contents?"

Peter asked, feeling a little perplexed.

"Nothing to worry about. Once you arrive, there are a series of tasks that need to be executed, in order, to properly establish the link back to the present. This envelope contains specific information about your part of the mission, and it is critical that no one else on the team is made aware of it. You must assure me, Peter, that you will keep this last bit of information confidential, even from Miss Frey. Once you open the envelope, everything will be apparent."

Peter paused. "Listen, General. You're in charge, I get that, but I have to question your motivations here. I can't tell anyone? How about when we get to 1942? I'm going to be spending weeks with the docs and a month with Julie!"

"Absolutely not. This packet contains . . ." Applegate hesitated momentarily, as if searching for the right words. "It contains a side mission."

"A side mission? I don't suppose you'd like to clarify," Peter said incredulously.

"No. Peter, it is imperative that you follow the instructions precisely as they are laid out in the envelope."

"I don't suppose I have a choice here."

"Yes, Peter, I think you do. It's called free will, but I hope that once you open the envelope, you will understand."

Peter listened and felt uneasy. "Come again?" he asked cautiously.

"I am merely stating that your choices in 1942 could have drastic consequences. Just keep that in mind while you handle all forms of currency."

Peter froze. Did the general know about Operation Abraham? He wondered if he should confess to his alternative motivation or play along with the ploy.

"All right. Nobody knows about the envelope and I open it in private, only after arriving in 1942," Peter agreed.

"Great. I'm glad we understand each other."

General Applegate focused on Peter for a few more seconds before turning and walking toward his car. He paused and turned back to Peter. "Be sure to be at the warehouse at 7:30 sharp. Tomorrow is going to be a day for the history books!" Applegate resumed his march to his car.

Peter stood on his porch a moment longer, watching the general drive up the street. Looking down at the envelope, he wondered if he should disobey his orders and go ahead and open it now. Before he could make that decision, Brett opened the front door.

"Dad? Everything OK? Your dinner's getting cold."

"It's all good, sport. I was just given some additional paperwork to take on my business trip tomorrow." He slid the envelope under his arm and followed Brett back into the house. Tonight was the night to savor all the memories, emotions, and love for his family. It was also a night wracked with the fear of never seeing them again.

———————— ～ ————————

It was that time of night where being up too late danced with getting up too early, and Peter was wide awake. He lay there glancing about the darkness throughout his bedroom; his mind on overdrive. His thoughts, mostly of the mission's success, continued to invade his rest ensuring sleep was a lost cause. Peter turned his gaze to the open window and stared out into the night. He wondered if Julie was having sleep trouble as well. Looking at the clock, it was just after 2:00 in the morning. Was it too late to call?

Peter swung his legs to the floor as he reached for the phone. He punched in her number and was surprised when she picked up on the first ring.

"Hello?" she answered questioningly.

"Hi. It's me. Did I wake you?"

"Peter? Is everything OK? It's 2:15 in the morning."

"I know. I couldn't sleep. I'm sorry – I shouldn't have called..."

"It's OK, really. I'm awake. Just laying here, thinking about the mission."

"Same here. I feel ready for whatever tomorrow brings, but

my mind keeps going over everything in slow motion," Peter paused, wondering if he should tell Julie everything that was keeping him up. "What if we don't make it, Jules? I mean, what if we die and nothing changes in the present?"

Julie was silent for some time before replying. "It's OK to have those thoughts, Peter. You have a family to think about. Honestly, I would be worried about you if you didn't."

"What about you? What's really keeping you up?" Peter asked.

"Same thoughts, I guess. More about my ancestors in France though. I also think that Griff and Brett are two of the smartest guys I know, and they are going through the machine with us. Have they shown any sign of nervousness or insecurity?"

"Well, no. Not that I've noticed."

"Neither have I. Peter, I think we are going to do great tomorrow. I think you will do great."

Peter thought about just how foolish he was being. "Thanks, Jules. I'm not sure if it's your words or just hearing your voice, but I think I'm good now. We should both get some rest."

"Wow. That was easy. I thought I'd have to whisper sweet nothings to you for at least an hour." Julie feigned mock disappointment.

Feeling more foolish by the minute for calling her, Peter said "Sorry to disappoint, but I really am fine. See you in the morning?"

"Good night, Peter."

"Night, Jules." Peter hung up the phone and leaned his head back to the pillow. Moments later, he was fast asleep, and he didn't dream all night.

CHAPTER 15
Five hours to Linear Shift

Peter awoke just a few hours after his conversation with Julie. He felt more rested than he would have imagined after limited sleep. A quick shower, and he was ready for his life-altering day to begin.

"What are the rules?" Peter asked Tori, as she finished off her bagel breakfast.

"Dad, we just talked about this last night. We'll be fine. It's not like you've never left us alone before." Tori retorted, without addressing his question.

"I know, kiddo, but it's just that I've never been away for an extended period of time. I know you'll do fine, but humor me, please?"

"Fine. Come right home after school. Do our homework every night. Nobody comes over. No parties. Lock the doors the minute we're inside. Don't answer the door... Do I need to go on?" Tori asked sarcastically.

"No, that's fine. I think you've got it." Peter replied, feeling somewhat relieved that his daughter actually remembered most everything they'd talked about over the last week. "I'll be home in a few days, so there's really nothing to worry about." he added.

"I know, Dad. That's what I kept telling you last week." Tori placed her dishes in the sink when she heard the sound of a car idling out front. "I think Trevor just pulled up."

Peter's eyes narrowed and worry lines pulled across his forehead.

"Dad. Just go. We'll be fine. GO!" Tori said with a reassuring smile.

"OK. I'm going. I love you. Tell Brett I love him too when he gets out of the shower." Peter said, as he hugged his daughter. Grabbing his jacket and bag, Peter walked out of the house, wondering if he would ever step back into this life again.

The drive in to the warehouse passed by, mostly in silence. That gave Peter time to assess his choices over the past few weeks. Had he spent enough time with the kids? He thought so. Did he leave his life in order, in case he didn't survive? The general assured him that things would be taken care of. Did he plan enough for Operation Abraham? He hoped so. Yesterday, he had spent the entire afternoon researching the final aspects of his personal mission. Yes, he had done everything possible, and all that was left was to move on. Complete the mission and get back to his kids. He had never felt more confident. This was life-changing. Peter's introspection halted as Trevor pulled up to the warehouse.

"Here you go, Mr. Cooper," Trevor said. "I wish you luck. I know you will be successful.

"Thanks Trevor. I mean it. Thanks for everything for the last month." Peter said.

"It was my pleasure, Mr. Cooper." Trevor said, adding more emphasis to Peter's surname.

Peter smiled, and then said "You know Trevor, I really thought you being my driver and constant presence was quite a nuisance. At first. But in hindsight, I am not sure I could have done it without your help."

Trevor looked at Peter graciously, "Thanks, Peter. That means a lot."

"Now, I've got to go! If I never see you again, it's nothing personal." chided Peter as he climbed out of the black town car for the last time. He was certain Trevor knew the team was going back to 1942 but wondered if he knew the implications of what they were about to do. For all Peter knew, their mission could potentially erase certain people forever. They might never exist. Peter suddenly realized that they were playing God, and that disturbed him.

Once inside, he glanced a final time at the French village and wondered how accurate it really was. He'd find out shortly. As usual, the streets were abandoned, but Ops was bustling. He was the last member of the team to arrive. Scattered about the large conference table sat the members of his team, the general, and a number of other military personnel Peter hadn't seen before. In addition, there were a half dozen assistants milling about, handing out folders and filling water glasses.

Peter strode in and sat next to Julie. She looked over at him and smiled. Her demeanor had changed since their briefing yesterday. Julie had been astonished and hesitant after hearing the French destination. Today, she had a giddy air that Peter found refreshing.

"Excited or scared?" Peter asked.

"Both! I couldn't sleep a wink last night."

"Me either. Until we talked, that is." Peter winked.

Before they could exchange another word, General Applegate called the room to attention.

"Good morning, everyone. It is now 7:40 and mission departure is in three hours. We need to be diligent. The schedule this morning is as follows: From now until 8:30, we will answer any last minute questions that may have arisen since yesterday's briefing. I suspect that any questions you might have were answered in the paperwork distributed yesterday. From 8:30 to 10:00, you will be in wardrobe. We have several clothing options for each of you. You will be transported with only the clothing we provide for you. You will be sent with adequate funding to purchase clothing for the remainder of your mission. After wardrobe you will report to sublevel six for mission departure."

Peter considered this. Was it going to be like boarding an airplane? Now boarding seats one through four, please, he imagined the crackled announcement. He found it funny that in that moment he was comparing time travel to an airport concourse gate.

Having thoroughly reviewed the briefing from yesterday, Peter had no questions. He wanted to get dressed and get on with the mission. His anxiety was manifesting itself with jittery hands and excessive sweating. He wondered if that would be a problem.

Peter looked about the room. Most everyone was sitting, experiencing the same discomfort. Several minutes passed and there were no questions. Peter's unease got the best of him.

"General, I'm feeling a little anxious this morning. I don't think it's anything to worry about, but not having traveled through time before, what should we expect?"

"Peter, I would be worried if you weren't experiencing anxiety this morning. After wardrobe you will each be given an anti-anxiety supplement. It should reduce your stress level and put you at ease for the jump. Your intellectual faculties should not be impaired."

Trying to quell his apprehension, Peter wondered how many others had taken this trip. After all, this wasn't as common as taking a plane to Vegas.

He leaned back and observed the visiting military personnel question the procedures leading to transport and the potential impact of cellular degeneration. They were obviously there to observe this monumental undertaking. The general answered the questions he could and sought assistance for the technical ones he couldn't. With that, the team was ushered off to wardrobe.

Two hours to Linear Shift

Since Peter had been down there last week, he was relatively unaffected by their desolate surroundings. He was certain that Drs. Lamb and Larsson had also been to the basement; neither of them showed any hesitation. If they are going to get us home, he thought, they better have studied the devices before today. Julie, on the other hand, was full of trepidation and excitement. Peter wanted to share his recent trip through the tunnel but kept his promise to the general.

Passing through the final security door, Peter stepped into the frigid confines of the long concrete tunnel. Julie's sudden realization of what lay beneath them seemed to motivate her. Her pace quickened.

While Peter followed and feigned interest in the aesthetics of the grey, concrete tunnel, he missed the rust colored stain covering a spot on the floor half way down the tunnel. Moments later, they arrived at a doorway opening to a long stairway headed down. Two by two, as if loading the ark, the team began to descend. Peter glanced ahead to General Applegate and wondered if he'd demonstrate his bizarre behavior that Benny and Stella talked about. Peter was certain that it was a nervous reaction of some sort, but the precise cause was unknown.

"Our first stop will be sublevel two for wardrobe," stated the general as he mechanically climbed down the worn steel stairway.

Going down a single flight of stairs only took moments. When they reached the level, the general slid an odd-looking key into the antique door lock. An audible *clink* echoed widely as the general pulled open the door. Peter could see that the initial layout was similar to SUB-10. The group walked down the corridor, which Peter assumed would open into a gathering room. He was half right; the corridor did open into a larger room, but it was enormous compared to level ten. The space had never been finished suitable for living quarters. He could see exposed steel beams on the ceiling and gritty concrete walls around the perimeter. In the center were a half dozen racks of antique clothing. To the left of the clothing racks were two temporary changing rooms, crudely constructed of waferboard.

"Gentlemen, these racks will provide you with clothing for the trip. You will only need one outfit, and be sure to include an overcoat. It will be raining when you arrive. Julie, the women's section is this way. Follow me." Applegate led Julie around the corner as Peter joined the two doctors inspecting the racks.

The screech of wire hangers sliding on metal rods echoed

throughout the cavernous level as the three men sifted through the vintage clothing. The diversity was sparse, mainly offering drab-colored sport coats and trousers with button-up shirts. Peter honestly didn't care how he was dressed, just as long as the clothing was date appropriate and fit properly. He pulled three pairs of trousers from hangers and picked out matching shirts before heading into one of the makeshift fitting rooms. Five minutes later, Peter emerged wearing olive tweed pants with a cream collared shirt and his black suede loafers.

"Well? How do I look?" Peter asked, walking up to the general.

General Applegate assessed Peter's attire and nodded. "Looks good, but you need to lose the shoes. Nothing from the present goes back. Did you grab a pair of socks and underwear from the bin?" Applegate pointed to a large box overflowing with undergarments at the end of the aisle.

"Are you serious? You want me to wear another man's boxers?" asked Peter incredulously.

"Yes. If you ignore the smallest detail, it could jeopardize the mission. They've all been washed, you'll be fine." General Applegate looked away, indicating the discussion was over. Peter returned to the clothing area and begrudgingly picked out the cleanest pair of tan boxers he could find, and grabbed a pair of brown socks before moving to the shoe bin. Discouraged, he stepped back into the changing room to complete his costume.

As Peter finished redressing, he heard a sharp *click-clack* echoing across the cavernous level and steadily growing louder. "What the hell is that?" he murmured to himself. A few minutes later, the clamor ceased. Peter re-emerged from the booth and was greeted by Julie.

"Hiya, Hubby," she said and twirled in a full circle. She was dressed in a beige cotton, pleated skirt and a navy-blue knit blouse. She sported a pair of vintage strap-back heels to complete the ensemble. "How do I look?"

"You look wonderful, Julie," Peter said without hesitation.

"Thank you, sir. Let's see you. Spin," demanded Julie.

Peter did so, and Julie nodded. "Very handsome, Peter. I approve."

"Thanks, Jules. But I'm not crazy about wearing another man's drawers. First thing we do in '42 is go shopping."

"Agreed," replied Julie, walking toward yet another box of vintage wear.

Peter's eyes followed her and saw what she was scrutinizing: a box of purses, handbags, and wallets.

While the team was dressing in their respective areas, the anti-anxiety pills were distributed and swallowed.

"Peter, I set aside a leather satchel for you," Applegate said quietly from behind. "It would be perfect for holding any important paperwork while on the mission." The general handed Peter the bag.

"Thanks, General. I'll swap things out while we wait for the doctors to finish."

Peter stepped aside and found an empty table. He nonchalantly looked about before moving the large manila envelope and his own vintage cash to the satchel. As he finished, General Applegate walked up.

"Peter. Here is an envelope with sufficient funds to complete the mission. Spend it wisely." Applegate handed Peter the envelope, and he slid it into the bag.

"Thank you, sir. Seeing as how we are about to depart, I would like to see Benny and Stella be released before we head down to level six."

General Applegate looked stunned at Peter's request. "That was not part of the agreement, Peter."

"Sure it was. You said that once we left, they would be free to leave. It's now 9:45 and we leave within the hour. I would like to say goodbye before I go."

"What you are asking doesn't fit into the schedule. I'm sorry, you will have to trust me; they will be released."

"Listen, General. I've been patient with you from the beginning. I have rarely questioned your motives, despite my doubts. And honestly, I don't trust you. You need to release them now, or your operation will be a man down, because I will walk out of here right now." Peter didn't break eye contact with the general.

"Fine. You will have to give me thirty minutes for their debrief and release." Applegate paused momentarily, as he considered the situation. "As soon as you are outfitted, head down to sublevel six. I will bring them up, and you can say your goodbyes from there."

Applegate stomped off, clearly frustrated at Peter's demands. Peter hadn't lied. He didn't trust the general, and regardless of what kind of *shift* occurred because of this expedition, he wanted to free his friends before he left.

Peter slung his new satchel over his shoulder and walked back to the dressing area. Dr. Larsson was dressed and waiting next to Julie, but Dr. Lamb was still trying to decide what shoes to wear.

"Please, Doctor. Just pick a pair and let's get a move on," Peter stated and headed for the stairway. Peter heard the *click-clack* a moment later and smiled at the sound of Julie hurrying to catch up.

Forty minutes to Linear Shift

Peter and Julie were greeted by a restless engineer when they arrived at the entry door to sublevel six.

"We've got tickets for the next flight out," Peter joked. He didn't receive the desired response.

"Why are you two down here without an escort?" asked one of the scientists.

"Relax, friend. General Applegate sent us down. He'll be along shortly. Lamb and Larsson are right behind us," replied Peter, just as the doctors walked up.

"So who here is going to get us up to speed so we can do this time jump thing?" quipped Peter, glancing at each of the scientists' faces one by one.

"I can give you two the tour," Dr. Lamb offered.

"Great. Show us where the magic happens." Peter noticed

his confidence increasing in the last ten minutes. He wondered if the pills had anything to do with it or if it was his own attempt to hide his nerves.

Peter brushed away the thoughts and took Julie's hand as they followed Dr. Lamb down yet another long corridor. The difference with this one was that it appeared newly constructed. The ceiling glowed, but Peter could not see any fixtures. Recessed lighting? Didn't have those in the forties.

As they neared the end, there was a sign posted that said, "NO ELECTRONIC DEVICES BEYOND THIS POINT."

"What's with this?" inquired Peter.

"Oh, that. It's meant for cell phones, tablets, and the like. There are computers being used in here, but the time-travel chamber is located in a clean zone. It's enclosed within lead-lined walls to eliminate interference."

"Aren't those to prevent radiation from harming people?"

"Yes, they are effective for that as well, but the sensitivity of the equipment running the time-travel program dictates it be used for this application as well," replied Dr. Lamb.

"If you need all this computer equipment to run the time machine, what did they do in 1942?" asked Julie.

"Well, Dr. Epson did, in fact, use a computer. It was not a digital device as you know it and largely occupied the majority of the surplus area throughout sublevel six. It was the size of a small house. Shall we continue?"

Dr. Lamb turned into another large room. Peter thought this area could be an auditorium or gymnasium. Built in the center of the floor area were two enclosures approximately ten feet by ten feet, with opposing doors for access. Along the perimeter of the room were a half dozen computers set up at work stations. On the far side of the enclosures were several rows of theater seating.

"Are we expecting a movie?" Peter asked.

"Not quite. As we were developing Dr. Epson's theory, we had a number of fellow scientists fly in to document the research." Dr. Lamb paused, as he activated a power coil. "We will not have an overly large audience today. Once everyone arrives, we will run through a brief explanation of the protocols and then we'll be zipped."

"Zipped?" Peter questioned.

"Just my term for the process. You know when you zip computer files to reduce their size, it's easier to send large amounts of information? Well, we're zipping ourselves to be sent back."

"I'm sure my kids would know exactly what you're talking about." Peter replied. "Don't we have a precise departure time?" Peter asked, trying to move passed the scientific jumble that Dr. Lamb was ever so excited to explain.

"Not exactly. You see, we can jump within a specific window of time. During that time, we can pinpoint our exact destination. That window will close at 10:42 this morning and it will not open again for another six weeks," Dr. Lamb explained.

"OK, makes total sense," Peter lied, not wanting to admit that the science was light-years beyond his comprehension. He looked at Julie, and she shrugged her shoulders.

Peter walked up to the twin chambers and examined the layout. He could see the lead lining and wondered just how safe this was. Who was the lining protecting, the scientist running the show from outside or the travelers inside?

As Peter rounded the outside of the chambers, they were joined by Dr. Larsson, General Applegate, and Mark. What the hell was Mark doing there?

"Peter? A moment," said General Applegate nodding away from the group.

Peter walked across the room and met Applegate near the entrance to the corridor.

"Peter, Benny is sick. We have physicians evaluating his condition as we speak. He won't be leaving today. However, Stella is here and desperate to see you. She has been brought up to speed rather quickly to meet your demands. Please don't tax her mental state. She is in shock after our explanation."

"Is he going to be ok?" asked Peter. "Benny seemed fine last week."

"He should be fine. Just some flu bug," replied the general. "Mark, you can bring Stella in now."

Mark nodded and returned moments later with Stella. When Peter saw the look on her face, he realized that the general had not been exaggerating. Shock was a term used too lightly for her condition. She looked haggard and disoriented. As Mark released her arm, she flinched and stepped away from him. Then she noticed Peter.

"Peter!" yelled Stella as she stumbled to him and hugged him tightly. "Oh, honey. You are so brave! They just told me all about what you're doing, and I think you're the most wonderful man."

Peter, confused, said, "How's Benny? The general said he was under the weather."

Stella fidgeted and looked nervously around the room. "He's, um . . . he'll be OK. Just got a bug or something."

Feeling a little relief, Peter continued "How about you? Are you ready to get out of here? It'll all be over in what, ten minutes or so?" he questioned the general, who was standing near listing to their conversation.

"That's correct. We have to jump in the next ten minutes, so please wrap this up."

"Right. Listen, Stella. Tell Benny that I hope he feels better and let him know how sorry I am that this all happened."

"I'll do that, sssweetie," slurred Stella. "You be currrful on your trip."

"Are you doing OK yourself, Stella?" Peter asked, concerned. "You seem to be a bit out of sorts."

"I'll bbbe jussst fine, Darlin'," she replied, not making eye contact.

Mark once again took Stella by the arm. He led her to the observation seats and sat next to her in the front row.

Dr. Lamb conveyed some last minute instructions to the attendant manning the computers and joined Peter and the general. "It looks like we are green across the board, General."

General Applegate called for Julie and Dr. Larsson to join them. "The time has come, and I want to thank each and every one of you again for your dedication to this mission. We only have a brief moment to explain the process. Dr. Lamb?"

"As we explained yesterday, we will each be reduced to a digital stream and sent through the nearest gateway. In order to reduce us to a digital format, we will be utilizing Epson's devices in the chambers." Lamb referred to the twin chambers which were beginning to leak some sort of cloudy gas.

"Are they supposed to be leaking like that?" asked Julie.

"Yes, that's an inert gas that is lowering the temperature of the lead surrounding the chambers." As Dr. Lamb spoke, Peter couldn't help but hear Stella weeping.

Peter looked to the general, and it was clear that he was trying his best to ignore her. The general remained focused on Doctor Lamb's explanations. Peter looked back to where Stella and Mark were sitting, concerned with her condition.

General Applegate cleared his throat in an effort to bring Peter back to the conversation.

"Once the chambers have dropped to the target temperature, we will enter the transmitter. Hope everyone is comfortable with each other, it's gonna be snug. Located inside the chamber are four titanium plates surrounded by multiple electromagnets. As the magnets begin to spin, the titanium plates will record their contents as digital data and begin sending the signal."

"Wait. Are we going to be deconstructed one layer at a time?" asked Peter.

"Not exactly. According to Dr. Epson's research, we will simply vanish after the recording process is complete," Dr. Larsson replied nervously.

"So this is untested?"

"Not exactly. As we stated yesterday, Dr. Epson tested it in a limited fashion. What you all are doing today has not been. That was made clear when we first approached you about the mission," stated General Applegate.

"Great. We're guinea pigs," Peter said sarcastically.

"Shall we begin?" asked Dr. Lamb.

Followed by a few assistants, the team moved toward the transmitter. As they did, Peter glanced at Stella. He was worried about her. Suddenly she jumped to her feet and screamed, "PETER, THEY KILLED BENNY!" She attempted to run, but Mark was quick. He reached out and grabbed her arm as she passed. She spun around and hit the floor, hard. As she tried to crawl away, Mark pulled her to her feet, a pistol in his hand.

By now, everyone in the room was stunned. Every eye on the room was fixated on Stella and Mark as the melee unfolded. Mark held Stella tightly, wrapping his left arm around her shoulders and covering her mouth with his hand. He pointed the gun directly at her head with his right hand.

"Now listen to me!" barked Mark. "All of you are going to get on those platforms and go on your mission. Stella here will be just fine as long as you all play along."

"WHAT THE FUCK IS GOING ON?" Peter looked at General Applegate and was surprised to see fear in his eyes. He had been certain that Applegate was behind everything.

"Listen to me, Mark," said the General. "There's no reason to hurt anyone else. Killing Benny was an accident, and nobody blames you."

"Shut up! You four, get in the fucking chamber now!" Mark yelled as he cocked his pistol.

Peter stood speechless. As he attempted to process what was going on, he could see Trevor slipping silently around the back of the observation area. He didn't recall seeing him come in with the rest of the group.

"Mark, what the hell do you think you're doing?" screamed Peter. "What did Benny or Stella do?" he pleaded, trying to keep Mark's attention while Trevor crept up from behind, his own gun drawn.

"You don't get it, moron? This mission was supposed to be mine, but the general here pulled the plug at the last minute," growled Mark.

Applegate didn't reply right away, and his eyes shifted to Trevor about twenty feet from Mark. Mark noticed and instinctively turned. As soon as he caught sight of Trevor crouching, gun pointed at him, he pushed Stella to the floor and swung his pistol around. He pulled the trigger twice. The first shot missed wide left, but the second shot hit home, piercing Trevor's forehead above his left eye. The impact of the bullet flung his head back as he fell to the floor. Mark now aimed his weapon toward the appalled crowd.

"Get in the chamber now!" he screamed.

Nobody moved except for Stella as she tried to crawl away quietly. Mark pointed the gun down and shot her in the back. She no longer wept or crawled. Mark leveled his gun at General Applegate next.

"Are you going to move, or do I need to keep shooting until there's nobody left?"

"You son of a bitch! Why are you doing this? Why don't you go?" asked Peter, as tears blurred his vision.

"Because I can't jump. We tried, didn't we General? My platoon was hit by an IED in Afghanistan, and I have a metal plate around my left eye. It reacted to the magnetic coils in the transmitter." Mark paused, as he wiped a bead of sweat from his forehead. "It hurt like hell, but I ain't no pussy. General Applegate here refused to let me travel after that. Said I could die. I call bullshit. Now my only chance is for you all to get in the chamber and change something-anything so I don't lose my men in that godforsaken place. No IED, no metal plate, I travel." Mark's voice had taken on an eerie, chilling calm. He pulled the hammer back on his pistol as he pointed it at General Applegate.

"Go!" Applegate yelled, and the team jumped into the chamber. They climbed onto the titanium platforms.

Silently, the four team members were strapped in by one of the assistants. All were either shaking, crying, or both. After the last belt was secured, the attendant stepped out of the chamber and latched the door. He nodded to the general, who was now standing by the control board watching Mark. He reached across the panel and lifted a red switch cover and flicked the switch beneath.

Nothing happened.

He flipped it again, and nothing happened.

Applegate turned to the large clock on the wall. It read 10:42. No, 10:43 now.

"Oh God, we're too late!" cried the general. All hope for the mission was lost. A solemn silence settled over the room.

Slowly, the power inverter began to hum and pop. All eyes turned to the large power coil and saw that it began to spark, turning faster and faster. As it reached critical mass, a loud grinding sound came from the back side of the device and a thunderous clap deafened everyone in the room. Smoke billowed about the room, as the resonance of the power inverter began to abate.

Applegate stumbled around the control bank and rushed to the door of the transmission chamber. He hit the latch, swung the door open, and rushed in. A moment later, he slowly walked out and said two words:

"They're gone."

PART 3

CHAPTER 0

July 24, 1942

The apprentice stood beside his mentor, analyzing the data from the spatial assembler. The smell of burned ozone permeated the room. The electro coils hummed loudly, just as they had with every one of the forty-three failed tests that preceded this one.

"Reorganization levels?"

Gallagher twisted a knob slightly to sharpen the display. "Levels optimal."

Dr. Bernard Epson stood at the large control panel, analyzing the switches and dials, verifying that they were correct. After a second visual sweep across the monstrous panel, he paused.

"Doctor?" prompted Gallagher. "All levels are within their optimal ranges. Shall we proceed?"

"Yes. Yes. I was just . . . reviewing everything before . . ." Epson's voice trailed off.

Michael Gallagher had been Dr. Epson's trusted assistant long enough to notice he'd gone into reflection mode. Gallagher assumed the doctor was contemplating the past failures, hoping that this test would be successful. All the years of arduous research and development had culminated into this single moment. This test had to work. Needed to work.

Epson took a deep breath before he engaged the master

switch. As he drove the brass and copper lever home, the lights throughout the laboratory flickered momentarily. Gallagher briefly wondered whether they would lose power to the test chambers, but levels remained constant.

Epson glanced across the control panel after the power surge, verifying nothing had changed. He nodded mostly to himself before looking to Gallagher, whose face was frozen in intensity.

"Mr. Gallagher?" Epson inquired.

"Levels are still acceptable but unstable. They should be off the charts, but they continue to deteriorate."

Epson stepped closer to see the telemetric readout for himself. "Can you boost the relativity modulator to compensate?"

"Not from here. And we shouldn't have to, Doctor. There is more than enough power coming through the electro coils. It's almost as if there's some kind of restriction . . . some kind of interference . . ." Gallagher stopped as the coils began to wind down.

The grating sound began to subside as the revolutions abated. Epson eased Gallagher away from the oscilloscope and leaned in himself. The assembly levels continued to drop, and there was nothing he could do to stop them.

Epson stepped away from the scope. "I don't get it," he lamented.

Gallagher stood silently as the doctor scrutinized the dials scattered across the control board for the third time in as many minutes.

"Mr. Gallagher. Did you calibrate the relativity modulator before engaging the inversion coupler?" questioned Epson.

"Y-y-yes, sir," Michael stammered through his lie. "The magnets were calibrated for optimal performance."

Epson moved from behind the control panel and began to examine the now-silent power inverter. He deftly removed the access panel and leaned into the base of the device. As he inspected various wires and tubes, Gallagher stood by, watching intently.

Epson backed away from the opening and squatted with his back against the dusty wall. His face shone fear and exhaustion. He sat for a long moment in silent contemplation.

"Doctor? Is something wrong?"

Epson remained on his haunches as he stared into space. "Where did we go wrong, Michael?" Epson began.

"I don't follow you, sir."

Epson slowly brought his eyes around to Gallagher. "You've been with me for how long, eight years? Have my equations been that far off?"

"No, Doctor. You've done everything right," Michael replied, avoiding his gaze.

"How, then, would you explain all the failures? We haven't had a solid success on any of our experiments since moving the lab here. I just . . . don't . . . understand." Epson again looked off into the distance.

Gallagher was conflicted. He knew that Epson had poured years of blood, sweat, and tears into the project, and on an emotional level, he felt sorry for the man. But his loyalties remained with the Society; his righteousness remained with the failure of the tests. The months of sabotaging the critical, yet minute, circuits and byways in Epson's device continued to pay dividends.

Not wanting to betray his feelings, Gallagher turned away from the doctor. "I'm sure there's a practical reason, Doctor. Perhaps the depth of the lab might have something to do with it. We are down six levels and encased in two feet of solid concrete. At least."

"Hmm. I suppose. But none of my theories should be affected by either of those circumstances." Dr. Epson stood from his crouched position and walked back to the control panel next to Gallagher.

"Frankly, I am beginning to wonder if my theories have any validity whatsoever. On paper, we should have completed a half-dozen test jumps." Epson paused as he pulled a handkerchief from his pocket and wiped the beads of sweat from his brow.

"But in practice . . ." Epson trailed off again.

"Don't beat yourself up, Doctor. We'll figure it out and try again," Gallagher said.

"No. No we won't. This was our final test. Unless we had achieved certifiable results, our benefactors are unwilling to continue funding." Epson slumped into his worn leather chair, and for a moment his eyes looked misty.

"So soon? I thought we had a year contract," asked Gallagher.

"Initially, yes. They promised a year's support, but seeing as each of our test runs have failed, the military has lost faith in my abilities and are ready to terminate our agreement. And, frankly, I revel at the thought. I've been at this for far too long, and what do I have to show for it?"

"Doctor, your research will be invaluable-"

"Invaluable for what? It doesn't work, Michael. It's a lost cause. I'm a failure, and I will count my lucky stars if the government doesn't come after me for reimbursement on their bad investment."

"No, they can't do that," Michael said. "Can they?"

"They certainly could—they're the government—but I don't think it would be prudent for them to do so. All it would take is a page four article in a random scientific publication exposing their frivolous spending, especially in wartime. However, I do believe they will certainly show me the door posthaste."

Hearing that his assignment from the Society was nearing its end left his mind spinning. Gallagher began to wonder what was next. For both of them.

"If that's it, Doctor, what will you do?"

Before Epson could answer, the sound of click-clacking footsteps echoed throughout the lab. Both men looked up to see Miss Stewart approaching.

"Good morning, gentlemen. How was the test?" she asked, oblivious to the sorrowful expressions.

"Unfortunately, the test did not meet our desired expectations," Epson replied as he straightened himself in his chair. "And, as I was just telling Mr. Gallagher, our time here in sublevel six has come to an end."

"I don't understand. You were so sure the test this morning was going to be successful. Even after you left last night, Michael stayed late to make sure everything was perfect. What went wrong?" asked Stewart.

"We'll never know," Epson snapped. "I've spent far too long chasing this dream, and if they want to throw me out onto the street, I'm not going to waste another minute tracking down another frayed wire. No, it all ends now."

"But, Doctor! You can't just walk away—" Stewart began.

"Why not? Haven't I earned the right? Isn't it obvious that I'm a failure?"

"Stop that! Stop that thinking right now," Stewart yelled, surprising both men. "The only thing you've earned is the respect from everyone surrounding this project. You've worked far too hard to just walk away. You owe it to yourself to see it through. There'll be other people looking for investment opportunities down the road. You're so close, and I will not stand by quietly and watch you throw it all away."

The lab was silent as Stewart's words sunk in. "I . . . I suppose we could record this last test before we file our report."

"Yes. That sounds more like it, Doctor," Stewart said, turning her frown into a smile. "Now, it's nearly eleven o'clock. Would you two like me to run over to the cafeteria and pick you up a sandwich while you proceed?"

"Yes, Miss Stewart. That would be fine," Epson replied.

She winked at the doctor and walked back down the corridor. Moments later, they heard the faint echo of the large steel door sliding shut.

"Well, I guess she told us," Epson said to Gallagher as they both began to chuckle. "Mr. Gallagher, please retrieve the records from my file cabinet, and we'll begin."

Gallagher had hoped to find some time to correct his latest sabotage in the transmission chamber before they began recording the data, but he masked his desires. "Absolutely,

Doctor."

As he began to cross the lab, the familiar sound of the power inverter kicked on. Time turned to molasses as Gallagher turned and noticed the gyration of the coils was much faster than previous tests.

"Doctor?" he yelled. "What's going on?"

"It appears that you forgot to disconnect the power feed after the last test. Again, I might add." Epson walked to the emergency disconnect switch mounted on the wall. But as he gripped the handle, he hesitated. He glanced back to the control panel and then to Gallagher, who was standing halfway between the panel and his office. With both men frozen in curiosity, a thunderous clap echoed throughout the lab. Both Gallagher and Epson covered their ears and hit the floor. Moments later, the ringing in their ears began to subside.

Epson struggled up and walked shakily to the master control panel. To his surprise, the teletype had just completed printing "ACQUISITION COMPLETE." He looked over at Gallagher, who was still standing in the middle of the lab.

"Mr. Gallagher . . . it appears that our latest test has been successful."

CHAPTER 1

July 24, 2013

The door closed abruptly, and the interior of the chamber was dark as a starless night. The sound of the latch securing the door resounded throughout the chamber, affirming the team's fate. The events of the last fifteen minutes crashed through Peter's mind like a runaway freight train. Hearing about Benny's death was devastating, but to see Mark shoot Stella, he had nearly lost the ability to breathe. He wanted to get up, needed to get up—to hurt someone—but the bindings were too tight, and he couldn't see anything.

"Jules? You okay?" Peter asked.

"Yeah, I think I'm all right. You?"

"I've been better. Docs? How are you two holding up?"

In the silence, Peter could hear faint whimpers from the direction of the two scientists. "Larsson! Lamb!"

"We're . . . f-f-fine. Just a little shaken up," Dr. Larsson said, answering for both of them.

"What the hell just happened?" asked Julie. "I always thought Mark was a little unstable, but holy shit, I had no idea he was capable of murder."

Peter stared in the direction of what he thought was the door, his mind retracing the interactions with Mark. Although they were clouded, he could see the warning signs. "I don't know, Jules. I don't get it either."

"I mean, all he had to do was wait patiently until we left. Everything would have been fine. We would have traveled and—" Julie stopped. "It was because of Stella. Her showing up forced Mark's hand."

"Let's not go pointing fingers," Peter snapped. "Stella's dead because of that bastard."

Quiet settled throughout the chamber. A moment later, Julie spoke. "I'm sorry, Peter. I didn't mean that it was her fault."

Peter wished his hands were free to wipe the tears leaking down his cheeks, but he was glad the team couldn't see him. He had loved Benny like a brother, and while he would have never admitted it, he loved Stella just the same. They were both dead because of him.

"Peter. Can you hear me? It's nobody's fault but Mark's," Julie said, as if she could read his thoughts. "Doctor, how long until we travel?"

"Well, if everything functions as planned, it should be nearly instantaneous," replied Dr. Lamb.

"Listen, Peter. We need to regroup, here, and quickly," Julie said professorially. "If they send us back and we come out emotional basket cases, we'll have a lot more to explain than simply traveling through time."

Peter squeezed his eyes tight in an effort to force the tears away. "You're right. We shouldn't say a word about anything that just happened. Agreed?"

Everyone agreed. "Then we wait. As soon as we zip, as Dr. Lamb puts it, we'll pop out of the chamber as originally planned, story intact," Peter said.

As they waited in silence, Peter began to feel a slight rumble originating in the base of the platform. As the vibration intensified, he could hear a muffled roar from outside the chamber. "Doctor?"

"It's fine, Peter. It's the power inverter ramping up. Nothing to be worried about," replied Larsson with a crackle in his voice.

A moment later, a muffled thump, then absolute silence. "Nothing to be worried about, huh?" questioned Peter.

"Um, I think we just traveled. Did anyone feel anything . . . peculiar?" asked Lamb.

"Why, were we supposed to?" asked Julie.

"No, no. Well, we're not entirely sure. We're not exactly clear on what happens during time travel," Dr. Larsson added. "Theoretically, we would lose a millisecond of consciousness, but our minds are not designed to recognize to recognize to recognize the missing ing mo moment."

"Are you all right, Doctor?" asked Peter. "You're stuttering."

"Fascinating!" exclaimed Dr. Lamb. "We have traveled. That was a momentary slip in Dr. Larsson's consciousness."

As Peter and the team lay strapped to the metal tables, Peter realized a flaw in the design of the device. Suppose nobody was home where they were going? Would they stay strapped to the tables until they were discovered? Peter's thoughts were interrupted when he heard the sound of the latch disengage from outside.

"Well, here goes nothing," Peter said as the door inched open, allowing light to spill in from a new timeline.

CHAPTER 2

As the door opened slowly, he half expected to see general Applegate—or even worse, Mark—standing just outside, but neither were visible. From his lying-down position, Peter looked out into a dusty laboratory straight from black-and-white Hollywood. He could see the back side of an enormous bench where the theater seating existed before he and the team entered the transmission chamber. Then, Peter saw a shadow dance across the floor just beyond the doorframe.

"Uh, hello? Is anyone there? We could use a hand if you have a moment," Peter said with a wry grin on his face.

A moment later, a greying man wearing a white lab coat and horn-rimmed glasses stepped into view. His mouth resembled that of a big mouth bass. He was clearly unprepared for their arrival.

"Hi there. Would you mind unstrapping us? Even though it was a short ride, titanium platforms are not the most comfortable mattresses to lie on for extended periods of time," Peter quipped.

"My God. It actually works!" the elderly man said with astonishment.

"Ah, yes. That it does. You must be Dr. Epson," Peter replied.

Epson staggered back a few steps, nearly stepping on his

apprentice's feet. "You know who I am?" he asked.

"Yes. We all do. I'd introduce you to my team, but it's quite awkward from this position," Peter said.

"Right. Hurry, Mr. Gallagher, give me a hand in here." Epson and Gallagher, whose eyes were edging on softball size, stepped into the receiving chamber and, one by one, unstrapped the four team members from the metal platforms.

Peter sat up and twisted his head side to side, untying the knots inside his neck. Relieved from his restraints, he dropped his feet to the ground and stepped forward toward Dr. Epson.

"Hello. I'm Peter Cooper and this is my team, Drs. Lamb and Larsson and Julie Frey. It's a great pleasure to meet you." He extended his hand.

Epson, spry for an older man, hopped back out of the chamber, followed by Peter and the rest of the team. His face had forgotten it had pigment, and he looked as if he might pass out at any moment.

"Don't worry, Doctor. Everything is going to be all right. We realize how much of a shock this must be, greeting four strangers inside your lab like this."

"Shock is an understatement. Overwhelmed might be more appropriate," Epson replied as he leaned against the edge of the nearby control panel. "How is it that you know who I am?"

"Well, Doctor," began Dr. Larsson, "we've traveled from the future, where we've reviewed all your records and lab reports. Quite impressive record keeping, I might add."

"F-f-from the . . . future? How far?" stammered Epson.

"Oh, not terribly far. Around seventy years," replied Dr. Lamb.

"S-seventy . . . ?" Epson asked for clarification.

"That's right, Doctor. We're from the year 2013," Peter added.

Epson stumbled to the side and luckily found a chair just behind the control panel. He pulled his glasses from his face and wiped several ponds' worth of sweat from his forehead with the back of his coat sleeve.

Peter looked at the man standing next to the doctor and was surprised that his expression didn't quite match Epson's. If Peter's instincts hadn't taken a wrong turn at Albuquerque, he'd think it tinged on fear. "And you are Michael Gallagher? Dr. Epson's assistant?"

"Yes, that's right," Gallagher replied curtly. "You say you're from the future, but why should we believe you?"

"Didn't you just unstrap us from titanium platforms inside a time travel device that you helped construct? Isn't that proof enough?" Peter replied with a disparaging tone.

Julie recognized the hint of sarcasm in Peter's voice and placed a hand on his shoulder.

"For all we know, some of the physicists from downstairs are just playing a cruel trick here," Gallagher said. "And furthermore—"

"That will be quite enough," Epson stopped his assistant.

"But, Doctor—" Gallagher begged Epson.

"Pardon me, but I have an element of validation for you," Dr. Lamb said, interrupting the conversation.

All eyes turned to the doctor as he stepped forward, reached into his front pocket, and pulled out a coin. "It's a ten-cent piece from the year we originated." Lamb handed the dime to Epson.

Epson took the dime and examined it as thoroughly as if he had discovered a new periodic element. Gallagher crowded in to see the dime for himself.

"Who is this on the face of the coin?" asked Epson.

Lamb looked to Peter to continue the conversation. "That is President Roosevelt. He died, or dies, in 1945. His bust was placed on the dime in 1946. The design of the dime hasn't changed since."

"The . . . the president dies in forty-five?" Epson asked in a whisper.

"Yes, unfortunately he dies after suffering a stroke," Julie added.

"Again, this could be just another fallacy to discredit our research," Gallagher said, stepping away from the coin as if it were tainted.

Dr. Lamb's presentation of the dime had caught Peter off guard because the general had made it explicitly clear to leave everything from the present in the present. He made a note to talk to Lamb and Larsson about it later. Presently, however, he needed to gain Epson's trust swiftly.

"Doctor, we are here to prove that your time machine does work. There are a few tweaks that need to be applied to the transmission chamber for it to become fully functional. That's why Drs. Lamb and Larsson are here." Peter slowed the information dump, taking care not to overload Epson. The team needed him as an ally. He also wasn't yet completely confident that Epson's assistant could be trusted.

"Dr. Epson, don't believe them," Gallagher yelled. "Can't you see they're playing with your mind? That dime was probably fabricated down on twelve. Their clothes are even from our time. Wouldn't you expect them to be wearing some kind of . . . futuristic suit?"

Epson nodded slightly. He was still holding the dime between his fingers. He looked at each of the four time travelers and nodded again. "Mr. Gallagher, I believe them. Why would those buffoons downstairs want to jeopardize my research? No, these folks are from the future, and we should welcome them with an open mind."

"I, for one, will not stand witness to their shenanigans. If you can't see it yourself, there's nothing I can do for you. I'm leaving!" Michael Gallagher turned and stormed out of the lab.

Nobody said anything at first. Peter broke the silence with a low whistle. "Is he always wound so tight, Doctor?"

"Ha. Mr. Gallagher has been in my employ for the better part a decade. That is the first time I've witnessed such an outburst. You four are really from the future, right?"

"Yes, Doctor. We are. Without the ability to give you any more proof, you'll have to take our word for it," Peter smiled at Epson.

"Well then. Welcome to 1942. How long do you plan on

staying?"

"We plan on sticking around long enough for the doctors here to help you get this contraption working and send us back. Julie and I are here to conduct historical research in the meantime. We're hoping to be on our way home in a few months," Peter said.

"Oh. A few months. I see." Epson looked pensively at the strangers in his lab. "How do you expect to remain true to your future if you're spending an extended period of time here? There could be some catastrophic consequences for the future if you change *anything*!" Epson squealed apoplectically.

"Dr. Epson, we're a highly trained scientific team. We've run hundreds of test scenarios to account for any time displacement," Lamb replied calmly. "We're prepared; nothing will disturb our timeline, or our mission."

"In addition to our research, Julie and I will keep our chronologic footprint to a minimum," Peter added.

"Oh, I understand. As long as you are all aware . . . Well then, we'll have to find you all a place to stay. As soon as Miss Stewart returns, she'll be able to help you out with whatever you need."

"Miss Stewart? Who is she?" Julie asked, not recalling the name from reading through Epson's research records.

"Oh, Miss Stewart. She's our personal assistant. She helps Mr. Gallagher and me with the nonscientific activities of the day. If it weren't for her, we'd likely forget to eat."

Peter smiled. "She sounds wonderful. I may have to get one of those for myself when we return." As the words left Peter's mouth, he noticed Julie's eyebrow arch slightly.

"Well, it might be a while before she returns, so it looks like we'll have a bit of time to kill. Tell me, Mr. Cooper—"

"Peter. Please, call me Peter,"

"Okay, then. Tell me, Peter. What's it like in 2013?" Epson asked.

CHAPTER 3

Michael Gallagher frantically guided his 1936 Plymouth coupe into the porte cochere at the corner of Allston and Shattuck and screeched to a halt. Before the valet made any movement toward his car, Michael sprang from the wheel.

"Where's Emmett?" Gallagher demanded.

"Um, he's at lunch," replied a man in a red suit laced with gold trim. "He'll be back around one. Are you staying at the hotel?"

Gallagher looked at his wristwatch and saw it was 12:13. "Damn!"

"Pardon? Would you like me to park your—" began the valet, but Gallagher cut him off.

"No! I need to talk to Emmett right away. Do you know where he eats?" Gallagher asked.

"He's . . . he's probably down in the lunchroom. I can send for him if you'd like."

"No. Just tell me where it is."

"It's for employees only, so—"

"I don't care! Tell me where or I'll just start opening doors until I find the right one," Gallagher snapped.

"All right, all right. Go through the lobby, past the front desk, and down the hallway to the left. Halfway down, turn right into the back stairway. The employee lounge is the first door at the bottom of the stairs," he replied, eyeing Gallagher questioningly.

"Thanks," Gallagher said as he sprinted for the entry door.

"Hey! You can't leave your car there," the valet yelled, but Gallagher was already gone.

Gallagher walked into the lobby of the Whitecotton Hotel for the first time since meeting Emmett there several years ago. Emmett had approached him while he was attending a lecture in the grand ballroom about a new theory on Einstein's general relativity and collapsed neutron stars. Little did Gallagher realize at the time that he would be swiftly recruited into the Society and begin leading a double life.

As he dashed past the concierge, he briefly glanced over his shoulder to see if any of the other hotel employees were watching. Not a single eye looked in his direction. Gallagher hustled down the corridor and easily found the stairway. When he arrived at the bottom, he found himself in front of another hotel employee.

"I'm looking for Emmett? The guy at the front desk said I could find him down here," Gallagher pleaded.

"In there," the employee said as he nodded his head toward the open door.

Gallagher walked past him and into the small employee lounge.

Emmett looked up from the book he was reading; shock and dismay flooded his face. "What are you doing here?"

"I had to see you. Something's happened," Gallagher cried.

"I don't care! You know how this works." Emmett stood and rushed to shut the door. "We're never to meet in person. You swore that you would abide—"

"I know, I know. But events from today made it imperative that I talk to you *right now*." Gallagher fidgeted with the keys in his pocket as he paced back and forth.

"Shh. Shh. Not here. Nobody can see us together. Did you talk to anyone?" asked Emmett, moving to close the break-room door.

"Just the valet. He told me you were down here," replied Gallagher. "Oh, and some guy that was walking down the hall just now."

"Dammit, Gallagher! Mandrake is not going to be happy."

"I don't think he'll be that upset after he hears what's happened," Gallagher proclaimed.

Emmett turned to face his agent. "Well, what's so important that you've potentially blown both of our covers?"

"It's the time machine. It works," replied Gallagher.

"We know this already. That's why you're there—to prevent the process of it from becoming fully functional."

"That's the thing. It is functional. Four people just appeared from the future, and there was nothing I could have done about it."

The color drained from Emmett's face as he leaned against the wall. "Is this confirmed?"

"As best as I could. They had all the right answers—"

"Wait, you talked to them?"

"Of course. I pressed them for some kind of proof that they were from the future."

"And?" Emmett coaxed Gallagher before he could finish.

"And one of the doctors showed us a dime from 2013."

Emmett looked at Gallagher in disbelief and began to pace nervously about the room. "More than seventy years."

"I didn't know what to do, so I came here," Gallagher said.

"Yes. It is good that you . . . came straight away." Emmett said reassuringly. "Wait. What did you tell them before you left?"

Gallagher scratched at the side of his face and said, "I . . . I think I said something about not believing them and—"

"Michael, you've got to get back there. You've got to observe everything, now more than ever. You've got to see why they're here. I'll contact Mandrake and see what the next step should be."

"Go back? Are you sure?" Gallagher asked.

"Yes, Michael. It's crucial that you find out as much as you can. And don't come back here. Ever! Send a wire the moment anything changes."

"I, um, I guess I could tell Epson that I panicked or something."

"Come now, Michael. You have a brilliant mind. I'm sure you can do better than that. Now go. Don't speak to anyone on your way out. Do you understand?"

"I understand. I'll wait to hear from you, then?" asked Gallagher.

"That's right. If there are new orders, I'll contact you."

Gallagher nodded his head and walked toward the door. Emmett unlocked it and held it open for him. Gallagher walked past him and, as instructed, didn't say a word to anyone all the way to his car.

CHAPTER 4

When Miss Stewart returned with the lunches and saw the four strangers visiting the lab, she assumed that Epson's concerns were validated. She feared that they were there to shut the program down. But as soon as she saw the look on Epson's face, she knew it was something quite different.

One by one, Epson introduced the team to her. And with each introduction, Stewart became more and more bewildered. With Gallagher gone and Epson preoccupied with the sudden revelation of the functionality of his time machine, he had no appetite. Peter and his team, on the other hand, were famished. The doctors shared one of the meals while Peter and Julie shared the other. They each took turns answering what questions they could for both Dr. Epson and Miss Stewart about their year of origin.

After some time of dancing around events and specific knowledge of the future, Peter decided that he and Julie would leave with Miss Stewart to find housing, while Drs. Larsson and Lamb would stay with Epson to discuss what adjustments might need to be made to his time machine. Epson agreed to drop the doctors off later.

Because the team had entered the secure military base by means that no one in 1942 could have fathomed, Epson was concerned about them leaving the facility. They decided that the best time would be in the midst of the lunch rush and hoped that the military police, or MPs rather, didn't ask too many questions.

Miss Stewart drove a 1940 Chevy deluxe coupe, which had an enormous trunk. Without having IDs, Peter concluded that they would ride there until safely away from the base. Peter chuckled; Julie was less than amused. But they knew the attitude on base was different in wartime 1942 than in their own timeline.

At just before 1:00 p.m., Miss Stewart led Peter and Julie up the familiar stairway from sublevel six. Peter had been in the stairway only twice before, but in his timeline the paint was faded and the treads worn from foot traffic. Now, as they climbed the five flights of stairs, everything looked shiny and crisp. He thought he could smell freshly applied paint and feel the grip of newly imprinted steel with each step.

As they exited the stairwell and passed through the blast doors, Peter's familiarity vanished. They entered the long corridor with the arched walls and roof, but it seemed . . . different. To begin with, it was only half as long as he recalled. There was no security door, no freshly painted walls blocking off the tunnel. To the left there were steel stairs leading up. But the stairway was different as well. In Peter's timeline, the stairway was a switchback style, where this stairway was straight up and landed at a large bulkhead. Peter assumed that there must have been some substantial remodeling over the years and ignored the differences. Still, it was trippy.

Once through the bulkhead, familiarity returned. They stepped into the large warehouse that had army green painted crates stacked to the ceiling. The mock village was nowhere in sight; Peter had known it would not exist in this timeline.

Stepping out into the sunlit afternoon, the base was buzzing with military activity. Thankfully, Miss Stewart's car was parked just to the side of the warehouse and away from prying eyes. They approached the car and slipped into the trunk without notice.

———————◇———————

Fifteen minutes later, the three of them sped along the Pacific Coast Highway, heading for downtown San Francisco.

"I think the first place we'll check is the Perry Hotel. I've heard that they have weekly and monthly rates," Stewart said.

"I don't want you to go out of your way, Miss Stewart. Anything will do, really. Just as long as the place is near shopping and transportation, we'll be fine," Peter replied.

Miss Stewart nodded her head as she drove in silence. Her face wore a mask of contemplation. "I know it's probably none of my business, but what are y'all really here for? I'm no scientist, but I understand Dr. Epson's work enough to follow along with conversations about it. I can understand why your two scientist friends came back. But you two are a mystery."

"Julie and I came back to conduct a little historical research," Peter said with their rehearsed response.

"Ooh! Sounds interesting," Stewart replied. "What kind of research, exactly?"

"Do you have a first name, Miss Stewart?" Julie asked.

"Oh yes. It's Gertrude, but everyone calls me Miss Stewart; it would be peculiar to hear anything else."

"Well, Miss Stewart, those two gentlemen are our coworkers. Peter and I are here for another reason. It's top secret, and we have to keep quiet for now. I'm sure you understand," Julie said as she smiled warmly.

"Say no more. I sometimes stick my nose where it doesn't belong," Stewart said as she blushed slightly. "You won't hear another peep from me about it, and your secret is safe with me."

Peter glanced at Julie and admired how she knew that speaking so directly would be the right approach with Stewart. He had been ready to expound on the ruse when elaboration was clearly unnecessary. Julie winked and smiled.

———————◇———————

Thirty minutes later, Peter unlocked the door to his room on the third floor of the Perry. Julie stepped in, followed by Miss

Stewart. It was a suite, which provided them plenty of space. Space that afforded them separate sleeping areas without raising suspicion.

"Are you two sure you can afford this?" Stewart asked. "A standard room is less than half the cost of this palace."

"We're sure. Even though we're coworkers, we're also newlyweds, and this is kind of like the honeymoon we never had," Peter said, wondering how much of the lie Stewart would buy.

"That's so nice. How memorable for the both of you," Stewart's smile glowed. "Now, what is your plan for clothing and other incidentals?"

"Well, we are going to need a few things. Clothing is a priority. We're also going to need toiletries," Julie said.

"And a car," Peter added.

"A car? Dear, San Francisco has the best transportation system. The trolleys are free."

"We're aware, but as we mentioned earlier, we plan on conducting research during the day," Peter said, disguising the real reason for needing the car. He and Julie would be spending the next several weeks preparing for the trip to France, and their own vehicle was a necessity.

"Are you two rich back in 2013? A car could set you back several hundred dollars."

"We'll be fine. We'll just sell it before we head back," Julie said.

Stewart nodded in understanding and then gave Julie an appraising look. "We'll deal with the car after Dr. Epson arrives this afternoon. First off, let's get you into something . . . a little more appropriate?"

Julie looked down at herself. "Is this outfit not correct for the time?"

"Oh, it's fine, dear. It's just a bit faded, is all. And last year's style. How about the three of us do a little clothes shopping?"

Peter cringed at the thought. "How about the two of you go shop for Julie. I'll wait for the docs to get here, and we'll go then."

"Are you sure?" Julie asked. "It won't be a long trip."

"No, I'm positive. Besides, I've got some studying to do," he said, hoisting his satchel up.

"Then it's settled. Us girls will go have a pleasant time buying wonderful things," Stewart said, a little too eager. It was apparent that shopping was her forte and that Julie was in capable hands.

Stewart started for the door as Julie followed. With her hand on the handle, Stewart glanced back to Peter and then to Julie and paused.

Julie grasped the awkwardness and returned to Peter. She leaned in and kissed him on the lips. "We'll be back, dear."

Julie sauntered back to the waiting Stewart, trying to suppress her giddiness.

Stewart on the other hand wore her smile ear to ear. "Oh, young love. I envy you both."

Julie pulled the door shut behind them, leaving Peter standing in shocked silence. His only thought was, I could get used to that.

CHAPTER 5

Finally alone, Peter sat at the small corner desk, emptied out the contents of his satchel, and tossed it aside. He scrutinized each of the three envelopes one at a time: an envelope of money he'd brought for Operation Abraham, another envelope of money that Applegate had given him for operating expenses, and the mysteriously large manila envelope that Applegate had given him the night before. Pushing the money aside, he stared blankly at the manila envelope, fear coursing through his veins. What kind of side mission could the general actually have planned? he wondered. With trepidation, he tore open the flap.

Inside, he found a letter written by Applegate, along with several smaller envelopes. He scanned each label as he set them aside: Julie Frey, Dr. Bernard Epson, Dr. Brett Lamb, Dr. Griff Larsson, Peter Cooper, Michael Gallagher, Gertrude Stewart, Mailing Instructions (open after returning from France), International Travel Information (open on the train to New York), Surplus Funds. Peter returned to the letter and began to read.

Peter-

If you are reading this letter, I want to congratulate you on making the mission a success, if for only the time travel portion. You and your team have accomplished something paramount in human history. That alone deserves merit. But without complete success, those merits may go unrecognized. It is important that you read this letter in its entirety, as well as the contents of the enclosed envelopes as soon as possible. Your success will depend on it. Additionally, this information is strictly confidential and is for your eyes only. DO NOT SHARE WITH THE TEAM.

I'll begin by briefly explaining the supplemental envelopes. In each, you will find additional information that will be useful on your mission and travels to France. For example, Julie Frey has strong familial ties that run deep in French culture. Inside her envelope you will find information outlining Miss Frey's ancestry. It may become useful when the two of you travel to Oradour-sur-Glane, from where her family originates. There are also surplus funds in the event the need arises. Finally, there is an envelope with mailing instructions. That is your passport to returning to 2013 and may very well be the most important piece of information in the entire dossier. Read it and follow the instructions very carefully.

Next, there are a few things you need to be aware of in 1942. First, there is a mole on Dr. Epson's support staff. We are unsure who it is, but we are certain one exists. After years of analyzing Epson's detailed records, we discovered a number of inconsistencies that can only be explained as sabotage. Also, a bomb was detonated at the warehouse on October 12, 1942. It was reported as an unknown munitions malfunction, but it happens to coincide with the same time and date of the disappearance of Dr. Bernard Epson. We feel the two are linked, and it is vital that you discover who is behind the attack.

He dropped the letter on the desk and leaned back, bewildered. *What the hell kind of mess did Applegate involve us in?*

Peter walked to the bathroom to fill a glass of water. He drank half, and refilled it. Before returning to the letter, Peter opened the drapes covering the small bay window. From his third-floor vantage point, he could see the busy afternoon traffic. Mesmerized by the hustle and bustle, an image of his kids flashed in his mind. He'd just said good-bye to them a few hours ago, but he felt a million miles away. Now, after reading the disturbing news from Applegate, he was sure he'd never see them again. The thought stabbed like a hot knife in his chest. He breathed deeply, calming himself for several moments, and returned to the letter.

Peter, you are authorized to use any means at your disposal to complete your mission. We attempted to prepare you for most situations, but this one we trust you will handle with subtlety and acumen. My advice is to investigate Epson's staff as quietly as possible. Once you find the culprit, and I trust you will, use your best judgment on how to handle the situation. I've enclosed additional currency for you to secure a firearm for apprehension of the mole and protection of yourself and your team. You may need this prior to leaving for France on the 21st of August.

Good luck, Peter. I have faith in you.

Harrison Applegate

Peter whistled softly as he let the information ferment. He knew there was much more to the mission than Applegate had let on, but he hadn't expected this.

Peter set the letter aside and picked up the "Surplus funds" envelope. To his surprise, there was more than double the amount he had originally been given by Applegate before leaving. *What kind of weapon does Applegate expect me to buy? Surely guns are cheaper 'now.'*

Next, Peter opened his envelope.

Peter-

I was reluctant to include an envelope with your information. However, it has been brought to my attention that you have devised a plan to secure some valuable currency from 1942 to bring back with you to the present. I cannot stop you from doing such a foolish thing. I can, however, advise you to reconsider.

First off, obtaining the desired currency in 1942 and returning it through the time machine would be fruitless. The linear nature of time and space would nullify any perceived value of the money. In essence, any item you acquire there and bring back could be—would be—deemed counterfeit. There are scientific tests that can be performed on any item, currency or otherwise, that would indicate the original production date within a few years. If you bring back money that was minted in 1942, tests will show it was printed within the year. It will have had no chance to age the seventy-plus years required to qualify its originality.

Notwithstanding the aging problem, there may be more pronounced repercussions from your actions. Suppose you take money from that timeline that has great importance in the decades between then and now. Those historical occurrences may never exist, and the money would cease to be more valuable in 2013 than it was when you obtained it in 1942.

In conclusion, Peter, please dispense with any aspirations of personal or financial growth from this mission. Although I cannot guarantee this, your personal life will be improved once you return. I would wager heavily on it.

Please reconsider.

Applegate

Stunned, Peter slowly folded the letter and reinserted it into the envelope. *How did he know?* Peter was certain that he had taken every precaution in his preparation for Operation Abraham. He didn't think Trevor knew anything, and if he did . . . It didn't matter anymore. Applegate knew about it, but there was nothing he could do to stop Peter now.

Peter tossed his envelope in disgust and flipped through the remaining pile. He paused momentarily on "International Travel Information" before settling on the envelope with Julie's name.

Julie's grandmother was the sole living descendant that survived the massacre in Oradour-sur-Glane. She was captured by the invading Germans at the age of ten. She was held captive for five years, until late 1947, when she was released. She was two months pregnant at the time. She delivered her child in the spring of 1948. Julie's mother, Marie-Claude, was considered a bastard of World War II, and life in France was hard. The family immigrated to the US in 1960.

Julie Pierrette was born in Sacramento, California in 1973. Her mother went through an ugly divorce four years later, but the ugliness didn't end. A large and rather lengthy custody battle ensued, but her mother maintained custody in the end. Julie's father swore revenge but abruptly left town for several years. A few years later, Marie-Claude remarried Frank Frey, who adopted Julie that same year. She was fifteen at the time.

Two years later, Marie-Claude's first husband returned to Sacramento. The night he knocked on their door, he was drunk and Frank wasn't home. Violence ensued, and after breaking down the door, he attempted to rape Julie. Marie-Claude shot and killed him with Frank's hunting rifle. That is all in the police report, and the case was closed. During the investigation, however, it was suspected that it was Julie who shot her father, without hesitation, the moment he broke through the door. It was believed at the time that both women had lied about the situation in order to protect Julie because she was still a minor. Nothing could be proven, so no charges were ever brought against her.

Peter, I am telling you this so that you know exactly who you are dealing with. Julie Frey is completely committed to her family and she is considered reasonably unstable because of her past. She was chosen for this mission because of her familiarity with the French region in which you two will be traveling. Since coming of legal age, she's been back to France every few years.

Because of her strong family ties to Oradour-sur-Glane, you must be mindful of every move she makes while there. She mustn't be allowed to make contact with her family. Her position on the team is for tactical, language, and regional support.

Peter leaned back, dumbfounded by the written grenade that had just exploded in his hand. He remembered Julie mentioning Applegate holding something over her, but wouldn't have guessed it was this big. As he contemplated his next move, he heard a noise just outside the hotel room door. He quickly scooped everything back into the satchel. The door unlocked and Julie stepped into the room a moment later.

The smile on Julie's face—bright and full of excitement—nearly made Peter forget what he had just learned.

"Oh my God! I think I love this time. Everything is so cheap, I could hardly stop buying clothes," Julie exclaimed as she dropped a half dozen bags to the floor. "And this was just from the store around the corner. Tomorrow, Gerty and I are going to—"

"That's great, Julie. Remember, we have a mission, and frivolous spending is not part of it."

Surprised at Peter's rigid delivery, Julie's smile quickly vanished, replaced with a look of concern. "Peter? Is something wrong?"

"Should there be?" he asked.

"Well, no. I was just excited about getting out of these horrid clothes. We need these things, and I am sure you'll feel the same after you and the boys can get some shopping done."

"Perhaps you're right," Peter replied. "I guess being cooped up in this hotel room for hours has made me edgy." Peter stood from the desk and slung the satchel over his shoulder.

"What's going on, Peter?"

"Nothing. I just need a bit of fresh air."

"But there is so much we need to talk about."

"Such as?" Peter questioned, fully realizing and regretting how much of an ass he was being.

"Well, for starters, Gerty lent us her car until we can get one of our own."

"Great. That'll help," Peter said as he stepped closer to the door.

Julie hadn't moved from where she was standing and just stared curiously at Peter.

Peter stopped at the door, and as he reached for the handle, he glanced back at Julie and asked, "Anything else?"

"There is, but you clearly need to leave, so we'll talk later."

"Great. I'll be back before the docs return."

Peter stepped into the hall, pulling the door closed. As he walked toward the stairway, he began to feel remorse for how he had acted. Regurgitating the information from Applegate, he tried to evaluate whether Julie was the person he thought she was. During the past three weeks, he had begun to truly care for her, and to read about her past only clouded his judgment. He needed time to think.

CHAPTER 6

Peter stepped into the pedestrian flow in front of his hotel. Out of habit, he glanced at his wrist. Seeing as Applegate hadn't allowed any of the team to wear anything from their timeline, he felt naked without his wristwatch.

As he drifted down the sidewalk, he had no particular direction in mind. He just needed to walk, clear his mind, think. Peter's mental stability was on the verge of being tapped dry. Hearing about Benny's death and just moments later witnessing Stella's murder should have been enough to push him over the edge. But it hadn't ended there. He'd also had to travel through the yet-to-be-proven time machine and then read some disturbing facts about the mission and Julie. If Applegate hadn't given them antianxiety pills, he would have certainly faltered.

Thinking of the pill, he realized it had been hours since he had taken it. He wondered how long the medication would last. He recalled how quickly the effects had kicked in that morning, and he checked himself. He felt enormous sorrow for all that he had lost in just a matter of moments. He was angry with Julie, yet he also pitied her. He found that he felt foggy, drowsy, and confused. Peter made a mental note to pass on taking any more pills from anyone ever again.

The familiar ding of the cable car moving along Powell Street grabbed his attention. Pausing only long enough to stare at the trolley passengers as they whizzed past, he continued his wayward journey along Powell until it crossed Market Street. He stopped at the intersection and decided to turn right onto Market. As he began to head southwest, he soon passed the historical Warfield Theater. He chuckled to himself at the thought of it being historical. It looked like an average, run-of-the-mill theater as he stood in front of the marquee. Looking up and down the block, the facade was certainly different than his own timeline. The Warfield looked grandiose compared to the neighboring buildings. In his timeline, the surrounding neighborhood had grown significantly. A few doors down from the theater—not 150 feet from the entrance to the Warfield— Peter found his previously unknown destination: a bar named Benny's. It struck him as quite appropriate.

Retreating out of the sunlight, Peter stood just inside the bar, motionless, until his eyes adjusted to the dimness of the pub. He moved up to the bar and sat next to a man with his head hung low. The bartender had his back toward Peter but still called out, "What can I get you?"

"Yeah, what's the time?" Peter asked.

"Ten till," said the man sitting at the bar.

"Till four?"

"Five. Can I get you something?" asked the bartender.

"Scotch. Neat," Peter said.

The man sitting at the bar glanced over, and Peter gave him a friendly smile. The man nodded before returning his gaze to his nearly empty beer glass. A moment later, the bartender slid the lowball in front of Peter. "Thirty-five cents."

Peter pulled two dollars from his pocket and handed it across the bar. "Keep 'em coming."

The bartender nodded as he grabbed the cash. Peter brought the glass to his nose and inhaled deeply. The warm smell of smoky peat danced with apples inside his nostrils. He pulled the glass away and then returned it again for another sniff. A moment later, Peter sipped along the edge, feeling the astringent burn to his lips and tongue as the tepid liquor slid down his throat. He closed his eyes, cherishing the warming sensation all over his body. Before opening his eyes, he tilted the glass back again, finishing off the scotch.

"That good, huh?" asked the man sitting next to him.

Peter looked over, meeting the man's intense stare in return. "It's been a long day."

"Aren't they all?" asked the man rhetorically. "You're not from around here, are ya?"

Peter nodded to the bartender as he slid his empty glass forward. "What makes you say that?" he asked.

"You're dressed . . . let's just say peculiar."

Peter looked down at the suit he'd picked out earlier that morning. "Really?"

"That thing looks like it came from the bottom of an old hamper, buddy."

"It was my uncle's suit. He gave it to me when I"—Peter stopped, thinking quickly about the story he'd impart to the barfly—"when I told him I was leaving Montana." Where the hell did that come from? he wondered.

"Well, good luck finding any work around these parts. Since the war came, good payin' jobs are few and far between."

"I'm not really looking for a job. Just passing through, really," Peter said casually. "What do you do?"

"I work construction. After working on the bridge in thirty-six and thirty-seven, I've kind of bounced around some. You?"

Peter hesitated, adjusting his worked backstory. "Me? I'm kind of a jack-of-all-trades kind of guy. I've worked a fair bit of construction myself. Nothing as elaborate as the steel harp, though."

"Yeah, that job was certainly a once in a lifetime affair. But, to tell the truth, I prefer wood construction much more. Take this job I'm on now. I'm building these detached houses south of town, and let me tell you, they are works of art."

Peter's attention was piqued. "What's the area called?"

"Eh? Oh hell, I can't remember. It's just off the highway, a few miles south of Daly City."

Peter's heart bounced. That was very near his own house. "Tell me, are these small houses?"

"Nah. We just finished the first floor of this one house, and you could fit my entire house in the basement."

"Size is relative. Suppose you live in a five-hundred-square-foot studio apartment . . ."

"Yeah, I see your point. I think the house we're on now is going to be around thirty-five hundred square feet total when we're finished."

Peter wondered what the odds were that the man he was talking to, in a bar called Benny's in 1942, could possibly be building his home. He knew the house was built in this year, and the size and location were a close match.

"So then why are you sitting here and not at the site? I know it's none of my business, but it's Monday afternoon."

The man looked at Peter with a steel gaze. "Copper shortage. We're shut down out there for at least the next week and a half until the next wire shipment comes in."

"Ah. Good ol' war efforts. I'm Pete, by the way."

"Cliff. Good to meet you," he said. "You're right, though. I should be at the site, but I didn't have the heart to tell the missus about the work delay, so I leave for work in the morning and sit around here until it's quittin' time." Cliff looked at his watch, finished off his beer, and pushed himself up from the bar. "And look at that. It's quittin' time now. Nice talking with you."

Before Peter could offer to buy him another round, Cliff walked out of Benny's. Peter looked forward again and saw the bartender had poured his second scotch. He smiled and sucked down half the liquid perfection.

Peter made a mental note to drive by his house sometime before leaving for France, just to see it being built. There's something you don't get to see every day, he mused.

As he sat alone at the bar, his thoughts returned to Applegate's dossier. He was so confused by everything he had learned. His personal mission was virtually a pipe dream now that Applegate had pointed out the flaws in his plan. How had he not thought of the implications of aging when he and Benny came up with the idea?

Then, Julie's face invaded his mind's eye. She was a beautiful woman, but despite his growing feelings for her, he couldn't help the sense of wariness creeping into his consciousness. How he could have been so mistaken about someone was beyond him. *A murderer.* She didn't even remotely resemble a person capable of taking another human life. What exactly does a person like that look like? he wondered. He had no answer.

After finishing his scotch, Peter contemplated heading back to the hotel. Before he could move away from the barstool, the bartender slid another drink in front of him. Peter nodded his thanks and swiped his hand horizontally across the top of the glass, to which the bartender nodded. He needed to be done.

Peter thought about reviewing more of the envelopes from his satchel but thought better of it. Applegate would shit purple Twinkies if Peter openly reviewed confidential information like that. He smiled and seriously considered it on that basis alone. *He can't do a thing from 2013.*

Applegate stained his thoughts as he sipped his scotch. Nearly everything that he had been told by the man had been a lie or an excessively fabricated truth. Nothing had been what it seemed. How did my life become so full of deceit, he asked himself. That's when it hit him. Maybe Julie's letter was yet another attempt by Applegate to deceive him. *Am I really going to judge her without hearing her side?* Peter knew better than that. He decided his next step should be to talk to Julie and try to coax the truth from her. With everything that Applegate had told them both, he hoped the truth would come out quickly.

He tossed back the remaining whisky and stood. The bartender glanced his way and held up his hand as he counted out some change from the register. "Keep the change, my friend," Peter said and smiled at the expression on the bartender's face as he walked out.

CHAPTER 7

Peter sat stoically behind the wheel of their newly acquired 1937 Packard Six, minding the speed limit. The hour and a half drive to pick up the car seemed worth it, since they had been able to buy it with cash, no questions asked. At $725, he felt good about not overpaying for a car that would inevitably be abandoned at the end of their mission.

Julie sat next to him as he drove, her eyes not on the road but on the train schedule she had picked up a few days earlier. "It looks like the train we want departs on August 12 at 4:24 in the afternoon."

Peter nodded his head. "I think we'll be ready. Hopefully Dr. Epson will have the security badges for the docs by then."

"I think he'll have them much sooner. Gerty said he's already started the paperwork and even put a rush on it. He's getting us all badges just in case."

"That makes sense," Peter agreed. "At least we'll be able to get in and out of the base until we leave and have easy access after France." He paused. "What were you going to tell me about Miss Stewart the other day? You said you had something important to tell me."

Julie looked up from the schedule before answering. "Oh, she said that she found it odd that we were newlyweds is all."

"How's that important? It's just part of our cover."

"She felt that we really didn't act much like a couple that had been recently married. I think the term she used was 'sterile.'"

Peter cringed at the word. "Really? I don't think we're sterile together."

"I guess she's used to seeing more affection between lovers. I assured her everything was all right between us. But maybe we should try to be a little more, I don't know . . . more in love?"

"But, darling, you are the apple in my pie," Peter said.

"You are the apple of my eye," corrected Julie.

"Right, that's what I said," Peter said as he touched her hand lying on the bench seat next to him. Julie smiled.

Peter hesitated briefly before deciding to delve into the informal interrogation. "Julie, now that we're out of the grasp of General Applegate, I feel like I need to share something."

Julie moved her hand and wove her fingers into his. "Okay. This sounds a little ominous."

"No, it's nothing like that. It's just that Applegate has something on me that, in effect, persuaded me to join the team." Peter paused. "You see, after my wife died, I nearly lost everything. I tried to climb into a bottle and forget about my problems for several years. If it wasn't for Applegate and this mission, I would likely be in a different place right now. He bailed me out of a jam I was in and has asked me to do things that I would have never agreed to do before."

"Applegate has his ways of manipulation, that's for sure," Julie said as she released her hand from Peter's.

"That's right. You mentioned that he's holding something over you . . ."

"It's nothing, really. Just something that happened a long time ago."

Peter's eyes remained focused on the road while his attention was affixed to the conversation. "Do you want to talk about it?"

"Like I said. It's nothing, really."

"We're in this together, Jules. Let's clear the air. Go ahead,"

Peter pushed.

"I . . . I, um, I kind of killed someone."

Peter's heart sank when he heard her words. "How is killing someone 'nothing'?" he protested.

"It wasn't malicious, if that's what you mean. There were circumstances."

"Like?"

Julie looked out the side window, away from Peter's glare. "It was my father. He was an abusive alcoholic. My mom had divorced him years before, and he actually left town. At the time we thought he was gone from our lives." She paused to wipe a tear from her cheek. "It was the week of my high school graduation, and I'm not sure why he thought he'd be welcomed back. He stopped by our house one night, and we were alone—just mom and me. She told him to leave, but he was too drunk to listen. He forced his way in and started to knock my mom around. I tried to pull him off her, but he hit me so hard, it nearly knocked me out."

Peter remained stoic as he listened, despite the anger building inside of him—anger at having to hear the wretched story, but also for Applegate's attempted deception.

"I laid there on the floor, playing dead long enough for him to leave me alone. When he returned to continue to beat on my mom, I snuck down the hall and grabbed Frank's shotgun. He'd taught me how to shoot it earlier that year, so I was comfortable handling it. I came back into the living room and told him to get off my mother. He did, and I thought it was over, or would be as soon as he left. He didn't leave, though. He stared at me and made some crude comments about both mom and me before he ran after me. I . . ." Julie stopped, her chin quivering with her sobs.

"Hey," Peter soothed. "It's okay. I'm sorry. You don't have to continue. I understand."

"But you don't. When he charged me, I pulled the trigger and missed. He stopped and had this look of . . . surprise, that I actually pulled the trigger. That's when I pumped another shell into the chamber and pulled the trigger again, hitting him in the chest. He was dead before he hit the floor."

Peter was silent once again.

"I killed my own father when I didn't have to. But I knew he'd come back again and again, because that's how crazy he was. Mom called the police right away and said she'd killed him. We fabricated the whole story by the time the police arrived. Mom said that I had my whole life ahead of me, and that it was nonsense for me to go to jail when that bastard deserved to die. In the end, the jury called it self-defense, and the whole thing went away."

"And Applegate somehow knew?" Peter asked.

"Yep. He confronted me about it a few months ago. He wasn't mean about it. He was actually very compassionate, but he said that he would make sure the problem would disappear forever if I went on this mission."

Peter noticed the familiar scenery sweeping by the car window and let off the gas pedal.

"I'm sorry, Jules. I never meant to bring back those memories. But . . ." Peter paused as he turned onto a side road. "But I had to know."

Julie looked around as Peter slowed the car to a stop. "Are we going somewhere?"

"Yeah, I wanted to drive by my old house, or new house. Depending on your perspective."

"Wait, what did you mean you had to know?" Julie said tensely.

Peter sighed.

"Julie, Applegate has been at it again. Before we left, he gave me an envelope with profiles on everyone on the team, as well as information on Epson and his assistants. He told me that it was for my eyes only. The information about you mentioned briefly what you just described, but it was not the complete truth. He skewed the facts, insinuating that I would need to keep an eye on you."

"That son of a bitch! What else did it say?"

"I'll let you read it for yourself when we get back to the hotel if you want. I contemplated not telling you at all, but I felt you should know. I knew you were a better person than how Applegate portrayed you."

Julie sat in silence the rest of the way to Peter's house. Peter felt it best to remain quiet. Don't poke the bear and all that.

Fifteen minutes later, he parked the Packard in the dirt driveway in front of 713 Glencoe Drive. The exterior walls were framed but the interior remained a mystery. The neighborhood was relatively new, with only a half dozen homes complete or under construction.

"Do you want to come look, or do you want to stay in the car?" Peter asked.

"What are we looking for exactly?"

"Nothing, really. It's just, how often do you get to see your own house being built? My architecture background is getting the better of me. I sort of get all third-graderish any time I walk through houses under construction." Peter smiled.

"Sure. I'll come," Julie said. "You're a goof, you know that?"

"What? I can't help it." He smirked.

Peter escorted Julie up to the house and entered through the garage. The interior walls were framed, but the lath and plaster had yet to be installed. As Peter walked through the house, he noticed a number of oddities. Some of the rooms were different from how they existed in 2013.

"How bizarre. This room doesn't even exist now. Someone, between now and when we bought the house, had removed this wall," Peter said, pounding his fist gently against one of the wood studs.

Julie didn't reply but walked around the floor, peeking around half-framed walls.

As Peter continued surveying his home, an idea began to form. The more he investigated, the more he recalled how his home was finished in his own time. It wasn't until he went into the cellar that his planning bore fruit. As he walked about the basement, he looked up at the framed floor above. In his own cellar, the framing looked identical. Down to the random knots in the lumber, it looked exactly like his did back in 2013. He paused near the furnace, and although his own furnace had been replaced, he recognized the behemoth as the one they tore out after buying the house. That's when his plan started to coalesce into the makings of a genuine possibility.

What if I hide the pennies here in the house somewhere? he wondered. It would solve all the problems that Applegate mentioned in his letter. They would sit here, stashed beneath some random piece of lumber until he returned from the mission. They'd have aged through the years and would be good to sell off one at a time, discreetly.

Peter stood in silent contemplation for much longer than he realized. It was Julie's hand that brought him back to the present.

"Are you okay? You've been just standing there staring."

"Oh, really? I was just imagining how the years have gone by. This is the first house we bought. It's just . . ."

"I get it, Peter. You miss your family. I miss mine too," Julie said as she wrapped her arms around him and hugged. Peter returned the hug, and the two stood embracing each other for several minutes.

"As nice as this is, Peter, we should probably get back to the hotel."

"Yeah. You're right. Thanks for indulging me."

"Thanks for listening earlier. I haven't told anyone about that, and it helped getting it off my chest. You have no idea. It feels like a huge weight's been lifted from my shoulders."

"Don't mention it, Jules. From now on, we shouldn't keep anything from each other. We're partners in this, and without each other, we'd be lost. Agreed?"

"Agreed. Let's go and get something to eat. I'm starving."

Peter led the way back to the car, and they were back on the road to San Francisco within minutes.

CHAPTER 8

As Peter lay on the sofa bed, he looked around the darkened room, waiting. Slivers of bluish moonlight cascaded through the partially open drapes, saving Peter from utter obscurity. He listened intently toward the bedroom door. Silence. Julie was sure to be fast asleep.

Wondering if it was time to get moving, he glanced at the nightstand, but the moonlight wasn't cooperating. He moved his wrist in front of his face, but he couldn't see the hands on his new watch either. It has to be after one, he surmised.

He dropped his legs off the hide-a-bed mattress and into a new pair of trousers he had purchased a few days earlier. He stood, sliding his feet into a pair of Oxfords, which were the closest to casual tennis shoes he could find. Finally, he grabbed the tattered leather jacket acquired from a secondhand store and stepped into the hallway.

The lights were dim because of the late hour, but they were bright enough that he could see his watch. It was 1:46—later than he'd anticipated but still giving him plenty of time.

Peter took the back stairway, which dropped him in the alley behind their hotel. The guest parking lot was just across the street. Peter had purposefully parked the Packard in the back row to avoid waking anyone when the engine rumbled to life.

As he slalomed his way through the parking lot, he

considered the leather jacket. The temperature was hovering around sixty degrees, but the humidity was high. He contemplated leaving it, but with only a white cotton T-shirt, it might be useful, if a bit uncomfortable. He slipped it on as he slid into the driver's seat. He chuckled at the reflection in the rearview mirror. He looked like James Dean from *Rebel Without a Cause*. It was one of Minnie's favorite movies. If she could only see me now, he mused. Of course, she wouldn't be born for another thirty years.

Peter eased out of the lot and turned toward his midnight destination. In all practicality, he could have walked the mile and a half to the bay, but the thought of lugging his supply bag made him rethink his mode of travel.

At nearly two in the morning, the streets were deserted. Without traffic, he could make it the water's edge and back with time to spare. The only unknown lay beneath the streets. His plan was simple. Tonight's excursion was Peter's "dry run" into the U.S. Mint.

Back in 2013, Peter had meticulously analyzed all potential entry points into the mint. Armed with Chet's fortuitous information, Peter had discovered the only feasible, yet incredibly unsanitary, approach was through the city's sewer system. According to the historical maps, there were several storm drain overflows that dumped directly into the bay. Because the sewer had recently gone through a major renovation, the outlets still remained uncovered. It wasn't until 1953 that the vulnerability was discovered and barriers installed. Since that wouldn't happen for another eleven years, Peter was free to enter the sewer at his leisure.

The ten-block drive was mundane, and within minutes Peter had parked along the pier. Considering whether or not to leave the car so close to his entry point, Peter opted for convenience. According to his schedule, he could make it to the mint and back within fifty minutes.

Peter opened the trunk and pulled out a large duffle bag. From its side pocket he slipped out a neatly folded packet. He slung the bag over his shoulder, stepped over the rope barrier, and climbed down the stone embankment. By the time he reached the water's edge, he had unfolded his map and was studying it in the moonlight. Once he had his bearings, he walked another twenty paces until he came upon a large concrete tube. Stepping over two rows of heavy riprap, Peter stood up in the mouth of the opening. Flicking on his flashlight, he strode into the darkness.

He had expected the ceiling to descend, but after a dozen steps into the bowels of the city sewer, he was still able to stand fully upright. Adjusting his map, Peter plotted his route and continued onward.

The map—the proverbial key to the castle—had been something of a windfall. Chet, the coin shop owner, had spoken of a flaw in the original security. The original documents had been sealed shortly after the flaw was discovered. Luckily though, the sixty-year confidentiality had serendipitously expired only a few months before Peter's trip through the time machine. He had examined every detail regarding the breach and had found an unaltered map of the city sewer system. Peter hadn't been able to take the map out of the records room, so he'd had to memorize it. His map was something he was quite proud of; he had drawn it completely from memory upon arrival in 1942. With his architectural background and razor-sharp memory, he'd been able to sketch the map with superior precision, even without the benefit of the original.

After a few hundred feet, Peter stopped to review his map more closely. He had been navigating smoothly for no more than five minutes before he came upon his first variance.

Peter rotated the map as he made a slight right turn before continuing straight for another fifty feet. As his eyes adjusted to the murkiness of the sewer, Peter pointed the flashlight toward the ground and let the light float down the tunnel. In the distance he could see his first obstacle. He had to jump across the main diversion tank to make it into the main sewer line, which ran straight to the mint. Stepping to the edge of the tank, the crevasse was not as far as it appeared on his map. At the reduced scale of his drawing, he'd anticipated the gap to be in the neighborhood of nine feet across. Thankfully, whether by his error or inaccuracies in the original map, the distance was closer to six feet.

Stowing the map in his inside jacket pocket, Peter tossed his duffle across. It landed with a muffled thump before rolling to the side. He took half a dozen steps back, turned, and ran for the divide. A split second before leaping over the opening, he heard a loud howl echo throughout the concrete network. His nerves clenched instantly, but his focus and training prohibited a catastrophic error and potential injury.

Reaching the edge of the opening, Peter leaned forward as his legs shot his body over and across the gap. He landed with an easy tuck-and-roll, standing at the conclusion of his acrobatics. Without hesitation, Peter reslung the duffle over his shoulder and moved forward. Not even a minute had passed when the screeching echoed through the tunnel again. Peter stopped and flashed his light through the darkness as far as the rays would reach. All he saw was a trickle of water at the bottom of the brick-lined cylinder. With no desire to meet whatever had made the horrendous sound, Peter trudged on. Based on his progress, he still had another twenty-five hundred yards of pitch-black labyrinth to navigate before reaching his destination.

As the minutes passed, Peter focused on his footsteps. His new shoes were completely coated with the gelatinous slime that coated the bottom of the storm drain. He wondered how he'd clean them so Julie wouldn't find out in the morning but decided to handle one obstacle at a time.

As he explored the dark underbelly of San Francisco, he wondered if he should have bought a gun first. But, he argued with himself, it's a practice maneuver; why the hell would I need a gun? However, the noise—whatever it was—sounded like it was getting closer.

Turn by turn, Peter noted adjustments on his map. He was able to circumvent the various discrepancies and make it to the mint in a little more than thirty minutes. He would have made it much faster if he hadn't brought everything and the kitchen sink with him. But he knew that preparation was the pivot point for the success or failure of his mission, so he had brought something for every foreseeable complication: extra batteries for the flashlight; dry clothes, in case the waste of the world decided to find him attractive; and a small arsenal of tools for any eventuality.

Finally he arrived at his destination—a large, open vault directly below the courtyard. From his estimation, it could hold several thousand gallons of water. As he surveyed the room, he quickly realized that there was only one exit—the way in which he had entered. He prayed the weather cooperated.

Peter opened his duffle, removed the tool pouch, and stashed the bag into a small niche in one of the walls five feet from the basin floor.

Two steel ladders were mounted on opposite walls, each leading up to cast iron grates at the top of the sewer vault. Peter recalled that the courtyard was situated so that in the event of fire or other catastrophe, the employees could escape into the center of the facility for safety. Because of the enormity, the courtyard required multiple storm drains.

Peter chose the ladder on his right for its proximity to the egress pipeline. Peter knew the height of the grate was seventy feet above the floor. He had never had an issue with heights before, but now his mind began to play tricks. The ceiling of the vault itself was only fifteen or twenty feet high, but the ladder continued up and split into two separate shafts. Each shaft led to grates on opposite sides of the courtyard.

"Here goes nothing," Peter murmured as he grasped the highest wrung within reach. As he pulled himself up to the first crosspiece, his weight was too much for the rusted steel rung, and he dropped to the ground as a dull twang reverberated inside the vault.

Concerned but determined, Peter tried again. He reached up and grunted his way to the second step before gaining purchase with his feet. Step by step, he scaled the ladder to the waiting cover. He concentrated on not looking down.

He moved methodically, not placing too much weight on any one rung. As he reached the top, the shaft tapered in, and Peter was able to lean his back against the wall as he stood with both feet on a single step. It was chancy, exerting so much weight on one rung, but he had no choice. He needed his hands free.

Looking up at the storm cover, he found that the grate was bolted from below, just as the city blueprints had indicated during his research. He untied the tool pouch and fished out a pipe wrench. After making a few minor adjustments, he fit the wrench snugly around the bolt and applied pressure. At first it didn't budge. Peter repositioned himself to get better leverage and tried again. On his second attempt, the rusty bolt budged slightly and then broke free. The wrench slammed into the concrete wall with a metallic clang.

Peter quickly returned the wrench to the pouch and rubbed his stinging fingers. He stood on the metal step, waiting. He heard nothing for several minutes. With a firm grip, Peter pushed up on the storm cover. The grate didn't budge. He didn't see any more bolts.

"Shit."

Peter stepped higher and leveraged his back against the grate before exerting pressure. After a strenuous moment, he felt movement. Unfortunately, it wasn't the grate breaking free, but the rusted rung pulling away from the concrete.

As it dislodged from the wall, gravity took over, yanking Peter downward. In a panic, he lashed out with both hands, trying to grasp anything, but the steel rungs were spaced a foot apart and his hands scrabbled at smooth concrete more often than the rungs. Finally, a few feet above the vault floor, he grabbed a rung and held on. His body stopped violently, slapping against the concrete wall. He quickly grabbed another rung with his free hand and placed both feet on the crosspieces below.

Discouraged , he dropped down the ladder and crossed to the opposite wall. With determination, he climbed straight up the concrete shaft, stopping just below the second storm cover. He smiled internally, as his second attempt went much smoother than the first. After the second bolt came free in his hand, he stashed the tools and attempted to dislodge the grate. To his surprise, the grate lifted freely, without any resistance.

Peter briefly popped his head above the ground level of the courtyard, and all was clear. Security lights shone throughout the plaza. As he peered through the slivered opening, he glanced at his watch. It was 2:58 a.m., and he was out of time. He lowered the grate and deftly climbed back down the ladder. Deciding to leave the tools with his duffle, he quickly re-secured his bag and began his trip back to the sewer entrance.

The trip out took half the time as it did coming in. Having kept a hold of the map, he only had to look at it twice the entire journey. The only disturbing issue was the continued howl of whatever wild animal was wandering the tunnels with him. He made a mental note to acquire a pistol before his full run at the mint.

Satisfied, Peter needed to get back to the hotel and rest. With the ID badges coming tomorrow, he knew the day would be packed. The team would re-enter the base for the first time since coming through the time machine.

Peter retraced his steps to the Packard and drove quickly back to the hotel. There wasn't a soul in sight when he stepped into the rear lobby. Moments later, he was undressed and back in bed. Delighted with the evening's accomplishments, he drifted off to sleep.

CHAPTER 9

The following morning came far too early for Peter. After his highly eventful late-night escapade in the dank sewer systems of San Francisco, he had only gotten a few hours' sleep before being rousted by Julie.

"Wake up, you bum. Everyone is going to be here within the hour," Julie said as she opened the drapes, allowing the morning sunlight to fill the room.

Peter rolled over and looked at the clock. It was 7:13 and Julie was far too bright-eyed and bushy-tailed for his liking that day. He rolled onto his back and stared at the ceiling. His mind began to review everything from the past twelve hours. From his trip to the hardware store to the depths of the vile sewer lines. He was thoroughly exhausted.

"Up! You really need to get cleaned up before they arrive. You smell like . . . well, let's just say it's not at all pleasant."

Peter glanced at Julie, who was clearing off their small dining table. He exhaled completely before drawing in a slow breath through his nose. Yes, he stank like the sewer.

"I'm up. I'm up," Peter said as he willed himself out of bed and into the bath. One of his great disappointments of 1942 was the fact that he had yet to take a long shower. Although they existed in the timeline, not many hotels had them installed. Not with the war efforts and all. So, he was compelled to take baths

207

instead. He honestly didn't mind taking a bath, but nothing beats hot water pounding a sore body after a strenuous activity.

Twenty minutes later, Peter stepped out of the bathroom, having bathed and dressed in clean clothes. Julie had already stowed the hide-a-bed back into the sofa and straightened the living area when she looked up.

"Much better, dear husband. Now, go across the hall and fetch the docs."

Peter nodded and followed her command. He was still a little too drowsy to protest her early morning bossiness. As he opened the door to walk across the hall, he was greeted by Dr. Epson and his apprentice.

"Good morning, Peter. We were just about to knock," Epson said, startled.

"Hey there. I was just going to go get the docs from across the hall. Come in and take a seat. I'll be right—"

Before Peter could finish talking, the door across the hall opened and Drs. Lamb and Larsson stepped out.

"Well, never mind, then. Let's all come in and get on with this," Peter said, stepping aside to clear the way for their guests. He hoped his tiredness wouldn't affect his mood too much.

As Lamb stepped into the room fully, he asked, "Wow. What is that smell?"

Shit, Peter thought. He didn't think that his shoes would still smell after last night; he'd made sure to rinse them off completely in the water from the bay before driving back to the hotel.

"That, my friend, is the smell of heaven," replied Epson. "I took the liberty of stopping by my favorite bakery on the way over. I picked up coffee and pastries for everyone this morning."

"Smells wonderful, Doctor," Julie said, taking the box filled with breakfast fare from him and setting it on the table.

As she began to empty out the morning treats from Epson, Peter's senses began to hone in on the wonderful aroma of freshly brewed coffee and of something yeasty. "Is that fresh bread?" Peter asked.

"Yes, Peter. That's the sourdough you smell. It's their specialty. I highly encourage you all to stop in for a bite before you, um, leave town?" Epson said.

"Yeah, I suppose our situation is a bit of quandary. We're not really going to be leaving town when we leave here, but . . ." Larsson added.

Peter sat at the table, poured himself a cup of coffee, and swallowed a quarter of the cup in one gulp, despite the intense heat on his mouth. He cleared his throat.

"Well then," said Epson. "I was able to secure civilian ID badges for you all, but I had to exaggerate a bit regarding your individual backgrounds. My reputation is on the line, so please, do be mindful while on base." Epson handed out the plastic-covered badges. "As you can see, it lists your contrived profession on the line below your name."

Peter took his and read his aloud.

"War department
The adjunct general's office
Washington, DC
Peter G. Cooper
Civilian TEC 4 MD"

Peter glanced at Julie's badge. Like his, it included her photo and signature.

"These are outstanding, Doctor. What does the 'TEC 4 MD' mean?" Peter asked.

"Well, that's where I had to fabricate. I had to tell them that you all were medical doctors assisting me in my research."

"If it's any consolation, Doctor, you only had to lie for those two," Larsson said, referring to Peter and Julie. "Dr. Lamb and I both have PhDs."

"I suspected as much. Unfortunately, to get these rushed, I had to tell the base commander that your transcripts would arrive in the mail within the month," Epson pursed his lips. "If you four plan on staying beyond that . . ."

"We'll cross that bridge when we get there," Peter said, not wanting to broach the subject just yet. "But, medical doctors?

Couldn't you have picked another profession? Like photographer or propaganda specialist?"

"Yes, yes. I certainly could have set a few of you up as photographers, but I was worried that once you were given the credentials, the base commander might reassign you to other activities."

"And you don't think he'll do the same with medical doctors?" Peter asked, concerned.

Epson laughed out loud.

"Am I missing something, Doctor? I'm having a hard time finding the humor," Peter said dropping the badge on the table.

"Relax, Mr. Cooper. That will not happen," Epson said, trying to suppress another giggle. "You see, in Britain, where I specified your education origin, an MD means something completely different."

Peter listened to the doctor intently.

"Here in the United States, MD is the designation for doctor of medicine. In Britain, an MD, or DO as it is sometimes called, is the classification for research physician. Since there was no way to specify 'research' on the form, I left it as MD and added the specific information later in the application. It's really one of my more genius moments."

Peter relaxed, picking up the ID from the table and looking at it once again. "So, I'm a doctor?" he joked.

"Only in title. As I said, these will only be used to gain access to the base."

Peter looked at his team, and they were all smiling at him. "What? I was worried that we'd be asked to remove somebody's spleen or something."

It was Julie's turn to laugh now, and as she did, she caressed Peter's shoulder. Turning her attention to Epson, she asked, "So, are we to act British, then?"

"Not specifically. Americans travel abroad frequently for medical degrees when they don't have what it takes to get into a US institution," Epson explained.

"Ouch," added Larsson.

"It's ok, buddy," Peter said to Larsson. "We all know you are the smartest man at the table. Except for Dr. Epson, of course."

Larsson nodded and continued to examine his ID.

With Larsson's ego repaired, Epson continued.

"Now, then. The next order of business comes from Mr. Gallagher. Michael? Would you like to speak?" Epson said, nodding to his apprentice.

"Um, yes. I . . . I would first like to apologize for my actions last week. It was Friday, and . . . and my emotions got the better of me after a long week in the lab. There is no excuse for my outburst, and I can only ask for your forgiveness. I am very excited to be part of this momentous occasion."

Peter stared at Gallagher questioningly. He knew the only way to find the saboteur was to keep everyone close. He adjusted his glare to friendly acceptance. "Hey. No problem. I suppose I'd have reacted the same if I were in your shoes. It's water under the bridge. Doctors? Do you all agree?"

Peter looked around the table and received nods from everyone, including Julie.

"See? Nothing to worry about," Peter said.

"Right then," Epson boomed. "How have you found life in 1942? I would imagine it is quite different from what you are used to."

"A little. I like the traffic here compared to our time," Peter said. "You can drive across town in half the time, even in rush hour."

"I, personally, love the shopping. I love the styles and I'm tickled with the prices," Julie added with an embarrassed grin.

"I am certain that you and Miss Stewart will become fast friends, because Lord knows she likes to shop."

"I think we're quite compatible, as she's taken me shopping numerous times since we've arrived."

Epson smiled and nodded. "How are your amenities? Is there anything we can arrange to make your stay here more pleasant?"

"Nice of you to offer, Doctor, but we'll be fine. The only

obstacle we foresee right now is the use of a bigger car."

"Can you elaborate?" Epson asked.

"We've purchased an old Packard from a gentleman in San Jose, and although it was affordable, it is a coupe. To get to and from the base all together . . ."

"Ah, yes. I see your predicament," Epson said, staring up at the ceiling as he deliberated. "I have a larger sedan that I would be willing to exchange with you while you are here, if that helps."

"We could never impose on you like that, Doctor. Besides, Lamb and Larsson will be heading onto base daily, whereas Julie and I will only be in on occasion. One of us can drive the doctors back and forth—"

"I can do it," Gallagher interrupted.

"Excuse me?"

"I can do it. I can pick up the doctors in the morning and drop them off at night. It's on my way into the base anyway," Gallagher added.

"Mr. Gallagher, are you sure?" Epson asked. "It's not very convenient for you."

"Yes, I'd love to. It'll give us a chance to talk about the modifications and such."

Peter looked at Dr. Lamb, who'd been silent all morning, and Dr. Larsson for their opinions on the matter. "Doctors? Thoughts?"

"I think that is the best option, aside from buying another vehicle," Larsson said.

"Good. Because we're not buying another one. The Packard is quite a piece as it is," Peter joked.

"Then it's settled. Mr. Gallagher will pick up the doctors from your hotel." Epson paused before turning to Peter and Julie. "I'm curious. I understand the doctors' reason for coming back through the device, but what about you two? Historical research? Would you care to expound on that?"

Peter knew Epson would press the matter at some point, and he was hesitant to let the good doctor in on their entire plan . . . just yet.

"Yes, we do plan on visiting a number of venues around the area to examine the various historical differences in time that perhaps our textbooks might have gotten wrong. But to be completely truthful, we're mainly here as damage control. It's all about the contamination we leave here in 1942."

Epson's facial expression changed from curiosity to acceptance. "Ah yes. You cannot leave a single trace of your existence here or . . ." he paused, as he returned his gaze to the ceiling in thought.

Peter looked up to where the doctor was staring and saw nothing.

"Don't mind him," Gallagher said. "He looks into the ether when he is trying to solve a problem or is thinking intently."

"Yes, yes. The effects of you presence here could be catastrophic," Epson said with a worried look.

"I wouldn't go so far as saying catastrophic, but you're correct; we can't leave a trace. Julie and I are here to make sure everything is as it was when we leave." Peter hoped his story would squash any further inquiries.

"Right, then. Shall we talk about device modifications? Despite your fascinations with 1942, I'm sure you'll tire of the novelty sooner than later and want to get back to your own time," Epson said, moving on.

Peter and Julie ate their breakfast while the doctors discussed their plans for repairing the device.

CHAPTER 10

Michael Gallagher pulled away from the base exit in a rush. The timing couldn't have been worse, as it was the first full day that Drs. Lamb and Larsson were in the lab for assistance. To make matters worse, Dr. Epson had been called into an emergency "all-hands" meeting with the base commander at precisely the same time a telegram was delivered from the Society.

The missive was short and precise: "Must Meet Immediately," followed by a new meeting locale. With Epson out, he'd had no other option than to leave the doctors alone in the lab. He pounded the steering wheel in frustration.

Turning north toward the city, Gallagher accelerated down the dangerously winding road. The message inspired haste, but only to a certain point. He backed off the accelerator but still kept it above the speed limit.

He wondered why the sudden urgency. He'd made it clear to Emmett that the team had not been allowed on base until that morning. Did the Society suspect something soon? he wondered. The two doctors had barely been in the lab for a few hours and had only been familiarized themselves with the most current experimental data, along with the collected algorithms during their arrival.

Gallagher swerved around a slow-moving convertible before

returning to his frantic speed. The thought of leaving them alone in the lab, where they might possibly isolate his creative deconstruction, made his heart beat faster. Realizing that the whole ordeal was out of his control, for the moment at least, he tried to focus on the morning traffic.

Ten minutes later, he eased off the accelerator and merged into the city. He reached into the glove box and pulled a city map from beneath a Walther PP. Flipping it open, he searched for his destination without pulling over. After nearly rear-ending the car in front of him, he maneuvered his Plymouth onto a side street.

With the engine idling, he laid the map across the seat next to him. In just a few minutes, he found the address of the meet in relation to his current position. Five minutes later, he pulled in front of the Pacific Telephone Building and was immediately met by a man in a grey suit.

"Hello, Mr. Gallagher. You are expected. Take the elevator up to the twenty-third floor, where you will be met."

Gallagher did as he was instructed, and upon entering the building, he turned toward the bank of elevators to the left. The polished brass elevator doors parted, and he was lifted to his destination in moments.

The doors opened, and before he could step out, he was greeted by another man in a grey suit. "This way, Mr. Gallagher."

Gallagher followed the man through a maze of windowless corridors until he came to a pair of large mahogany doors. Without hesitation, the man thrust open both doors and stepped inside.

The room was enormous. It was nearly half the size of Dr. Epson's entire warehouse laboratory, and the side walls were lined with floor-to-ceiling bookshelves. At the far end of the room sat a single desk with two chairs. Behind the desk was a window that captured a view of Bay Bridge.

"Ah, Mr. Gallagher. Please come in. Thank you, Cornwell. That will be all."

Gallagher stepped nervously into the excessive office and walked toward the welcoming man. He was middle aged, dressed in a suit, but nondescript. He stood as Gallagher approached.

"Please, have a seat. Can I get you anything, Michael? Can I call you Michael?"

"Uh, sure. And you are?"

"I'm Asher. Asher Mandrake," he said as he extended his hand.

Michael took his hand but nervously avoided the man's face.

"It's quite all right. I won't bite," Mandrake joked. "You've done a wonderful job shadowing Dr. Epson; I felt it was time for us to meet."

Michael sat across from Mandrake and nodded.

"I would imagine that things are very exciting right now in the lab. Do you have anything to report?"

"I . . . I really don't. Just what I relayed to Emmett a few days ago."

"Right. Something about the scientists from the future gaining unrestricted access to the military base? And to Dr. Epson's research?"

"That's right. In fact today was the first day that they've been allowed on base," Michael said before adding, "and, unfortunately, I had to leave them alone in the lab to come here."

"Alone?"

Michael feared a reprimand was coming. "That's right, sir. Dr. Epson had been called into an emergency meeting. There was no alternative."

Mandrake contemplated as he listened to Michael explain the situation. After a moment, he said, "Although that is unfortunate, no harm will come of it. It's not like they're going to flash back to the future today, right?"

"Um, no. From what I've gathered, their return isn't scheduled until late September or early October. It all depends on when they can get the device functioning properly."

"See? Nothing to worry about. Are all your precautions still in place?"

"They are, but the two scientists are extremely sharp. They appear to know more about the machine than Dr. Epson does himself." Gallagher paused. "They somehow knew that the issues with the machine were isolated to the transmission chamber and that the receiving chamber was in working order. All from the future, I might add."

Mandrake listened, staring at Michael intently. "And you fear they'll find out what's been causing the test failures?"

"I do. Not right away, but they'll figure it out eventually."

"I see. I see," Asher said as he nodded in agreement. "What of the other two? Are they as bright as the two doctors?"

"Peter seems to be their leader. The doctors talk science, while Julie tends to follow Peter's lead."

"And what about Julie? Julie Frey?"

"Yes, that's right. She's Peter's wife, but strangely, she has a different last name."

"Peculiar. What is their function here?"

"That's the odd part. Peter mentioned that they were going to be conducting some kind of historical research and that they were here to eliminate any trace of their existence while here in our time."

"And you don't believe them?"

"I don't think so. I feel like they're hiding something. Who would risk their lives to come back in time just to provide cleanup and wander around like tourists throughout the city?"

"Frankly, I believe him, Michael. If they left any sort of trace of their existence here in the past, the ripple effects would be vast. If they are as wise as you say, they'll effectively be ghosts while they're here."

"There's something else," Michael began. "Peter has left the hotel a few times, late at night, alone."

"Have you been following him?"

"I tried to one night, but he eluded me. He drove north from their hotel, and he must have made a turn I missed, and I lost him."

"Thank you for trying, Michael. You certainly weren't trained for that sort of thing. You're dedication has been admirable. We'll put someone at the hotel so you can focus on your own objective."

"And what might that be?"

"To keep them from returning to 2013, naturally. We cannot have them report back that the time machine works. Before long, it would be opened like a highway through time."

"I've tried, sir. I truly have. But I'm not sure what else I can do to stop them, short of . . ."

"Short of . . . murder? Is that what you were going to say?"

"Y-yes."

"Michael, I appreciate your dedication to the cause, but you know the Society doesn't condone taking another human life. No matter what the stakes. No, we need to find another way."

"I'll try my best to stop the machine from functioning, but unless you have a better idea . . ."

"Well, we are working on something. Something that I'm hesitant to —"

"I'm all ears, sir. If I'm—or hell, we are—to succeed, anything you can give me will help, I'm certain."

Mandrake pondered Michael's request and nodded. "I suppose you're right. We need to convince the travelers that they should not return to their own timeline, whether we tempt them monetarily or instill them with trepidation."

"I don't follow, sir," Gallagher confessed.

"If bait won't work, we may have to trap them. *Persuade* them to stay until the war ends."

"You mean kidnap them?"

"Kidnap is such a harsh word," Asher said. "We'll just . . ." his words drifted off.

"Yes?"

"Michael, I need you to return to the lab. I've got another idea, but I will need Society approval before we can proceed."

Michael nodded. "Okay. I'll wait for word from you, then?"

"Yes, Michael. You'll hear from Emmett or me shortly," he said as he rose from his desk.

Michael stood as well, recognizing the end of the meeting.

"Michael, I need you to be sharper than ever. If any new

developments arise, do not hesitate to contact Emmett."

"Contact Emmett?" Michael asked. "Shouldn't I get word to you directly?"

"No, no. It's far too risky. This meeting today was an enormous risk, but it was a calculated risk. Until you hear from me directly, Emmett will continue to be your contact."

"Yes, sir," Gallagher said as they approached the large double doors.

"And, Michael? Keep that devilish machine from working. I know you have it in you to evade detection. You are much craftier than you give yourself credit for."

Michael appreciated the words of confidence from Mandrake. "I will, sir. I'll make sure they don't suspect a thing."

CHAPTER 11

Peter slipped out the side door of the hotel lobby and into the night. He opted to walk the dozen or so blocks from his hotel to the bay to help calm his nerves before breaking into, arguably, the most secure facility in 1942 San Francisco.

The night was cooler than it had been since they'd arrived, but Peter didn't mind. At his brisk pace, he would normally be covered in sweat within minutes. The chill kept the perspiration at bay.

The walk had an additional benefit: it gave him roughly forty-five minutes for a final review of his plan for breaching the mint. He'd reviewed the blueprints for countless hours before leaving 2013 and felt that he knew the floor plan better than anyone.

He knew that the closet in the basement housed a safe containing an artifact taken by the US government from Tutankhamen's tomb. He also knew that the second floor housed not only the clerical department but also a secret office for the governor of California when he was visiting the city. Peter had researched the whereabouts of the governor at the time and discovered he was in Bakersfield; no extra security would be present.

Lastly, he knew exactly where the misprinted monies and coin overruns scheduled to be voided were kept. It was a small anteroom next to the coining repository. The small chamber might very well have been mistaken for a utility room or janitor's closet. He had Chet to thank for the bulk of his research. Between his tales of working in the mint as a tour guide, and Peter's own blueprint, his plan was rock solid.

As Peter neared the Embarcadero, he slowed his pace and tried to maintain control of his breathing. His planned forty-five minute walk had taken only thirty minutes due to his brisk pace.

Stopping along the rope barrier near the edge of the bay, Peter surveyed the surroundings, looking for any night owls that might be hunting. Satisfied with the solitude, he dropped down the embankment and proceeded to the sewer outlet. He pulled out his flashlight and walked into the gloomy abyss.

Peter began his route toward the mint much like he had on his first trip through the sewer. He was much more confident on the second foray into the city's underbelly, as he now carried a sidearm that he had bought from a pawn shop the night before. Although he never saw what made the disturbing sounds on the night of his dry run, his mind certainly explored the gruesome possibilities, and he adjusted the holster at his hip.

Without the need of his map, Peter was able to navigate past many of the discrepancies that he had previously found throughout the storm drains. He leaped across the diversion chamber without hesitating or faltering, continuing past it without breaking his stride.

When Peter made it to his halfway point, he heard the first guttural howl of the night. Since stepping into the tunnel system, he'd been prepared for the eerie assault on his eardrums. Still, the sound made his bones tingle. He hastened his pace, with his right hand resting on the grip of his gun.

It wasn't until he arrived at an unfamiliar Y-intersection that Peter unfolded his hand-drawn diagram of the sewer system. After several minutes of backtracking, he arrived at the vault below the courtyard.

Peter waved the beam of his flashlight along the chamber

walls, refamiliarizing himself with his surroundings. On the right he noticed the rusty stair treads lying on the floor from his previous visit. On the left was the other set of rungs leading straight up the concrete wall. Before beginning his assent to the courtyard above, he reached high up the side wall and pulled his stashed duffle bag down. He rested the flashlight on the ledge and changed into the stowed clothing.

Moments later, Peter climbed up to the storm grate, reaching the courtyard within moments. Sliding the drain cover to the side, mindful to keep it from grinding across the pavement, he hoisted himself up to a crouched position. He replaced the grate and quickly moved to the side of the courtyard.

Hunkered next to the wall, he visualized the blueprint of the main floor. The courtyard was surrounded by stone edifices on three sides. The fourth side was open to the street, which was blocked by a two-tier gate system. Throughout the courtyard were several ventilation hoods. They were ducted to the basement level of the facility, one of which was Peter's entry point. He explored each hood until he located the fresh-air duct located along the north wall. He left his cover and began to walk across the courtyard when he heard something. He froze instantly. A moment later, the familiar clank of a metal door closing echoed in the night. Peter rushed to the space between the van and the wall and waited in silence.

"I don't care what you say, I'm never gonna pay twenty-seven cents to see a movie about a baby deer. Paying that much for any movie is highway robbery," said the first man coming into view.

"What about your wife and children? Don't you think you owe it to them?" asked the second man, following a few paces behind.

The first employee pulled a pack of cigarettes from his pocket and offered one to his friend. Peter seized the opportunity to get out of sight. He quietly dropped to the ground and rolled under the van, but the toe of his boot struck the rear quarter panel.

"What was that?" asked the man pulling a cigarette from the pack.

"What was what?" The other man glanced about the empty courtyard.

"I thought I heard something."

"I didn't hear anything. Maybe it's your mind playing tricks on you. Maybe it's Bambi's mother coming back from the dead."

"Very funny, wise guy. I'm telling you, you'll get great mileage with the family if you take them to the show."

"I'm sure I would, but all I'm sayin' is, I'd have to work an extra four hours just to pay for the damn cartoon. That's just not practical."

Peter lay silent as the two workers debated the merits of whether or not to see the Disney film while they smoked their cigarettes. From his prone position, he could see their feet a few yards away. As they talked, their feet shuffled in a small semi-circle around the drainage grate he came through just moments before. Patiently, Peter waited.

A few minutes later, their conversation ended and the last of their cigarette butts having been thrown into the storm drain, the men walked out of sight. Peter scrambled out from beneath his cover to see which door they entered. It was the single door in the west wall, and from Peter's recollection, it led into the main corridor that ran along the perimeter of the facility.

Noting the door's proximity, Peter quickly reevaluated his plan. If he didn't have to dismantle the vent hood to gain access, so much the better. He sprinted to the west wall, sticking to the shadows as best he could. Leaning against the wall next to the door, he tried the handle. Unlocked. Peter's pulse rose as he pulled the door open and peered in. The corridor was clear in both directions. Without hesitation, Peter stepped through the opening and casually walked in the direction of a janitor's closet at the end of the hall.

Peter reached for the door handle, hoping for an easy access. It was unlocked. Don't they lock up anything around here? he mused. Stepping into the small closet, he flipped on the light and closed the door behind him. After a cursory examination of the cramped room, Peter found what he was looking for. He pulled the largest of the three freshly cleaned overalls from a hanger and quickly stepped into them, zipping the front over his clothing. Pausing long enough to take a few deep, calming breaths, Peter backed out of the closet, pulling a garbage cart with him.

He made his way down the corridor toward the coining room, occasionally stopping to empty various wastebaskets into his cart. As he turned the corner, he came face-to-face with one of the mint employees. Peter's anxiety strangled his throat, but they simply nodded to one another as they passed. Peter released a huge sigh and casually walked into the coining room.

As expected, the room was empty. From his research, he knew the midnight to 6:00 a.m. shift had no staff pressing coins. He continued toward the anteroom on the far side of the repository. Peter glanced over his shoulder as he reached for the door, and to his satisfaction, he was alone.

The anteroom was smaller than he had expected. So small, in fact, that Peter had to leave the garbage cart parked conspicuously outside the door. With the windowless door closed, he wasted no time pillaging the various drawers and cabinets, hoping to find that single penny pressed from a bronze planchet. His research of the famous penny indicated that its minting date was within the timeframe of his visit.

As he thoroughly examined each compartment of each drawer, Peter only found nickels, dimes, and quarters. A handful of steel pennies were found with the pressing misaligned, but no bronze penny. He moved to a small wall cabinet and began to rummage around the open shelving. Unfortunately, all he passed over were paper bills. That's when he noticed a small metal box on the top shelf and pulled it down. Upon opening the box, Peter's anxiety threatened to burst a blood vessel. Inside was a plastic tray with blank bronze planchets. He quickly sifted through the blanks, hoping to find a pressed penny. There were none.

Lifting the plastic tray out, Peter found the mother lode. There were a half dozen rolls of pennies lying at the bottom of the till among a few rolls of other denomination coins. He picked up the first roll and peeled away one end. His heart skipped a beat. It was the wheat side of a bronze penny. Flipping the coin out with his thumb, his eyes darted to the date: 1942. His heart sank. Tossing the roll aside, he grabbed another roll and opened it. Again, 1942. He continued to open each of the six rolls, finding the same date each time.

Deflated, Peter tossed the box aside and contemplated plan B. He didn't want to resort to it if he didn't have to. Frustrated, he tossed the penny rolls back into the box and replaced the plastic tray. Before closing the box, he slid the blank bronze planchets into his pocket. He returned the box to the top shelf and exited the coining room.

And came nose-to-nose with a familiar face. Peter instantly recognized Bartholomew Canter from his Operation Abraham research.

"What are you doing in there?" barked Canter.

"I . . . I was just cleaning out the trash—" Peter began to explain.

"There's no wastebaskets in any part of this area. You should know that. Who is your supervisor?"

"Well, that's an interesting story," Peter scrambled. "I'm actually not an employee here. I'm . . . I'm a private contractor for the government."

"Come again? A private what?"

"I'm a private contractor. Hired to find possible . . . security weaknesses in . . . various government facilities. As you can see, I've been able to make my way into the depths of the US Mint without being detected," Peter said confidently.

"I've been in the mint for nearly four years, and this is the first I've heard of it. I need to see your identification," Canter demanded.

"Well, Mr. Canter—or should I call you Bart?" Peter paused

to judge Canter's reaction.

"I, um, Bart is fine. Do you know me?"

"I do, Bart. I know about all the employees here," Peter said, not lying. He just prayed that he could remember all the names. "I know the staff tonight consists of twelve employees. I know that there is no janitorial staff on this shift and that the coining room was unattended. I also know that the entire second floor is vacant this time of night."

"That could be just a lucky guess on your part," snapped Canter. "So I'll ask again. Show me your ID."

Peter paused, not quite sure whether he should show his military ID or not. Figuring he was in deep now, he made for his back pocket. He handed the ID to Canter.

"I'm Pete. Pete Cooper." Peter cringed at the thought of actually telling a person his real name in 1942, something that he had been ordered to keep confidential throughout the entire mission.

Canter examined the ID, and although he wasn't familiar with military IDs, he was smart enough to know a real one.

"I, um, I'm not quite sure what to say," Canter said as he handed the badge back to Peter. "We've not had any security issues for as long as I've been here."

"It's not just for the protection of the mint. My task force is investigating multiple installations throughout the nation. In fact, my West Coast team consists of more than a dozen men and women," Peter said, building his ruse.

For the first time, Canter looked fearful. "I suppose that your presence here means we failed miserably?"

"That's an understatement. When I began my surveillance of the site, I found multiple avenues of entrance, some less conspicuous than others. Once I breached the perimeter, I found many more disturbing security deficiencies."

Canter hung his head in embarrassment. "I don't suppose we can just get a warning? I mean this really is a first for us."

"I'm afraid not. It's all going in my report when we complete our investigation next week," Peter said.

Canter found an empty chair and slumped into it. "Well, I guess that's it. I'm through."

"Bart, this is not completely your fault. True, it is your shift, and you are the on-site supervisor, but the entire staff has its part of the blame. I'm sure they'll go easy on you."

"I'm not so sure. I've been given a written warning already for another . . . incident . . ." Canter trailed off.

"I am aware, Bart. Something about giving a personal tour . . . to a civilian female after hours," Peter said, recalling the humorous file from Canter's employment record.

"You must think I'm a horrible person," Canter stated.

"What I think has no impact on this situation. Sure, bringing a woman into the mint—a woman for whom you had romantic intentions—was certainly a lapse in judgment."

"Oh God. Oh God. Oh God," Canter mumbled as he rested his forehead on the edge of the table.

"Listen, Bart. Keep your head up. My report isn't going in for a few days, and . . ." Peter paused, realizing that Canter was nearly at his tipping point.

"And?" Canter begged.

"Well, I really shouldn't," Peter said, letting out a bit more line.

Canter raised his eyes to Peter. "Anything. I'll do anything to make this go away."

Peter began to pace slowly for effect, keeping his eyes down as if dissecting a complicated equation.

"There is this one thing that you could do for me."

"Name it . . . uh, what was your name again?"

Peter smiled. He had him. "Pete. Pete Hooper."

CHAPTER 12

The following day, Peter and Julie spent the better part of the morning and all afternoon gathering supplies for their trip to New York. They purchased luggage, clothing, and toiletries throughout the bay area. Although Peter had been out shopping with the doctors shortly after their arrival, he had been shocked at the cost of things, even with prior knowledge of the economy.

"Miss Stewart showed you all those stores?" Peter asked Julie as they hauled the last of the bags up to their room.

"Yeah, and I didn't even take you to all of the shops. Gerty has a thing for shopping and knows nearly every clothing store owner in town personally," Julie said before carrying two arms full of clothes into her room.

Peter slid his suitcase into the closet and began hanging his shirts. "You two have really bonded, I'd say."

"What? Oh yeah. Gerty's wonderful," Julie said, walking back into the living room. "You know, I think she and Dr. Epson are in love, but neither of them know it."

Peter didn't respond. It was none of his business, and he felt awkward talking about other people's love lives. He changed the subject. "So, I think this should about do it for clothing until we leave on the twenty-fourth."

Julie nodded. "There are a few more things I'd like to get,

but it's stuff I can pick up on my own." She lowered herself onto the arm of the sofa. She looked down at the cushions concealing the hideaway bed that Peter slept on. "There is something I'd like to know, Peter."

Peter had hung the last of the new shirts in the wardrobe before turning to face her. "What is it, Jules?"

"I've noticed . . . you gone at night. Last night, for one, and a few times last week as well. Is there anything going on?"

Peter stood motionless. He'd expected her to become suspicious if she found him gone but hoped she hadn't notice. Yet he was surprised at her directness.

"Uh, yeah. About that. I've been . . . tracking some things down for General Applegate. It's really nothing to worry about."

"Things like what? I thought you said we weren't going to keep anything from one another."

Peter considered her statement. She was right.

"So I did," Peter returned to the wardrobe and pulled his satchel from the top shelf. "I wasn't going to mention any of this until we were on the train, but I suppose now is a good a time as any."

He sat on the sofa and pulled out the manila envelope from Applegate. "The general gave this to me the night before we left. He told me not to open it until we arrived, which I did the afternoon we checked in."

Julie dropped off the arm of the sofa and slid closer to Peter, eyeing the envelope curiously. "What's in it?"

"It's, um, it's the additional information for the mission I told you about. Along with dossiers for everyone on the team. There's information on Epson and Stewart, as well."

Intrigued, Julie picked up the envelope. "Information like what?"

Peter slipped the envelope back from Julie and pulled out the various smaller envelopes. He handed them to Julie one by one until he came to the envelope with her name on it.

She dropped all the other envelopes into her lap and studied her own.

"What's it say?"

"Pretty much what you told me the other day about your past. The general thought I should know about everything that could potentially compromise the mission."

"How would my past compromise anything?" Julie demanded. "I'm completely dedicated to this mission."

"I know, Jules, but Applegate felt that you were . . . unstable because of your parental incident and your ancestors in France. After reading this, at first I thought so, too. But it's just how he manipulates things."

Julie wiped a tear from her eye, not looking up. "And now?"

"Now I trust you completely. I know you're a good person. Julie, why would I share any of this if I felt otherwise?"

Julie looked into Peter's eyes and smiled. "Thank you, Peter." She pulled the letter from the envelope and read. A few minutes later, she crumpled the paper in anger.

"What gives him the right to judge me like this?" Julie demanded.

"It's okay, Jules. I said I believe you. Let's not focus on Applegate's mind games."

Julie nodded and smoothed out the letter and hastily stuffed it back into the envelope. "What about the other envelopes? And what does any of this have to do with you leaving at night?"

Peter handed Julie the letter in which Applegate had informed him of the mole, and as she read it, Peter removed the remaining envelopes from her lap. He nonchalantly found his own and slipped it back into the larger envelope, along with Julie's. She didn't seem to notice.

Frown lines grew on her face as she read, but Peter remained quiet until she finished.

"So he thinks one of Epson's assistants planted a bomb? I can tell you this, it wasn't Gerty," Julie stated confidently.

"I don't know what to believe, Jules. I've been out at night tracking down where they live," Peter lied.

"What good will that do?"

"I don't know. But it's a start. You never know when we'll

need the information. It's not like I'm going to bust into their houses and interrogate them. Not yet, at least."

"Not ever," demanded Julie. "I think there are better ways to figure this out."

"Such as?"

"Well, first thing we need to do is share this with the docs. They are with Gerty and Michael every day and should be aware of this."

Peter nodded. "Agreed, but we need to be careful. I'm not sure how well the docs can play dumb knowing there may be a bomb in their future. How much of this other stuff should we share with them?"

Julie contemplated Peter's question. "Well, I don't think they need to know about our past or what's in their envelopes. I think we should just give them enough information so that they can observe the entire situation."

Peter nodded again. "Sometimes less is more. Certainly in this situation." Peter returned the remaining envelopes to the large manila envelope.

"What about our travel. What's it say?"

"The general doesn't want us to read that until we are on the train to New York."

"And you think that's the best move? Considering all the lies he's told?"

"I s'pose you're right," Peter said and pulled out "International Travel Information." He opened it and began to read aloud.

Peter-

If you are reading this, I assume you are on the train to New York and everything in San Francisco is in order. Let me first say that what you are about to read may come as a shock, but in the end, I am positive that you will agree it is necessary for the success of the mission.

Once you and Miss Frey arrive in New York, you need to

check into a hotel for a few days before the boat departs for France. During that time, you will need to track down two people and persuade them to surrender their travel documents. I know this sounds ominous, but because international travel by civilians was mostly suspended during wartime, obtaining their travel documents is the only practical solution to get you two across the Atlantic without leaving a paper trail.

The two individuals are Warrant Officer Alexander Cain and Miss Alicia Hamilton. Cain is responsible for war-related news reporting and is a civilian with military clearance. He should be referred to as Mr. Cain; no military title is necessary. Miss Hamilton is his personal assistant and has no military designation. They will both be staying in New York until their scheduled departure on Friday, September 4. Because they are both technically civilians, we feel that obtaining their travel documentation should pose no significant complication.

I recommend your first approach be covert appropriation. If you can lift the paperwork from their hotel room, so much the better. By the time they realize their paperwork is missing, you'll be boarded and on your way.

If your first approach doesn't work, you are authorized to detain them by any means necessary to obtain the documents. Because we are unsure of their temperament, we cannot not advise you on whether to use lethal force. Bring your weapon and use your best judgment. Peter, I need to express the urgency of this segment of the mission. If you are not on that boat on September 4, the mission will fail.

For obvious reasons, Miss Frey should be advised of this letter. Best of luck to you both.

Peter and Julie sat quietly as the implications sank in. It was several moments before either could speak, and it was Julie that broke the silence.

"I, um, I'm not sure what to say. What did he mean 'by any means necessary'? Does he really expect us to kill them?"

"Of course not," Peter said, hoping his confidence was

believable. "I think Applegate just wants us to be very persuasive, is all."

"Then why did he say to bring a weapon? Do you think we'll need one?"

"I have no idea, Jules. I hope not, but we'll take a side arm just in case."

Peter refolded the letter and slipped it back into its envelope. As he and Julie sat privately waltzing with the possibilities in New York, they heard murmurs from the hallway. From the sound of the voices, it was the two doctors returning from their day at Epson's lab.

"We've got to tell them about the mole," Julie said as she rose and moved toward the door.

"Wait, Julie. I agree, but not a word of anything else."

Julie opened the door, startling Lamb and Larsson. "Hi, there. Can Peter and I have a few words with you?"

"Sure thing," replied Lamb. "What's up?" he asked as he and Larsson walked into their hotel room.

"What's up, docs?" Peter said with a smile. "Why don't you take a seat. There's been a . . . development."

CHAPTER 13

Michael Gallagher stood motionless as the elevator arrived at the third floor of the Perry Hotel. Even though the ride up was short, agitation overwhelmed him since he'd just been here five minutes ago, dropping the doctors off. But one of them had forgotten an attaché case, and now he had to return it. Initially, he'd thought about just giving it to them the following morning when he picked them up. But upon second thought, returning it now might give him an opportunity to chat with Peter and Julie and potentially learn something new. Even though Dr. Epson had provided them with military IDs, neither had been back to the base since their arrival.

The chime of the elevator bell returned Gallagher to the task at hand as the doors parted at the third floor vestibule. As he approached the doctors' room, he slowed and brought his hand up to knock. Before he did, voices echoed from across the hall— Peter and Julie's room.

". . . imperative . . . to the mission . . ." Peter's familiar baritone voice reverberated through the wood panel door. Gallagher couldn't quite make out all the words, so he delicately pressed his ear to the door and listened.

"I think we understand. You just need us to keep our eyes and ears open. Report anything out of the ordinary back to you and Julie ASAP," Lamb said. "Do you have a hunch who it is?"

There was a pause before he heard Peter. "I think it's best not to speculate until we know more. You agree, Jules?"

Gallagher imagined Julie nodding her head, since there was no reply.

"Great then. Stay sharp and keep your nose down. There's no need to raise any suspicion until we know for certain," Peter ordered.

Gallagher felt apprehension steal through him but left his ear planted on the door. Dr. Larsson finally spoke.

"How are your plans coming along? Are there any updates on your travel?"

"We've just about wrapped up our shopping, and let me tell you, planning for two months abroad isn't easy," Julie said.

"That's because you want to bring everything under the sun," Peter said, obviously making a joke at his wife's proclivity for excess.

"That's not so. I just know what it's like to travel to France, Peter . . . and you can never be prepared enough."

France? They're going to France? There was no mention of this before, Gallagher noted.

"Well, Jules, traveling to France in 2013 would certainly be a lot different than it's going to be now. We're probably going to be limited on the number of bags we can take on a navy ship. Most of what you're bringing will likely be left on the docks. You may want to start deciding now what you're gonna leave. Lord knows it will take at least a couple weeks to work that out."

"You guys still scheduled to leave on the fourth?" Larsson asked.

"Yep. Why do you think I want Jules to start now?" Peter quipped.

My God, Gallagher thought. They're going to France, and soon! The fourth of what? He listened, praying for more.

"Be that as it may, Mr. Smart Ass, at least next week's train will be graced with my amazing ensemble!"

Crap! Gallagher thought. They're leaving on a train next week? What day? What day? he fretted.

"That's all great, guys, but do you have anything on the mission itself?" Dr. Lamb inquired.

The following silence unnerved Gallagher.

"No, nothing new on our end. The plan is still to get to Oradour-sur-Glane by the end of September. Once we get to Normandy, we'll determine the best way to get there and complete the mission."

Gallagher inhaled sharply and quickly covered his mouth.

"All right, then. Anything else we need to discuss?" Peter asked.

Gallagher felt he should get word to Emmett now, but he stayed, hoping for more information. He only heard a series of murmurs for the next few moments, and he assumed everyone was shaking their heads. Then he heard movement. He darted away from the door and tiptoed down the hall as fast as he could. Just as he got to the corner, he heard a door open behind him. He ran the last few steps, hoping he wasn't seen. He flew past the elevator and plunged into the stairwell, dropping two steps at a time. Bursting into the lobby, he instinctively slowed to a casual pace and headed for the front entrance.

As he slid behind the wheel of his car, he realized he was still carrying the doctor's attaché. *Forget it,* he thought and sped down the road. He needed to get word to Emmett immediately. Mandrake would not be pleased.

CHAPTER 14

Peter walked the ten blocks from his hotel to Grace Cathedral flushed with nostalgia. The last time he'd visited the cathedral was with the kids only a month ago, but it felt like an eternity. Since arriving in 1942, he'd had to keep his family from his thoughts. He knew he'd have to compartmentalize his feelings while on the mission, but the closer he got to the granite steps of the historic sanctuary, he realized the difficulty of the task. A sense of abandonment began to seep into the corners of his mind. The mental invasion was something Peter was prepared for.

Trying to focus on the present, Peter forced the feelings aside. From his southerly approach, he could just make out the spires of the cathedral inching above the rooftops of the surrounding buildings.

Continuing up the steep incline toward California Street, he wondered how much longer he would be able to deceive Julie. The lie he'd told her about his surveillance of Epson's assistants could only last so long. He knew Julie was smart and would begin to figure it out, given enough time. Just a few more trips would be all he needed; today's encounter to get the pennies and the 'entrovement' in a few days would be the culmination of Operation Abraham.

The burn in his thighs stole his attention as he ascended

the final block. Peter smiled appreciatively at the architectural beauty as the cathedral came into view. Crossing the street, he wondered if he'd made a mistake by arranging the meeting here instead of someplace more inconspicuous. At the time, his attention had been so focused on obtaining the pennies themselves. Thankfully, his quick thinking and ingenuity brought up a location he was familiar with.

To Peter's pleasant surprise, Canter had reluctantly agreed to run an entire roll of bronze pennies through the stamper with the date of 1943. His plan all along was to secure just a few of the valuable coins, and never in his wildest dreams had he imagined obtaining fifty.

Peter glanced at his watch and saw he was on time. It was three in the afternoon, and the bells began their toll from the apex of the spires. Before entering the church, he surveyed the grounds for anything conspicuous, but everything seemed in order. He chuckled. *How would I know what was out of place in 1942?*

Trusting in fate, Peter walked up to the south entrance and entered the partially completed edifice. He immediately noticed a number of differences. First, the famous labyrinth was nowhere in sight. That part of the cathedral would not be constructed until many years later. The pews throughout the nave were also temporary, smaller, less elaborate versions of the pews he had known.

At that moment, Peter realized how powerful the cathedral's presence had been throughout his life. It was part of his college years and his time with Minnie. It had even been part of his time with his children. Now here he was, standing on the precipice of great change. He knew he had chosen this location wisely.

Peter walked to the rear of the nave, looking for Canter. He scanned the faces of the dozen or so other patrons but came up blank. He sat on a creaky pew in the back row and waited. From his vantage point, he would be able to see Canter, or anyone else for the matter. As he waited, he marveled at the breathtaking arches sweeping across the ceiling and the beauty of the ubiquitous stained glass windows. Peter felt a comfort he hadn't known for some time.

"An interesting place to meet, Mr. Hooper," Canter said, startling Peter as he slid into the pew next to him.

"Ah, yes. I am a fan of"—Peter paused to choose his words carefully—"of architecture. This is something special. I can only imagine what it will be like when it's complete." Peter smiled at the irony of his own comment.

Canter looked about impassively. "Yes, I'm sure it'll be nice."

"Did you have any problems?" Peter asked.

Canter shook his head. "Nope. No problem."

Peter tried to read Canter, but he was stone-faced. No emotion, no concern—nothing.

"I assume you have also corrected the flaws in your security?" Peter asked.

Canter flinched slightly and turned to Peter. "I have. I just don't understand how you knew of any of this. Unless you had plans of the mint, how would you have known the layout of the building? How *did* you get in?"

"I did have the plans. That's all part of my job. I know everything about the mint, as well as many other government facilities. As for the how . . . well, that's classified."

"But wouldn't that be an unfair advantage? How would the common criminal know how to breach the facility without any of the information you had?"

"Why would you assume they don't? Suppose they were able to appropriate a set of blueprints from the designing architect; wouldn't that give them all the information they'd need?"

"Not really. They would only have locations of walls and doors and such. They would still not have the information on staffing and shift personnel that you were privy to. It just seems that we were set up to fail, and I find that quite unfair."

"I'm sorry you feel that way, Bart, but if you would prefer, we can just forget this meeting, and I can file my report—"

Canter cut him off. "No, no. I just want you to understand how bizarre this all is. Don't file the report. You obviously know you have me over a barrel. It just doesn't make sense." Canter pulled a roll of coins from his pocket. The sheath was opaque but looked about the right size. "If you were going to blackmail me about this, I would have thought it would be for a lot more money than fifty cents' worth of unusable 1943 pennies."

Peter smiled. "I have my reasons, and it's best we leave it at that."

Peter held out his hand and waited. Canter glared suspiciously and then handed him the roll.

"How do I know you won't file that report anyway? For all I know, this whole penny business might be all part of your plan to get me fired."

"Why would I do that? You can trust me, Bart."

"Can I? I don't even know you. This all seems so . . . so cloak and dagger."

Peter smiled reassuringly. "I'm not interested in seeing you or anyone else fired from the mint. My only concern is security. I want the best people in place to ensure the security of our national economy. Sure, I should report everything that I've encountered, but from where I stand, you've done nothing wrong here. I know your family counts on you. There is no funny business going on. The pennies here"—Peter dropped them into his breast pocket—"are just a token. If I wanted to really blackmail you, I would have asked for a stack of hundreds or something ridiculous. This roll of pennies will never see the light of day. As you say, it's fifty cents. I just needed to see how far you would go."

Canter was stoic. "Are we done here?"

"Sure thing, Bart. Just remember. I, or another member of my company, could run another test at any time. There will be no second chances. If we breach your security again, there will be hell to pay."

Canter sat for a moment longer before standing and walking away. He didn't acknowledge Peter again.

Peter remained seated for several minutes, contemplating his attitude toward Canter. He hoped that he had instilled a significant level of fear, enough that Canter would not breathe a word of any of this to anyone.

As he stood to leave, Peter pulled the pennies from his shirt pocket, deposited them into his front pants pocket, and walked toward the side exit leading to the gardens. It was still early, and he wanted to see more of the differences between cathedral's past and present.

Stepping out into the daylight, Peter shielded his eyes until they could adjust. Once normal vision returned, it was too late to see the men standing on either side of the doors. The last thing he saw was a glimpse of yellow roses before the darkness.

CHAPTER 15

A hood was cinched tight below his chin, and Peter was grasped firmly by both arms. He tried to resist, but the more he did, the harder they squeezed.

"Hey!" Peter yelled.

The assailants forced him to move through the gardens, half dragging him, half carrying him. Despite the blackness, he could still smell the sweetness of the rose bushes.

"What's going on?" Peter asked, trying a more subdued approach. Still, he was met with silence from his captors. "Who are you? Come on, you've got to give me something."

"Quiet, if you know what's good for ya," replied a gruff voice.

"Not until you tell me what's going on," Peter demanded.

Instead of silence or another order to be quiet, Peter received a sharp crack on the back of his skull. He instantly saw a cluster of dancing stars. Peter momentarily lost his balance, and in turn, the guys holding him gripped even harder.

"All right, all right. I can walk on my own. Just let up a little, will ya?"

The vise grips released slightly, and the feeling began to return to his hands. They guided him forward and then left into the alley. As he stumbled up a few steps, he began to hear street traffic. Peter tried desperately to think of a way out. If they were going to shove him into the back of a car, he'd only have moments for an escape attempt when they released their grip. He had to time it perfectly and trust his instincts.

Which direction should I run? If he chose correctly, he could dash toward the south and into the afternoon pedestrian crowd. If he chose unwisely, he could run directly into the stone wall of the church—or even worse, into street traffic.

As they made their way up the alley, Peter tried to visualize his surroundings. His captors' pace slowed and he began to hear the sound of an idling car. The moment was imminent. If he could just break away—

"Don't try nothin' funny, buddy," said the man with the gruff voice as he shoved Peter into the back of a sedan and slammed the door. Peter's head hit the opposite door, and the car lurched forward. With his arms free, Peter instinctively tried to loosen the hood. But before he could get to the knotted rope at the back of his neck, he heard another voice.

"Please, Peter," said the new voice—a much calmer, more educated voice. "Just leave it on for a few moments longer. I promise no harm will come to you."

"Easy for you to say. You weren't just hit in the back of the head."

"Ah yes. For that, I apologize. I asked them not to harm you, but only to . . . persuade you to come quietly."

Peter rubbed the growing knot on the back of his head. "I was persuaded, all right." He felt uneasy, but there was nothing he could do about it at the moment.

The car ride passed quickly, and Peter guessed they had only traveled a dozen blocks at the most. He also felt they were probably near the water, because most of the travel had been downhill.

A few minutes later the car stopped, and he heard the front doors open. Then one of the back doors opened and he was once again dragged by firm hands. Peter relaxed and halted any further protest.

He could hear the educated man whispering to someone behind him. He couldn't quite make out the conversation, but he thought he recognized the other voice . . . but from where?

A moment later the man said, "It'll only be a moment longer, Mr. Cooper. I promise, everything will be explained shortly."

"You obviously know who I am. Would you care to tell me who you are?" Peter asked, hopeful to glean something from the bizarre situation.

"In time."

The men holding his arms guided him up a number of steps and through a doorway. By the sound of their echoing footsteps, Peter realized they must be in an atrium of some sort, most likely with marble floors and high ceilings. The men stopped and stood beside him silently. A moment later, a mechanical bell rang before they all stepped into an elevator. As the doors closed, Peter felt one of the men loosen the hood and yank it from his head.

It took a moment for Peter's eyes to adjust to the light of the small elevator. He blinked away the blur and focused directly ahead. The elevator car was lined in brass, and there were three other men in the car with him: two men on either side of him and one standing behind him. Peter could not make out the face in the reflection on the door, so he turned his head to face the man. Staring back was a middle-aged man with salt-and-pepper hair. He smiled and returned his gaze forward as the elevator reached its destination.

With much less shoving, the men guided Peter down a long corridor lined with mahogany. At the end of the corridor were a pair of massive wooden doors. The man in charge stepped forward and walked inside. Peter and the henchman followed inside, where his arms were released.

"That'll be all, gentlemen."

"You want us to stay close, boss?"

"Just near the lobby will be fine. I don't expect any problems from Mr. Cooper."

The two men backed into the hallway and closed the doors.

"Please have a seat, Mr. Cooper," said the man, motioning toward the chairs placed on the opposite side of the desk.

Peter sat down and crossed his arms.

"What's going on here?" Peter asked.

"I wanted to talk with you, Mr. Cooper. I know all about you and where you came from. Or should I say *when* you came from?"

Peter was shocked but didn't let on. "Come again? When? I just came from Grace Cathedral, where I was praying for—"

"Come now, Peter. I know everything about you. And your team, for that matter."

"If you know so much about me, you should know I am here with my wife on our honeymoon."

"Ah yes. Miss Frey, is it?"

"Yes, that's right. She kept her maiden name when . . ."

"You can stop the antics now, Peter. They won't work."

Peter stared intently at the man. His eyes darted about the room and then back to the man. "So who are you, then?"

"I'm sorry, Peter. Where are my manners? I am Asher Mandrake." He stood and extended his hand. Peter reluctantly took it and gripped firmly.

"I think you might have me confused with someone else," Peter said, trying a different tactic.

"No, no. I am positive I have the right person. You're the man that has traveled from the future."

"What! Are you insane?" scoffed Peter. "What on earth are you talking about? Traveled from the future? Like in some kind of space machine?" Peter asked, laying it on thick.

Asher chuckled. "No, not in a space machine, but through Dr. Epson's time machine. I know all about it."

Peter wasn't sure how to react. General Applegate had assured him that their mission was virtually foolproof. *Another deception?* Peter wondered.

"That is the craziest thing I've heard in a long time. Who is this Epson fellow, anyway?" Peter asked.

Asher's smile faded to a stern glare. "I really don't have the time for charades, Peter. I know you and three others came through the time machine almost two weeks ago, and I would like to know why. There is no use in denying it any further. I could easily send my men to pick up Julie if you would prefer."

Peter flinched at the mention of Julie's name. "No, that won't be necessary."

The smile returned to Asher's face. "Good. So, what is the reason you and your companions have traveled back from . . . 2013, is it?"

Peter nodded slowly. "Yeah, that's about right." He wondered how this man knew so much. Applegate's letter about the mole came rushing back to him.

"I'll assume that your ploy about 'historical research' is just some clever cover, and your reason for being here is much more elaborate," Asher stated.

Although Peter was well rehearsed for this kind of interrogation, he had hoped to avoid it. He prepared the necessary responses in his mind.

"It's obvious that you have someone close to Dr. Epson. What have they said?"

"I'm asking you, Peter. Never mind how I know about your existence."

Peter realized he wasn't going to get much from Asher. "It's true, but it's not as elaborate as you might think. Two scientists, Julie Frey, and I came through Epson's time machine. We arrived on July twenty-seventh. Our purpose here is to help Dr. Epson complete his research on time travel and then return back to 2013."

"You expect me to believe it takes four individuals to help fix the time machine? What exactly is your part in repairing the device?"

"I . . . I'm not a scientist, if that's what you are asking."

"Then why are you here? And how about Miss Frey?"

"Julie and I came back to help control the situation from a nontechnical standpoint. Julie and I are here for damage control—to make sure nothing is changed that could affect the future."

"That, Peter, I believe," Asher said. "But what has me

perplexed is why you need to travel to France."

The blood drained from Peter's face. "France? What makes you think we're going to France?"

"I am aware of the travel plans for you and Miss Frey. From what I understand, you will be traveling by train next week and departing from, I can only assume, New York on or around the fourth of September."

Shit! Peter thought. How did he know so much? Did he get to one of the docs?

"I . . . I have no idea . . . how'd you know?" Peter was caught completely off guard. *There is no sense in denying the trip now.*

"I have my sources, Peter. What I don't know is, what is the purpose of your *mission*?" Asher asked.

"I'm sorry, Asher, but I can't tell you that. It's best that you know as little as possible about our purpose. The fact that you know about me and my team is already laced with disaster."

"I couldn't agree more. For that reason, I cannot permit you to return to your time. Too much has changed in the present, and the further you contaminate the timeline, the worse you are making things for the future."

"So far the only thing that has not gone as planned is you, Asher. It's up to you to stop the contamination by minding your own business and letting me complete my mission."

"What is your mission, Peter?"

"I'll say it again: I cannot tell you."

"Why?" Asher prompted again.

"Contamination, remember?" Peter shot back.

Asher did not look amused. "Peter, you leave me no choice but to contain the situation. I'll have to have your time-travel mates picked up and the four of you detained until the threat of—"

"You can't do that!" Peter burst out.

"Oh, yes I can. And I will. You've given me no other choice," Asher said.

Peter studied Asher's face as he worked through his next response in his mind.

"Okay, okay. Julie and I are planning on going to France, but our reason isn't as sinister as you would like to think. You can believe it or not, that's completely up to you, but Julie and I are history professors for the Jeffersonian Institute. We were sent back to gather information on life in France during the war," Peter said, pausing long enough to catch his breath. "You see, there are several inaccuracies during the time in question. Julie and I are here to confirm, or deny, certain political situations during the last few weeks of September."

"What sort of activities?" Asher asked, his curiosity provoked.

"Asher, I can't. I've already said too much."

"And as I've already said, you don't leave me with much choice—"

"Who are you to think you can control people's lives like this?" Peter asked.

"I head a private organization of individuals with the sole purpose of preventing situations like this from advancing."

"How on earth could you have realized that time travel was possible, let alone have the time to create a militia to prevent it?"

"We were established long ago, for other reasons. It just so happens we were in the right place at the right time to handle your situation."

"So then, what is your purpose? To prevent scientific advancement? Are you Amish with an attitude?" Peter asked sarcastically.

Asher chuckled. "No, we're not Amish. We are here to prolong the existence of man and to ensure a rich, full life for everyone. Anything that threatens that, we deal with swiftly."

"I suppose you have a plan in place to prevent the atomic bomb, too?" Peter asked, knowing that the Manhattan Project was already underway.

"Yes, we are aware of the development of the A-bomb, and unfortunately, that is out of the reach of our society," Asher said as his brow tightened. "In a perfect world, Peter, there would be no war, but some things are out of our control."

Peter saw an opening. "Suppose we could help each other?"

"How on earth could you help me?" Asher asked incredulously.

"Well, you see, our mission has a lot to do with the war. Allow my team to continue on as planned, and you might get exactly what you desire most."

"I'm listening. Continue."

Peter stood and paced about Asher's office for dramatic affect. He stared into the void as he began to speak.

"It's true that Julie and I are to observe life in France. I'm not denying that. However, because of our vast knowledge of historical facts, we know a lot about the war, including how and when it will come to an end. Now, suppose we could accelerate the end of the war by several years—"

"Several years?" Asher blurted. "It continues on that long?"

"You know I cannot tell you when it will end, but I believe my partner and I could devise a . . . a plan, something, that could benefit both of our interests."

"Wouldn't you risk changing the outcome of the war as well?" Asher asked.

Peter thought about the question and realized how close to the truth the whole conversation really was. If he and Julie did accomplish their mission as planned, just how much would it change the outcome? He pushed the thought from his mind, trying to prevent Asher from controlling the conversation.

"Not necessarily. With the knowledge that Julie and I possess, the outcome could remain relatively unchanged, but the timeline could be shortened tremendously." Peter took his seat again. "I need to confer with Julie about all of this before fully committing to anything, you understand."

Asher contemplated their conversation for several minutes in silence.

"Suppose I let you and Miss Frey continue with your mission. Who is to say that you don't simply run and never return to San Francisco?"

"Wouldn't you just love that! Have us complete our mission

and not return to 2013? That's a win-win for you, Asher."

"Okay, Peter. You win. I'll permit you and Miss Frey to continue to France. In the meantime, I will meet with the other members of our 'militia,' as you call it, to determine the future of you and your team. I will say this: your actions in France will greatly determine your chances of returning to your time. I suggest that you and your wife prepare an impressive plan for us to review prior to your departure on September fourth."

Peter felt relieved for the moment. At least he would be able to make it back to Julie . . . and the docs. He would deal with returning through the time machine when he arrived at that bridge.

"Great," Peter said, standing to leave. "Don't mind if I show myself out."

"Not so fast, Peter. I have some stipulations, of course. I will need to send someone to accompany you and Miss Frey. I need to keep tabs on you to make sure you stick to your plan."

Peter sank back into his chair. "A babysitter?"

"Not exactly. Consider it a chaperone."

CHAPTER 16

Peter was escorted from Asher's office by the two goons that had detained him hours earlier. *Has it been hours?* The conversation he'd just had with the leader of the Society had passed in a blur. The exchange of information between himself and Asher made his head spin. Peter knew he would have to tread lightly for the remainder of his time in San Francisco.

Stepping out of the elevator, Peter glanced back at his two escorts and said, "You know, I'm quite capable of making it back to my hotel on my own. It's only a fifteen-minute walk from here."

The two looked at each other, obviously confused.

"Are you surprised? You brought me in with a bag over my head. And yet, I still know! It's magic!" Peter flourished, not expecting a response. "The cat was let out of the bag, so to speak, when I sat across from your boss with that breathtaking view behind him. You see, I know that to have a view that impressive, we had to have been pretty high up. Maybe even in the tallest building in San Francisco?"

"Yeah, whatever. Mr. Mandrake asked us to see you back to your hotel peaceful-like," replied the muscle of the two. The other fellow was more of a squirrelly guy and remained silent.

"Suit yourself. I just thought I'd let you two off the hook. Come to think of it, do you mind if we stop by the drugstore? I need to pick up a few things."

Neither of Peter's escorts said anything. Muscles simply guided Peter toward the door of their waiting chariot. It was a 1941 Lincoln Zephyr with the unmistakable rear suicide doors.

"Wow, nice ride, boys. The boss lets you drive this all by yourselves?" Peter asked, almost certain his sarcasm and intellectual jabs were bound to trigger some kind of reaction. Surprisingly, they were both well-tempered on the drive to his hotel. In fact, the short jaunt up Market Street passed in complete silence.

As they pulled up to the hotel, the Squirrel turned around to Peter and said, "Listen, I'm not sure who you are or what you're all about, but neither me nor my friend here want to play any games."

Peter stared blankly at him. "I'm sorry, but what games?"

"Mr. Mandrake said for us to keep tabs on you and be ready for anything. He thinks you're a pretty slippery guy. I'm just sayin', we don't want any games, and everything will be fine. Just fine."

"Okay, then. On that note . . ." Peter unlatched the door and stepped out onto the sidewalk. He walked away from the car, leaving the door wide open. Seconds later, he heard the car hastily pull into traffic. "Dipshits," Peter mumbled as he stepped into the hotel foyer.

The lobby was empty, save for a bellhop that must have recognized him, because he returned to reading his newspaper the moment he saw Peter.

Peter shoved his hands into his pockets and wondered what his next move should be. His right hand felt a cylindrical paper tube. The pennies.

"Shit," Peter said aloud. His plan all along was to drive to his house and stash them somewhere . . . creative. He looked at his watch, and it read 2:30. It can't be that early, Peter thought. He tapped at the face of his watch, and as he did, the second hand moved a few ticks and then stopped again. *Damn mechanical watches!*

He walked up to the bellhop. "Got the time?"

The bellman looked through Peter and onto the wall across the lobby where a large clock with Roman numerals showed 6:34. He didn't respond but just nodded his head in the general direction.

"Thanks, buddy. Remind me to tip you a few bucks for all your help."

The bellman straightened up and said, "Excuse me?"

"Sorry, kid. I'm just messing with you," Peter said as he walked through the lobby toward the back stairway. He wondered if he still had time to get out of town to make the stash. Deciding that he did, he kept walking straight out the back door and into the parking lot.

———————

The traffic was lighter than he'd expected. The normally forty-minute drive to his old neighborhood took him slightly less than half an hour, and he was thankful that the construction workers were gone for the day.

He parked in the yet-to-be-poured driveway and entered through the garage, which was still void of an overhead door.

It was near sunset, and deep shadows began to loom through framed window and door openings throughout the main floor. Peter guessed he had fifteen minutes of usable daylight to find an adequate hiding place.

Starting in the kitchen, Peter searched for a place that he hoped would not be discovered during the remaining construction activities. Between plumbing and electrical runs that still needed to be completed, he dismissed the room and moved into other parts of the house.

Passing by the main floor powder room and dining room, Peter entered the living room. The room was enclosed by framed walls, and the lath installation had begun on the ceiling. Hiding the roll of coins above the ceiling plaster would have been ideal, but Peter couldn't find anything to climb on. Determined, Peter continued to search the room. As he moved toward the end wall, he noticed a small opening in the stone hearth. Kneeling next to it, he could see that the mortar for the stone was still tacky. He assumed that the masons had just set the stone earlier in the day.

As Peter knelt next to the fireplace, he missed the car that crept slowly by the front of the house.

He scanned the room, searching for something. To the left of the fireplace, he saw a scrap of tar paper. Grabbing it, he wrapped the impregnated paper around the pennies. Hoping that the extra layer of protection would endure the seventy-plus years before he could recover his precious trove, he leaned close to the hearth and attempted to slide it into the void. With the thick wrapping around the pennies in his hand, his closed fist would not squeeze past the surrounding stones. He maneuvered the roll between his fingers, rotated his wrist, and tried again. Success, but not without scraped knuckles.

With his hand deep into the void and his body leaning into the hearth, Peter tried to drop the pennies. The space inside the hearth was so tight he could not release his grip. He tried to shift his hand to the side and try again, but it was useless. At that moment, his vision blurred and the room began to spin. He tried to pull his hand back, but it wouldn't budge. He tried to tuck his thumb into the palm of his hand, hoping to make it as small as possible, but the effort was in vain. He was stuck.

Seconds later, the spinning subsided and he regained focus. He realized he was no longer alone. With his right hand lodged securely in the hearth, Peter was unable to turn in the direction of the visitor.

"Hi, there. I suppose you're wondering—" Peter began.

"Stehenbleiben! Nehmen Sie langsam die Haende hoch. Machen Sie keine ploetzliche Bewegung oder ich erschiesse Sie," said a harsh female voice in an unrecognizable language.

"Come again?" Peter asked as he tried to contort his neck to see who the voice belonged to.

With effort, he was able to glimpse a woman wearing a military uniform of unfamiliar origin. All the insignia were completely unrecognizable. Startled at her appearance, he began to thrash his hand wildly inside the stone hearth in an effort to free himself. As he did, he heard a gun being cocked.

Peter froze. He slowly twisted his head again to see the woman holding a machine gun pointed at his face. It was a German MP40, the weapon of choice for the Nazi army.

The woman moved to Peter's left, pressing the barrel into his cheek. "*Was machen Sie hier? Das ist ein Sperrbereich der Deutschen Befreiungsfront,*" she asked.

"I'm sorry. I don't speak German," Peter said, guessing at the language after seeing her weapon.

"Vhat ah you hea for?" she repeated in heavily-accented English.

"I . . . I was looking for something . . ." Peter managed, as he tried to figure out what the hell was going on.

"Show. Me. Yor. Hends," she said very slowly, as if constructing each word in her mind before speaking.

Unable to release the roll of pennies, Peter began to work his hand free of the hole, not without trouble. He twisted his wrist a quarter turn and pulled again. His knuckles left bloody streaks around the hole as his hand finally broke free. As he began to raise his hands and face the woman, the room suddenly lurched, causing Peter to lose his balance. His head struck the edge of the hearth and darkness enveloped him.

Blackness and pain abounding, Peter tried to focus. There was nothing.

"Peter? Peter! Are you all right?" said a familiar voice. Then a soft shake of his shoulder. "Peter. You're scaring me."

"I, uh, what . . . what's going on?" Peter said. He tried to sit up but was held down by a firm hand.

"Lie still. You hit your head."

"Jules?" Peter asked as he reached for his face. His hand found a cloth draped over his head. "I can't see—"

"It's me. Don't try to move. You were bleeding pretty bad when I found you. I found a rag in the back of the car to clean you up."

Peter held Julie's hand while he pulled the rag from his face. Twilight had come and gone, and the room was almost as dark as it had been with the cover over his eyes. Almost. From somewhere outside, a light shone through the windowless openings around the room.

"Wha . . . uh, what happened?" Peter stuttered.

"I don't know, Peter. You tell me. I followed you from the hotel," she said.

"You followed me?" Peter asked, lifting his head from Julie's lap and turning to face her.

"I did," Julie shot back. "Ever since we've arrived, you've been deceitful. I know what you're up to, and let me tell you, you can't. Just don't."

"What do you know? I . . . I'm here . . . because . . ." Peter said, trying to come up with a reason.

"Peter. Stop. I figured it out. I just want to hear it from you."

"I . . . I don't know what you're talking about," Peter said, feeling a little déjà vu.

"I know you're going to hide something just so you can retrieve it once we get home."

Peter's eyes had fully adjusted and he could see Julie's face. Her eyes were intense and concerned. "Is there anything wrong with that? I mean, I've had a miserable last few years. I just want to make things right for . . ." Peter paused, feeling his emotions overtake him. "I want to make it right for a change. For them. I have two great kids back home, and . . ."

Peter slumped against the fireplace. He'd been so focused on either the mission or Operation Abraham, he'd forgotten about the kids, and he felt sick. "I miss them badly, Jules. I'm here, an entire lifetime away, and there isn't a single thing I can do for them." Peter wiped tears from his eyes.

"I understand that, Peter, but you can't go changing things like this. Once you open Pandora's closet, there's no looking back."

Peter smirked, thankful for the humor to turn off the waterworks.

"What's so funny? I'm being serious. You can't—"

"You mean Pandora's box, not closet, and I think you mean a paradox," Peter said, taking her hand into his.

"Well, obviously. Just . . . just shut up. You know what I mean."

"Yes, I know. But what difference does it make what I hide here? Nobody will ever know."

"I'll know, and that's enough to make all the difference in the world. Besides, something very strange happened when I walked in."

"You felt it too? It felt like . . . like the room was twisting and turning, and . . ."

"Everything was fine, and when I walked into the room, you were kneeling there, and as you slid your hand into the hole, the whole room blurred and you vanished for a moment. It was like you were simply erased from existence."

"Did you see the woman? The German?"

"No. The room was empty. Come to think of it, I'm not even sure it was the same room."

"So strange," Peter said, trying to understand.

Julie rolled to her knees and sat face-to-face with Peter. She extended her hand, holding the roll of pennies.

"Oh, so you found my stash?"

"Seriously, Peter? All this work for a roll of pennies?"

"It's not just any roll of pennies, Jules. These are special pennies. This roll could potentially be worth millions of dollars-"

"No."

"But all we have to do is hide them now, and . . . wait a minute," Peter leaned forward, his face inches from hers. "You said you walked in just as I slid my hand into the hearth?"

"Yeah, why?"

"That must be it. If you hadn't seen me do it, I don't think anything would have changed. But because you saw what I was doing, another linear shift occurred, even for just a brief moment."

"I don't understand. What shift?"

"When you saw that I was about to make a substantial change in the timeline, your knowing is what shifted our current reality."

"I get that. But how is my knowing so important?"

"I don't know. Maybe it has something to do with what will happen on our mission. When the linear shift occurred, I saw a German officer holding a sub-machine gun. But as soon as I pulled the roll of pennies back out, everything shifted back. So weird."

Peter took the roll of pennies from Julie and moved to the hearthstone.

"Peter, don't!"

"It's okay. I'm not going to leave them there. I just want to see if it will shift again when I try."

Holding the roll of pennies, Peter twisted his hand a quarter turn and slid it into the hole, just as before. He looked directly at Julie, but nothing changed. No tilting of the room, no blurred vision.

"Huh. I was sure that it would have—" Peter began.

"But we both knew you weren't going to leave them in there. It totally negates the fact that a change was going to be made."

Peter nodded in agreement, pulled his hand back out, and slid the pennies into his pocket.

"I'm sure one of the docs can explain it all when we get back to the hotel," Julie said, rolling to her feet.

"No! We can't tell them anything," Peter insisted.

"But why? You're not still planning on going through with this, are you?"

"No, no. I won't. It's not that. We can't tell them anything," Peter said. "Jules, there's something I need to tell you. It's about the mole in Epson's lab. They know about us—our team, our mission, everything."

"Who knows about us?" Julie asked.

"There's this secret society. They call themselves The Global Nation Initiative, and they've known about us from the moment we arrived. My money is on Gallagher, but Stewart is still a suspect."

"Peter, we've been through this. Gerty is a good person. Hell, she even lent me her car to follow you."

"She knows about this too? Jules, what else have you told her?"

"No, she thinks you're off gallivanting around San Francisco, but she doesn't know why. I kept that to myself after I figured things out."

"Well, at least there's that."

"How do you know about this society, anyway?" Julie asked.

"Well, I, uh . . . met their leader. Asher Mandrake. Nice fellow. His thugs? Not so much."

"When did this all happen?" Julie asked, concerned.

"Just this afternoon. I got nabbed by a couple of their guys, and . . . Jules, I've got a *lot* to tell you."

Peter spent the evening telling Julie everything he'd learned from his captivity. After several rounds of Q&A, Julie followed Peter back to their hotel. They hatched a new plan and hoped surprise was on their side.

CHAPTER 17

Peter stepped onto the sidewalk in front of the Perry Hotel, surveying his surroundings. He ignored the pedestrian hordes scurrying like ants about their hill. He focused on the parked vehicles in front of the hotel. One by one, Peter scanned each of the cars, evaluating. On the seventh car, he found them. Two men sitting, watching, waiting. There was no question who they were waiting for.

Satisfied, Peter turned up Powell Street. As he got to the end of the block, he heard the car start and pull into traffic. He smiled. *So far, so good.* He continued his leisurely stroll, only picking up his pace slightly. *Keep comin', fellas.*

After several blocks, Peter slowed as he approached his destination. The heavenly scent of baking bread emanated from the entrance as Peter stepped inside. He found a booth with a view of the street and sat. As he watched the traffic flow outside, he wondered if he'd given Julie enough time for her part of the plan. He could only hope.

Moments later, his pursuers pulled to the curb across the street. Squirrel exited the vehicle, lit a cigarette, and leaned discreetly against the car, staring. He bored a hole through the front window of the bakery. *Hello, boys.* Peter smiled again as he was greeted by the waitress.

"What can I get ya?" she asked.

"Just a coffee, thanks."

She nodded politely, but before she could turn to go, Peter asked, "Where's the men's room?"

"Down the hall, second door on the left."

"Thanks," Peter said. He glanced back toward the waiting car and noticed Squirrel was no longer in sight. Getting impatient, he looked at his wristwatch. It had been twenty minutes since he and Julie carried their bags to the back entrance of the hotel.

"Here you go, dear. Want anything to eat?" the waitress asked, setting a steaming ceramic mug in front of him.

"Excuse me? Oh, no. Just the coffee, thanks."

She pulled out an order pad, scribbled on it, and tore away the page. After dropping his check on the table, she turned and retreated to the kitchen.

Peter glanced at it, saw the coffee was ten cents, and placed a dollar bill on top of the check. Wishing he could see her face when she saw the exorbitant tip, Peter exited the booth and made his way toward the back of the café. As he neared the restrooms, he glanced over his shoulder to see if anyone was watching. Seeing no one, Peter headed straight out the back door. As expected, Julie was parked across the alley.

As he climbed into the passenger seat, Julie asked, "Well? How'd it go?"

"We couldn't have planned it any better," Peter replied. "How about you?"

"After loading the bags in the car, I went back to the room and made one last pass before sliding the letter to the docs under their door. Peter, are you sure we couldn't have told them in person?"

"I'm positive. If we had let them know, they might inadvertently let it slip to Epson, Gallagher, or Stewart. No, we need to split town quietly."

Julie dropped the car into gear but held her foot on the brake. "I guess you're right. It just feels like we're being dodgy with our own friends."

"They're smart enough; they'll figure it out. Now, what time does the train leave?" Peter asked, pulling out the railroad map.

"There's one that leaves for Seattle at 11:14, and there's another at 12:35 for Flagstaff. The last one departs for Ogden, Utah just after 2:00."

It was just before ten in the morning. "We'll, it'll be tight, but let's try to make the first one. We can always head west out of Portland. I want to disappear before Mandrake figures out we're gone."

"Agreed," Julie said as she let off the brake and accelerated through the alley. As she approached the cross street, she stopped, waiting for a break in traffic.

Peter was still looking at the various routes across the United States when Julie suddenly threw the car in reverse and stomped on the gas pedal. "What the—"

"It looks like our friends got impatient for you to come back out," Julie said, nodding toward the alley entrance.

Peter looked up and saw Squirrel staring back, his cigarette barely hanging on to the rim of his lips. As recognition washed over his face, he sprinted out of sight, most likely to join Muscles to continue the tail, or something worse.

Julie surprised him as she deftly swerved the Packard in reverse at such a high speed. Peter hoped no unsuspecting person stepped into the alley. Thankfully, Julie hurtled the car onto the cross street without killing anyone, flinging the steering wheel in the direction of the oncoming traffic. Smashing the brakes, she looked forward, slammed the car in drive, and hit the accelerator.

"Where are they?" Julie begged.

Peter whipped his body around and watched out the small rear window of the coupe. "I don't see them. Hold on—there they are. They're about a block back, but they're gaining!"

"Shit!" Julie exclaimed. "Which way should I go?"

Frustrated at the sudden urgency, Peter managed to maintain his cool. "Just focus on the road. I'll keep an eye on them while I think. Just drive faster."

Julie already had her foot to the floorboard as the Packard roared down the road. "Hold on!" Julie screamed. She blasted through an intersection, launching the car a foot in the air as the road dropped toward the wharf.

"Great, Jules. Head west. Let's try for the Golden Gate Bridge."

Julie leaned on the gas pedal, and with the steep decline in the road, the speedometer rose quickly, inching toward sixty miles an hour.

"Won't that take us in the wrong direction? If we want to make the train—"

"New plan, Jules. Let's lead them away and try to lose them in Sausalito. We can cross the Richmond-San Rafael Bridge and head down into Berkeley."

"No good. That bridge hasn't been built yet. We'll have to take the long way around the bay. If we're lucky, we'll just barely make the last train by the time we get all the way around."

Peter stared out the back window as he considered their options. "They slowed down a bit, but he's still back there. Hang a left on Broadway. There should be less traffic."

"Maybe not. We're pulling away from them heading downhill. If we turn up Broadway, we're going to slow down."

"That's okay. I've got an idea."

Julie passed several blocks before letting off the accelerator and tugging on the steering wheel. She merged into the traffic flow on Broadway with ease.

Peter looked ahead and saw that the traffic was far worse than he'd hoped, but it was too late to change the plan now. "Can you pass some of these—"

Before Peter could finish speaking, Julie swerved into oncoming traffic and passed three cars as she crested the next intersection. Peter glanced back, and just before his vision was cut off, he saw their followers' car screech to a halt and turn up Broadway in pursuit.

"Damn. Almost lost 'em," Peter moaned. "Quick, turn right onto Webster."

Julie skidded toward the intersection and turned just in the nick of time. The steep decline launched them into the air once again, and their angled momentum nearly caused her to lose control.

"Easy, Jules."

"I've got this!" Julie snapped. "Can you see them?"

Peter looked back as Julie made another turn onto Vallejo. With their drop in elevation, it was difficult to see any cars on Broadway. "I think we're good. For now, at least."

Julie spun the steering wheel again and pulled the car into a sublevel garage, stopping inches from the wall of the house.

"Jules?"

"Relax. We're just going to sit here for a bit."

From this position, no one could see their car unless they were on the street directly behind them. "Okay. I think this'll do."

"Come on, Peter. This is genius! They'll never suspect that we parked in someone's garage, let alone Frank's garage."

"Frank?" Peter asked.

"Yeah, this is my stepfather's house in the past . . . er, I mean the future," Julie smirked.

"Ah, very clever. Now, as long as we don't run into the current owner, we'll be okay," Peter said.

Julie nodded, turning the ignition off.

They sat in silence. The only sound was the ping and ticks of the car's exhaust adjusting to the temperature change. Peter glanced at his watch and was surprised to see that it was only 10:15.

How long should we wait? If they left too soon, they might be seen by their pursuers. If they stayed too long, the current homeowner could discover them and either call the police or confront them. Neither were good scenarios. Julie must have been thinking the same thing as she reached for the ignition.

"I think we should backtrack a bit. That's our best option," Peter said.

"Just a few more minutes. With any luck, the goons are still headed up Broadway."

"Either that or they're doubling back. It's hard to say."

Julie nodded and started the car. "Here goes nothing."

Backing up the steep driveway, Julie pulled back onto Vallejo and headed in the direction they came. As she stopped at the intersection, she asked, "What if we head down to the wharf and get lost in a parking lot for an hour or so?"

"That was my first thought, but I think we just need to keep moving. Let's head south for a few blocks and then head east. If we aren't being followed, we should make a beeline to the train station."

Without another word, Julie followed Peter's suggestion and began driving. As she passed Broadway, Peter looked up and down the street for any sign of Asher's minions. Five minutes later, Julie made a left turn. The street was vacant of all traffic, pedestrian or vehicular. Julie continued to drive for several blocks before pulling over.

"Well?"

"I think we did it, Jules. I think we lost 'em," Peter said, patting her leg. "Let's head to the train station and get the hell out of Dodge!"

She looked into his eyes. "Let me catch my breath first. All this excitement has gotten me a little flustered."

Peter returned her gaze, then leaned in and pressed his lips firmly on hers. She responded with equal passion. As they kissed, Peter stroked her hair and she leaned further into his embrace.

As the moments passed, Peter knew they had no time for frivolities, but he couldn't bring himself to pull away. It was Julie that ended the moment of passion. "We, um . . . I think we should continue this once we're on the train. If we plan on catching the 11:14, we'll need to hurry."

Peter held his face only centimeters from Julie's, basking in the moment. "Yeah, I think we definitely need to continue this. But I think we'll be fine catching the next train," he said before kissing her again. "Besides, I like the idea of traveling south instead of north."

Julie fluffed the side of her hair in an attempt at regaining her composure. "Can you drive to the station? That chase really took it out of me."

"Sure thing, Jules. You deserve the rest. Your driving skills were quite impressive, though."

"Driving is not the only thing I'm good at," she said as she swung her leg over Peter's lap, straddling him momentarily. Before shifting the rest of her body to the passenger seat, she kissed him once more while sitting on his lap.

Peter beamed like a schoolboy with a crush. He slid behind the wheel and pulled away from the curb.

Julie sat close to Peter the entire forty-minute drive to the train station. The ride across the bay bridge was breathtaking, and Julie nuzzled his neck as they reached Berkeley.

After unloading their luggage at the curb, Peter parked in a lot across from the train station. By discreetly stashing the keys behind the spare tire, one of the docs could retrieve it as instructed in their letter.

Once Peter returned to Julie, they found a cart for their bags and made their way toward the ticketing counter posthaste.

As they approached the line, neither of them noticed the black sedan pull to the curb. As the car sat idling, Emmett climbed from the back, momentarily stopping to get last-minute instructions from the other passenger. Asher Mandrake glanced toward Peter and Julie and nodded his head before pulling the rear door shut and speeding away.

While standing in line, Peter analyzed their route to New York. As there was no true direct path stretching across the country, he anticipated two transfers along the way.

"Well?" Julie questioned Peter, seeing him look up from the schedule.

"It looks like we'll be good. We'll take the 12:35 to Flagstaff, which continues on to Denver. We could continue on from there through Chicago, and into New York via Philadelphia, or"—Peter paused to flip through a few pages—"or we could stay south and go through Kansas City and a few other stops along the way. Have any preference?"

"No preference here. Whatever you think is fine," Julie said, sliding her arm into Peter's.

"If you don't mind, I have a suggestion," said the man behind them in line.

"Pardon me?" Peter said turning to the stranger.

"I'm sorry. I didn't mean to eavesdrop, but I understand you're heading to New York? I've made this trip many times, and the route through Chicago is much more scenic. Definitely a better way to travel," said the man. "In fact, I'm heading there myself."

"You don't say? Hmm. What do you say, dear? North through Chicago?" Peter asked.

"That's fine, darling. It's been a while since we've been through the Windy City."

"That's it, then. It's settled. Thanks for the advice, uh . . ." Peter said to the man.

"Oh. Emmett. Emmett DuBois. It's my pleasure," Emmett said, extending his hand.

"Peter. And this is Julie, my wife. Pleasure." Peter accepted his hand and shook it firmly. "Perhaps we'll run into one another during the trip."

"I'm sure we will," Emmett replied. "I can almost guarantee it."

Moments later, the ticket agent called "Next," and Peter and Julie stepped forward to secure passage for the next step in the adventure.

PART 4

CHAPTER O

July 24th, 1942

Mr. Mandrake-

As per your request on August 12th, I am sending you this correspondence, outlining my observations of Peter Cooper and Julie Frey's travels from San Francisco.

Fortunately, I was able to make early contact prior to securing passage and boarding the train. That initial meeting, although brief, gave me plausible acceptance with the couple, which opened the way for future conversations throughout the trip across country.

After departing San Francisco, Peter Cooper and Julie Frey (whom I will continually refer to as 'the target couple') remained in their sleeping car for the majority of the first two days. Initially, my sleeping quarters were in a different train car, but I was able to persuade the coachman to relocate me to the same car as theirs, albeit a few compartments away. Being near them gave me the opportunity to closely observe their activities through most of the trip.

During that first day and a half, they remained in their cabin, taking all their meals in privacy. I tried to listen outside their door when I could, but only moaning sounds could be heard. Finally, in late afternoon on the third day, they emerged from seclusion and made their way to the dining car for drinks in the bar. I arrived moments later and was able to reintroduce myself. After a brief dialog, we agreed to dine together. During our dinner conversations, they revealed to me that they were history professors, married to one another, and would be traveling abroad after arriving in New York. I pressed them for more information as delicately as possible, but they remained relatively secretive about their ultimate objectives.

During the remaining few days of the first leg of the trip, they began to spend more and more time outside of their cabin. During the four-hour layover in Denver, the three of us ventured into downtown, which was a mere mile away. During that walk, the two talked as if they'd been there before, but were surprised at how much had changed since their last visit. Had I not known about their time traveling origins, I suppose their observations could possibly come across as odd.

The route from Denver to Chicago passed with two more shared meals and a few chance meetings in the observation car, but no new information could be gleaned. After relocating to the connecting train in Chicago, I was unable to acquire a compartment in the same sleeping car so my precise observation was limited.

The remainder of the trip from Chicago to New York, however, resulted in the most information. I learned that they would be staying in New York while they waited for their travel documents to be prepared. I pressed on about the documents, but they were evasive with their replies.

There was one night in particular that was quite fortuitous. After another mutual dinner, we retired to the bar for an after dinner drink. During that evening, Mr. Cooper inadvertently shared the names of two people that they needed to meet with to obtain their travel documents. I am certain that had he not consumed copious amounts of alcohol that evening, he would never have divulged that information. After that evening, our chance meetings came to mere chance, and we did not dine together again. We happened to meet in the observation car once or twice after that, but Mr. Cooper was much more subdued during future conversations.

Upon arriving in New York, I wished them the best on their travels forward and politely dismissed myself. Once out of sight, I began to follow them covertly. Their first stop was The Riker Hotel, where they booked a room. I was able to bribe the concierge afterward for their room number. I also learned that they had paid for their room until September 4th. Not wanting to be discovered, I booked a room across the street, on the side facing the Riker, so that I could potentially see when they came and went.

Their first night in New York, they had dinner in the hotel dining room, and then retired to their room. As had been true on the train, they remained very amorous. That first night, they failed to close their drapes and I am embarrassed to admit that I watched their night of lovemaking.

The following morning, they had breakfast at the hotel and walked several blocks to another hotel on East 43rd, where they simply walked in, crossed though the lobby and exited on the opposite street. They continued to walk around the hotel along the surrounding sidewalk before reentering. They remained inside the Webster Hotel for nearly twenty minutes before exiting and hailing a cab. I was able to follow them to the Empire State Building, where they became tourists and visited the observation deck. I maintained my distance, but was able to keep them in sight. After an hour of mingling with the crowd on the 102nd floor, they disappeared into the elevator. By the time I was able to follow them down, they were nowhere in sight. My only option was to return to their hotel and wait for them to reappear. On my way there, I stopped back at the Webster Hotel to inquire with the concierge as to the nature of their earlier visit. After a small bribe, I learned that the couple that Peter had mentioned on the train were staying in that hotel, and that Peter and Julie had inquired about them.

Upon returning to my hotel, I waited in the main floor café until the targets stepped out of a cab around four in the afternoon. I retreated to my own hotel room only to catch another episode of their romantic diversions. Deciding that there wasn't much to be learned from their lovemaking, I ventured back to the Webster Hotel to see what more I could learn out about the mystery couple. Having no idea what they looked like, I inquired with the concierge on duty that evening to indicate to me who they were as I hid behind a newspaper in the lobby. After I had waited for several hours, they were discretely pointed out to me when they returned. I casually followed them into the elevator and struck up a conversation with them. I learned that he was a propaganda officer with the Army, and she was his assistant. They were on station until their departure for France on September 4th.

At first I was confused by my targets' visit to the hotel, the purpose of which seemed only to inquire about the other couple's identity. Armed with this latest bit of intel, I surmised that my targets planned to appropriate the other couple's identities and travel papers in order to board the boat to France. Over the next several days, I continued to follow and observe the target couple and concluded that my original deduction was correct, as it appeared that they were observing the daily activities of the mystery couple. It appeared to me that they were looking for some kind of rhythm in their behavior—almost as if they were waiting for the right time to apprehend them.

The days passed, and their travel date approached. I knew that my targets would be making the grab without delay, but they only continued to observe. They must have had a plan, but for the life of me, I could not figure it out. Finally, going against your specific instruction not to interfere with their intention of traveling to France, I intervened. Having spent a considerable amount of time with the couple on the train ride to New York, I concluded that my targets were of the nonviolent type, and were most certainly challenged by how they would obtain the travel papers from the mystery couple. A few nights before their departure, I broke away from following my targets, and met up with the mystery couple. Certain that I wasn't being watched, I was able to 'take care' of the situation. The less you know about what happened to them, the better. I was able to secure their room key and locate the travel documents and leave them in plain sight. I packed their bags and left them sitting next to the armoire.

The following day, my targets made their move. They took a cab to the Webster and were in and out of the hotel room within ten minutes. The look of surprise on their faces was something to behold, but they were still very cautious. After hailing another cab, they traveled throughout Manhattan for an entire afternoon, not stopping for too long at any one place. Finally they returned to their hotel, and I to mine. I could see them analyze the documents from my room, and it looked like things were finally proceeding to their plan.

The remainder of their time in New York was spent in their hotel room. I can only imagine what their room service tab was like.

On September 4, Mr. Cooper and Ms. Frey boarded the *Queen Mary* and joined a convoy of ships scheduled to cross the Atlantic. Prior to eliminating the mystery couple, I was able to determine the targets' destination, assuming that they do not deviate from their travel documentation. After a stop in Casablanca, the *Queen Mary* is scheduled to arrive in Sete, France on September 21st.

With my current assignment at an end, I shall remain in New York until I receive further instructions.

Regards,

Emmett DuBois

CHAPTER 1

As Peter drove his battered Astro van toward his house, he was astonished that nothing had changed since he had returned to 2013. He had traveled back in time, completed his mission with expert precision, and returned to his own time. He had expected that something would be different—anything to make it appear that the whole ordeal had been worth it. But as he drove toward his home—to his family—everything seemed abnormally regular. He noticed that certain landmarks or instances from his own past still remained, but were slightly different.

Just then, Peter passed the intersection of Forest and Windermere and recognized the repaired streetlight. The very streetlight that had played an inactive part in the horrific accident involving his wife several years previously. He'd almost expected to see it differently once he'd returned, regardless of what Applegate had told him. Applegate had said that even though certain things would change from what Peter remembered, some things would inevitably remain the same. And that there was no scientific way to determine what changes had taken place.

Peter pushed the sorrowful thoughts of his dead wife from his mind, and turned into his neighborhood. As he maneuvered through the vaguely familiar streets, he finally began to see some variances. He was still a dozen blocks from his own home when the first major anomaly presented itself. A familiar house that was one of his favorites in the neighborhood wasn't there. It just didn't exist. In its place stood a more modern version of the house. Instead of to the traditional bungalow he remembered, it was a concrete and stucco monstrosity. It didn't fit the neighborhood or the surrounding homes. With each additional block he drove, more of the bizarre homes began to appear.

Finally, as he pulled onto his own street, things seemed to get back to normal. His neighbor's house was as he remembered, and so was his own. He pulled up to the curb and shut off the engine. For the first time since returning through Epson's time machine Peter felt anxiety. He wasn't sure what he expected to see when he walked in. Applegate had warned him that his family might be different—even by the slightest margin, and that he should be prepared for the worst. Taking a deep breath, Peter slid from behind the wheel and made for the front door.

As he approached the front door, he recognized the rosebushes that he and Minnie had planted the year before her accident. They were growing vibrantly now, and he could even see where he had pruned them not more than three weeks ago. Peculiar. When he stepped onto the wooden porch floor, the familiar creak echoed, and he knew everything was going to be fine. He smiled and pushed open the front door.

Stepping inside, Peter instantly sensed a strangeness that he couldn't quite put his finger on. He glanced down to the floor and saw a pile of mail that had been dropped through the mail slot. Picking it up, he scanned the various envelopes and noticed that they were all addressed to him. He tossed them on the table in the foyer and moved further into the house. As he turned the corner into the kitchen, his heart rose into his throat at what he saw before him.

"DADDY!" screamed Tori.

Peter looked around the room, and saw that Brett was tied to a dining chair, and Tori was being held by the very same female German soldier who had existed in his *linear shift* experience back in 1942.

"Velcome beck, Mr. Cooper," said the soldier. "We've been expecting you." She stood, holding a pistol to the temple of Tori's head.

Peter's anxiety shot through the roof as he quickly analyzed the situation. He couldn't think clearly. All he could see was the fear in Tori's face as her tears dropped to the floor.

"What? What is it that you want?" Peter begged. "Whatever it is, please leave my kids out of it."

"It's you thet ve vant, Mr. Cooper," she said, thrusting Tori forward as they both moved toward him. Brett wiggled in his chair, trying to break free, but his bindings were too tight.

Peter glanced around for something—some kind of advantage. All he could see were dishes and silverware sitting on the kitchen counters. He moved slightly toward the kitchen island before he replied.

"Why me? What is it that I can do? Whatever it is, just let my kids go, and I'll go peacefully," Peter said, stepping further into the kitchen. Out of the corner of his eye, he saw what he wanted. What he needed. The butcher block full of knives.

"Halt! Do not make another move," snapped the German.

Peter froze mere inches from the knives.

The soldier twisted Tori's body in front of her own, so that she was a living shield between herself and Peter.

"Hey, hey," Peter protested. "I'm just standing here. I'm not going to do anything." He rested his hands on the kitchen counter, hoping to show he was no threat.

"Ve know you can travel through time. You must go back and fix this mess!"

"I ... I don't know what you're talking about. I'm an architect, not a time traveler," Peter said as he threw his hands up in exasperation. Before dropping them down, he tossed a quick wink at Tori. She nodded slightly a split second before Peter dropped his hands and grabbed the 8-inch cleaver from the butcher block.

The soldier jumped back, yanking Tori with her. Tori screamed.

As the soldier shuffled her feet backward, Brett did the only thing he could—he tossed his foot out, tripping the crazy German.

Everything moved so quickly. Peter lunged toward them, pointing the cleaver toward the soldier. As he dove toward her, the gun discharged, forcing Peter to close his eyes tightly. The loud report dissipated quickly and Peter regained focus. It was too late, though, as Tori slipped to the floor, blood oozing from the side of her head.

"No!" Peter screamed. He began to thrash, screaming over and over again, "NO! NO! Oh God, NO!"

Peter rushed to Tori's limp body and dropped to his knees. He slipped her delicate hand into his own and cried, "You've taken her. You've taken her from me!" Peter closed his eyes tight, forcing his tears to fall. "Why? Why, oh why?"

Peter felt a hand gently rub his shoulder and shake him slightly. "Why what, Peter? It's okay. I'm right here."

Peter rolled over and looked into Julie's eyes. He lurched up, tossing the covers from his naked body. He brought his hands to his face, and there were no tears. He rubbed the sleep from his eyes and looked around. He was lying next to Julie in a drably colored room.

"What, where ... Where are we?" Peter asked, not fully awake from his nightmare.

"It's okay, Peter. You just had a bad dream, is all. You scared the shit out of me, though. Probably scared the people in the room next door as well."

Peter looked back at Julie as reality finally began to seep in. He was safe. "We're in France?"

"Yes, dear. We arrived late last night. We checked into the hotel and fell right into bed," Julie said as she continued to rub his shoulder.

He leaned back, dropping his head into the pillow. "We're safe. We made it," Peter said, remembering more.

"That must have been some doozy of a dream," Julie said. "Of course we're safe. We were really never in danger."

"That was no dream. It was a hellish nightmare. They killed Tori."

"Who killed Tori?"

"It was that German soldier. The one I told you about, when I tried to hide the pennies?"

"Yes, I remember. But that wasn't real either," Julie said.

"It wasn't real to you, but it certainly was real to me—at the time," Peter said, rubbing his eyes again, thankful that the nightmare was fleeting from his mind. "My God, it just seemed so real."

Julie slid her hand across Peter's stomach as she rested her head on his bare chest. "It'll pass quickly enough. Until then, we should start to think about food. Skipping dinner last night and heading straight for dessert has left me famished," she said with a giggle.

Peter's senses had fully returned to him and visions of the night before filled his mind. They had in fact waved off dinner and had gone directly to their room, and right into bed. Spending two weeks apart on the boat from New York had been taxing on his manhood. The previous three years of sexual dry spell were nothing compared to being away from Julie on the boat. The moment they entered the room, their clothes had flown off, and passion had taken over.

He smiled and began to stroke her hair.

"That feels good," Julie admitted as she caressed Peter's chest.

Peter kissed the top of Julie's head and pulled her tight against himself, feeling her warm skin against his. She leaned her head back and accepted another kiss from him, this time on her open and waiting mouth. Their hunger for breakfast was overtaken by their hunger for each other. Food could wait.

CHAPTER 2

Peter dug through his suitcase, looking for the journal he'd bought in New York. It was the quintessential impulse purchase, but with so much going on with the mission, he'd felt he needed to record some of his thoughts along the way. It had been years since he'd kept a journal regularly—from when Minnie was still alive, when he'd had aspirations of being a writer. Those hopes and dreams had vanished along with his wife. Peter hoped to renew his passion for writing, as he was certainly creating an entire new life for himself and his family by accomplishing this mission.

Finally, at the bottom of the suitcase, Peter's hand grasped the leather-bound ledger tucked underneath too many pairs of itchy wool pants. He pulled it out and tossed his clothing back in, orderly enough to get the suitcase to close once again. As he sat at the side table to write, the door leading to the hallway opened. Peter looked up to see Julie step in, her eyes immediately focusing on the open journal.

"No, sir. No time for that this morning. If you hadn't wanted seconds of last night's indulgence this morning," Julie said playfully, "you'd be fine. But seeing as it's nearly eleven in the morning, I think we should check the train schedule and get a bite to eat."

Peter sighed as his shoulders slumped against the chair.

"But, Mom. Just a little?" He winked at her as she stowed her toiletries in her suitcase before leaning in and kissing him on the cheek.

He leaned into her kiss, wondering if they had time for a third round.

"Maybe, if you're good, you can write once we get on the train."

As he listened to her plea, he could feel his stomach rumble and realized that nourishment was a priority.

"Okay, but only if you promise," Peter said before closing the journal and sliding it in the front pocket of his suitcase.

———————————

They stepped out of their hotel and began walking in the direction of the train station. They had passed it on the way to the hotel the night before, just a few blocks away. As they walked, Julie slid her hand into Peter's, weaving her fingers with his. He smiled and gently squeezed her hand.

Peter had been to France once before while traveling abroad for a semester in college. His academic trip had been through northern France, so he was delighted to be in such a historic town as Sete. If he hadn't known better, he'd have thought they were in Venice because of the canals snaking throughout the small town.

Despite the country being at war, Peter was happy to see so many locals out, milling about. There was a level of military presence, but it wasn't at all overpowering. Unless you were looking for them specifically, the Vichy Army were barely in sight.

Just as those thoughts crossed Peter's mind, a military convoy turned up the street that he and Julie were walking on, forcing them to step back onto the sidewalk. There were six troop-hauling vehicles and two jeeps in the caravan, and as nearly all the pedestrians stopped to stare as they drove by, none of the soldiers paid them any attention.

Peter glanced back to Julie. Her concern was clear on her face.

"I'm sure it's nothing. Probably just a routine sweep of the town to show solidarity to the villagers," Peter said, trying to convince himself at the same time.

Julie nodded but said nothing.

They continued along the cobblestone street, and all the while, the reality of the situation began to sink in. They were in the middle of a war. A war in which 60 million people would die before it was over. Peter recalled those statistics from one of the many briefings the general had given during their limited training. What was most startling about that statistic was that nearly 40 million of those deaths were civilians. Folks just like him and Julie. They could certainly end up being a statistic if they weren't careful.

Peter pushed those thoughts aside as they walked by one of a half dozen restaurants or cafés he'd noticed since leaving the hotel.

"How about this place for lunch?"

Julie didn't respond right away, and Peter assumed she was having similar thoughts.

"Hmm? Oh, yes. This'll be fine," she replied. "Let's check out the train situation first. If we can catch an early departure, we might even make it to Oradour-sur-Glane before nightfall."

"You do realize that we're in 1942, right?" Peter questioned sarcastically. "It's most likely going to be a two-day trip."

"Yeah, that's what I meant. Nightfall tomorrow," Julie replied with a wink. "I only wish Applegate's historical data included this leg of travel. I know we're a few weeks away from intercepting that memo, but I want to get there sooner rather than later."

"Having an off-chance meeting with a distant member of your family has nothing to do with that either, am I correct?"

"I have no idea what you're talking about," Julie pouted. "I know the risks, because Applegate incessantly reminded me about them before we left. I promise to be a good girl."

They stepped back across the street as the train station came into view. As they approached, they could see a passenger train stretching out from behind the station.

"Before we head back to the hotel, I'd like to pick up a newspaper as well," Peter said as they moved past a soldier walking away from the station.

"What do you need a paper for?"

"Nothing important. I'd like to make note of a few things from this time in my journal, is all."

When they walked into the station, they found it busier than either of them had anticipated. The line to the ticket counter was nearly twenty people deep. The line to reach the platform was almost twice as long.

"Well, then. I think we're close to boarding time. Any chance we'll make the train today?" Julie asked.

"I suppose we should first find out if this train is even heading in our direction before we start to rush."

"Agreed. I'll go wait in line if you want to go get your newspaper," Julie suggested, pointing to a small newsstand across the station lobby.

"Great thinking, Jules. I'll join you shortly," Peter said, then turned away.

"And, Peter," Julie called after him. "Don't forget we're in France. Be sure to use you French speaking voice." She winked at him. He smiled before heading through the crowded terminal.

Julie looked around and found the shortest of the ticketing lines and began to make her way through the crowd herself.

"*Excusez-moi*," she said in French as she stepped around an elderly couple. She repeated the apology several times as she made her way toward the line. As she bobbed and weaved through the crowd, she wondered why so many people were boarding the trains.

As she neared the line, she found a number of gentlemen with their backs toward her, blocking her way. "*Excusez-moi. Puis-je obtenir par?*" Julie asked.

A man in a suit turned and said, "Why, certainly you can get by," in perfect English.

Julie froze in alarm. How was it that this man had known she'd understand English? Perhaps he'd overheard her and Peter talking before they split up.

"*Excusez-moi?*"

"It's quite all right, Ms. Frey. I'm sure there'll be plenty of time to catch tomorrow's train," replied the stranger.

"I'm sorry, do you know me?"

"In a roundabout way. My name is Asher Mandrake."

Feeling the blood drain from her face, Julie went numb at hearing the name.

"I see by your reaction that Peter has told you about me. Have no fear, Ms. Frey. I mean you no harm."

"But how did you ..."

"It's easy. Peter told me everything."

"I doubt that. I think ... you guessed and got lucky." Julie paused a moment to consider another option. "Or you had us followed."

Mandrake smiled. "How I arrived at your destination is irrelevant. I am here merely to ensure that you two had a safe trip."

"You traveled halfway around the world to see that we arrived safely? Somehow, I once again doubt that."

"Your skepticism is certainly understandable, but it is unwarranted," Mandrake said.

Peter stepped up to the newsstand and perused the various editions of newspapers offered for sale. *La Depeche, Paris-soir, Le Martin*, as well as *Stars and Stripes* were all present. All emblazoned with news of the war. He certainly hadn't traveled through time and halfway around the world to find a newspaper written in English, so he picked up a copy of *Paris-soir* and handed the clerk a coin from his pocket. The two nodded at a completed transaction, and Peter retreated without having to say a single word in French.

He looked across the terminal and saw Julie sitting on a bench, staring into the ether. He wondered how she could have made it through that enormous line so quickly. Suddenly, a man walked though his gaze, and for the briefest of moments, Peter could have sworn it was Squirrel. He quickly shifted his gaze toward the man, but he was gone. Anxiety began to creep into the back of mind, but he quickly dismissed the notion completely. The odds of Squirrel, or Muscle for that matter, being in France were slim.

He maneuvered his way toward Julie, being polite as possible along the way. As he stepped around the last of the crowd separating him from Julie, he noticed that the look on her face was now laced with fear.

"It's okay, Jules. We can catch the next train out tomorrow," Peter said.

"I. Um ..." Julie stammered, still looking straight ahead.

"Julie? What's wrong?" Peter asked, but got no response. He lowered himself onto the bench next to her before following her gaze. Sitting across the aisle from Julie was the cause for her alarm.

"Good morning, Peter," Mandrake said before standing up. "Or should I say *bonjour?*"

Peter bolted upright. "What are you doing here?"

"Well, Peter, you really left me no choice. I thought we had a deal, and the next thing I hear is that you two have skipped town."

"Our train schedule moved up. Out of our control. Sorry about that," Peter replied, less than sympathetic.

"Does Ms. Frey here know about our deal, Peter?" Mandrake asked.

Peter looked at Julie momentarily before returning his glare to Mandrake. "Yes. I told her everything ... after our *conversation.*"

"Good. Then she's aware that you two might be stuck here in 1942 unless you can come out of this country victorious."

Peter stepped forward, narrowing the gap between himself and Mandrake. "Do you think it's wise to speak so openly about this?"

Mandrake glanced around the crowded terminal. "No, I suppose you're right. Perhaps we should take the conversation someplace a little more private. I know just the place."

CHAPTER 3

At a sidewalk café near the train station, Peter and Julie sat rigid across from a relaxed Mandrake.

"So, tell me, Ms. Frey," Mandrake began. "Have you been to France before?"

Julie glanced at Peter before responding. He nodded his head, agreeing that it was all right to share a bit of their past. "Yes. I have. A number of times."

Mandrake nodded as the waiter left a loaf of bread and a dish of oil-covered olives before retreating. Once the waiter was out of earshot, Mandrake continued. "And how does it compare across the span of time between your visits?"

Julie shrugged, not entirely in the mood for small talk. "As different as one might expect."

Mandrake nodded again before focusing on Peter. "And you, Peter? Have you been to the region before?"

"How about we cut the crap, Asher? What is it you really want here?"

"As I told Ms. Frey a few minutes ago, I just flew in to check on the two of you, seeing as we didn't have a chance to talk further before you left."

"And as I already stated, our departure was out of our control," Peter lied. "We had no time to ask for your permission and all. You know how it goes."

"There's no reason to be sarcastic, Peter. I'm just concerned that our agreement might be in jeopardy. We reach an agreement one day, and you flee the city the next. What am I to think?"

Peter remained silent.

"I'll tell you. I think you two have much bigger plans than the historical research line you gave me in my office." Mandrake paused long enough to sip from his glass of water. "I agree, Peter. We should cut the crap. Just tell me what you two have planned, or ..."

"Or what? Or you'll sic one of your cronies on us? Pull our fingernails out until we talk? Is that it?"

Mandrake winced at the image Peter had painted with his words. "No, Peter. Our society is non-violent. I am, however, prepared to take you two back to the US if you don't cooperate."

Peter smiled. "Feeble words, Asher. I know you want this war over sooner rather than later, and if there is the slimmest of chances that Julie and I can make that happen ... Well, I know you'll leave us to our business."

Mandrake studied Peter for a long moment before replying. "You're right, Peter. I won't take you two captive, and I won't interfere with whatever your plan is. Just know this—I will be watching you. I'll know what you're doing every step of the way. If whatever it is that you two are up to seems the least bit disingenuous to our country and the success of the war, believe you me, I will not hesitate to put a halt to your escapades by whatever means I deem necessary." Mandrake leaned forward, his eyes drilling a hole in the back of Peter's head. "Do I make myself clear?"

Peter held Mandrake's steely gaze a moment longer before looking down at the plate of food at the center of the table. He picked up his fork, stabbed an olive. He held the fork inches from his mouth, and just before he took the bite, he replied, "Yeah, we hear you. Crystal clear." Peter then shoved the salty fruit into his mouth before dropping the fork onto his plate.

As Peter chewed, Mandrake released his tense stare and

leaned back into his chair.

"Now, if you don't mind, Julie and I would like to be alone for the rest of our meal," Peter said, motioning for Mandrake to leave.

Mandrake stared at Peter with a bemused look. He then folded his napkin into quarters before placing it on the table in front of him. He stood, but before he walked away he spoke once more.

"Just remember, Peter. My reach extends far and wide. One slip-up, and I can snatch the both of you back faster than a snap of my fingers," Mandrake said as he demonstrated the action with his hand. When neither Peter or Julie responded, Mandrake walked away down the sidewalk.

Peter watched him until he was completely out of sight. Moments later, he could see Squirrel and Muscle trotting to catch up.

"Okay, I get your point with that guy," Julie said. "What a piece of work."

Peter turned to face Julie. "How did he find us? I've said nothing about where we were going."

"I haven't said a word either."

"Not even to Gerty? You two certainly spent a lot of time together. Maybe you let it slip."

"No, Peter. I haven't said anything. Why is it that you don't trust her?"

Peter shrugged. "Lately, I'm not sure who I can trust."

"You trust me, right? When I tell you she's fine, you'd better believe it," Julie snapped, her voice louder than either of them expected.

Peter placed his hand on Julie's. "I trust you, Jules. It's just the others that I'm not sure about."

Julie didn't reply. She slipped an olive into her mouth and chewed slowly.

"New plan. I think we should get something to eat. I mean a full meal here. Then we should split up and find another means of transportation."

"But the train will take us into Oradour-sur-Glane in a day or two."

"Yeah, and Mandrake will certainly have someone on that train with us. We need to get out of his grasp ... again. It's just you and me from this point forward. I think we need to deviate a little from our plan. If we drive straight to Oradour-sur-Glane, we might not be able to complete our mission without Mandrake interfering."

Julie nodded. "What do you suggest?"

"I think we need to zigzag our way to Oradour-sur-Glane. If that means it'll take us a few days longer to reach the town, then so be it. We've got time to burn before the memo is set to go out, anyway. Let's take advantage of it."

"We could still do that on the train," Julie pointed out.

"Yes, but that would still allow whoever it is that Mandrake has following us to keep tabs on our every move. No, I think we need a car."

"And how do you expect to get a car in 1942 France?"

Peter smiled at Julie. He tossed another olive into his mouth and said, "We'll steal one if necessary. What are they going to do? Arrest us? They'll be more concerned with the war than dealing with a stolen car."

Julie shook her head. "You're certifiable, you know that?"

CHAPTER 4

Journal entry #12, September 24, 1942

Julie and I finally reached Sete after a far too long boat ride across the Atlantic. If the ocean liner had been cruising around in my own time, the trip would have most certainly been much more relaxing. But because the world is at war, everyone was on edge. Even though we've landed in an unoccupied seaport in France, the country is still heavily occupied by the Nazis.

There's a sentence that I never imagined I'd ever write.

So, yeah, we arrived last night, and since I'd been separated from Jules for the last two-plus weeks, our animal instincts took over, and we made up for lost time. What can I say— I think I'm wild for that woman. And the best part? I think she feels the same about me. But who really knows. I've been off base before.

Right now, it's a little before 10:00 p.m. here, and we're still in this little French hotel we stayed at last night. Our initial plan was to spend just the one night here, and then be on the train to Oradour-sur-Glane today. Well, plans change. And today was no exception.

Despite our best efforts, that bastard Mandrake seems to fuck everything up. To say we weren't caught off guard today would be a lie.

For now, I think we're okay, but Julie and I cannot effectively complete our mission with him and his goons following every move we make. Oh, yeah, he brought Muscle and Squirrel with him. Those two are about as dumb as a stump. With their sudden appearance here, we're going to be forced to do something deviating from our initial plan. Something that I'd never thought possible. We're going to steal a car. Both Jules and I tried to find a car to buy or borrow to get to the next town at least, but it's nearly extortion what these locals want for a simple ride of 200 kilometers. The fact is, nobody wants to do it. They're afraid of being consumed by the war. I suppose I can't blame them. So Julie and I scouted the town, and we've settled on an older Fiat that's a half dozen blocks away. It's nestled in between a small café and an abandoned factory of some sort. We watched the car from a distance most of the afternoon, and it appears to be used by a nearby business. From what we could tell, it will run, and all we can hope is that it has enough gas to get us to the next town. Once we're out of Sete, we can reevaluate the situation.

Well, that's enough for now. We're planning on getting a few hours of shut-eye before the big heist around 3:00 in the morning.

Peter stood in the shadows of the moonlit night. Making the quarter-mile hike through the sleepy French town was the easy part. The hard part was yet to come.

After standing in silence for nearly thirty minutes, Peter was confident there were no prying eyes in the vicinity. As he stepped to the side of the car, he slipped out a pocket knife and extended the blade in one swift motion. Before slicing the ragtop of the Fiat, Peter first tried both the driver and passenger side door handles. Locked. Without missing a beat, Peter placed the tip of the knife at the lower right corner of the rear tonneau cover and pushed the blade through. The polished steel of the blade reflected glints of moonlight before disappearing into the canvas. With a little back and forth movement, Peter was able to create an opening large enough for him to crawl through and gain access.

After a final glance around the shadowy alley, Peter separated the opening and slipped inside the car. Thankfully, the space behind the front seats was empty, otherwise he'd have had some difficulty maneuvering inside the cramped interior of the Italian two-seater. Once inside, he climbed into the front seat and dropped straight to the floor beneath the dash. On his way down, he quickly familiarized himself with the dash layout, noting the location of the ignition switch. Peter sighed as the challenging part was upon him.

Reaching up, Peter felt through the wires and cables hidden behind the dash. It only took a minute to find the right cluster. The ignition wires were practically invisible to him in the darkness. As he pulled them down for better access, he felt each of the three wires. After tracing the smallest wire to the instrument cluster, he sliced it free and removed a portion of its sheathing. The next wire he felt for was the largest in diameter—the power wire. He quickly repeated the cut-and-splice procedure. With those two wires ends exposed, Peter twisted them together, instantly noticing a glow from various lights and gauges on the dash. Finally, he cut and exposed the last of the three wires—the starter wire.

With the main procedure of hot-wiring complete, Peter unfolded his body from beneath the dash and into the driver's seat. A quick seat adjustment and he was ready to roll. He gently held the exposed wires before mumbling, "Here goes nothing."

The moment he touched the two exposed wires together, a spark flashed brightly beneath the dash as the starter engaged. Even though he'd been prepared for the event, Peter forgot about the clutch, and the car lurched forward as the starter engaged with the engine. He quickly pulled the wires free and put his foot on the brake. With his other foot now on the clutch, he touched the wires together once again, and the starter turned freely, forcing the engine to life.

The sound of the four-cylinder engine was much louder than Peter had anticipated. He quickly slipped the car into reverse and backed out of the alley. Once on the street, he hit the light switch and proceeded down the road. Glancing in the rearview mirror, Peter saw no house lights illuminate. After he'd gone several blocks, he was confident that nobody had been roused by the sound of the engine. Peter turned toward the hotel and his waiting companion.

As Peter pulled to the curb, Julie stepped out, carrying the first of their two luggage pieces. Peter set the brake but left the car running while he helped Julie with the other bag.

"Any problems?" Julie asked.

"Piece of cake. Other than a little surgical precision on the ragtop, everything went as planned."

Peter grabbed the bag from Julie and slid it behind the driver's seat. While inside the car, he reached across and unlocked the passenger door. By the time he made it around to the other side, Julie was coming back out of the hotel with their other bag. As Peter took that bag from her, he heard a loud yell.

"*Arrêtez!*" echoed from down the street.

Both Peter and Julie glanced up and saw a man running toward them. He was still a few blocks away, but was coming from the direction of the heist.

"Shit!" Peter exclaimed.

"No problems, huh?" Julie asked sarcastically.

"Well, none till now," Peter snapped. He threw the bag behind the passenger seat before climbing across and into the driver's seat. Julie jumped in and the wheels were rolling before Julie's door closed. The momentum of the car lurching forward launched the suicide door fully open. Peter tapped the brake long enough to swing the door closed before hitting the accelerator again.

Peter shot past the man running toward them, most likely the car's owner. At the end of the block, Peter yanked the wheel and headed north, toward the road out of town. Within minutes, they were cruising along the vacant streets, the only sound coming from the rumble of the engine.

"Well, that was fun," Julie said.

"What? I thought I zigzagged enough before doubling back. Hell, I even drove several blocks the other way before I came back to the hotel," Peter confessed.

"Mmm-hmm," Julie mumbled. "You think he saw our faces?"

"Hell, Jules. Does it really matter?"

Julie didn't reply right away. "Yeah, I guess not." She looked out the window at the passing village buildings. "I still don't know why we had to steal a car in the first place."

"It's like I said. If we paid someone for a ride into the next town, there'd be a trail. Don't we want to get away from Mandrake's grasp?"

"Mmm-hmm."

Peter ignored her cynicism and focused on the dark road ahead. By his estimation, they'd reach the next town by sunrise. He leaned back and enjoyed the silence.

CHAPTER 5

The sky above faded from dark cobalt toward the west to a warm salmon hue in the east. The sun was rising. Peter anticipated another thirty minutes' drive time through the French countryside before they pulled into Castelnaudary.

Julie was fast asleep, and had been so for most of the drive. He glanced over and saw her legs pulled tight to her chest and her head leaning against the side window. He smiled, and knew then that once they were back in their own timeline, they would discuss their future together with the kids. The choice was inevitably his, but having come so far back from the bottom of the bottle, he wanted their approval. He needed their approval. He'd been unhappy for far too long, and he felt he could have a future with Julie.

Focusing ahead once again, he crested a hill, and for the first time, Peter could begin to see civilization return to the barren land. He'd always imagined that the French countryside was more picturesque than what he'd seen over the last three hours. Granted, the bleakness of night had masked most of the scenery, but now that the sun was rising, he wasn't terribly impressed.

Peter came upon a curve in the road that forced him to downshift before pulling on the steering wheel. The four-cylinder engine rattled louder as he re-engaged the clutch, causing Julie to stir.

"Mmm. Time is it?" she mumbled without opening her eyes.

Glancing at his watch, Peter replied, "Just before six in the morning. Did you have a good sleep?"

Julie lifted her head and squinted her eyes open, looking at the terrain all around them. She stretched her legs, pressing her feet to the floorboard. "Like a baby. Want me to drive for a while? You've been behind the wheel all night."

Peter shook his head. "No need. we're close. I'll grab some shut-eye once we have a place to lay our heads for a few days."

"Suit yourself," she said, leaning her head onto his shoulder as he drove.

———— ◦∕ ————

Twenty minutes later they pulled into the small town of Castelnaudary. From what Peter could see, their hospitality choices looked grim. He glanced at Julie's face and saw the same worried look he'd been wearing displayed in the furrow of her brow.

"It can't be that bad, right?" he asked, trying to stay positive.

"Well, I've been here before, and I know of a few boarding houses ..." She paused and shook her head. "But that was a few years ago, in our timeline."

"It doesn't look like we've got much of a choice. Let's start looking closer to the train station. It'd make sense to have a hotel or something near there."

Julie nodded. "Sounds logical to me."

Peter had followed along the rail line as they pulled into the small town. As they neared the train station, worry crept over him as he passed a number of barricaded side streets running parallel to the approaching platform.

"Hmm. What do you suppose those are for?" Julie asked.

"It's probably just precautionary. We *are* in the middle of a war."

"Yeah, I suppose," Julie replied, but said nothing further. She just stared at the gray military vehicles parked behind the barricades.

Peter slowed the Fiat, turned up the first side street that wasn't blocked off, and pulled to the side of the road. He reached up under the dash and untwisted the ignition wires, and the engine cut off, leaving them in an eerie silence.

"You think it's too early to go knocking on doors, looking for a room?" Peter asked.

"That there, it reads *room-for-let*." Julie pointed to the faded words stenciled across the side of a rundown brick cottage a few houses away from where they were parked. "I'd think we should start there."

Peter nodded as he surveyed the rest of the quiet street. "Okay, then. We'll park the car down near the train station and then walk back here."

"Why not just leave it here? Are you concerned ..." Julie began.

"We can't be too careful. I'm not exactly sure how grand theft auto works in France, or if it was even a big deal in 1942, but I'm not willing to take a chance."

Peter leaned forward and sparked the wires together, and once again they were moving along the cobblestone streets. Ten minutes later, he and Julie walked side by side, carrying their baggage, heading for the boarding house.

———————～———————

Peter pulled his journal from the side pocket of his suitcase and dropped it on the nightstand next to his twin bed. A plume of dust kicked up as he did so. Ignoring the lack of cleanliness, he fell onto the bed, and the moment his head hit the pillow, he could feel his eyelids being pulled closed, as if magnets were forcing them together. Before he succumbed to sleep, though, he glanced across the room at Julie, who was sliding her suitcase under her own twin bed.

"Don't you think we could just slide the beds together?" she asked.

"Sure thing, Jules. We'll do that first thing tomorrow. Right now, I'm spent. If I don't get some shut-eye, I might drop my cover and start speaking English, and ask who won the Super

Bowl last year."

"You do know it's already tomorrow? It's a little after nine in the morning."

Peter's eyes had just closed, but he was still in the conversation. "I know, I know. Just a few hours' sleep, and I'll be good as new. We'll get up and have a late lunch, then we'll start planning ..." Peter's words drifted as exhaustion overtook him.

Julie grinned. "That sounds like a well-thought-out plan," she said as she leaned down and kissed him on the forehead.

He puckered his lips and made a kissing face toward her without even opening his eyes. He was unconscious a minute later.

"Stop. Right. There!" the German soldier said as she pressed the barrel of her gun against Tori's temple.

Peter did as he was told, and dropped his hands onto the kitchen counter. He looked around and recognized the room as his own kitchen, feeling a wave of Déjà-vu course through his mind.

"Whatever it is you want, just let my kids go," Peter said, recognizing those exact words as if he'd just said them moments before.

The German woman twisted Tori's body in front of her, using her as a human shield. "You know what ve vant."

Peter thought for a moment. He knew the answer, but he couldn't pick it out of the jumbled thoughts dancing through his mind. "Um, you want me to ... go somewhere? You want me to travel? Back in time? Is that right?" he asked, predicting the soldier's next few words.

"Very good, Mr. Cooper. If you vant to see your children again, you go now!"

"But. Um." Peter blinked at his young daughter, at her pleading eyes. "I'm not a time traveler. I'm just an ordinary architect—"

The German soldier lifted Tori high in the air by her collar, adjusting the gun around her face. "You must change the history of time," the woman screeched at him in a harsh German accent.

Peter reached back toward the wall. He felt the room tilt. His son, tied up at the dining room table, and his daughter across from him, with the gun directly in her face, pleaded with him: *Save us. Save us.* But he couldn't. The room started to darken around him. He tried to force himself to see it all—the dining room table he and his wife had picked out, the German woman's finger pointed directly at him...

He then felt a hand on his back. Chaos surged through his head. He felt sweat rising to his forehead in great drips. They descended down his nose. He realized that his throat was vibrating—that he was very nearly crying. "TORI!" he screamed. "BRETT!"

"Shh," came a familiar voice, echoing in his ear. "Shh."

He blinked several times, recognizing the small, European-style hotel room around him. He gasped, tasting stale oxygen. "Julie?" he whispered. He spun onto his back to see Julie next to him, wearing her thin nightgown, rubbing his back. "What's going on?"

"You were having a dream," she murmured.

"The German woman—" Peter sputtered. "She wants me to change something from history. She said—she said I'll never see my kids again if—"

Julie shook her head. Her small face scrunched into a worried, skeptical look. She whispered again. "Listen, Peter. We need to get dressed. The Germans. They're coming."

Peter shook his head quickly, shooting up in bed. "They can't be. Applegate said they didn't come this far south. Not yet. Not till next year—"

Julie leaped from the bed and started grabbing at clothes. "We need to move fast. We need to figure out what's changed in the timeline. Anything that differs now could alter what we're meant to do in this timeline's future. Do you understand?"

Peter was still lost in the confusion of his dream world. He wiped the sweat from his palms and steadied himself. Why was he having such terrifying dreams? What had happened to his mind during that time lapse, when he'd seen that German soldier? Had she entered his psyche somehow, altered his perception of the world? Could he continue with the mission if he constantly dipped into this terrifying dream world? He needed to be careful. He needed to stay alert.

He joined Julie and pulled his aging pants over his hips. He peeked outside the window and saw a short, precise line of German soldiers marching through the cobblestone streets below.

"They've been coming for about an hour now," Julie murmured. She tugged her shoes over her feet. "We need to figure out what's going on and then get the hell out of here. Do you think we can make it to the car?"

Peter nodded. He grabbed his satchel and started toward the door, with Julie rushing up behind him. He spun on his heels and looked at her. "The café by the train station. We can sit out in the sun and watch them, listen to them. Ask the barista if this was expected." He looked at the strength behind Julie's ever-beautiful hazel eyes. "If anything happens, we have to run. This isn't part of the plan. We're off the path."

Julie nodded as they descended the back staircase and burst into the sunlight of the early afternoon. They stayed in the shadows, lingering behind buildings and drifting toward the center of town, where the railway station was situated. Peter noted that several cafés and restaurants had been quickly boarded up as the Germans arrived. He could see eyes peering out from the windows, gawking at the terror arriving like one would gawk at a fire. Peter's stomach trembled for a moment. Every German face he saw seemed to resemble that terrible woman in his dream, pointing a gun at his daughter.

They arrived at the café and bounded inside, away from the searching eyes of the German soldiers. The Frenchman who would normally be waiting on customers was hiding behind the counter. He placed his finger over his lips and he told them to hide. "*Cachez*," he whispered harshly.

Julie grabbed Peter's hand and darted into the back of the

café, behind a crooked red curtain. The tattered drape didn't reach the floor, which meant their feet could be seen beneath it. "Why do you think they're here?" Peter asked Julie quietly.

"*Parlez le francais,*" she murmured back, her eyes bright with fiery energy.

Peter bit his lip, hoping beyond anything else that the Nazis wouldn't come bursting into the café. If only Mandrake hadn't have followed them; if only they'd been able to shoot up to Oradour-sur-Glane as they'd planned.

Suddenly, he heard it: the sound of crashing glass. Julie grabbed Peter's shoulders and peered up at him, petrified. They had to leave. The Germans were coming. Searching.

"*Bonjour,*" someone with a German accent called into the empty café. "*Je cherche les Jews...*" His words were harsh, rude. He sniffed the air, and Peter could hear snot lingering deep in the man's head.

Peter peered beyond the tiny hallway in which they stood. He saw a bit of light glancing in from the exterior. He knew they could run; they could get out that way. He mapped it in his head: it was only a quarter mile back to the hotel, back to the car. They could bolt from this formerly sleepy French town. He blinked several times, feeling deep fatigue. He'd only slept a few hours that morning. But he knew the time for sleep was over.

He gestured with his head at the window in the back. Julie crept toward it, keeping her eyes alert. They could both hear the soldier out front, harassing the café owner. A sudden crash of glass told Peter that the German soldier had slashed his arm through the air, knocking dozens of beer glasses to the floor, where they shattered into pieces. Peter could hear the café owner weeping softly. His terror was obvious.

Peter snuck his hand into Julie's as they crept closer to the window. They would make it out alive, his grasp told her. They would be fine. As long as they stayed together.

CHAPTER 6

Peter and Julie hoisted themselves through the open window at the back of the café. Peter could already feel the sun on his face as he launched his body into the clean air. They were far more exposed than he was comfortable with, although they were away from the main road.

He looked at Julie, ready to say something in high spirits, something that would reassure her. He watched the slim arch of her neck as she peered up at something, and then her face turned to stone. His heart beat fast in his chest as he followed her gaze.

There, at the edge of the building, stood two unfamiliar men. They were leaning against the old brick of the wall, their dark eyes staring back.

"*Bonjour,*" Julie murmured. She nodded at them.

Peter's mind was rushing. The man on the left was wearing the familiar dark gray, slim-fitting Nazi uniform. He was tall, a bit burly in his chest. The man on the right was slim-hipped, wearing the colors of Vichy France.

"*Ah, oui, madame. Bonjour a vous,*" said the Nazi man, grinning at Julie in a way that made Peter want to punch him in the face. He felt a surge of negative energy, the anger he'd had when he was training for the mission back in San Francisco.

"*Qu-est-ce-que vous avez fait?*" the French officer asked Julie and Peter. He gestured toward the window, asking them what they'd been doing. Peter grabbed Julie's hand, hoping the men would turn their attention toward him. He could be strong enough for the both of them, he thought. He could lead them to safety.

"*Ah, oui,*" Julie began. Her body didn't betray a hint of anxiety. "*Moi, j'ai un peu de peu pour cette situation.*" She gestured, speaking about her fear of the Nazi situation. She smiled, appearing a bit sheepish, nothing like her actual self. "*A chez moi, oui.*" She shrugged, meaning she was going back to her home, back to safety. She turned toward Peter, looking at him curiously.

"*Est-ce que vous savez cet homme?*" the Vichy asked her, wondering if she knew Peter, standing beside her.

"*Non. Il est mysterieuse pour moi. Il etait dans la café, mais pas avec mois.*" She turned her head back toward the men, nodding. She didn't know Peter, she'd said. They weren't together. Peter tried to track the story she was telling the men, trying to stay on track.

But the Vichy officer and the Nazi didn't appear to buy her small talk, her childlike nature. They began to advance toward Peter and Julie. The Vichy's eyebrow was raised high on his face. "*Ah, oui. Okay. Et vous? Vous n'etes pas avec cette femme?*" The Vichy turned toward Peter then, forcing him into an immediate moment of panic. He searched for the words to say. The French ones he had practiced (albeit half-heartedly) for so many hours.

"*Les papiers?*" the Vichy asked him, bringing his fingers together.

Peter searched through his pockets, looking for his identity papers. He breathed a sigh of relief when he found them. Maybe he and Julie would make it out of this after all. Maybe they'd would be all right.

"*Ah, oui. Vous visitez cette ville?*" the Vichy asked Peter then, peering at his papers. He asked if Peter was visiting this town from somewhere else, since his papers clearly illustrated he wasn't a local. He certainly didn't look like a local, he knew.

Peter cleared his throat, preparing to respond as easily as possibly. *"Oui. Um."* Think! Think! *"Je suis de Paris. Je suis un architect de Paris a—"* He felt the American notes in his voice, and he watched the eyebrows of the men before him descend toward their eyes. He could see panic swelling in Julie's eyes, as well. This wasn't going well. He trekked on, feeling like he was walking the plank. *"Je dois documenter les architectures de cette region—"* he said, saying that he'd meant to document the beautiful architecture of the region. He brought his hands out, gesturing to it—to the slumped-over café beside him, to the crumbling ground beneath his feet.

They weren't buying it. The German leaned toward the Frenchman, whispering German into his ear. Peter understood the words, if vaguely. They thought he was a spy.

The Frenchman wrapped his arm around Peter and led him to the side of the building. Peter felt like he was being ripped away from Julie. His heart began to tremble, and his head tried to find where she was. He could hear her continue her talk with the German solider. She was murmuring her affirmation that she didn't know Peter; that she lived in the town. That she was, indeed, French.

Suddenly, he heard her scream. He started squirming in the hold of the Vichy. "Get your hands off me!" he yelled, pushing against the Frenchman's incredible strength.

The two men grabbed his arms and brought them around to his back. They quickly tied his wrists, and he fell to the ground, nearly slamming his head into the brick wall before him. He could hear French words humming around him. All was lost, he knew in that moment. All was lost. He and Julie would be murdered here in 1942, and nothing would ever come to pass the way it was meant to. His children would live on in the future, perhaps. Or maybe another timeline would open; Minnie would meet someone else, have a different set of children. Maybe she wouldn't die.

Peter felt tremors all over his body as his vision descended into blackness. There was no hope.

———— ∽ ————

Peter's body flew through the air, then slammed into something solid. The vehicle swayed a bit with the weight of his body. He felt blood flow through his mouth as he sat up, trying to make sense of his surroundings. He'd bitten his tongue.

To his right, he saw her: Julie. She was strapped to the side of the German Jeep into which they'd been thrown. His heart surged with happiness, even as they looked at each other with tremendous fear. They'd been captured. All their best-laid plans couldn't have saved them from this horror. But they couldn't speak; they couldn't allow the Germans to understand that they knew each other. They needed to stay as surreptitious as possible. Maybe, maybe they could escape. They could go on with their mission. But Peter couldn't help but feel that with each moment that passed, they were creating new timelines, new elements of this brand-new past. He shuddered as he looked toward Julie.

Julie stomped her foot in anger. Peter could feel the same anger coursing through his body, through his arms. Through his legs. His heart forced him to calm her with an assured look. He mouthed the words to her in English. "It's going to be okay."

Peter heard a laugh and turned his head quickly to the left. His eyes widened. The German soldier sitting in back with them peered at them malevolently, his gun slung over his lap. He'd seen the small moment between them; he'd seen it all. He grinned a bit stupidly, as if he were a child. He was missing a tooth on the left side of his mouth. He called up to the front seat in a rough, rollicking German voice. *"Ich denke, dass sie sich gegenseitig kennen."*

Two German soldiers turned back from the front seat and eyed their captives, the beautiful woman and the grizzled American man with her. They looked at Peter and Julie hungrily. Lying spies.

Peter turned back toward Julie, his eyes searching. He felt like he couldn't get enough oxygen. She whispered to him slowly. "They know we know each other," she said in English.

The soldiers up front snickered, holding their bellies as they laughed. They kept peering back at the pair, knowing the trouble to come.

Peter lowered his head, feeling utterly hopeless. Their lives, he knew in an instant, were over. He peered out the window beyond Julie's small, pointed face. The countryside of war-torn France glowed outside the car as they darted down the bumpy dirt road. A castle gleamed in the distance. Maybe this past world wasn't so dismal-looking, after all.

CHAPTER 7

The Nazi Jeep swept out of the small village. Fear seemed to bleed through Peter until it became all-encompassing, and he was sure the same was true for Julie. Nothing he experienced seemed real. He thought he was in a sort of hellacious dream once more—like the one with the German soldier in his dining room, holding her gun at his daughter's head. Maybe he'd wake up any moment, feeling Julie's warm fingers on his back. "It's just a dream, baby," she would murmur.

But this was all too real. When they reached the compound, a low gray building seemed to sprawl out ahead of them, crawling with soldiers. Peter felt the car door burst open behind him. A German soldier grabbed him by the shoulders and pulled him backward sharply, and his neck snapped back. Another soldier grabbed at Julie's upper arms, forcing her to hit her head against the exterior frame of the jeep. Peter's throat ached as he screamed at them. "Stop it! You're hurting her!" The stakes were too high; he had to speak. He had to make his feelings known.

The soldiers shoved him and Julie toward the compound. He could see the deep footprints of Nazi boots surrounding them: all the soldiers who had marched round and round without a single thought of 2013, of the way his life had been. Of all that could be. Their eyes were directed toward German dominance. Would they get it in this newly created timeline?

The soldiers seemed not to notice them, this new round of "spies" who were being dragged toward the interior. The sun arched above them in strange juxtaposition to their terror. Peter peered up at the sky, remembering a time when he and Tori had launched a kite into a similar blue sky, watching as it arched back and forth. He and his daughter hadn't had a care in the world.

The German men pulled them into a stone structure and led them down a narrow hallway. Peter continued to turn his head back toward Julie, who had begun to cooperate, marching forward in subtle anger. Her eyes were dark and turned directly toward him.

Another soldier emerged from an opening as they passed. "Halt!" the soldier called toward the men who thrust the two Americans down the hall. He marched forward toward the man who held Peter's arms behind his back and spoke to him in stark, direct German. "*Was ist die Bedeutung dieses,*" he snapped. *What is the meaning of this?* Peter recognized the insignia on his uniform as that of a higher officer of some sort.

"*Feindliche Spione,*" the soldier replied. Enemy spies.

The German official nodded. "*Gute Arbeit,*" he said. Good work. "*Nehmen Sie sie mit der Kammer,*" he ordered.

Peter tried to peer back toward Julie. What were they saying? His German was so elementary. He cleared his throat as the German who held him tight forced him forward, further down the hall. The strange, bleary notion that this hadn't happened before in this timeline—that this was happening to him, now, in real time, hurt his head. Blood pounded in his ears.

The men who held Peter and Julie forced them into a small stone cell. A splintered wood table sat in the center. Three chairs surrounded it. Two of them had shackles on the armrests. The German soldier forced Peter into the chair on the left and snapped the shackles around his wrists. Peter's wrists were far too large for the cuffs, and his bones crunched together as the restraints locked shut. He started straining against them, wondering if it would mean something if he fought his own death. If it would mean something rather than nothing.

The German pushed Julie forcefully into the chair next to Peter's. Her supple, beautiful body strained in the seat. Her eyes darted around like the eyes of a small animal in the forest, ready to flee from its impending demise.

A Nazi soldier guarded the doorway and glared at them as the other soldier left them alone, muttering to the man by the door. It was clear they'd be questioned before they were murdered, Peter thought. He felt an emptiness in the room. He couldn't reveal anything; he didn't want to put Dr. Epson in danger. He didn't want to jeopardize the welfare of anyone in his life.

Julie's eyes were brimming with tears. Peter thought he understood why. They hadn't been able to go to Oradour-sur-Glane. They hadn't been able to save her family. After all she'd sacrificed to be here, nothing had played out as planned. They'd simply come to France and been captured. Peter wondered how many other times in the history of the world this had happened: when training led to nothing. It was almost like dying in a car accident during the driver's test. What was the point?

They heard great strides outside the door, Nazi boots hitting hard against the floor. Peter saw a visible shudder from the soldier guarding the doorway. Who was approaching? He felt the blood begin to pool in his hands; it couldn't escape due to the shackles. He was growing light-headed.

In the doorway, suddenly, stood perhaps the most attractive man Peter had ever seen. He seemed to be *glowing*. His skin was tanned and beautiful; his blue eyes were animated as he looked toward Peter and Julie, grinning with broad, white teeth. His Nazi uniform was trim at his thin waist and then pulsed outward at his great, muscled arms and chest. His neck was thick, holding a great head and its curling blond and brown hair. His face was clean-shaven and wide.

"Oh, hello, American people," he called to them. His accent was incredibly German, but his English was clear and accurate. He strode toward the front of the room, eyeing them fiercely.

"My, my. What a beautiful woman you are." He leaned toward Julie and kissed her hand, even as it splayed useless, strapped in the unyielding shackles. Peter's face burned.

Julie spat on the ground at the man's feet. Her aim was true.

"Well, well, well," the man murmured. "We have a feisty one, don't we?"

He turned toward the German soldier at the door. His eyes grew dark. "Fritz. You'll be wanting to get the mechanism."

Fritz nodded and spun around, eager to leave the room. He shut the door behind him, leaving Peter, Julie, and this strange German alone in the echoing chamber.

"So. Allow me to introduce myself," the Nazi said. "My name is Friedrich Manstein. I am head general of this—shall we say—exhibition in the lower French region. And may I say, I'm quite pleased to meet you both. Such fine American people, traveling through Nazi-occupied France. What a wonder." He tapped his ring finger for a moment on the table, allowing the sound to echo against the stone wall. "We haven't captured spies in quite a while. So you might say you're quite like celebrities right now in this camp. All the men are talk-talk-talking about you. Wondering what it is that will happen to you. You know—they are so much like hungry dogs. Always down in the pit. Looking up at you with these big eyes." Manstein made large eyes himself, aiming a look of pleading at Julie and Peter. There was a lot of malice behind his eyes, Peter thought.

"Anyway. You might say it's good that we've found you. To boost morale, so you say. Oh. You also might wonder how it is that I speak such profoundly wonderful English." His voice bounced with zeal as he spoke. He seemed nearly giddy. "You see, I was actually born in Berlin, but I grew up in New York. Amongst the Jews, amongst the Irish, amongst them all. Which gives me quite the advantage, here in Nazi-occupied Europe." One eyebrow rose high on his forehead. "I know how they operate, you know. I know how they think." He tapped his temple with a long, thin finger. "Ah, well. That's beside the point.

What we're really here to do is talk about you. You both, of course."

He collapsed on the chair in front of them, smiling heartily. Peter felt he'd seen the smile before; something about it twanged at his stomach. He swallowed, hoping he wouldn't throw up.

"Now. Now. Now," Manstein murmured, rubbing his hands together. "I need to know why you're here. Who the hell you are. And what your mission is. Why are you spying on this small French town? What is to be gained?"

Peter bit his lip. His eyes lurched toward Julie. Blood rushed to his head. He longed to bring his arms forward, to strangle this man sitting in front of him. He wouldn't say anything.

Manstein began to laugh. "I see, I see. I don't know why I thought it would be so easy. You'll forgive me. It's been a while since I had an interrogation on my hands." He sprang up from his seat and brought his body forward, toward Julie. Peter felt a bead of sweat roll down his face, into his mouth. Almost unconsciously, his throat started making small, guttural noises.

Manstein leaned toward Julie and breathed into her ear. "Darling. Can you tell me why you and your sad-looking fake husband over there are lying to my soldiers and wandering around the countryside?" His lips were just inches from Julie's ear. Julie began to shudder. "What are you up to?"

Julie didn't speak. Peter thought fleetingly that perhaps she was too frightened, that she was overcome with fear.

Manstein brought a finger up toward Julie's face and wiped a small tear away from her cheek. "Fear is nothing, my darling. Nothing compared to what's about to befall you." He spun toward Peter then. A grin formed across his face, bringing great, white, wolf-like teeth into view.

"And you, my strong soldier. Do you want to relinquish the truth?" Manstein appeared to be orchestrating them almost like pawns, like puppets. He could do whatever he wanted to them; he could say whatever he wanted. They were at his mercy.

Manstein stood directly in front of Peter, then. "What are you doing here, sir? What are your real names? What is your mission?"

Peter shook his head back and forth, looking directly at the man in front of him. Manstein brought his long palm up toward Peter's face and smacked him lightly, playfully on the cheek. Peter felt fear sizzle down his spine. He knew what was coming next.

"You like that, don't you?" Manstein said. He cleared his throat. "Let me do it again. I rather like it, too." He brought his hand back and slapped it hard across Peter's cheek, across his mouth. Peter tasted blood once more. He blinked wearily up at Manstein, seeing stars swirl around his head.

Julie had started to scream quietly, as if she couldn't allow anything else to exit her throat. As if she couldn't get enough air. Manstein seemed to adore the sound. He brought his hand back once more and slammed it into Peter's face. This time, Peter felt something crack deep inside his mouth. A tooth had come unlodged, and he felt blood begin to course down his tongue, into his throat. He started spitting it up.

"So. I take it you aren't going to talk, no?" Manstein said. He rubbed his fingers together, considering his options.

Peter swallowed the metallic taste of blood, longing to rip this man to shreds. He couldn't allow him to know about the mission; he couldn't allow any information to get out. If he and Julie were going to die here, they would die with the details of the mission still locked in their minds. Nothing would ever be known.

Manstein clapped his hands ominously. The sound ricocheted from side to side in the great room. The soldier who had left a short while ago pulled the door open quickly and peered into the room, a look of fear on his face.

"I think we'll move into the second phase of the interrogation," Manstein murmured, bringing his eyes slowly from Peter's bleeding face to Julie's pale, squinched one.

"Right away, sir," the man said. He turned back toward the hallway, and Manstein grinned at the two Americans in front of him, bringing his bright blue eyes from one to the other. He eyed them like they were his dinner: fresh meat.

Peter's heart was ricocheting in his chest. He began to hear a subtle screeching down the hallway. He swallowed as the screeching came closer and closer, like a crescendo. He felt a tang—the blood—rise in his mouth. Julie, next to him, had a dribble of sweat coursing down her nose. She couldn't stop shaking.

"Ah, yes. Thank you, soldier," Manstein said. The door opened to reveal the soldier, pushing a screeching contraption. A large, very old mattress sat on a cart with wheels that spun haphazardly, taking the cart forward slowly, hesitantly. The cart seemed like it would collapse at any moment.

The mattress's springs pushed high into the air, their points gleaming. Peter's head spun. He tried to lurch in the chair, to speak. But the cart crept closer and closer to him and Julie. He knew it was time.

"Now. I understand, of course, that I won't be getting any information out of the two of you. Where you came from, what your mission is. What you were up to back in that small French town. Ah, what a beautiful village, no?" Manstein brought his arms forward and cracked his knuckles. He bent his head this way, then that. Peter could hear his vertebrae popping. "And so. We'll move on. I think—Peter first." He smiled at Peter, showing his great teeth.

The other soldier came forward, past Julie. He grabbed Peter's wrists and unclasped him from the strain of the shackles. He spoke in German, spitting out insults to Peter. Peter's head hung low. He could see Julie, see her eyelids close over those beautiful hazel eyes. He wanted to hold her; he wanted to tell her they'd be all right.

The solider led him forward forcefully and tossed him onto the mattress. Peter could feel the cart nearly collapse beneath his weight. He could feel the small spokes of the mattress springs dig into his shirt and poke his skin. He closed his eyes, arching his back against the pain.

"Ah, yes. Not so easy to take, is it?" Manstein asked him. He chuckled.

Peter's mind raced. He thought he could handle this; it was just the coils of an old mattress digging into his skin. He wouldn't tell them anything. He could take it.

"But, of course, we'll have to increase the pain. Just a bit, no?" Manstein said. He gestured toward the soldier once more. The soldier brought forth an elaborate contraption, one that plugged into an electric socket. Peter watched as he snapped the electric cord to the wires of the mattress. He started laughing, realizing what was about to happen. It would all be over soon, he thought. He would die.

Manstein held the switch in his hand, peering down at the laughing Peter. He clucked his tongue. "Peter, Peter. Now. Before I do this. Before I—" He giggled for a moment. "Before I electrocute you. Is there anything you want to answer for? Do you want to tell me what you and this lovely woman were doing in France, on my watch?"

Peter peered up at this German man, at his shining blond hair. He bared his teeth like a dog. "I won't tell you anything," he snarled. "Electrocute me as much as you want."

"Suit yourself," the German man said. He flipped the switch back and widened his eyes, peering down at Peter.

Peter felt his spine jolt with electricity. He tried to remember all he'd learned about electric units in school; he tried to remember how the flow worked. He tried to focus. But the pain seemed to numb his skull, his brain. He almost didn't realize that he was screaming.

Finally, the electricity stopped. Peter was still shaking. He felt blood oozing out of his tongue once more, where he'd bitten it. He blinked up at Manstein. He wanted to speak, to say something, anything. But he couldn't find the words.

"How did that feel?" Manstein asked him. His eyebrows were wagging. "Are you ready for another round?"

Peter didn't think he'd live through another round. He felt like he could feel the earth spinning beneath him. He stretched his arm to the right, toward Julie, and tried to make eye contact with her. But her eyes were closed; her head hung low over her chest. When he died, would they electrocute her, too?

"Let's try again," Manstein said authoritatively. He grabbed the switch and flicked it once more, allowing the electricity to jolt through Peter's body.

Peter felt like his stomach was on fire. He felt laughter bubbling from his gut and he closed his eyes, remembering the day his son was born. How joyful they'd been, he and Minnie. He'd always wondered what that sort of was like, the pain of labor. Minnie had said she'd felt close to death, during those tense moments. And then, it had all been over. She'd been holding Brett in her arms.

In that moment, suddenly, Manstein had flipped the switch back. He raised his eyebrow to the sky, assessing the situation. Then he stomped toward the soldier and spoke harsh words to him, gesturing toward Julie. The soldier nodded curtly and turned toward Julie, then pulled her up from her slumped-over position in the small chair.

Peter watched as they took her away. Where were they taking her? His heart jolted in his chest. He couldn't live without her. He couldn't. "Julie!" he screamed. But she was gone. He could hear her feet dragging down the dirt hallway as the soldier pulled her along. "What are you going to do to her?" he howled at Manstein. "WHAT ARE YOU GOING TO DO?"

He was no longer worried about himself. He could die; anything could happen. But he couldn't allow anything to happen to Julie. Was she strong enough to endure this?

Manstein lumbered forward. "I don't have time for this," he blurted. He spat on the ground, and with that, his sweetness was gone. Then he disappeared down the hallway.

Peter scrambled up from the mattress, feeling the blood drip down his back from where the mattress had punctured his skin. He felt tears form, hot, in his eyes. From somewhere down the hall, in a sort of dreamy haze, he heard the screams: Julie's screams. They were different from anything he'd ever heard, so animalistic. They represented real, incoherent pain. He began to shake with anger. He started pounding at the wall of the cell, feeling bruises begin to form on his hand. "AHHHHH." His howls joined with hers in a strange, disconcerting duet. "AHHH. STOP TORTURING HER! TAKE ME! TAKE ME!"

The locked door burst open behind him once more. The younger soldier from earlier grabbed him by the neck and pushed him against the wall, choking him until his screaming subsided. "STOP." The single syllable was harsh, jagged.

As the oxygen left Peter's lungs, darkness formed over his eyes. The pain flew away; the howling from down the hall halted. He felt himself collapse onto the floor.

And that was all.

CHAPTER 8

Peter awoke without any comprehension of the time, the day. It seemed he could have been sleeping for an eternity. What year was it? He blinked, eyeing the room around him. He'd been taken to a different cell, he knew that much. This cell was smaller, with a single cot leaning against the wall. He shivered, standing up from the flat mattress. He could feel dried blood caked on his back from the torture, and remembered the terror he'd experienced. He remembered pounding on the stone wall as Julie screamed down the hall. He wondered if they'd killed her. He wondered if he'd ever know.

He paced the room, maintaining a route, back and forth from wall to wall. If Julie was really gone—and he had no reason to think that she was still around, after all—then he felt no devotion to the mission any longer. Everything was off kilter. He didn't give a fuck about going to Oradour-sur-Glane and carrying out Applegate's mission. He just wanted to go home. He wanted to go home and take it all back.

Suddenly, he heard footsteps down the hall. Someone was coming. He leaned against the far wall, his arms crossed over his chest. He wanted to look angry, to look tough. He wasn't going to go down without a fight.

The soldier on the other side of the door was a bit scrawny. His blond hair and his small blue eyes created a portrait of the perfect Arian baby. The soldier nodded curtly at Peter as he placed a small plate down on the ground. Peter made no motion toward him as he shut the door, returning him to darkness.

Peter walked toward the meager piece of bread, the small cup of water. He felt an emptiness in his stomach. He hadn't eaten in something like two days by that point, he calculated. He wanted to eat, but he didn't want to give his captors the satisfaction. If he died in captivity, they wouldn't be able to get any information out of him. If he died, he was safe.

Just then, however, he heard another door open, then close—the sound of the soldier entering the cell next to his, it seemed, and tapping a plate on the ground. Peter's ears perked up, trying to hear who was on the other side of the wall through the chinks between the stones. Another prisoner? He tried not to get his hopes up. The soldier left, then, and Peter didn't hear another sound from the adjacent room. He pictured the two of them—this mysterious captive and him, standing far back against the wall, staring at the only piece of food that would allow them to live on in this terrible hellhole.

Finally, Peter heard the person take a single small step forward. Peter matched this step, as well. He listened closely for a minute before he heard the person taking one more step. He followed. He felt his blood pressure rise. He could nearly feel the weight of the person behind the dark stone wall.

Unable to handle his curiosity, he leaned toward the wall and scratched at it with his fingernail. A bit of dirt collected beneath it, creating a muddy half-moon. "Hey," he whispered. "Is anyone there?"

Peter waited. He listened as the person crept forward. He held his breath, hoping. Hoping.

Finally, he heard the words. "Peter. Is that you?"

Julie.

His heart leapt into his throat. How had she survived? He couldn't find the right words. "Did they torture you? Are you all right?" He bit his lip, feeling dizzy.

"I'm all right, Peter. Peter ... I thought surely you were dead.

Your face. It was so pale. It was like all the life went out of you."

"I'm all right, Julie. I'm all right." He longed to hold her, to tell her they were going to escape these Nazi brutes. They were going to get out of here. He longed to hold her hand and walk along the Bay. He longed to tell her everything about his life, about every feeling he'd ever had. He held his tongue. "What did they do to you?"

"It doesn't matter. What do you think went wrong? Why do you think they captured us? Did they see the car? Did they know we stole it?"

"I guess that could be it. I did think of that," Peter murmured. He was very wary of saying too much. He tried to listen for any footfalls outside the room. He thought they were alone. "I'm so sorry for getting you into this mess, for stealing the car. I wouldn't have done this if I knew—"

"Don't worry about it."

"No. Listen. I think—I think I felt like I was outside of time. Like I was free from the repercussions of what we're doing. I'm so sorry."

Julie was quiet. Peter knew it didn't matter that he'd apologized; nothing mattered. They were stuck, then. A great stone wall separated them, and their whispers were muffled, like they were whispering through time.

"It still doesn't make sense. I don't think the car is why we were captured, Peter," Julie murmured. "I think they know something. What tipped the Vichy and the Germans off? They know that we're up to something. That's why they tortured us."

Peter swallowed slowly, feeling the swelling bite marks on his tongue. He wondered what state Julie was in; he didn't want to imagine it. In his head, she was still ripe and beautiful, the woman he'd met all those months before.

Julie went on. "I think they know something, yes. Do you think Mandrake told them something? Would he put our lives in danger like this?"

Peter thought about how Mandrake had met them at every phase of their journey thus far. He realized that Mandrake probably knew where they were at that moment. "I don't know what he would gain. He wants us to finish the mission, remember?"

"Still. We can't trust anyone except each other," Julie whispered.

"I know. I know," Peter said. He slammed his hand against the wall, desperate to eliminate the barrier between them. He longed to see her face, to make sure she was okay.

"Who else could it have been?" Julie said, trying to calm him down.

"Maybe it was just our demeanor, Julie. Maybe I was just too American," Peter whispered, leaning his head against the cool rock. His hand throbbed.

"I don't think so, Peter," Julie said, laughing with nervous energy. "You were wonderful."

Peter knew she was lying to make him feel better. He knew that his French had been dismal, that no matter how hard he'd tried (which wasn't so hard, really), he'd never really captured the appropriate French inflections. He sighed. "Well. Remember how we lost track of that couple in New York?"

"Right. Their bags were packed, like they were waiting for us," Julie said.

"Yeah. It was almost too convenient, like they knew we were watching them. I'm sure they set up a trap for us, to grab their passports." Peter nodded, trying to buy into it. He needed a reason to rely on; he needed a purpose for all the torture, for all the pain he'd experienced.

"It was a trap, after all," Julie said.

"Are you going to eat this bread?" Peter asked her. He gestured toward his own sad-looking piece of bread, the small glass of water, though he knew she couldn't see the movement.

"It's our only sustenance, Peter. We have to stay alive as long as we can. If we can escape—if we can continue with the mission—"

"Fuck the mission, Julie," Peter said earnestly. "I just want to get out of here. And then I want to go back. I want to take it all back."

"It's not an option, Peter. And you know that."

Peter swallowed. He thought back to their first date, all those weeks before and all those years in the future, when he and Julie had sat together at the French restaurant, eating more than just a chunk of bread. He picked up the small piece and sniffed it. The smell of yeast filled his nose. "You'll eat with me?" he asked her.

She chuckled on the other side of the wall. "It's a date, Peter."

"You aren't alone, Julie."

"I know."

CHAPTER 9

Peter and Julie ate the piece of bread over the course of the following two days. The second piece they received was so moldy, they thought it would be far too detrimental to their stomachs to eat.

Peter sat on his bed and whispered stories to Julie to keep her mind off her hunger. He told her about helping Tori learn to ride her bicycle—all the scabs, all the Band-Aids. She spoke about her best friend growing up, a young girl she'd lost touch with. The scrapes they'd gotten into. They talked about their favorite records, about music that would never reach the ears of the people of this decade, of this century. They laughed through the hunger that gnawed at their stomachs.

After several hours had gone by on the fourth day, Peter thought Julie had fallen asleep. He felt so woozy from hunger and dehydration that he was ready to drop off himself. He whispered the words to Julie: "Good night."

But instead, Julie spoke back. "Peter. I have to tell you something."

"Sure, Jules. Anything." Peter stared at the far wall, at the five stripes that went down the wall—the only remnant of the previous captive who had lived in the cell. He imagined the man scraping his fingers down the wall, screaming at the Nazis for a freedom he would never receive. Peter shivered.

"Um. I think my arm might be broken."

Peter sat up on his bed, his ears ringing. "What? They broke your arm?"

"I think it was an accident. They um. They pushed me up against the wall during the—the torture. It's really not a big deal. Maybe it's dislocated? I might have just landed on it wrong."

"Why didn't you tell me sooner?" Peter demanded.

"I thought I could hold out. Or that we would die or something before … But here we are on the fourth day. I don't think I can take the pain anymore." Julie's voice broke as she spoke.

Peter's world began to crumble. His head spun from the lack of food, of nourishment. He brought his dirt-caked hands to his face and felt his tears falling fast. "I'm going to tell them everything," he said. "I'm going to tell them everything about us, about you and me. About 2013."

"No!" Julie snapped. Her voice was again thick with pain. "No, Peter. You can't. We can't give up on the mission yet. Not yet. We can escape! I know we can."

"It's no good, Julie. Can't you understand—"

"No. I can't. I just think that you're about to lose your mind. You're hungry. Exhausted, yes. But you can't give us away. Not yet."

Peter allowed his chin to graze his chest. He felt himself grow dizzy. He was going to fall asleep, and he wasn't sure he was ever going to wake up. He longed to tell Julie he loved her, but he couldn't find the strength.

Peter woke up when his cell door burst open. On the other side of the door, he saw a great, hazy shadow. The man stepped into the subtle light of his cell. Peter pulled himself up abruptly, shocked by the man standing before him. Manstein. Peter had almost thought that the Nazi had been a part of his dream—just another in a long stream of scary Germans, lingering somewhere in his subconscious.

Manstein stomped into his room, his large boots making

great indents in the dirt floor. "Vell, vell, vell. I see you are awake," he said.

Peter stood before him, next to the sad cot in the corner. He tried to look tall, to look proud. He thought of Julie in the next room, and he wanted to be a pillar for her, someone for her to hold on to. "What do you want?" he asked Manstein.

"I wouldn't use that tone with me, sir," Manstein said. "You are ultimately at the mercy of the Nazi regime, and you know that."

Manstein paused once more, considering. He grinned down at Peter, the smaller of the two: never a war hero, even during his days in the army. Peter felt like an ant, just as he had when he was in the ranks, ever at the mercy of the higher-ups. His face burned.

"I'm not a spy," Peter spouted. "Sir."

Manstein started laughing then. He closed his eyes and turned his face toward the sky, holding his stomach. Peter could see a large, thin baton strapped to his leg. He tried not to imagine what it would feel like to have that stick smacked against his face. Would the rest of his timeline be filled with darkness? It was no use thinking otherwise.

"No, no," Manstein finally said. "I know you're not a spy. I know you're both not spies. I know you're absolutely not married, that's for sure. That beauty, with you?"

Peter maneuvered his weight from foot to foot. He cleared his throat. What was Manstein getting at?

"Anyway. I know that you're not a spy. I know precisely why you're here in France, in fact."

Peter's mind rushed. How could Manstein know why he was there? He couldn't possibly know. Surely this cookie-cutter Nazi general couldn't comprehend time travel.

Manstein took a step forward and leaned down, nearly touching his nose to Peter's. "I even know Dr. Epson personally."

Peter leaned back and spit on the ground at Manstein's feet. "I don't know what you're accusing me of. But it's completely false. I've never heard of a Dr. Epson."

Manstein held his stomach and chuckled once more. "Yeah. Yeah, you have." He walked toward the wall and placed his fingers on the fingernail lines that swept from the ceiling to the floor. "You know what happened to this guy? This prisoner who was living in this beautiful place before you?"

"Couldn't guess," Peter murmured. His voice was laced with sarcasm.

"No. I suppose you wouldn't be able to imagine. But I can still hear the screams in my head at night." Manstein pointed to his forehead, showing his teeth. "We've lost a lot of good men in here. And for what reason? Because of their pride, of course. They were too good, thinking their secrets meant more than their life. But it wasn't true." Manstein grinned at Peter. "Ah, well. Really, we can get everything we need out of your little lady friend next door. Isn't she beautiful, that girl?"

Peter's head jolted to the right, and suddenly, he heard Julie scream. He grabbed his face and dug his fingernails into his cheeks, nearly falling to the ground as the screams continued. They were so much more intense than they'd been the last time.

"What are you doing to her?" he bellowed.

"Just say the word, and the torture will cease," Manstein said. His eyes looked expectant; they were glowing. His lips arced into a wolf-like smile.

Peter knelt once more, leaning his body into the wall. He felt her wails—so full of anger, of sickness—ripple through the wall. He felt like he was spinning, like he couldn't escape. This was it; this was his only reality. "Stop!" he finally cried. "Stop! I'll tell you anything you want to hear."

"Ah, yes. Well, then. You want this to stop?" Manstein asked.

Peter nodded his head vehemently. He made eye contact with the man in front of him, allowing tears to cascade down his face. "Yes!"

"Then tell me about the time machine," Manstein whispered.

Peter could hardly hear him over the bloodcurdling screams coming from the other cell. "What?"

"The time machine," Manstein repeated.

Peter swallowed slowly, trying to gain the energy to answer him. "After. After you stop the torture."

Manstein nodded, raising his eyebrow high into the air. For a moment, Peter thought he'd done well. He turned back toward the door, walking slowly even as the screams continued like a great train, streaming toward them. He called down the hall, toward the other cell. *"Mit der folter!"* Manstein shouted in German.

Silence fell over the room. Peter's ears felt like they were bleeding. He brought himself up to his full height once more and took his hands away from his cheeks, blinking slowly at the man in front of him. His heart ached. He needed to go get Julie; he needed to hold her. To console her. Was her arm okay? Was she going to survive?

"Now. That's much better, isn't it?" Manstein asked him. He strutted toward Peter, looking at him expectantly. He acted like he had all the time in the world, like a war wasn't raging across the beautiful countryside. Like the entire continent wasn't in upheaval. He leaned toward Peter, whispering once more. "Zee time machine."

Peter brought his head back and gazed into this evil man's eyes. In the back of his mind, he wondered what Applegate's historical documents said about this Manstein fellow. Would he be a part of the Nuremberg trials? Would he pay for what he was putting innocent people through?

"A time machine?"

Manstein waited. *"Ja."*

Peter shrugged. *"C'est un idée trés stupide,"* he murmured with what he hoped was a *blasée* attitude. "It's a stupid idea." He looked at Manstein like he was the height of stupidity, like the mere idea of a time machine was crazy talk. He tried to emanate Tori—the way she would look at him when he tried to get information from her. *Where were you all afternoon? Where did you put your tennis shoes?* Such sass back to him. It always made him feel so small.

It appeared to work, at least for a moment. Manstein reared back, giving a strained smile. "Ah-ha. A stupid idea, is it? I have to say, your French accent is *trés* terrible. *Vous etes un americain* stupid. *C'est* normal, *non*?"

Peter leaned his head to the left. "All right. All right. You can call me stupid. But I've personally never heard a more idiotic idea in my life. Not in America, France, or Germany. A time machine? Ha. Much more likely that I'm a goddamned spy and that beautiful woman in there loves me. And those things aren't even likely, mind you."

"Okay. Okay. Well. How likely is this?" The German took the small baton from its thigh strap. He placed it against Peter's face and tapped it evenly, softly, against Peter's cheekbone.

"I'd say pretty likely," Peter said. He felt rash; he didn't care anymore. He couldn't let this man know anything about the time machine. It was his only route back home. And home, right now, was the only thing on his mind.

Manstein reared his hand back and smacked the baton against Peter's upper arm. Peter fell back onto the cot, nearly toppling it to the ground. He could hear Julie on the other side of the wall, then. Sobbing. "Hit me again, asshole," Peter said. His rage was hot in his neck, his face. He felt sixteen, ready to take on the world. "Hit me, motherfucker!"

Manstein reared back once more and struck him on the back, on the side. Peter's screams dissolved into laughter, even as Manstein reared back over and over.

Manstein paused. "You won't tell me? Then what use are you?" He grinned at Peter, and pulled out a pistol from its holster at his waist. He placed the barrel of the pistol directly on Peter's temple.

Peter could feel the cold, round barrel just to the left of his eyebrow. He smiled up at the man, breathing loudly through his nose. He felt a complete lack of passion about what would likely happen in the next few moments. "Do it, Manstein," he whispered. "Do it. *Je vous défie.*"

"You dare me, you do?" Manstein said. He cocked the pistol.

His hand was steady; he'd clearly done this many times before.

Peter swallowed heavily, preparing himself for oblivion. He started a countdown. *Eight. Seven. Six. Don't think about your children. Five. Four. Don't think about Minnie. Three. Two.*

And then, all of a sudden, a loud explosion erupted outside. The barrel of the gun lifted from Peter's skull, and he placed his hand over the spot it had touched, rubbing at it. Manstein's eyes had grown wide. Alarms began to blare from all over the compound, and Peter heard soldiers running through the hallways, many of them speaking in loud, panicked German.

The soldier who'd been beating Julie burst into the room and saluted Manstein. "Sir."

"Vhat's going on?" Manstein asked.

The man spoke in rushed German. "*Es geschah.*"

Manstein turned toward Peter and raised his eyebrow, bringing his pistol back to its holster. He bolted out of the room and locked the door behind him.

Peter fell back on the cot, his heart racing. His mind began to shut down as he understood, beyond anything else, that he had almost died, just then. He placed his hand on his stomach, appreciating each breath.

From the other side of the wall, he heard silence, even as the rest of the compound seemed in a state of panic. He placed his hand on the stone that still separated him and Julie. Everything else seemed to fall away. "Julie?" he murmured. He longed to hear her voice. "Julie? Are you all right?"

The other room seemed immense, empty. Peter heard screams and crashes from outside, and he curled closer to the wall, preparing to die in the fire that was surely going to consume the compound.

"Julie?" he called again.

"I'm here," she murmured. He could hardly hear it. "I'm all right."

Peter breathed a sigh of relief. "I don't know what's going on."

"Me neither. They hurt me, Peter."

"I know. He almost shot me."

"I know. I was preparing for us both to die."

"Me too," Peter said.

Outside, another explosion rolled through the ground. Peter felt the building shake much more this time. The bombs were getting closer.

"I'm sorry this happened."

"He says he knows Dr. Epson?" Peter whispered.

"He's lying, Peter. Everyone's lying. You know we can't trust anyone."

"But then, how could he know about time travel?"

"It doesn't matter."

Another bomb went off. Peter whispered to her in a voice he was certain she couldn't hear, couldn't comprehend. "I want to hold you, Julie."

She met that with silence.

CHAPTER 10

Suddenly, the door burst open. Peter brought his head up from the wall, blinking wearily at the brightness and the smoke that crept into his cell.

The man who stepped into the room looked strangely familiar. Peter scrubbed at his eyes with his hands, trying to rise to his feet.

"Peter? Peter? What's going on?" Julie called from the next room. But he didn't know yet. He peered into the smoke.

Emmett, the man from the train ride across the country, stepped forward. Peter was shocked to see him. He brought his hands up into fists, certain he'd found the enemy—the man who'd ruined them, who'd given them up. "Get the hell away from me!" he barked.

But Emmett turned around, toward the hallway. He seemed rushed, worried. "Listen. We have to hurry. You want to get out of here alive, don't you?"

Peter began to lower his arms.

"Come on. The Nazis and the Vichy are confused. They think the Nazis are attacking, and there's mass confusion outside. The Nazis are angry because they think their own are attacking. Listen. We have to move. This is our only goddamned chance."

Peter thought for a moment, his mind rushing. He took a couple of fast steps forward, watching as the smoke continued to course into the room. Outside the room, he saw Nazis grabbing their guns, holding their uniform caps. They were shrieking in German, "*Nicht schieben!*" *Don't shoot!*

Peter lurched around, feeling the adrenaline pulsing in his blood, and burst toward Julie's room, finding it unlocked as well. As he opened the door, it creaked, and she cringed at the sound as she scrambled to her feet. He gasped at the state she was in. She looked so thin, so haggard. She looked like she'd aged ten years since he'd last seen her three days ago.

"What are you looking at?" she muttered. "You don't look so hot yourself. And what the hell is he doing here?" She gestured toward Emmett. The smoke had started to make her cough.

"Honestly, Julie, I have no idea. But we need to go. We need to move, now. This is our only chance." Peter offered her his hand, and she brought her good hand forward. He watched as she pressed her other arm to her chest, swaddled in a small bit of her torn clothes.

He grabbed her fingers, and they found themselves running through the confusion. As they rushed out of the compound, they passed many Germans who were running back in. Several of the Germans had lost an arm, and they were screaming, their eyes wide. Peter saw a Nazi without an ear trying to talk to someone over a walkie-talkie; his jolting German couldn't be heard in the chaos.

Emmett gestured to them as they waded through the soldiers. He ducked inside one of the German Jeeps and pushed a dead man from the back seat, allowing the two weak Americans to hobble into the back. Julie collapsed into Peter's arms as Emmett turned the key in the ignition, then sent the Jeep jolting forward. Peter peered around, watching as the great compound erupted into flames. He thought about the wire mattress, about the way the electricity had shot through the wires and into his spine. He shivered, holding Julie's head close to his chest. He kissed the back of her head.

"What happened in there?" Emmett called back to them. His voice was raspy, harsh.

"How the hell did you know we were here?" Peter called back. They hadn't seen the man since the train in New York—since before so much of this had happened. That had been before Peter knew he was going to die; before he'd miraculously come back from the dead in a different time.

Emmett didn't answer. He maneuvered the bulky Jeep around another Nazi vehicle that lay on its side; a German soldier was hiding in the front seat, peering out at them with fearful, little-boy eyes.

"War really tears the world apart, doesn't it?" Emmett said, shaking his head. He coughed for a moment. "Tell me. How did the two of you wind up there?"

Peter understood, then, that Emmett wasn't yet willing to deliver any information about how he'd found them. He had to understand as much about their situation as possible. "Two Americans in New York. They gave us the slip. I can only imagine that they were on to us somehow." He wiped his sweating upper lip with his free hand, watching as Julie's lids began to close over her hazel eyes.

"That's impossible," Emmett replied. As he spoke, Peter could hear another explosion in the distance. "I took care of them—the people you stole the identities from, back in New York."

"What do you mean, you took care of them?" Peter asked. He felt dizzy, like he was living in another reality.

"I eliminated them."

Peter and Julie made eye contact. She looked so frightened. Peter wrapped his arm around her. They understood, in that moment, that Emmett was not to be trusted. They brought their eyes forward, nearly in unison, and eyed the road before them as Emmett charged ahead, away from the erupting blasts. Peter rolled his arm over Julie's back, trying to reassure her, to let her know everything was going to be all right.

"What's your plan?" Peter finally said to Emmett. He didn't want to be in the dark any more. He'd been a prisoner, completely resigned to certain death. But now, in the sunshine, away from the fire, the crippled Nazis—the screams—he could focus once more.

"We'll stop at a local village," Emmett said gruffly. "I drove past it on the way in. Nobody will question me. After all, I'm from this time. I can head to town, get some supplies. You both can get some rest."

Peter tightened his grip around Julie. How did Emmett know about them? But it seemed that more and more people were coming out of the woodwork, declaring they knew exactly what he and Julie were up to. He shuddered.

Julie spoke, apparently noting that Peter was too involved in his own revolving thoughts to respond. "That sounds wonderful, Emmett. Thank you for your help today. You saved our lives."

She shrugged toward Peter. He knew they were both at a loss for what to do, and they were also mentally and physically exhausted. They needed to regroup, to heal.

The Jeep rushed down the country road. Dust revolved all around them. Emmett suddenly took the Jeep in a crisp turn, skirting it among a cluster of trees. In the distance, they could see a small town. "Best if we walk from here," Emmett said with authority. "We don't want any questions asked about this Jeep."

He popped out from the front seat and rounded back, then opened the trunk and removed a few bags. Peter walked steadily away from the car with Julie, his muscles and bones aching. Peter's head was throbbing. He held Julie's hand as they walked, feeling so grateful. He'd thought he'd never feel the sun on his face again; he'd thought he'd never feel her fingers clasped in his. He was so grateful for this moment of human interaction, he felt he could cry.

The town was one of the smallest Peter had ever seen. All the buildings were uniquely French, with beautiful facades and decorative window shutters. A bakery stood on the left-hand side of the street, a single café on the right side. He watched Emmett as he gestured toward them, asking them to follow him up some steps to the right of the bakery. If he hadn't known where to look, Peter was sure he wouldn't have seen them.

Haggard, they walked up the steps, smelling the bread baking just beyond the wall. Peter's mouth was watering. He realized that they hadn't eaten in days. He clutched Julie's hand in his and felt her shaking. They were so close to survival.

Emmett opened the door and revealed a very small flat. A double bed was pushed toward the wall, and sweet, cool country air whipped in from the field through an open window. In Peter's eyes, this was paradise.

"I'm going to head downstairs, grab some food, fill a bucket of water," Emmett said, nodding to them.

Peter couldn't comprehend how this man had found them, or why he was helping him. But there was so much, in this lost timeline, that he couldn't readily understand. "Thank you, Emmett," he murmured. He turned to see Julie fall delicately onto the small bed, looking out the window at the green fields as she stretched out and relaxed. Her profile was so beautiful in the light. "See you soon," he said to Emmett, distracted.

Emmett was already gone, hurrying down the steps on his way to save their lives once again. Peter walked toward this beautiful woman—who held her hurt arm with her other hand—and draped his arm around her slim waist. He kissed her cheek, tasting the dirt, the salt from her tears. "Everything's going to be all right now," he told her, knowing full well that his words were empty—that they were still trapped in an empty age, in a different timeline.

CHAPTER 11

Peter and Julie lay together on the sagging bed in the small room above the bakery, smelling the delicious smells and falling into a dreamlike state. Peter touched Julie's cheek, loving the way she lay there, half-asleep and almost smiling. Even after all they'd been through together, there was still such passion, such heart behind her face. The Nazis couldn't rip that away from her.

After an undeterminable amount of time, they heard Emmett clamber up the steps. He knocked on the door first—a polite murderer, Peter thought—before entering. Peter rose and walked toward him, stumbling a little, to help him with the groceries.

A baguette. Delicious éclairs, filled with chocolate and crème. Fruits and vegetables. "There was a market down the road, and I couldn't resist," Emmett said, smiling. "Fresh cheese, as well. I hope you like Brie."

Peter's stomach rolled over. He ripped at the bread and placed a great slather of the soft cheese on top, then brought it to Julie. Julie took a bite and her eyes rolled back in her head. "Oh, god," she murmured.

Peter and Julie ate ravenously as Emmett got to work making a salad and pouring wine. He handed them each a glass, and Peter sipped at it, allowing the wine to course over his tongue. He could still feel the pain radiating through his body from the torture, from lying on that cot in the cell staring at the barren ceiling. But he felt himself forgetting; he felt his body relaxing. He swallowed the bread; he drank the wine.

Emmett was whistling as he chopped the vegetables. He didn't seem to have a real care in the world. Peter considered him, bleary-eyed by the window. He wanted to ask Emmett so many things. But he also felt he couldn't readily trust this man, even as Emmett nourished them, even as he rescued them from that dreary Nazi prison.

"Oh. Peter. I know of a doctor in this town. I wondered if you might consider going with me tomorrow to track him down and bring him here to look at Julie," Emmett said, gesturing toward Julie, whose arm did look worse for wear, hanging down a little lopsided against her hip.

Julie's eyes seemed a bit empty; she was falling in and out of consciousness, Peter understood. The mix of pain and wine was forcing her eyes closed.

"Sounds good," Peter murmured. He took the glass from her fingers and helped her lie back, positioning the bad arm across her stomach. He leaned down and kissed her on the cheek. He whispered a few words in her ear: "I'm going to keep you safe." But he didn't allow Emmett to hear them.

Peter walked toward Emmett and leaned against the counter, setting his empty glass next to the wine bottle.

"Can I tempt you with another?" Emmett asked Peter.

Peter tipped his head, uncertain of what to say. "Yes, Emmett. Please do." He listened to the glug-glug-glug as the man filled his glass. They clinked their glasses together, sending a strange dissonance through the apartment.

"Why are you here?" Peter finally said. The wind had picked up outside, making him feel strange, like he was living in one of his German-occupied dreams.

Emmett paused, considering. He swirled his wine around in his glass. He cleared his throat. "I'm here to help you on your journey. My mission is to make sure your mission is successful." His left eyebrow rose high on his forehead. "And that's really all the information I can tell you at this time."

"So you've been following us this whole time?"

Emmett nodded. "I did lose you for a moment, of course. When the Nazis took you. I didn't expect that at all. Expert work stealing that car though." He tapped his nose, giving Peter a knowing look. "I didn't know you had it in you."

Peter felt oddly proud. He shifted his weight from left to right, looking down. "Well. It might have been part of the reason we were captured," he murmured, shrugging. He thought about it, remembering that Manstein had known about their foray through time. How had he known? And how much did Emmett know?

He began to ask him, then. But Emmett had already turned back toward the window. He shook his head. "You'd better get some rest, Peter. We'll be leaving in two days' time, to stay on schedule. I've brought your bags from the last town. I picked them up from that boarding house you were staying at."

Peter felt his heart sink. He felt like he was on a Ferris wheel, unable to get off. He would have to ride this disastrous, chaotic ride until it spit him to the ground. He turned back toward the bed and curled up onto it, molding himself around Julie. He felt his eyes close serenely; he fell asleep almost instantly.

———~———

The next morning, Peter felt a light touch on his mouth. His eyes opened to the brightness of the window. Beside him, Julie was awake. She was touching his mouth with her pinky finger, gazing at his face. Peter blinked, trying to figure out his surroundings. What a beautiful feeling, he thought. He leaned toward her and caught her lips with his. Their intimate embrace was a moment of solace before he remembered why they were there, what they were doing.

Peter pulled himself from the bed and shuffled his hands over his face, feeling the dirt and grime from the cavernous Nazi prison. He noted that Emmett had brought them a bucket of water and some soap. He'd set it by the windowsill. Peter picked up a washrag and started dipping it into the water, scraping at his dead skin, the caked blood on his back. Julie brought herself forward on the bed. Without speaking, she grabbed the rag and guided it toward the places Peter couldn't reach on his own. She scraped the dried blood away lovingly, without hurting him. Peter closed his eyes, feeling the tenderness of her touch. He longed for it to go on forever.

But it couldn't.

Emmett burst into the room. He was carrying a fresh baguette, and his face was pinched, serious. "Good morning," he said quietly. He placed the bread on the counter and leaned against the wall.

Julie removed the rag from Peter's back and rinsed it in the pail. Peter watched as the blood formed small trails in the water. "Good morning, Emmett," Julie said. Her voice was serene, cool. It held no trace of the screeching and screaming she had done during the past few days, back in the prison. "Is something wrong?"

Emmett scratched his chin. "Maybe. I've noticed more activity with the Vichy in both this town and the next one down the road."

"Are they looking for us?" Peter asked.

"It seems they're not," Emmett said. He hesitated. "Which allows us to find the doctor today, Peter. To look at Julie's arm."

Peter nodded. "But you're saying this isn't a good thing? What could this mean?" Peter asked Emmett, unsure. His brain was still muddled; he needed seventy more years of sleep. He wanted to wake up in the year 2013.

"That depends," Emmett said. He ripped off a piece of bread and started chewing it slowly. His eyes looked dead. "It could mean that the Vichy are preparing to ship out. Most of them, this time. A great battle, perhaps."

Peter stood. "But there isn't supposed to be a battle here. Not yet."

Emmett bit off another piece of bread, shaking his head. "No certainty in war," he murmured.

Peter wanted to grab him, to shake him. There was certainty. There was meant to be certainty. He was from the future; he should know. He took a deep breath and rose, then grabbed a clean shirt from the bag that Emmett had thoughtfully recovered from their last lodging. As he did so, his leather-clad journal dropped to the floor. He picked it up and briefly flipped through the blank pages, settling in on his last entry. After a moment of scanning through his written narration of their trip, he closed the book and tucked it under his pillow, vowing to record some of his thoughts, his horrific memories of the last few days.

"We should move quickly, then," he said. "If we're going to get to Oradour-sur-Glane by tomorrow."

Emmett nodded his head curtly. "It's a ten minute walk to the doctor. You ready?"

Peter nodded. He followed Emmett out the door, stopping for a moment to peer back at Julie. She was still holding on to her bad arm, wincing a bit. She looked at him meekly, mouthing the words, "Go. Be careful." She didn't trust Emmett, he knew. But Emmett was all they had.

Peter strode outside in his fresh clothes, his back and face completely cleansed. He felt renewed. He walked quickly alongside Emmett, noting that many of the soldiers who had been there only the day before had abandoned their posts for other mandates. In the field beside the town, he could see Vichy lining up, conducting drills. His heart quickened at the severity of the war—a war that hadn't been at all tactile or real to him in 2013.

Emmett hardly spoke as they walked. He pointed out small things in the town, saying that his research had shown this was a sleepy place, one that had suffered from the introduction of the Nazi party. A pretty fountain was in the center of the village, turned off. A beautiful Greek statue stood in the center: a naked woman leaning forward, pouring her pail into the basin. But no water flowed. A small chip in her cheek gleamed in the light, showing that she held less vitality and youth than she had in previous decades.

The doctor lived in a cottage outside of the city. A big old cow stood outside. It mooed at Emmett and Peter as they approached. Its udders were inflamed and drooping toward the ground. Peter reached out to the cow and stroked its head.

Emmett rapped on the weather-beaten door, and Peter could hear creaking inside the old house. The door opened slowly, revealing the small, timid head of the oldest man Peter had ever seen. The old man lifted his finger toward the two of them. "*Qu'est-ce que vous voudrez?*" he asked them. *What do you want?* Behind him stood a young woman. His daughter, certainly. She whispered to her father not to trust anyone, that anyone could be Vichy, could be Nazi.

But her father turned back around. Emmett explained to the man in rough French that they required a doctor immediately for the assistance of their friend who'd fallen on her arm. The doctor nodded. He turned back around, grabbed his coat and slipped it on. He blinked at the two men before him as if to say, "Lead me." His daughter grasped the door and watched them go, a worried look on her face.

The men walked slowly on either side of the old French doctor. When the doctor saw the Vichy practicing in the field, he began muttering under his breath. Neither Emmett or Peter understood his words, and the doctor apparently didn't intend them to. His eyes darted back and forth with certain anger. Peter wondered if the doctor had been involved in the first World War in any way, if he'd grown an intense hatred for war.

They reached the bakery. Peter helped the old man up the steps, saying, "Pardon," one of the few French words he knew—one that Julie jokingly said didn't really count because it was, technically, also an English word.

Emmett opened the door behind Peter as he made his final, backwards step. He guided the old man into the room. The old man placed his doctor's bag on the counter, and Peter remembered the sheer brilliance of modern medicine. His stomach clenched. What was this man going to do to Julie?

The man reached Julie's bed. She looked up at him and gave him that beautiful smile. *"Bonjour, monsieur,"* she whispered. Pain glimmered in each of her words.

The doctor knelt before her and began feeling her arm, touching it with soft fingers. He turned his face up toward Julie and said, *"Désarticulé."* And then, all at once, he manipulated her arm with a strength Peter would have sworn he didn't have and popped her shoulder back into place.

Julie screamed for a moment and then looked toward Peter in shock. It was over. She moved her arm gently back and forth, kneading at her hand. "He said it was just dislocated," she whispered. And sure enough, the arm now matched its partner. It was still a bit bruised, but it seemed to be fully operational.

Julie turned back toward the doctor, who was bustling toward the door. *"Monsieur. Merci beaucoup,"* she said. *"Du fond de mon coeur."* From the bottom of her heart.

The doctor nodded curtly. He had done his business, and he was ready to head back home. His eyes glazed as he looked at the American men. Then he flung open the door and walked down the steps, his body creaking as he went.

Julie stood. Her eyes were flashing. She picked up the bucket, still filled with bloody water . She flung the water out the window in a wave of red, and Peter heard it splash against the ground. "Let's get back on track, shall we, boys?" she asked.

Peter took it as a challenge.

CHAPTER 12

The next morning, Emmett, Peter, and Julie rose early. They sat in the kitchen and pored over the map, noting they were still two hours away from Oradour-sur-Glane, their destination. Peter watched Julie's slim finger trace the route as she thought, biting her lip.

"Well. We absolutely cannot take the Nazi Jeep," she said, refuting Peter's initial suggestion. "They know we've taken it. It's not safe."

Emmett nodded. "You know, there's French resistance all through this part of the country. If we explain to them that we must get to Oradour-sur-Glane—for their benefit, only—then I'm certain they'll help us."

"How will we convince them?" Peter asked.

Julie thought for a moment, tapping her finger against her chin. "That doctor ..." Her eyes moved from Peter to Emmett. "Surely he isn't involved in the war efforts."

Peter and Emmett thought of the woman who'd been standing behind the doctor—his daughter. She'd said something about not trusting anyone. She was clearly on the side of the resistance, and even if she wasn't, she might be their only hope. He began folding the map, preparing for a future he couldn't predict.

They donned their traveling clothes, picked up their

344

suitcases, and closed the apartment door tightly behind them, then began their trek back to the doctor's cottage. Peter said goodbye to this version of paradise, the only place in which he'd felt safe since their arrival in France.

The Vichy were still in the field, marching back and forth. Their boots seemed to create an earthquake beneath their feet a sensation that was truly ominous. Julie reached toward Peter and held his hand as they walked through the village, feeling the emptiness of the place as it echoed around them. The fountain seemed even more dead than it had the day before.

The doctor's shack appeared in front of them once more. The cow mooed at them, just the same as before. Before Peter had a chance to tap on the door, the door whooshed open, revealing the doctor's daughter. She held a knife in her hand, and her eyes were dark. "*Pas au'jour'dui,*" she said. Her lips were large, feminine. She was such a strange convergence of fierceness and soft beauty.

Julie walked toward her, unafraid. She didn't smile, choosing instead to speak with gentle authority. "*Mademoiselle,*" she began. "*Je suis d'un mission secrete des americains. J'ai eu un petit accident, et ton pere a assisté beaucoup. C'est tres gentille.*"

Peter tried to follow her words. She'd said she was on a secret American mission, that the doctor had helped her a great deal after her accident. Peter tried to make his face look calm and nonthreatening as they stood in the doorway.

"*Alors. Maintenainent, nous sommes coincés ici. Nouse avons besoin d'aller a Oradour-sur-Glane. C'est tres important.*" Julie's eyes pleaded with the young woman who stood scowling at her.

Finally, the young woman lowered her knife. She spoke gently toward Julie. "*Vous n'etes pas les espions, oui?*"

"*Non, non,*" Julie said, shaking her head. She wasn't a spy.

The young girl bit her lip, clearly having some sort of inner struggle. She gestured for them to follow her into the cottage. Inside, the doctor was sitting in a grand chair. His eyes were closed, and his mouth was slightly open. He was sleeping.

The house smelled like baking bread, like aging wood. Peter gazed around at this intimate portrayal of 1940s France, of the way the war had ripped into simple people like this and changed the very way they lived their lives.

The woman felt beneath a cupboard and brought out a key that she took to Julie, placing it in her outstretched palm. *"Pour la voiture,"* she said. *"Si vous plait. Allez."* She gestured for them to leave, all at once. Her eyes had begun to grow dark and frightened once more.

The doctor in the corner let out a long, strong snore. *"Maintenant,"* his daughter said again. *Now.*

The three Americans hurried out of the cottage into the clean, fresh air. Julie held the key in her hand, and they wound around to the back of the cottage, where they found a sad-looking yellow car. They bounded into it, with Peter in the driver's seat. Emmett sat next to him, and Julie sat in back.

"God, Julie. That was perfect. Just amazing," Peter said, shaking his head. "I didn't know what you were saying half the time."

Julie glowed in the back seat, but got down to business immediately. "We need to get going. *Allez-Allez!*" She hit the back of his seat hard, forcing him to place his foot on the gas pedal. The car made a creaking sound as he turned the engine over, spinning the wheels forward. Peter breathed a sigh of relief as they picked up speed. He wasn't sure if they'd gone through all that for nothing.

The French countryside began to glide past them at an alarming rate. Emmett pointed out a castle on their right hand side, one that had stood the test of time, of war. Peter gazed at it, knowing they were getting closer and closer to a terrifying future. Everything was about to change.

Peter's heart skipped a beat when he turned the corner, giving them a better view of the surrounding countryside. At the foot of the castle, tents stretched throughout the field. Nazi soldiers stood in ranks, practicing drills, pumping their knees toward the sky. Peter, Emmett, and Julie watched them in silence for a moment before Julie spoke.

"You know, I really think things have escalated much more quickly than Applegate suggested."

Peter nodded. "He said there wouldn't be much activity for many more months, that our trip up to Oradour-sur-Glane would be generally uneventful." He swallowed. "Clearly he was mistaken."

"Or that's what happened in the old timeline," Julie said, still gazing out over the field. The gray uniforms seemed so foreboding in the midst of all the green grass. They had marched until the grass—and all of Europe—had died beneath their feet. "I don't think we can take anything like that into account anymore. Historically significant dates are no longer dates at all. Things have begun to change."

Peter knew she was right.

They continued north until the Nazi army was out of sight, all of them still pondering the weight of what they finally understood. They were in a gray area of history. They didn't know what was going to happen when they arrived at their destination—or even if the now-future events would allow them to complete their mission.

They kept their eyes on the horizon, not at all certain it would arrive.

CHAPTER 13

They reached Oradour-sur-Glane just before nightfall. The beautiful French town seemed like a ghost to Peter. Soft light glowed from the windows; children were playing in the streets. Old men and women sat out at cafés, their bodies curved over their wine glasses and cheese plates. The whole place seemed like a memory, stripped from an idealistic old movie.

As the three of them drove down the street, it didn't seem to Peter that the war had affected these people at all. He yearned to save that, in a way. He yearned to hold this moment, with Julie—the only living descendant of this paradise—in the back seat, close to his heart forever.

They parked the car outside of a café, knowing it was too late in the evening to find the man who had written the memos. They could do all of that tomorrow, they agreed. But there was no time limit. They decided to enjoy one last night all together, to process the last few days. They walked toward a café and sat outside in the deepening sunset. A waiter came toward them and delivered three glasses of wine, some baguettes, a cheese plate.

Peter curled his arm around Julie's chair and spoke to her as Emmett busied himself with his food. "So. This is what we've been working for the entire time. Do you think it looks anything like the model Applegate had back in San Francisco?"

Julie laughed, tossing her head back. She was so pure,

here. She looked just as beautiful as everyone else. "Not even close," she said, shaking her head.

"How's your arm?"

"Just fine. He popped it right into place."

"Incredible."

"Who needs modern medicine?" she shrugged, smiling.

Peter and Julie had been gazing into each other's eyes for just a few moments before Peter's stomach lurched at a strange sound. A great blast from a horn—ferocious strength behind it. All three of them turned their attention toward the center of the square, where a young soldier was stationed on the cobblestones. Peter grabbed Julie's hand, afraid. The man brought the horn back to his mouth and blasted once more. All around them, people had scattered. They stood up from their chairs and scurried inside. All the young men stayed out on the street, reaching for their pistols.

Emmett leaned across the table, erupting from his chair. "You must hide!" he insisted.

Peter and Julie jolted from their chairs. In the distance, all the way down the country road, they could see the Nazis. Five Jeeps were headed straight for them, guns positioned toward the historic town. Peter reached down to gather the bags. "He's right," he told Julie. "We have to finish the mission. We can't get in the middle of whatever this is."

"This wasn't supposed to happen," she cried.

Peter tugged her inside. "I know. But we're improvising through time, now," he said, his eyes intent.

Emmett stayed out in the street. He reached for his own gun and brought himself alongside the other resistance soldiers, ready to protect the small French town.

"Why is he helping?" Julie asked as they took refuge in the back of the café, behind a wood-burning stove. They peered around, still in view of the coming skirmish.

"This is his timeline," Peter whispered. "This war is all he's ever known."

Julie nodded. The French people around them were huddled

close together. Women wrapped their arms around their children, trying not to shake visibly, trying not to frighten the little ones while their fathers and older brothers stood outside, waiting for the coming attack.

Julie wrapped herself in Peter's arms. Peter knew she was thinking about her own family. She wouldn't recognize them if she saw them, but if they died in front of her, he knew she wouldn't be able to take that pain, that loss. He rubbed her back, feeling the bones of her spine as they shook with the weight of her passionate cries. War wasn't fair, no matter whether it had already happened or if it was happening around you.

The Germans moved closer. Peter could feel the tension growing on the streets. At least a hundred of the resistance men, the Oradour-sur-Glane crew, stood outside, bravely preparing for the skirmish. And then, the first shot was fired. All the women and children gasped in the café, crying out. Shots began to explode back and forth. The line of Jeeps had reached the town perimeter, and the Nazis had bounded from their vehicles and begun shooting.

Peter watched Emmett as he ducked behind a table and took shot after shot. The men beside him looked calm, steady. Peter lurched forward from Julie and found himself gazing out the window at the terrifying battle—a battle he wasn't sure had actually taken place in his own dimension, in his historical timeline.

The men of Oradour-sur-Glane were sure in their shots—country and town boys with good aim. They struck and killed many German soldiers in the street that day, losing only a few of their own. The battle was swift, ending almost too quickly. It was almost a waste. Peter watched as the remaining German men scooped their dead into the backs of the Jeeps and rounded back, toward their home base.

The Oradour-sur-Glane resistance lurched from their hiding places and began leaping up and down, blasting gunshots into the air. "*Victoire!*" was the word on everyone's lips. "*Victoire!*"

Peter spun around and found Julie's tear-drenched face. He reached toward her and wrapped his arms around her, spinning her in a circle. "*Victoire*, Julie," he murmured, kissing her. His heart felt light. He carried her out into the street, where they met with Emmett. Emmett's goofy grin was youthful, triumphant. Peter grabbed him by the shoulder and shook him, smiling madly. This man—this man who had saved their lives—had done it once more. "Goddammit, Emmett. What would we do without you?"

All around, men met with their wives, their sisters. There was kissing; there was laughter. A sense of assurance washed over the three Americans as they walked through the town, gazing at the truly resurrected evening. The moon had risen over the town, allowing the windows to gleam, the puddles from a recent rain to shine.

"I just—I couldn't not fight, you know?" Emmett said, then reiterated the events of the previous hour. "I just felt I had to. I was called to."

Peter and Julie grinned at him. Julie leaned toward him and kissed him on the cheek, making him blush for a moment. "Thank you for protecting my family," she said.

On the outskirts of the small village, in the moonlight, they saw a small, delicate farmhouse. Julie stopped when she saw it. Peter could feel her pulse quicken at her wrist. "What is it?" he asked her.

"That farmhouse. It seems so familiar," she said.

The two men followed her as she walked toward it quickly, her eyes bright beneath the stars. She ascended the worn steps, wiping her sweating palms on her dress. She flicked her brown hair behind her back and rapped on the door lightly, carefully.

The three waited on the steps expectantly. A single tear had descended Julie's face, Peter noticed. She wiped it away before she thought anyone could see.

Finally, the door creaked open. On the other side, a beautiful young woman—a woman who looked incredibly like Julie; it was undeniable—greeted them. Her face was a bit worn, a bit tired from the events of the day. "*Bonsoir?* she inquired.

"*Oui. Bonsoir,*" Julie whispered back.

Peter knew, then. He knew they'd found Julie's past. Her family. His mind began to panic. Would this mess up the entire timeline? Their entire mission? Applegate had said she shouldn't find her family, that Peter had to watch her every inch of the way. But he'd been distracted. And with everything so out-of-whack anyway, did Applegate even exist anymore?

Julie continued, clearing her throat. "*Nous sommes les americaines avec un mission secrete de la resistance.*" She said they were Americans on a secret mission for the resistance. Peter thought it was a good plan; find shelter somewhere. But here? Was Julie out of her mind?

The woman nodded, looking at Julie through strained eyes. Surely she felt she was looking into a mirror. She gestured, allowing them to enter. Peter removed his boots at the door, feeling the rough wooden floor beneath his socked feet. Around him, the farmhouse glowed. A fire burned bright in the fireplace. A young girl sat before it, playing with a small doll. The young girl was dark-haired, the most beautiful little girl that Peter had ever seen. She looked like an angel.

"Marion," the mother called to the young girl. "*Nous avons des visiteurs. Si ti plait, il y a des verres la—*" The mother gestured toward the cabinet, where the young girl found some glasses. She set them on the counter, gazing up at Julie.

Julie bit her lip so tightly, Peter thought she was going to draw blood. She knelt before the young girl as the girl worked. The girl stopped, a glass still in each hand. "*Coucou,*" she said.

Marion, the young girl, smiled at Julie sheepishly.

"I'm sorry. She is quite shy," the mother began. "And my English—it is very bad."

"No. It's wonderful," Peter said, giving her a reassuring look.

The mother, whose name they soon learned was Marie, poured them each a glass of wine. "My husband is still in the city," she said. "He had to fight today with the resistance." She handed the glasses out to her visitors.

"They fought bravely," Julie said. She brought her glass forward in a toast. The others in the room clinked their glasses. Then Julie turned her head toward the little girl, Marion—her grandmother—and winked at her. The little girl gave her a secret grin.

"You'll all be comfortable in the guest room?" Marie asked, bringing her fingers together.

"Absolutely," Peter said. "It will be perfect for us to prepare for the mission."

"*Un mission secrete*," Marie said, raising an eyebrow. She was so sassy, so French. Peter found himself attracted to her, if only because she was so much like Julie.

"*C'est trop importante pour les hommes, seule*," Julie said to the woman, eyeing Peter.

Peter tried to work out the words she'd said as the women laughed together, but he found that he couldn't keep track. He didn't really care, anyway.

Marie led them to the guest room, where Emmett situated himself on a mat on the floor and Julie and Peter sat on the bed, whispering together.

"I can't believe I've found them," she said.

"Well, I think we should leave as soon as possible tomorrow to finish the mission. We can't mess up any more timelines," Peter replied. His voice was firm. He knew this had all been a very bad idea, even if it was sort of magical here—like a secret portal through history.

But Julie wasn't paying attention. She fell into the covers as if in a daydream. Peter kissed her shoulder as she fell into a deep sleep.

He couldn't sleep for a long time, filled with fear and curiosity about the coming day. He knew everything was coming to a head. He had to be vigilant. Finally, he surrendered to insomnia and opened his journal to write. As soon as his fountain pen began to scratch along the yellowed paper, his mind was fully engrossed.

Nearly two hours had passed before Julie rolled over,

prompting him to focus on sleep instead. Reluctantly, he obliged, slipping the journal back into his satchel and dousing the light. He was asleep within moments, dreaming once again of his kids and the brutish German soldier.

CHAPTER 14

The next morning, Peter woke, blinking into the sunlight outside of the small farmhouse. The bed was empty beside him, and his throat constricted as he realized Julie was missing. He sat straight up, lurching his head left, right, eyeing the simplistic, 1940s style of the bedroom on the top floor. Emmett slept on, dreaming into the late morning.

Peter raced toward the door, his heart pounding. He cracked it, searching down the hallway, down the steps. He heard a small string of laughter emanating from somewhere far away, and he held his breath, trying to pinpoint the laugh.

Sure enough, it was Julie. He shook his head, trying to calm himself. He brushed his hair with his fingers and began to walk down the steps, feeling the rickety house splinter around him. He wondered if they could save this house, if they could save the village by changing that memo. Perhaps they already had, in this altered timeline.

Outside, in the waking sunlight, he could see Julie, the young girl, and Marie, her mother. They all stood next to a cow. The young girl was showing Julie how to tug at the udder easily, squirting milk into a pan below. Peter drifted through the green grass, feeling completely natural in this environment. He walked up behind Julie, who'd begun to lean down to try her hand at it.

Marie brightened as he approached. "Oh. *Bon matin*," she

said, smiling. She looked at him shyly. Peter wondered where her husband was. Had he been injured in the previous day's short battle? "I hope you sleep well?" she asked him.

"Oh, yes," he said, eyeing Julie's slender fingers as she tugged at the udder and produced natural, steaming milk.

"*Pour le petit dejeuner,*" the little girl explained to him brightly. Because Peter had memorized a lot of French words associated with food, these hit him where it counted.

"*C'est tres bien,*" he said in his sloppy American accent. Everyone, including Julie, laughed into the bright blue sky.

He loved seeing Julie like this: so happy, so completely fluid in her surroundings. She'd always held a quiet shadow beneath her eyes—something that told about her wayward past with her father. But during the recent days in France, since they'd arrived in Oradour-sur-Glane, that shadow had nearly vanished.

She lifted the bucket toward Peter's face, nodding toward him. "*Boire,*" she murmured. *Drink.*

His eyes were on hers as he began to sip, and the still-warm drink passed his tongue, down his throat. He felt nourishment filter through him. He felt refreshed. "*Merci,*" he said, wiping his mouth with the back of his hand.

Marie suddenly leaped up, pointing toward the side of the farmhouse. "Marc!" she called. She lifted her skirts and darted toward the man, wrapping her arms around him when she reached him.

"That's her husband," Julie explained, falling back into English. "I read about him in the family mementos. The letters my grandmother wrote." She turned her head toward the young girl, Marion, who'd spun around to spot her father. "He's said to be a stern, if loving man. He died fighting in the battle at Oradour-sur-Glane, protecting my grandmother." Julie shuddered for a moment, peering at Peter. "You feel okay?" she asked.

"Of course. Just … The battle yesterday has me worried."

Julie shook her head. "Anything that happened in the past isn't guaranteed to happen again. We have to proceed with the mission today."

"And then? We go back together?" Peter said. He noted a hint of passion in his voice. He tried to hide the fear he had—that Julie would choose to live here, without him.

"Of course," Julie said, taking his hand. She gave him a reassuring look. "Let's head inside, yeah? *Petit-dejeuner*? I know you know that one." She winked at him.

They walked inside. Emmett stood in the dining room, strapping his suspenders over his shoulders. He reached out to shake the hand of the man in front of him: Marc. Julie's great-grandfather. "*Enchanté*," Emmett said.

"Please. I speak English," Marc said, bringing his hands out wide in explanation. "I think I saw you at the battle yesterday."

Emmett blushed, placing his hand the back of his neck. "Anything I can do to help out," he said.

"We appreciate it. We try to keep Oradour-sur-Glane strong, even in the wake of the Nazi terror." Marc wrapped his arm around his pretty wife, Marie. "We will not fall to such treachery."

"I understand," Emmett said firmly.

Marc began to sit at the table. He drew a napkin over his lap. "We've just learned this morning at the town meeting that the Vichy are joining ranks with us, with the resistance. After the Nazi attempt to destroy us yesterday—after all the events in the south and in Paris—the Vichy have decided to right their wrongs, so you say." Marc tapped his forehead with his finger.

A feeling of heightened emotion passed through the room. Peter swallowed. He knew that the Vichy weren't meant to join ranks with the resistance until at least a year after this time. What would happen to the timeline now?

"Well. We must get you some food before you go out on your mission secrete," Marie spoke up, inserting her way into the tension like a knife. "Or. *Le petit-dejeuner*, like you said," she said with a smile, tapping Peter on the shoulder.

Julie whispered into Peter's ear, noting his small moment of shock at Marie's intimate touch. "Don't worry. The French like to flirt. With everyone," she said, laughing.

They sat at the table and enjoyed a multi-faceted conversation, with many different dialects, many different flavors of speech coming together. Peter watched as Julie laughed with her family members, giving them such a brilliant smile. He realized that this was the first family reunion she'd ever had, really. So much had happened between 1943 and 2013 in her family's timeline. She'd been given a chance to reboot, to see the castle before the ruin.

Marc and Marie said they were meaning to walk to town that day, that they could show Julie, Peter, and Emmett around on their way to find the memo maker. Julie tapped Peter's knee, her eyebrows waggling. She wanted this more than anything, Peter knew.

"We'd love to," Peter said finally. Emmett looked at him with wide, loaded eyes. He was, perhaps, angry. He wanted to get on with the mission, to complete their time here. But Peter was split. He wanted to make Julie happy, beyond anything.

"Just a quick trip," Peter whispered to Emmett on their way from the farmhouse.

Emmett nodded. "I'm getting anxious, Peter. One wrong turn after another. And we're finally here." He rushed up to grab some of their equipment.

Peter felt like his stomach was gnawing at him, that he was forgetting something. He grabbed Julie's hand as they left the farmhouse. He looked back at the house for only a moment as Marion reached toward Julie's other hand, asking her a timid question that only Julie could hear.

The farmhouse seemed to gleam, like it was wafting, lost in the clouds just a field away. The window shutters flapped briefly in the breeze. The cow still stood in the yard, churning her cud and watching them go. Peter took a deep breath, trying to focus. Today was the day they'd been working toward since he'd signed up on that fateful day—since he'd understood, finally, that he was meant for something bigger than himself, bigger than his problems. Since he'd said that goodbye to his children.

He watched Julie engage with the little girl walking alongside her. He tried to draw up an image of his own children in his mind. What did they look like, again? Tori's blonde hair; that way she smirked at him when he did something so parent-like, so annoying. He didn't really feel like a parent anymore.

Marie and Marc were far out in front of them, now. Emmett, Peter, Julie, and Marion hurried to catch them. The French couple were holding hands and gazing into each other's eyes as they spoke. Their love was intimate, fully-formed. "We've lived in this village since we were born," Marie said, turning toward Peter and Julie. "We met when we were children."

The town appeared before them, then. It was so beautiful, sunlit and sparkling in the beautiful day. Peter saw young children playing in the streets, old people eating at cafés. It was like the previous day's events hadn't even occurred. Like the war was raging on somewhere else, without affecting this beautiful place.

Emmett elbowed him out of his reverie. "We need to go," he said. His eyes looked glazed over, serious.

"That's Marion's school," Marie interrupted, nodding toward a small schoolhouse across from a bakery.

Marion started speaking rapid French to Julie: about her classes, about her friends. Julie nodded along; not a bit of interest in the memo of Project Sledgehammer showed on her face. Peter didn't know what to do.

Peter stood next to Emmett, feeling a little nervous. Everything around him seemed too perfect, too serene. The bakery next to him emitted such tantalizing smells. He peered in and saw an old man bringing freshly baked baguettes into the world. They shone in the light.

Peter noted, as he stood waiting to get away, to proceed with the mission, that several Vichy soldiers were stationed at various points throughout the town. They stood in lines, ready to protect. Ready to maintain the structure of this timid place.

Marc walked toward him and gestured. "If anything is to happen, they'll protect us. Now," he said.

Peter nodded.

"You care for a cigarette?" Marc asked. Peter agreed, and he found himself leaning against the wall in casual intimacy with this long-dead man. They smoked quietly, watching the women as they spoke near the schoolhouse. All at once, Marion scurried back toward them and rushed into the bakery. Julie and Marie followed her slowly, speaking to each other in a way that made Peter think they were sisters.

Inside, Peter could see little Marion gazing at the small pastries as they glistened. The red marmalade in the center was puddled high, making Peter's mouth water. The old baker approached the little girl and leaned toward her, whispering a secret in her ear.

Marie laughed as the five adults watched this. "They have quite a friendship," she said. "He gives her sweets; she gives him smiles." She shook her head, and the adults laughed in the sunlight as little Marion ducked into the back room, where Peter assumed more sweets were lurking. Perhaps the baker would let her lick the spoon, like Peter's mother had all those years before.

Suddenly, they heard it again. That noise. That horn. Peter brought his arm around Julie, trying to protect her. Marc tossed his cigarette to the ground in a way that reminded Peter of a cowboy in an old western.

Marie threw her arms around her husband, crying out, "*Qu-est'ce que c'est?*"

"It's the Nazis. They've come back."

The adults from both this past and this future listened as they heard the horn again. They heard the crunching of boots against the road; they heard great wheels. "Tanks," Emmett said. "They have tanks."

Peter ducked around the building with his arm around Julie. He gestured toward Marie, toward Marc. Toward Emmett. From this side, they were protected from the coming army. But they could see them as they approached. This time, there were several hundred of them. They were in Jeeps, in tanks. They had strapped enormous guns to the sides of their vehicles. They came forward like an enormous wall of hate.

"They are angry about yesterday," Marc whispered. He pushed his wife against the wall, then kissed her passionately, on her mouth, on her cheek. "*Mon amore*," he murmured. And then he was gone, rushing down the street with other men who'd heard the alarm, who understood: now was the time they had to protect their town. Yesterday had only been a trial run.

Marie seemed completely tormented with this knowledge. She pulled at her hair. Tears rushed down her cheeks. Peter knew they needed to get to safety. He turned toward Emmett, but Emmett's eyes were dark. "This is it," he said.

Suddenly, Marie leaped up from the wall, howling. "*Mon bébé!*" She rushed around, into the bakery. She had to find Marion, they understood.

Julie was looking at Peter with frightened eyes. "What should we do, Peter?"

Peter felt the pounding weight of the past few weeks on his shoulders, on his chest. He felt like he was going to pass out. He tried to search through his rushing mind, to find an appropriate thought. He turned toward Emmett, and they both nodded at the same time. In that moment, they knew this was the only timeline they had. They had to fight.

Peter kissed Julie passionately, just as he'd seen Marc do a minute before. "Run inside, Julie," he said. "We'll be back soon. We'll stay alive," he assured her. She nodded at him, her eyes brimming.

He spun around and followed Emmett toward the road. He paused for just a moment as he saw Julie follow Marie into the bakery to find little Marion. They would to be safe.

Emmett and Peter met up with some men from the resistance at the corner, huddled together, barking orders. They had weapons strapped to their bodies. A few extra weapons had been thrown to the side, and Peter and Emmett grabbed them, slinging rifles over their shoulders. The resistance didn't have much to them; they were thin, so French. Used to a different way of life. But the passion in their eyes was strong.

The men began to fall into rows. Peter could hear the tanks getting closer. Their wheels were spinning faster, stronger. Their great noses—those penetrating rifles—were pointed right at them. Peter felt naked.

The resistance started to march forward, to meet the Nazi regime at the edge of the city. Peter tried to count them. They were outnumbered in ways he couldn't comprehend. He swallowed, watching Emmett's face as they marched. They weren't trained soldiers; they hadn't been meant to die on the battlefield of Oradour-sur-Glane—a town that officially had no hope.

The resistance stopped, then. Their marching feet landed solidly in the sand. A single tank—an antiquated one from the previous World War—was wheeled forth on the resistance side. Peter didn't hear a single sound on the battlefield. The Nazi faces held no emotion.

Suddenly, Peter began to hear something—like an itching in the back of his brain. He felt the tension grow around him and the other soldiers; he felt his anxiety rise. Then they saw it: a plane. It skirted closer and closer, soaring across the incredible blue sky. Peter brought his gun up, his eyes following the plane as it came closer and closer.

It dropped something. It shot toward them, coming fast. Peter's mind raced. A V-1 flying bomb, he realized. They'd sent a bomb directly toward him, toward all of Oradour-sur-Glane. He felt a scream beginning in his stomach.

But the French had realized it, as well. They'd begun to charge the Germans, to outrun the bomb that was heading their way. Shots were fired on both sides as the bomb flew closer—a consistent shadow, a feeling of rushing anxiety. Emmett lurched forward, toward the Nazi army, fear blazing in his eyes. Peter followed him, his rifle poised. He wove through resistance soldiers, and he cocked the great gun, firing toward the Jeeps that were now so close to him—just the length of a football field away.

The blast deafened Peter, nearly throwing him to the

ground. He tucked his chin to his chest and braced himself for the shockwave. The seconds passed eternally slowly, and just as Peter felt like the concussion wouldn't come, the wave knocked them forward, into the cobblestone road. He dropped his rifle in the fall, but groped after it as he rolled to the side.

Next to him, a man let out a great cackle, a great hiccup. Peter lurched his head to the right and watched the man as he fell on his back, a hole forming in his chest. He brought his hand toward the rushing blood. The Frenchman's body looked so small. He was losing air, losing blood. The war drained him, closed his eyes.

All around Peter, people were falling, dying. They screamed empty French words into the raucous day. War wasn't meant for such a beautiful morning.

Peter urged himself forward, toward the Nazi army. Another guided bomb was rushing toward them. He saw it to his right; it was closer, sent from the ground. Emmett suddenly spun. The whites of his eyes were stark when compared to the blood coursing down his cheeks—other people's blood, Peter knew. He wondered how much of it was on his own body.

But Emmett knew. He knew that the bomb was heading right for them, that Peter was too out of it, too shocked in this strange, other dimension. Emmett flung himself onto Peter as the bomb shook into the earth to Peter's right, taking arms and legs and hearts and minds from all the soldiers around them.

Peter could feel the shudder, the silence, as Emmett pushed him to the ground, to safety, protecting him with his body. Peter's arms and legs were covered completely, and his face was tucked beneath Emmett's chest as Emmett fell upon him.

Peter coughed, bringing the first noise into the now-hushed field. "Emmett," he whispered. Emmett was a dead weight on his body. Didn't he know it was over? "Emmett. God, you saved me. I was an idiot—"

But Emmett didn't answer. Peter felt something warm begin to fall on him, dripping. He began to lurch back, to push Emmett off him. His heart was racing. He pushed Emmett up, and he could see that his eyes were pulled open, that his ear had been stripped clean off by the bomb.

Peter leaned Emmett against the ground, jostling his shoulder lightly. "Hey. Buddy?" Emmett still wasn't answering. His lips were so loose on his face. Peter looked around him, noting that his was the only movement in the field. A huge cloud of smoke had taken shape around him. He couldn't see the Nazis anymore, nothing but the outline of a single Nazi tank. They would keep coming; they would keep destroying, until the last resident of Oradour-sur-Glane was dead.

Peter turned back toward Emmett. His head lolled to the right. Blood oozed from his back, from his side. Everywhere Peter looked, the field was pulsing with blood. Emmett was dead, Peter knew. He closed his eyes, feeling his mind fall into a state of panic. What the hell was he going to do?

Peter leaned over Emmett, trying to think of something to say—something meaningful. This man had saved him, had followed him across the earth just to make sure he was okay. And now he had paid the ultimate price.

He spun his head back, toward the town. He noted that the original bomb had landed in the city. His heart lurched. *Julie.* He leaped from the battlefield and started to run, trying not to look at the dead men in the field. Their arms. Their legs. He tried not to realize that he was the only person who had survived the attack, that he didn't deserve his life.

Peter found himself in the center of town. The great strip of buildings had been struck by the bomb, and everything was on fire, spewing billows of black smoke. He brought his blood-drenched shirt over his mouth and made his way down the street, thoughts only of Julie in his head. He couldn't be the only one here; he couldn't do this on his own.

The bakery was on the corner. Peter lurched toward it, trying not to see all the dead in the street. The beautiful schoolhouse they'd seen earlier was caught in its own fit of flames across the street. The bakery's top windows had burst, and the glass lay in the street below. Peter stomped through it.

The entire bottom of the bakery was completely blackened. The back kitchen was spitting flames, and Peter started coughing. "Julie! Julie!" The steps before him led upstairs. He wondered if the women were there.

He rushed forward, but his first step on the stairs told him he needed a different plan, a different route. The steps had already fallen in.

It was getting difficult to breathe. Peter rushed outside to take a few earnest breaths. He realized that the Nazis hadn't gotten any closer. And why would they? Around him, the city was nearly all destroyed. The bomb had landed mere minutes before, and already the world around him was conquered. People had died in an instant. The anonymity of a bomb was incredible to Peter. Someone had dropped it and floated on through the sky.

Peter heard a crash. He looked toward the steps, where he'd just been. He saw her. Julie. She was rushing from the top floor carrying a small person in her arms. She held a rag over her mouth. Her eyes were bloodshot as she ran. But her feet were so purposeful, so true. She burst into the air beside him and fell into his arms. Peter wrapped his arms around her and brought his mouth to her forehead.

Julie was shaking. She turned her head toward him, her eyes shining. The young girl, Marion, looked up as well. Her face was covered in soot; a small bit of pastry was stuck to her cheek. "Julie?" she murmured.

The smoke hovered around them, and Peter knew they had to get moving.

CHAPTER 15

Peter and Julie walked quickly away from the smoke, out onto the field by the farmhouse. They didn't speak. Marion had descended into a sort of shock, and Julie cradled her in her arms. Her body strained with the weight of her young grandmother.

Peter was surprised when he saw the farmhouse. It was far enough away from the town that it had been hardly affected by the attack, but for one thing. The shockwave from the bomb had struck the front windows. They were all smashed, sending their glass into the charming home.

Julie burst through the front door and laid the young girl on the couch, tucking her tangled hair around her face.

Peter watched her, longing to interrupt the silence between them. He wanted to reassure Julie, but he didn't know how. He was just so goddamned grateful that she was alive. She shouldn't have lived, he knew. He shouldn't have, either.

"The mother—"

"Dead," Julie said. She rubbed her nose with her finger, like a nervous tic. "I blacked out for a moment and woke up in time—in time to grab Marion. The entire room was on fire." Her voice quivered. "We didn't save them, after all," she groaned.

Peter wrapped his arms around her. "You saved her. You were meant to be there. She survived in the previous timeline, which means—which means everything happened the way it was meant to." His words were meant to make her feel better, to make her feel like she'd done the right thing. But her eyes were dark, her expression unyielding.

"Where's Emmett?" Julie suddenly asked, turning her head to look out the window. The fire in the city had sent a huge ball of black smoke into the air. Everything was gray, cloudy. So unlike the morning had been.

Peter hung his head, explaining Emmett's fate. Julie nodded. "It's just us, now," she said. "What do you think we should do?"

"Continue with the mission. We have to. We've made it this far," Peter said, wiping at the dried blood on the side of his face. Emmett's blood. "You know where they're stationed?"

Julie nodded. "South of town. Marc told me."

"We should go as soon as possible. And then get the hell out of France." Peter swallowed, eyeing the sleeping girl on the couch. He knew they'd have to bring the girl with them to find the Vichy, to find the memo-maker. She didn't have anyone. But perhaps after they returned, they could find someone to raise her, to help her on her journey. After all, if Julie's grandmother didn't live through this, then Julie's timeline was all out of whack. Then her mother wouldn't be born. And Julie wouldn't be, either. She'd never be born to kill her father, to go on this mission. To grow to love Peter.

Julie and Peter cleaned up, washing the blood and soot from their faces at the sink. They hardly spoke. Peter began to regain his strength, and reached for the baguette that the family had been meant to eat for lunch. In a way, with each bit he ate, Peter felt he was robbing them of the life they had been meant to live. This farmhouse was going to fall to ruin. It was going to turn to nothing.

Julie wiped the young girl's face and arms, and Peter wrapped her in a blanket. As the late afternoon fell around them, they began to walk south of the city, where they knew members of the resistance were located. There, they would find the memo-maker. They would tell him to promote Operation Sledgehammer. The plan to covertly replace the memo had long since been abandoned. After this latest timeline anomaly, they just needed to convince him to make the appropriate recommendations. The French could be strong. This way, the terror that Peter had just experienced firsthand could be over. Families wouldn't be ripped apart.

Peter knew what the three of them looked like as they approached. Their clothes were blood-splattered; they looked lost. A member of the resistance walked toward them, holding his weapon in his hand and looking at them with worry. He spoke to Julie. "*Ca va?*" he asked, gesturing toward the child.

"*Oui,*" Julie replied. Her eyes were serious. "*J'aime bien a parler avec Oscar Gionnoccaro.*" Peter nodded, remembering the memo-maker's name, as well.

The man eyed her suspiciously. "*Pourquoi?*" he asked. His eyes darted.

"*J'ai un importante message des les americains,*" she said.

"*On ne peux pas entrer,*" the soldier answered. Dusk was falling around them, and the conversation felt ominous, like a grand pause before more battle, more murder.

"*Alors, il peut venir ici,*" Julie argued.

The man thought for a moment. He nodded curtly and spun around in a single motion, retreating back toward his comrades. He spoke to another man, who considered his words for a moment. They marched back to the center of the great tent village that stretched over the countryside. Peter and Julie stood quietly next to each other in solidarity in this strained moment.

Finally, the memo-maker, a Frenchman named Oscar Gionnocario, stepped out from a large, open-sided tent. The man pointed toward Peter and Julie, standing in the distance. Gionnocario nodded and advanced toward them, unafraid. His chin was high in the air.

"*Bonsoir,*" he said, nodding politely. "*Vous etes americain?*" he asked.

Peter stepped forward. "*Oui.*"

"I speak English," Gionnocario said, nodding again. "Please. Proceed with what you must say."

Peter's heart was beating fast. This was it. This was why they were there. Was it worth it? "We must tell you. You're considering an operation. Operation Sledgehammer."

"It doesn't matter what we send, now," Gionnocario replied. His voice was strained. Peter wondered if he'd had family in the destroyed town. "Oradour-sur-Glane was destroyed. It is done."

"No." Peter shook his head. "You must tell Churchill to proceed with Operation Sledgehammer. It will make all the difference in the world."

"Why should I?" Gionnocario asked. His eyebrows rose high on his face. His eyes were cat-like, alarmed.

"It is of great urgency to the Americans and to the greater French army to proceed with the operation," Peter said. His voice was hushed. He adjusted the girl in his arms. She slept on. Would she ever wake? he wondered. "If you don't want things like that—entire towns destroyed in one afternoon—to happen again, you must tell Churchill that Operation Sledgehammer is essential for the end of the war." Peter swallowed. "You must."

Gionnocario thought for a moment. He bowed his head toward Peter and Julie. The moon had appeared over them, then, giving the entire scene a sort of surreal sense. "I appreciate this sentiment. I will make greater consideration over the operation and what it will do for my country."

Peter nodded. "It's the only option. You don't have many. Not after today."

"Truly not," the man said with a sigh. He leaned toward Julie and kissed her hand. "You must be strong, my lady," he said. "It is the time to be strong."

"*You* be strong," Julie said, her voice full of passion. "And change the damn memo."

The man listened as she explained the virtues of the operation he was considering, and how critical it was to ending so much death and destruction. So much pain. She and Peter took turns pleading their case for nearly an hour.

Finally, Gionnocario spun back around. He marched back into camp vowing to change the memo that night, putting an appropriate cap on Julie and Peter's mission in France. Peter draped his arm around Julie as they walked back from the moonlit field. He helped her lay Marion in bed, then they watched her sleep for a moment, holding hands in the darkness. They were missing so many people, that night. It was just the three of them left.

The couple lay together in the guest room, Julie stretched out on Peter's chest. They listened to the beating of each other's hearts for a long time into the night, feeling the enormous brevity of being alive.

CHAPTER 16

Peter awoke the next morning, noting that somehow, he was still alive, and sweating in the sheets. Julie's side of the bed was empty. He swung his feet to the floor, holding his head in his hands. His legs ached from all the running the previous day on the battlefield.

He heard something from the other room. Concerned, he grabbed a shirt and flung his arms through it, then rushed toward the source of the sound. He found Julie leaning over a small pot, vomiting. She brought her hand around, waving him away.

"Can you give me a minute?" she asked.

Peter didn't want her to feel this way; he didn't want her to be ashamed. He wanted to take care of her. But he obeyed her wishes. "Please. Tell me if you need anything," he said.

He walked from the bathroom and peered into Marion's room. The little girl was still sleeping, surely not wanting to return to this treacherous world without her parents. He wondered what they would ultimately need to do with her—if they would need to take her to Paris, to an orphanage. A small part of him feared Paris, of course. He knew that the Nazis had taken over much of it, if the timeline had stayed true in that part of France.

He made the bed swiftly and washed his face, waiting for

Julie. Finally, she appeared in the doorway, her face flushed.

"Julie. Are you all right?" Peter asked. He sat on the bed, tapping it to ask her to sit beside him. She was so frail-looking in that moment. He was worried that maybe she had contracted some 1940s disease that hadn't been wiped out yet.

She sat next to him, and he rubbed her back, feeling a small quiver in her spine. What was going on?

Julie cleared her throat. She was preparing to speak, and then she closed her lips once more, shaking her head.

Peter tried to fill the empty tension in the room. "I was thinking we could take the girl somewhere safe. Do you know of any towns around here—towns with orphanages? I didn't think we were too far from Lyon."

Julie turned toward him, her eyes flashing. "My grandmother isn't going to grow up in an orphanage," she said. Her voice sounded weary, far away.

Peter's mind lurched. Would they need to bring the girl back with them, to the United States? He cleared his throat. "I want her to be safe, just like you. But we need to go back to our own time, to allow the timelines to work themselves out." He placed his hand on hers and she clung to it, nodding. "I'm sorry. I know this is hard for you."

Julie turned toward him. "Peter. I'm going to stay behind. I'm going to raise Marion. It's the least I can do." She shrugged, her eyes pleading with him.

Peter felt like he'd been punched in the gut. He had to convince her that this was a tremendous mistake—that she was robbing them both of something truly special: this relationship they'd built together.

Peter brought his hand to the back of her neck and gazed into her eyes. She'd been his guiding force ever since this adventure had begun. "Julie. You know I can't let you do that," he said. "We had a mission, and it's finished. You know what Applegate said."

But Julie shook her head vehemently. "Fuck Applegate," she said. Her voice caught in her throat.

Peter couldn't say another word. The young girl appeared at the door, creaking it a bit as she entered. She yawned into the light coming through the window. "*Bonjour, mes amies*," she said, smiling at them.

Julie was on her feet, brighter and more vibrant than she'd been only moments before, when she'd hung over that basin to vomit. She lifted Marion into her arms and carried her down the steps.

Peter remained there, sitting on the bed, gazing out the window, feeling his heart breaking.

Julie knew that she had to tell him; that she couldn't leave so many of these things unspoken. She cared for him a great deal. He was the only man she'd ever loved. She'd seen the worry in his eyes; she knew the heartbreak she was causing him.

She sat her grandmother, little Marion, at the kitchen table and began buttering a piece of bread for her, speaking quietly in French, trying to distract Marion's mind from her parents. It wasn't easy, of course. The girl was gradually remembering the events of the previous day, and she dropped the piece of bread on the table. Tears rolled down her round cheeks.

Julie reached toward her and brought Marion onto her lap, stroking her hair. "Shh. Shh," she said. "*C'est pas grave. Je suis ici.*" She told Marion she was there for her, that she would care for her all the days of her life. Julie knew, in her heart, that she was telling the truth.

A wave of nausea passed through her. She fought it; it wasn't as bad as the others. The morning sickness had only begun the previous week. She remembered waking as Peter slept on beside her and rushing to the basin. A moment of surprise had passed through her mind. It was like she hadn't believed that biology, that life could follow her all the way back to 1943. But here she was: pregnant.

Of course, she hadn't taken the birth control pills. She'd loved the freedom: the freedom to be with Peter, to love him in this altered timeline, without worrying. Of course that lack of care, that lack of worry had caught up to her.

She imagined it, then: the two of them, caring for young Marion, living on at the farm. He'd have to learn better French, certainly, but she and Marion could help him with that. When she was ready to have the baby, they could find a doctor from a local town. They could help build Oradour-sur-Glane back to its former glory—something Julie knew hadn't happened in her own past.

Marion leaned back from her, wiping her eyes and asking to go see the cow. Julie nodded, smiling for a moment. Her heart was full of love for this little girl. She carried her outside, imagining Marion becoming the older sister to the child growing in her body. What a family they would make.

Marion patted the cow's soft nose, gazing into the doe-like eyes of the creature. The cow chewed at the grass as if nothing had happened, as if no wars raged on. Julie stood beside her, waiting for Peter to come outside. Waiting. What could she say?

Finally, he appeared beside her, shifting his weight from foot to foot. She couldn't tell him about the baby, she knew. Not unless he agreed to be with her, to carry on with her in 1943. She couldn't stand the thought that he would know about this child growing in her womb and decide to stay only because of the baby. She didn't want to trap him with the news.

So she began casually. "Peter," she said. He turned toward her, looking at her with wet eyes, his expression drooping and sad. He didn't want her to stay. "You can stay here with me. We can be a family, in this other time," Julie said. Her voice quivered.

Peter brought his hands up to his chest. Julie could tell he was conflicted. He wanted to stay, she knew. But...

"Julie. I love you so much." He shook his head, hesitating. "I just ... I have two kids at home, back in 2013."

Julie nodded. She smiled through her tears, feeling the weight of his love for her. She brought her lips to his, and they kissed for a moment. Her heart hurt desperately. So much of her wished that time could stop, that she and Peter could live on in this moment, holding each other close.

This was the only time they had. This was all they could create. This moment.

She helped him pack, gathering his clothes together and feeling her tears drip down her cheeks. Marion sat in a corner of the room, playing quietly with her dolls.

Peter paused from the packing for a moment and played with the little girl, making small voices for her toy animals and cooing at her. Julie could tell that he was a wonderful father— that Tori and Brett were lucky to have his love. She placed her hand on her stomach, feeling small flutters deep within. This baby would be here soon, for her. And yet, the timing would be so far away, for Peter. This three-dimensional, living reminder of Peter would be all she could see, forever. She wouldn't have a photograph of him; she wouldn't have anything.

She had an idea, suddenly. She grabbed a small pad of paper and a pencil, and she began to draw him as he played with Marion. She captured his nose, his crooked smile. She captured the beauty of little Marion's round, lovely face as she and Peter gazed at each other with the intimacy of family, of love. Julie was so caught up in the drawing that she felt jilted when Peter finally stood up and looked at her, bringing his hands together. "It's time."

CHAPTER 17

Peter kissed Julie good-bye for the last time on the farmhouse porch on the outskirts of the decimated city of Oradour-sur-Glane. Some hesitation in her made him peer at her, shaking his head. Why were they doing this—ruining something so beautiful? She bit her lip, watching as little Marion told him goodbye, kissed his cheek, and handed him a dandelion she'd picked from the yard. Peter used the last bit of French he'd say in front of Julie: "*C'est tres belle*," he said, rotating the flower in his hands. He tried to imprint their image on his mind forever.

Peter could sense Julie's eyes on him as he walked away; he could sense that something had been left unsaid between them—that their story wasn't complete. But he knew that when he returned to 2013, she wouldn't be there. She would be dead. He pictured visiting her grave, visiting the grave of the little girl, as well. He hoped that Marion would take care of Julie, just as much as Julie would take care of her. He hoped that this strange, cyclical life would bring comfort and joy for Julie. He only wanted her to be happy.

He tried to shake these death-filled thoughts from his mind; they were elements to be dealt with on a different day, in another time. Soon, he was on the road, walking toward the nearby town. Julie had told him it was only five miles away. He felt a shroud of loneliness follow him as he headed west, wondering what the hell he was going to do now. He tried to imagine being back home in the United States after all he'd been through. In comparison, his old life had always been easy and serene.

Once he'd reached the nearby town, he found that the Nazis had destroyed much of it, as well. A few people lingered on, walking like ghosts along the cobblestones. He walked meekly among them, feeling almost apologetic for still being alive. He knew he shouldn't have been.

Peter found a car parked away from the city street, and he stole it easily. He felt anger growl in his heart, in his stomach at the sheer fact that he had come so far—and yet he hadn't done a single thing, really. In fact, he felt he had less, then, than he'd had before he left.

He journeyed south, beyond Lyon, beyond small French towns with picturesque French bakeries and marketplaces. He made sure to avoid the Vichy and the Nazis; after all, he wasn't sure if he could trust the Vichy, yet, despite what Marc had told him a few days before.

He traveled mostly in darkness, occupying himself by remembering the lyrics of weepy songs from his youth. For the first time in many years, he thought about somber breakup songs—songs he remembered listening to in his bedroom in high school, aching after one girl or another. The music was in his mind—in his soul.

As the miles passed, so did his dedication to the mission. Every time he stopped to get gas or supplies, he had to struggle through French phrases and watch the men and women he spoke with snicker at him. He realized he no longer looked like a spy. Rather, he looked like a dirty, sad American—without any hope or any prospects.

He found himself back in Sete, the canalled city in the south of France. He parked the car by the water and wandered along the canal, his mind lost in a sea of regret. He picked up a stone and tossed it into the water, watching it bounce. A man in a boat just a few feet away raised his hand in greeting. The sun had peppered the man with freckles.

A few hours before his ship was scheduled to leave, he climbed up the small mountain around which Sete had been built. He stood next to the monastery at the top of the hill and gazed down at the wild stretches of turquoise water. The people in Sete didn't seem bothered by the war efforts up north. At one point, he thought about remaining here, about summoning Julie and the child. But he didn't feel right about it. He needed to get back; he knew his place in the world.

Peter found the liner he was meant to take back to the United States, and he shuffled aboard, thinking of the words Julie had said about Sete all those weeks before. Her voice sounded like an echo in his head. How long had they been in France? he wondered. How long had this been happening? Decades? Years? A day or two? He felt the scars on his back from his stint in the Nazi prison, and his heart ached, remembering Julie's fear, the sound of her voice through the wall. Back then, he'd thought he'd never see her again. Now, he was certain he never would. They were purposefully drawing a curtain between them. He thought of the journalist Edward R. Murrow's words: *Good night and good luck.*

He felt the boat lurch from the dock, and he rushed from his cabin to the deck, where he watched the sun-filled Mediterranean city drift away from him. The sea was turquoise beneath him. He leaned heavy on his elbows as the sunlight penetrated his skin. Closing his eyes, he tried to imagine a different life for himself.

Throughout the long voyage, Peter continued to write, documenting his and Julie's journey through World war II. The exercise was difficult, as with every word, every line, his mind was continually centered on Julie.

He sat on the deck often, gazing out at the horizon. A few other people were on the liner, as well, mostly French people traveling to live in the United States after their war-torn country had collapsed around them.

One afternoon, Peter sat outside, smoking a cigarette he'd

purchased from a Frenchman who lived across the hall from him. He blew smoke into the air, creating small rings that floated overhead. He hadn't done that since college, and he loved the familiarity of it—the feeling that he was rooted to himself, to his past, even as he mulled over the strange events of the past few months.

Nearby, a young French woman and her husband stood gazing out over the water. The man was American, and the woman was French. Their conversation was spotty. It was clear to Peter that they couldn't quite communicate yet. The woman nodded at the man, her eyes lowered. She appeared to be crying. She placed her hand on her stomach as she turned, and Peter understood that she was pregnant. She strode away, allowing her hips to swivel this way, then that. She was far along, and Peter was mildly curious about it, remembering the months when Minnie was pregnant. How uncomfortable she'd been. To be on an ocean liner with a baby in your womb certainly couldn't be ideal.

The American man saw Peter watching, and walked toward him, sitting a few feet away on the deck bench. He lit a cigarette as well and spoke out of the side of his mouth, allowing the smoke to drift from his mouth easily. "Motion sickness. Home sickness. Morning sickness. You name it, she's got it."

Peter grunted, acknowledging the words. He remembered that his grandfather had been a man of very few words, and he'd tried to emulate that on the ship. He owed no one his words.

The man beside him continued to blow smoke. "I'm injured, yeah. That's why I'm heading home. You?"

Peter tapped his leg. "Bum knee."

The man nodded. "I met her in Paris. I was stationed there. She was such a beauty. Now, I knocked her up, asked her to come with me. She agreed, but I think she's having second thoughts." He scratched the area between his lip and his nose. "She's a timid girl. Not sure how she's going to get on with my mother and sisters in Boston. They're a loud bunch. Going to eat her alive."

Peter nodded. His mind had begun to whirl, and he took another long drag from his cigarette. The man excused himself and followed the pregnant woman.

Peter understood, then. He lit another cigarette as the words revolved around inside his head.

Julie was pregnant.

He hadn't caught the signs. Too much had been going on. But she'd been feeling ill, showing symptoms. He remembered her poised over the basin, vomiting. He remembered her holding her stomach with her hands during the day as she spoke to him, as if she was trying to tell him something.

It was true that before the trip became dire—before it involved actual Nazis, actual bombs—he and Julie had made love to each other as often as they could. They couldn't resist each other. It had been their intimate time together—a time that didn't exist anywhere else.

Peter knew that she wouldn't have been taking her birth control pills during their travels; the pills didn't fit in the timeline. And yet: he hadn't used any condoms, hadn't taken any precautions. They had thrown too much caution to the wind already. What was one more thing?

Peter hung his head in his hands as the boat steamed west, away from his love and their baby. He would be leaving them in this rocky past, a past that wasn't even written yet. His heart ached for them. But there was nothing he could do, nothing he could say.

He wondered if the baby would even learn his name. If he or she would ever know what he looked like. He imagined what Julie would tell the baby as he or she grew older. Would she tell the baby that his father loved architecture, and take him to the renowned buildings in Paris to learn where architecture had been and where it was going?

Peter spent most of the following days in his room, feeling the weight of this knowledge on his mind and in his heart. He couldn't believe he hadn't seen the signs. His brain itched as he wondered, had Julie allowed him to leave because she didn't truly love him? Had she wanted him to leave because she didn't see a future with him?

He tried to orient himself, to allow himself to heal. That was the only way he could survive.

CHAPTER 18

Peter arrived at the port, in New York City, after what seemed like many weeks at sea. It was strange to him how unchanged New York seemed from when he'd last been there all those months before.

Essentially, nothing about the war seemed to affect the city. He saw burly men in suits walking down the sidewalk, speaking quickly with their hands, articulating something essential, something that had been important back in this clouded past. He bought a beer for 39 cents near the train station, thinking about the long road back to San Francisco. He imagined Jack Kerouac as a young boy, walking the New York streets and already imagining the open road, crossing the country.

Did anyone know about Oradour-sur-Glane? Did anyone know about Marion, about Julie—trying to move forward with their lives on the outskirts of that little town? Did anyone think beyond their New York City lives, beyond their American dreams?

Peter boarded the train and daydreamed all the way back to San Francisco, gazing across the plains and feeling his heart widen at the grandeur of the Rocky Mountains. What a country they had. And it would grow stronger, perhaps stranger, in the next seventy years. The coming century was so essential to Peter's very existence. In just a few decades, his father would learn that his mother was pregnant with him; his father would be faced with a future of children, of struggles, of both happy and sad times. As the train rambled ahead, Peter felt like he was at the bottom of a well looking up into the sky. The sky was his future.

The train arrived all too quickly, returning him to his home. San Francisco would be the place he and his wife, Minnie, would meet; it would be the place they would decide to raise their children. Their discussions of moving anywhere else in the world would be brief. *Why would we?* they'd ask each other. And then their family life, their home, became too perfect to ever leave.

Until, of course, Minnie had died. Until Peter's life had collapsed around him.

Peter sighed heavily as the train doors opened, trying to orient himself to what he still had to do. He had to reach Dr. Epson; he had to return to 2013. His mission was nearly complete, and he wanted it to be over. As if he was waking up from a nightmare, he was ready to begin his day.

He strode from the train station, suddenly in the California fog once more. He had gone on the longest journey of his life, and now he felt the overarching sadness of that journey coming to an end. So much had ended, really: his relationship with Julie, his mission, his purpose. He didn't even know if his children still existed in 2013, yet, and he didn't even know if this all had been worth it. He tried to remember the chances Applegate had given him for his children's continued existence. Fifty percent? Sixty? Could he really bank on these chances, or should he head back to France, to a woman and a child who needed him, wholly, in the here-and-now?

The hotel room was still reserved for him, for Julie, and for the doctors. He found his key in his pocket, and he entered, finding the room undisturbed since he and Julie had left the continent. He opened a window, bringing light and air into the stuffy room. He began removing the clothes from his bag, aligning them on the windowsill, allowing them to flap in the breeze. He pulled his overflowing journal from his satchel, stroking the leather cover before placing it at his bedside.

He lay back on the bed, hearing the tick-tick-tick from the clock on the bedside table. He felt his body aging around him, in a way: he felt wrinkles growing, felt his skin sagging. He wondered what all that would mean when he passed away in some year in the greater century moving forward. Would his skeleton, his sagging skin, still contain any resonance of this year 1943, when so much love and passion and anger and sadness had passed through him?

He thought for a moment about the doctors who had had the hotel room across the hall. He stood and walked toward their room, and rapped his knuckles against the door. Suddenly, the door creaked open; it hadn't been closed all the way. "Hello?" Peter called. He leaned in and sensed that the room hadn't been lived in for some time. "Hello?" he called again.

All across the hotel room, papers had been strewn about. The bed had been torn apart, as if someone had been looking for something. Peter felt a wave of alarm course through his body. What the hell was going on? Each of the dresser drawers had been searched and torn from the dresser. He brought his hand to his head and remembered that he'd kept some papers in his own dresser. He panicked and turned, running back to his own room. He opened the wardrobe and found that the papers were still there, along with the final envelope from Applegate—"Mailing Instructions", all undisturbed.

But there was something else.

The roll of pennies he'd gotten from Canter, so long ago, was lying in the drawer. He knew he hadn't been the one to put them there. He held them up, noting the image of Lincoln and the year: 1943, right where it ought to be. They glinted in the light from the San Francisco sky.

Beneath the roll of pennies, Peter found a folded note. His heart beating fast, he brought it toward him, leaning back on the bed. The letter was from Julie. Her handwriting made his stomach clench. He pressed the paper to his chest for a moment, unsure if he wanted to read further. Why had she left him this? And would it help him get over her? Would it make anything easier on him?

Finally, he dove into the letter.

Peter,

You're reading this on the other side of the mission. We've gone to France, to Oradour-sur-Glane, and I'm hopefully stationed there, now, with my French family, just as I'd always planned.

You must listen to me, Peter, and you mustn't grow angry. I've tied everything up in 2013. I was fully prepared to take the leap into the past. Too much had happened to me in my lifetime. I felt like an alien in my own land, in my own apartment. I said goodbye to my stepfather, and I'm officially ready to orient myself in the past and to save my family from certain death. I hope you can understand. I want to rewrite the future, to create a better life for my family's bloodline. I feel like I owe it to my mother, to myself.

You'll notice I left the pennies, of course. All but one (which I've kept for myself as a memento). It's ultimately up to you what you do with these pennies, Peter. But I'd wager that your mind isn't on the pennies right now. It's on whatever's happened to you back in France, or the fact that I'm still living on there, while you've come back here to be with your family.

You're a good man, Peter, a man I could have truly loved. I wish I could have met you in another lifetime, where things could have worked out perfectly for us, where we were meant to have our meet-cute in a café or something other than a secret government mission.

Remember that I care for you, Peter. Remember to have strength as you move back into the future. I'll be thinking about you, always, as I live the remainder of my life in this antiquated past. (I never got into the Internet thing, anyway.)

Yours,
Julie

Peter swallowed. He felt the weight of the pennies in his hand as he refolded the letter slowly. He kissed it on the corner and tucked it into his journal. This was his final reminder of her, this woman he now loved. She'd written it even before they became lovers who'd gone through hell and come out the other side, hand in hand. He missed having her in bed with him; he missed hearing her voice in his ear—those raspy, secret whispers.

But there was another letter demanding his attention.

Peter,

I assume that if you've opened this letter, the mission was a success! Congratulations to you and your entire team. I am certain that the repercussions associated with your memo swap will be world-changing, and in the most positive way, I am sure.

Now, for the final leg of your mission—the journey home. In order for you and your team to return to 2013, there are a few simple procedures that you must complete. First, you must erase any trace of your existence in 1942. Depending on how vigilant you've all been about not sharing your identities throughout your assignment, this should be fairly straightforward. Leave no trail. Nothing from you or the team must remain in 1942.

The most important action for you to complete now is mailing the enclosed envelope. Do not tamper with or alter it in any way. Do not open the envelope, and specifically, DO NOT edit the mailing address. The address has been vetted thoroughly prior to your departure to 1942. It is an address that exists both then and now, and one to which I will have full access in the future as you see it from 1942.

Briefly, I'll explain the urgency for this mailing. It contains information for me about the team and the mission. When you come back to 2013, the world will have moved on along a different path, and I will not have any recollection of you or the mission without that envelope. It will give me instructions to receive you and your team at the appropriate travel window.

As for that time frame, it is slightly different for your return to 2013 than it was for your travel to the past. We had a very specific slot we had to transport you all through in order to introduce you to Dr. Epson at precisely the right moment. With your return, we'll be able to leave the device on and in receiving mode.

Again, Peter, I am very thankful for your devotion to this mission, and will be eager to meet you, Julie and the doctors upon your return. I am sure your stories will be legendary.

Regards,
Harrison Applegate

Suddenly, Peter rose once more, his mind racing as he broke from his reverie. The doctors! He realized that they'd been taken by Mandrake—and that Mandrake had certainly had their room ransacked before taking them. He'd known that everything had been some sort of elaborate scheme, and now at the end of the mission, Peter needed to get to the bottom of it—why Mandrake was so heavily involved in everything, even when they hadn't heard his name spoken in the initial proceedings back in 2013.

He grabbed his coat and rushed from the building, sliding the roll of pennies into his pocket and holding his journal in his grasp.

CHAPTER 19

Peter sped across town, toward Mandrake's office. He remembered the fateful day when Mandrake had kidnapped him from the church and taken him there, to question him, to demand answers. Mandrake had said that he didn't want the four of them to return to the present because it could alter the timeline. Peter thought perhaps Mandrake was using them further: that he and Julie had perhaps halted the war, made it end much sooner than it would have. But they wouldn't be rewarded with being able to go back. Mandrake's society was interested in the greater good of the world, not in what Peter wanted.

He rushed into the building. As if they'd expected Peter at that very moment, a man leaped upon him, grabbing his upper arms with strong hands. Peter had been moving so fast that this sudden stop made him lurch forward, made him lose his breath for a moment. "Hey!" he cried. But the man held him tight.

"We've got a situation," the man said to his fellow security guards. They began to drag him from the room as Peter kicked and struggled.

"Get Mandrake! I have to see Mandrake!" Peter screamed.

The guard allowed Peter to stand on his feet, to straighten his shirt. When that was done, Peter looked at the men angrily. "Tell me where he is."

An entourage of security guards escorted Peter up the elevator and down several corridors to Mandrake's office. As they traversed the familiar maze of corporate hallways, Peter noticed the odd expressions on the guards' faces. He knew that he looked different, far more rugged than he had only a month or two before. He'd lost so much, and he was biting and fierce, like a cornered dog.

Mandrake appeared at the end of the hall, as if he'd known to expect Peter. He crossed his arms and waited, a slight grin appearing on his face. "Peter," he called. His voice echoed menacingly. "I didn't expect you so soon. How was your luxurious French vacation?"

Peter wanted to spit on the ground at his feet. Mandrake led him into his imposing office with its memorable wall of windows displaying the San Francisco skyline. He poured them both small glasses of whiskey, and handed one to Peter. Peter drank it gladly, loving the burn in his throat.

"I'm glad you came, Peter. I have much to speak with you about," Mandrake began cordially.

But Peter interrupted him. "Asher. Where are the doctors? Doctor Lamb and Doctor Larsson. What have you done with them?"

Mandrake raised his hands slowly, palms out. "I don't know what you think I've done. I can assure you that the men are completely fine. I hardly know where they are, myself." He flashed a smile.

"I just came from our hotel. They're gone, and their room has been ransacked. From the looks of it, I'd say they've been missing from their room for some time now," Peter said. "So I'll ask you again—where the hell are they? I know you're behind this."

Mandrake sipped his whiskey, listening. When Peter's tirade was over, he spoke.

"I'm sorry about that, Peter. A few of my associates may have overstepped their bounds over there. I gave them specific orders to observe only. It appears that your two doctor partners may have fled to safer havens." He paused momentarily. "Perhaps to your trusted colleague Dr. Epson's facility?" Mandrake adopted a sincere facial expression, but Peter knew better. He was convinced it was Muscle and Squirrel who were responsible.

"So ... you're telling me that the doc's aren't with you? They're safe?"

"As far as I know, Peter. Must I remind you again about our non-violent nature here at the society?"

Peter chuckled heartily, recalling Emmett's ability to kill in New York—for the society. He sipped the whiskey once again, longing for another shot of it. And another. God, it had been such a long journey.

"Let's get down to real business, shall we?" Mandrake said, changing the subject. "I'd like to offer you something—a once in a lifetime opportunity," Mandrake began. "I'd like to offer you the chance to stay here, in 1942, and work for this society." He spread his arms wide. "You, Julie, and the doctors would all work here, for me."

Peter raised an eyebrow. "What makes you think any of us would want to work for you?"

Mandrake smiled. "Well. Truly, I'm not certain. After all, you have so much to do in your own timeline, I'm sure. What I'm offering you is a full one-hundred-thousand-dollar-a-year contract. This is about—oh—one point four million dollars in your 2013 timeline." He leaned toward Peter once more. "I'm offering you the chance to be a millionaire."

Peter's hands grew clammy at hearing the amount. A millionaire? He'd lived for so long without anything, struggling with bills all the time. He swallowed. "I don't know."

"But wait. In this contract, I'd make you second in command of the society. The doctors would be lead scientists. Julie can—can have a role that we'll decide at a later date. But still—one hundred thousand dollars a year. Which is far more than any woman could possibly make in this decade. Probably in yours, as well." Mandrake leaned back in his chair, looking cocky.

Peter considered the offer. "Why would you trust me to be a part of your society? You hardly know anything about me. You haven't even asked how our trip to France went, and you don't whether anything I would tell you is true. Get on the radio and learn for yourself that Oradour-sur-Glane—the very French town we wanted to save during the process of ending the war—was still destroyed. What does this mean for our mission? Was it futile?"

Peter shrugged, closing his eyes. He didn't care about Mandrake anymore; he had no fear. "There's no way we can know if it was futile. But I can tell you one thing. Emmett was killed in France. And he wasn't killed at the hand of a Nazi; he was killed by me." Peter leaned forward over the desk, the lie fresh and real on his tongue. "Now that you know I killed your informant—yes, I knew about Emmett—would you say the offer is still good?"

Mandrake didn't hesitate. "Of course it's still good. My offers remain. All of them." He flashed his teeth, like a wolf.

Peter leaned back, considering. "Okay. Okay. So. Say I want to work with you. But I demand five hundred thousand dollars a year. Each. For all four of us. And I demand to be leader of this fucking society." He thumped his finger on the desk between them, feeling the anger of their exchange fueling his voice.

"Of course. Whatever you like," Mandrake said.

That wasn't at all what Peter had expected; he was stunned that his demands had been met with such nonchalance. He'd even said he'd killed Emmett—that poor, sad man who'd ultimately died fighting for France—and he hadn't seen a single reaction from Mandrake.

"All right. Whatever I want, huh?" Peter began. "All right. I want you escorted from the building. Right now. I'm in command, and you're out of here." He leaned toward Mandrake. "And I never want to see your face again."

Asher Mandrake paused, gazing at this new, angry Peter. A few moments passed by slowly. Then Mandrake leaned back and began to laugh. It echoed from the window to the wall, sending shivers down Peter's spine.

"Well," Mandrake said, obviously understanding that Peter was fucking with him. "I can run this by the higher-ups, of course. I highly doubt they'll go for it, but that doesn't mean I can't ask them."

Peter smacked his thighs, fed up. He knew that the scientists weren't there—which was enough to propel him from the office. "Well. Get back to me when you talk to your higher-ups," he scoffed.

He walked toward the door.

"You know we can hold you here by force," Mandrake said.

Peter wheeled around and glared at the man. "What did you say?"

Mandrake stood, still holding his whiskey glass. The ice cubes jangled against the sides. "We have the greatest power in this city. You really think we can't hold you here if we want to?"

"You sure didn't stop us from arriving," Peter shot back.

"Sure, sure. But we *can* stop you from ever entering that little box again. You wouldn't want this for yourself, would you? You wouldn't want this for little Miss Julie Frey?"

Peter glowered at him. "Julie has already made up her mind to stay. And she's securing safe passage for the rest of us to return to our time. You know she'll expose the society for everything it is if you prevent our return." He brought his glass up to his lips and drank the rest of the whiskey in a single gulp, then set the glass down on the table with a sharp rap. "Remember, Mandrake. I've killed before. I can do it again."

Then Peter winked at him, nearly smiling. He knew that Mandrake didn't know that Julie had remained in France, too far away for ready contact.

But as he moved toward the door, Mandrake spoke. "I'm prepared to do anything to keep you here, Peter. I will sacrifice anything and everything. And you know I'm crazy enough to do it."

Peter turned back toward him, unalarmed. He knew

Mandrake wasn't bluffing. He did hold real power. But what had he done since they'd arrived in the timeline? He'd had Peter and Julie followed. But then, Emmett had actually *saved* their lives, not hurt them.

Therefore, Peter chose the next words carefully before slamming the door behind him and stomping from the society grounds.

"Fucking prove it."

CHAPTER 20

Peter felt the energy from his encounter with Mandrake surging through his muscles, making his heart beat fast, strong. He slammed the door of the car and sped across town, ready to find Dr. Epson at the lab and discuss his return home. He was finally pushing forward from the depression he'd felt during the previous few weeks, on the long trip from France to the United States. He'd begun to hear his children's voices in his head; he'd begun to feel focused on a single purpose: returning to 2013.

He parked outside the lab where he and Julie had trained for the mission. Now that the mission was over, the place didn't seem so scary. It was his portal back home. He turned off the engine and hurried down the steps, through the older part of the warehouse. He remembered this part had been rather new in his 2013 timeline. He shuddered, wondering what that meant for the future of the structure. He assumed the bomb would go off in this general area, that the devastation would happen soon.

He entered the tubular tunnel—the extent of the first sublevel—hoping that the doctors from his timeline would be down on sublevel six; he needed to tell them about Mandrake. He was thrilled that Mandrake hadn't already taken them. He was still ahead of Mandrake, if only by a few steps.

Passing the heavy blast doors, Peter began to descend the final five flights of steel stairs, hoping that it would be for the last time. As he arrived at sublevel six, he couldn't help the emotions that began to take over.

The bright lights felt so sterile, so stark as he entered the lab. He found himself face-to-face with all of them, and he wanted to hug them—the first familiar faces, besides Mandrake's, that he'd seen in many, many weeks.

"Peter!" Dr. Epson said, bouncing a bit as he entered. "Why, we're surprised you're back so soon!"

Peter nodded, feeling a bit awkward even in his excitement, like he didn't know where to stand. Before him stood both the doctors from 2013, Dr. Epson, Ms. Stewart, and Gallagher. They all greeted him eagerly, shaking his hand and congratulating him on the mission. Only Gallagher was a little overzealous in his movements as he spoke, shaking Peter's hand a little too hard.

As the excitement died down, Peter turned toward Dr. Epson and the two doctors from his timeline. "Would you mind if we spoke in private?" he asked.

"Of course," Dr. Epson said. He led them down the hall, toward his private office.

The office was filled to the brim with filing cabinets. A small portrait of a cat stood on a shelf beside Dr. Epson's chair. He tapped at it, adjusting it. "Peter, I must say, you look a little the worse for wear. What happened in France, if you don't mind me asking?"

Peter collapsed into a chair, feeling safe for the first time in many weeks. He looked at the doctors from his timeline and explained the mission. "Mandrake had us followed by a man named Emmett from the very moment we boarded the train. He agreed to allow us to go, only if we had this 'companion.' He wanted us to stop the war as soon as we could—that was the only reason he allowed the mission to continue. He needs everything to coincide with his society's mission, his plan."

"Very interesting. A secret society. And did you file the memo?" Dr. Lamb asked, stroking his beard. His eyes were large. "Did you halt the progression of the war?"

Peter nodded, remembering the memo-maker, Oscar Gionnoccaro. "We think we did. We did as much as we could do. But that companion I mentioned—he was killed during a battle at Oradour-sur-Glane. He saved my life."

Peter could feel the brush of death, the weight of that bomb going off so close by. It reminded him of the bomb he knew would go off in this very laboratory, very soon. He needed to alert Epson and the others, but he didn't know how. He didn't know when it was all set to occur. He didn't want to create panic in the situation. Instead, he continued to speak about France. "Mandrake doesn't seem to care, really, about his death. What's more, Julie's decided to stay on in France—"

The doctors looked at each other, alarmed. Peter hated to hear the words come out of his mouth; they seemed so real, this way. He cleared his throat. The cat on the shelf behind Epson's desk seemed to glare at him.

"And Mandrake has just offered us millions of dollars in order to stay on here. He said it's absolutely essential that we don't go back to our timeline. And I—I thought he'd surely taken you," Peter said, turning toward the doctors beside him. "I went into your room, and I found it had been ransacked."

Dr. Larsson nodded. "We found it trashed as well. Luckily, we had all important documents with us and we moved in here, down on ten." He gestured toward the floor. "It's good, living so close to the lab. And Dr. Epson stays here most nights."

"Ms. Stewart will tell you I'm married to my work," Dr. Epson said, smiling.

Peter couldn't take the joking, the humor. He needed to reiterate the importance of Mandrake's words. He'd scoffed at Mandrake before, but the urgency of the situation was catching up with him. "He said that—that he'll stop at nothing to keep us here, away from our own timeline. I need to go back. I have my kids; my life is there. There's nothing for me here. Not anymore."

He thought about Julie, then. He wondered if her morning sickness had ended. He wondered if little Marion was recovering from the deaths of her parents. There was so much to consider, and Julie and Marion were worlds and decades away.

"We'll get you back—" Epson began.

But Peter shook his head vehemently. "I wouldn't put it past Mandrake to murder one of us to keep us here. He doesn't want to meddle with the timeline. I think—I think we need to be careful." He lurched his head up, blinking wildly. "I think we need to make sure Gallagher doesn't hear another conversation between any of us. Epson. He's the nefarious rat. He's delivering information to Mandrake."

Epson scratched his head for a moment. He ratcheted his chair back and rose to his feet, then charged down the hallway. His anger could be seen in the way his back lurched as he walked, in the way his feet pounded on the cement. The doctors rushed alongside Peter as they followed Epson down the hall, back toward the lab, and Peter wondered what it was like to work with someone for so many years, only to find out he'd been sabotaging you the entire time. *What a waste*, Peter thought. *What a waste of time—time, the only thing we truly have.*

Dr. Epson stormed into the lab. Peter and the doctors followed. They found Ms. Stewart standing there smiling at them.

"Ms. Stewart. Where is Mr. Gallagher?" Dr. Epson spoke slowly.

Ms. Stewart bit her lip. She opened her hands to them all, a trace of confusion on her face. "He's gone."

CHAPTER 21

The lab seemed to darken with the tension between Dr. Epson and Ms. Stewart—something, Peter sensed, that didn't normally happen. Epson brought his fists together in front of his face, growing more and more angry. "Where the hell did he go?"

Peter watched as Ms. Stewart seemed to fold before them, clearly afraid she'd done something wrong. "I'm so sorry, Doctor. The moment he saw you step into your private office, he began gathering his things. He just—he ran toward the stairs." She held her head in her hands. "I didn't know what was going on. He wouldn't listen to me when I asked him questions."

Dr. Epson began to pace. "He's been sabotaging me this entire time." He shook his head, muttering, "What the hell could he be up to?"

But Peter already understood. He knew the bomb would be going off shortly, that Mandrake and Gallagher had been working together all this time. He felt the ticking of time in his heart, in his mind, and he knew he had to tell the group the truth. He cleared his throat. "Everyone. I have something to tell you—something I should have told you long ago." He swallowed. "I know that a bomb will detonate in this lab, very shortly."

His voice held such authority. Everyone turned toward him with widened eyes. "We don't have time to figure out what Gallagher's doing. We can only search for the bomb I feel sure he and Mandrake have left for us. To keep us here in this timeline, dead or alive."

Ms. Stewart cried out; the situation was apparently too much for her, and she sat in a lab chair, wrapping her arms around her body. The two doctors had brought their heads together in intimate discussion. Only Dr. Epson turned toward Peter with fear and anger burning in his eyes. "When will this occur? Where is the bomb meant to go off?"

Peter breathed deeply, thinking. "I don't know the exact time or location. But the results of the bomb are catastrophic. The time machine might be destroyed, leaving us here in the past. But I'm sure the bomb will go off on sublevel one, toward the stairwell. It looks different in the future. But, as I've already experienced, bits of this past are different from the recorded past of my future. So this bomb could go off, or it might not. Either way, we're wasting time. It's here, somewhere."

"If you say it goes off upstairs, why do you think it's here and not up top?" Epson asked.

"I … I don't know for certain. But it does stand to reason that Gallagher would put it here in hopes of destroying the time machine completely, along with all of us," Peter guessed.

Ms. Stewart let out another cry of dismay. The scientists whispered on about timelines, about alterations in the future and the past.

Peter moved closer to Epson. "You should really say something to her." He tipped his head toward Ms. Stewart, whose tears were spilling down her cheeks. Dr. Epson approached her tentatively and placed his hand on her back. "Gertrude," he said quietly. "I apologize for being so forceful earlier. I just—I didn't expect to have such excitement today. We weren't even meant to run tests today." He shook his head.

She peered up at him. "I care about you a great deal. In case—in case we die in here."

Epson let out a great laugh of surprise. Peter looked down at his shoes, noticing the way Dr. Epson and Ms. Stewart had begun to look at each other. They'd been hiding their love from each other for all this time, in this lost decade.

"We have to move," Peter said. "Start looking!"

"What are we looking for, exactly?" Larsson asked.

"Not sure. I guess anything that looks out of place," Peter replied, thinking that everything in the lab looked out of place to him.

They began the search, through the many cabinets and hiding places in the lab. With every step, Peter knew that they were losing time.

To his right, Dr. Epson and Ms. Stewart had begun to hold hands and search together, dashing in and out of various offices. Peter tried to imagine the blast that would overtake them; he wondered if it would be similar to the explosion at Oradour-sur-Glane—all-encompassing, leaving few to no survivors.

Peter found himself in the great stairwell, climbing up the familiar army-green steps. He remembered this place from its future days, its massive subterranean levels. On this day, the only employees hard at work were Dr. Epson, the doctors, and Ms. Stewart. Luckily, not many would perish, Peter thought—if, in fact, Mandrake succeeded with this mission.

As Peter searched for the bomb, his anger at Mandrake for trying to force him to stay in this past, to never see his children again, grew exponentially. He turned over tables, scouring the level, the cabinets, the various small offices for the bomb. He would see his kids again; he had to. He had given up too much already to die here, in the explosion in 1942.

Peter rushed forward and found the steps once more, then hurried back down to sublevel six to find the others. Their time was running out. Everything had been turned over, filtered through in order to find the ticking bomb. But so far they'd found nothing.

Dr. Epson came toward him, his face bleak. "Peter, I think it might be time to consider evacuation. I'm sorry. But if what you're saying is true—I can rebuild the time machine. I can make it stronger and better, someplace else."

Peter shook his head. "No. We have to find it. This is my

only chance." He knew that Mandrake would find a way to stop the rebuilding process in the future, and he didn't want to linger on in this uncertain past. For all he knew, Mandrake was out in front of the lab that instant, waiting to ignite the bomb. What a grand show he would have, Peter thought.

Suddenly, they heard a scream from down the hall, in the control room. Ms. Stewart was crying out: "I'VE GOT IT!" The words echoed through the halls.

Peter and Dr. Epson darted from their positions and raced toward the control room. The doctors were already there, peering at the bomb and shaking their heads. "No deactivation, Doctor," Dr. Lamb said, shaking his head fearfully at Dr. Epson.

The thing was monstrous, with clusters of yellow, green, and red wires encircling it. Its tick-tick-ticking made it seem antiquated and truly frightening as it rested in Ms. Stewart's hands. She held it delicately, like a baby. Peter ran his hands through his hair, certain they were about to die, that the bomb would explode between them.

"What the hell am I supposed to do?" Ms. Stewart whimpered, her eyes moving toward Dr. Epson—the only man she'd ever trusted. "What can I do?"

CHAPTER 22

No one spoke as the bomb beeped before them. The tension filled the entire control room. Peter's thoughts were only on Julie, on their baby, on his children. He thought about them and closed his eyes, wishing them all a somber goodbye. He would go down with the ship; nothing else could be done. He wouldn't even see the end of the war.

But suddenly, Miss Stewart darted between him and Dr. Epson, still holding the bomb, carrying it out before her, like a beacon. Peter was so distracted with his own thoughts, he hardly noticed. Dr. Lamb and Dr. Larsson rushed forward, already chasing after her. "Where is she going?" Dr. Lamb called out.

Dr. Epson was panicked. He launched himself in front of Peter, his white coat flying behind him like a cape. "Gertrude!" he screamed to her. His voice cracked. "Don't do this!"

Peter ran behind him, part of his mind lost in reverie. So much of this reminded him of Oradour-sur-Glane—of the instant before the disaster. He rushed down the hall, watching as Miss Stewart powered forward with the bomb in her hands. She didn't have anything to live for except Dr. Epson, Peter knew. And the only thing Dr. Epson lived for was his work. It would be her ultimate honor to die for him, to allow him to keep going: to learn the secret of time travel and give the world a lasting legacy. She didn't know he was meant to die in his lab; she didn't know that all would be lost, even if she died today in order to save him.

In many ways, Peter thought, this act of kindness was so much like Julie. Julie had remained in France, taking the baton forward on the strange path of raising her grandmother, of helping her family create a strong and healthy bloodline. She'd accepted this duty wholeheartedly, throwing herself into a fire and wrapping her arms around young Marion, allowing her another chance at life. When Peter had asked her to take back the life she already had, she'd refused it. Who would care for Marion if she did that?

Peter knew that Miss Stewart was gifting them a free and safe world, even as she worked to sacrifice herself. She was far too quick for them to catch her, darting on toward the stairwell— the very stairwell, Peter knew, that was altered in the future after brand-new reparations. History was going to repeat itself if the bomb did, indeed, explode.

When Miss Stewart reached the stairwell, she looked to her right, toward a great wall of books. The bookshelf was tall and thick, with hundreds of science books stacked far and wide. Peter watched as the young woman carried the bomb with in hand and lifted the other to the bookcase, shaking it back and forth and allowing it to crash to the ground as she darted into the stairway.

Dr. Epson gasped as he reached the bookcase. It was completely blocking the heavy steel door, and its books had fallen, making it nearly impossible to clear the mess in time. Peter and the doctors began tossing the big, bulky books wildly to the side: physics books and time travel books and chemistry books. They all slid down the hallway. Peter understood that the books would be fodder for the fire that was about to erupt from the bomb in Miss Stewart's hands, just a few rounds of stairs above them.

Epson sweated as he worked toward the door, quivering in his passion and love for Miss Stewart. Peter wanted to assure him that it was going to be all right, but he knew his words would sound empty. He hadn't wanted to hear anything on the voyage from France to the United States except his own sad, lonely thoughts.

Finally, they flung the last book to the side. Dr. Epson reached out and spun the handle to the right, creating a dark portal into the five flights of stairs. They could hear Miss Stewart crying up above, and they darted into the stairwell and up the flights of steps. Peter felt his thighs screaming as he ran faster and faster. Dr. Epson passed him on the left, a look of passion and fear etched through his eyebrows, on his lips. His breath came in jagged inhales and exhales. "Gertrude!"

Miss Stewart had reached the top and had disappeared around the bend of the steps. She wouldn't stop. Where would she go?

Peter realized that the two doctors hadn't followed him and Dr. Epson. He assumed that they'd raced outside, trying to save themselves from this horror. But Peter wouldn't be able to live with himself if he allowed Miss Stewart to die. He continued to run, to feel the pain in his thighs, in his knees. Keep going. Keep going, he continued to think. He wondered if this was how Emmett had felt all those weeks ago on the battlefield. Emmett was meant to be an enemy to Julie and Peter, at Mandrake's direction. And yet, he'd become a friend, certainly a protector. He'd flung himself over Peter, allowing him to live. Peter longed to give Miss Stewart a chance at life, as well. After all, he was the reason all of this was happening. She shouldn't have to die for him, just as Emmett shouldn't have had to give up his life for Peter.

But time seemed to repeat itself, over and over again, in a series of insane patterns.

Dr. Epson and Peter reached the last step. Dr. Epson was a few feet away, tearing down the hallway. He lurched to the right, toward the first sublevel. Peter followed, ready for the end with every step he took. He would be there for this grand moment in time—for this end of all things.

CHAPTER 23

They found Miss Stewart standing at the end of the long, shadowed tunnel. She was cornered. She held the wiry, ticking bomb in her hands, and she stood gawking at the man before her: Gallagher. His face was harsh, and he was spitting as he screamed at her. His hands flapped wildly around his stout body. "You can't mess with time, Miss Stewart! It's the only thing that holds this world intact!"

But Miss Stewart was crying. Her face was scrunched, and she held the bomb tightly in her hands. She wouldn't let go. She shook her head vehemently. Her only chance was to cling to the bomb and make sure Dr. Epson didn't die in the resulting fire, to make sure the time travelers could make it back home.

Miss Stewart began to say something. Her words came in spurts between her tears. "You can't control time any more than I can, Gallagher," she said. "We have to let things play out their course, without violence." She shuddered.

Peter and Dr. Epson crept close to the two people at the end of the tunnel. Dr. Epson brought up a hand, halting Peter from going any further. He shook his head. "Don't. You need to go back. Let me."

He walked forward with confidence, his white jacket floating behind him. "Gallagher," he said, his voice resounding through the hallway.

Gallagher lurched back, toward the doctor. He looked fearful. "Dr. Epson. You know what needs to be done. Use that massive scientific brain of yours. Think of the consequences."

Dr. Epson strode forward. Every time that Peter had seen him, he'd been crouched over his time machine, always frowning at the various screws and wires. And now he walked forward like a sort of knight, ready to save Miss Stewart, the only woman who'd ever understood him.

"I don't know, Mr. Gallagher. And you don't know either." Dr. Epson swallowed.

Peter hung back, unsure of what to do. He wanted to rush down the steps and into the time machine, but he knew he needed to wait. These were his people, now. He knew in his heart that what Miss Stewart was saying was right. They had to allow this timeline to play out without violence, without fear of what would change in the future. He knew that Mandrake's entire society was rooted in that fear. Those people glaring at things they could never change, at the way Dr. Epson's new comprehension of time could end wars early, could make people never be born. They were busying themselves, trying to ensure those changes wouldn't take place—when change was really the only thing that ever happened, all the time.

Dr. Epson continued, "I know you've been working for Mandrake all this time. Altering my calculations and messing my tests up just enough—just enough to make me unsuccessful." Dr. Epson brought his hands forward, adjusting his fingers as he crept closer to the couple. "But all it did was make me work harder, deep into the night. And always for a greater purpose. To comprehend this universe we live in. And to perhaps solve serious crimes against humanity. Wars, for example. As I understand it, your Mr. Mandrake is keen on this idea: to keep people safe."

"In this timeline. To keep people safe in the *now* so that it can flow naturally into the future. You're an old fool if you can't understand that the monstrosity you're making down there is going to fuck up everything. This life—this one with you and

Miss Stewart, here—and the lives of our children and grandchildren," Gallagher said. His voice shook a bit as he reached toward the bomb. He needed to carry it toward Peter, Peter understood—needed to destroy both Peter and the time machine.

Miss Stewart started muttering to herself, gazing down at the bomb in her hands. She looked as if she was losing her mind. Her fingers curled around it.

Peter looked at his watch. It had been too long, at that point. He felt the tension creeping up around all of them. Peter's mind spun, pulling him into a sort of daze. As Dr. Epson spoke to Gallagher, trying to reason with him in a harsh, authoritative voice, Peter came up with a plan. They had to get out of the blast if they were going to survive—if this mission was ever going to be worth what everyone had sacrificed. To the right of Dr. Epson, he spotted a blast door that led into another, unused laboratory.

His eyes moved from Miss Stewart to Gallagher to Dr. Epson. He had to act quickly.

Miss Stewart had begun to quiver, holding the bomb still in her hands much like a woman presents a main course at a party—so delicately, so precisely. Gallagher was still flapping his arms wildly, angry at Dr. Epson, trying to reason with him. Their voices were echoing through the hallway. Their anger was consuming them, causing them to forget that death was only moments away.

"Put the bomb down!" Peter jolted forward, toward the three of them. He reached Dr. Epson first, and caught the attention of Miss Stewart, who gazed back at him with broad, bright eyes. Her lips had come apart, like she was about to ask a question.

But Peter lurched into Dr. Epson, and they tumbled into that vacant laboratory. Peter brought his hand up and grabbed the blast door, slamming it behind him. The explosion outside burst against the door, but the door held firm.

Dr. Epson had fallen to the ground as Peter slammed into him, and he lay on the ground during the blast, banging his hand against the ground in fury. "NooooOOOOO!" he wailed.

But it was too late. All around them, test tubes and lab equipment crashed and clanked and fell to the ground. It seemed like the end of the world, if only for a few moments. Peter felt his heart racing as the noise and vibrations of the bomb fell away, leaving the floor beneath them solid and steady once more. He slid down the door, feeling beads of sweat drip down his forehead, through his eyebrows.

Dr. Epson went on slamming his fist against the floor, drawing blood now. His screams had turned to silence. The chaos around them turned into unbroken silence—like every ounce of energy in the room had been sucked into the explosion.

Peter gazed down at his hands, noting how fragile and pink they looked. How youthful he still was, even after all that had happened to him. He'd been surrounded by dead soldiers on the battlefield in Oradour-sur-Glane; he'd seen their dead eyes gaze into the sky as he marched back toward freedom, toward life.

And now, he'd flung himself away from death once more. He'd allowed Epson's beautiful assistant and the good-for-nothing Gallagher to die in the explosion outside the door. He couldn't have reached them, he told himself over and over. It couldn't have happened.

Finally, Dr. Epson righted himself, peering at his hands much like Peter had. His right fist was slathered in blood. Peter knew that the pain probably felt good; it fit with everything else Dr. Epson was feeling. It fit with the pain in his heart.

"I tried to reason with him," Dr. Epson began to whisper, shaking his head back and forth. "I tried to make it work."

"You can't do this to yourself, Doctor," Peter said. He stood up then, placing his hand on the door. All around him, the lab had been torn to pieces. "There was nothing you could have done. Mandrake was out for blood."

Peter longed to tell the doctor that they'd won against Mandrake, that they'd beaten him at his own game. But he knew that in Dr. Epson's eyes, they hadn't won anything. He'd lost the only woman he could have truly loved in this world. And Peter knew that feeling all too well.

He opened the door and allowed Dr. Epson to stand, bumbling to his feet with enormous sadness written on his face. They coughed into the haze, the blackness that surrounded them as they stepped into the once-white hallway. Much of the floor and the stairway had fallen in, crushing some of the laboratories below. An electrical unit above them had begun to crackle and hiss, emitting small jolts of electricity into the air. Peter pulled his shirt up over his mouth. He didn't want to inhale anything. He alerted Dr. Epson to do the same. Dr. Epson did so slowly, his eyes still red above the white lab coat.

They moved down the hall, toward the other staircase—the staircase that didn't exist in the future. They stepped lightly, toward the side of the hall, where much of the floor was still intact.

Peter felt his mind rushing in overdrive as they moved up the steps to the ground floor. He burst through the door into fresh air and helped Dr. Epson out behind him.

They were outside, in the fresh light of San Francisco. This was peace.

CHAPTER 24

Peter put his arm around Dr. Epson as they stood and coughed in the sunlight. Behind them, Dr. Lamb and Dr. Larsson ran up from the parking lot, calling out to them.

"Oh my god! Where did the explosion come from?"

"Is everyone all right?"

"Where's Miss Stewart?"

But Peter and Dr. Epson just looked at the doctors, their eyes hazy. The doctors understood, then, that Miss Stewart was dead—that she'd sacrificed herself by running with that bomb. She'd run away from the time machine and away from the time travelers, protecting them all. She'd been lost in the struggle against time.

Dr. Lamb and Dr. Larsson volunteered to go downstairs and make sure Dr. Epson's lab equipment was all right after the explosion. They came back with good reports and cups of water which they passed to Peter and Epson.

"It all looks good. Not a single inch of the place was disturbed by the bomb." Their voices were quiet as they spoke, as if they'd just returned from war.

Peter and Epson drank without speaking, then wiped their mouths with the back of their hands. The sun had lowered in the sky, moving toward the ocean. The day was ending, and it seemed they were left with nothing but questions. What were they going to do now?

Peter laid his hand on the doctor's shoulder. Dr. Epson turned, startled by the touch. "She was a wonderful woman, Doctor," Peter said softly. "She saved our lives. You both meant the world to each other. We all know that."

Lamb and Larsson both nodded but said nothing. Everything felt so tired, so void of energy. Peter wanted to crawl into bed and sleep for the next twelve hours. Maybe, the next twelve days. He felt like he hadn't had a day of rest in months.

"But now ... There's nothing for you here," Peter continued. "We know you don't have family, that you've thrown yourself into this work. We can't allow you to enter that lab anytime soon, not when we know how the machine works in the future."

"And what was the purpose of all that work, in the first place?" Epson said, his voice croaking a bit. "It seems all this machine did was create devastation."

Peter shook his head. "Because of this time machine, the war will end much sooner in Europe. Thousands of people will live as a result. You can't understand the good your machine did. But I've been in that future, and that past in Europe— beyond anything else—was devastating. Because of you, it isn't any more."

Epson lived with that knowledge for a moment, staring at the darkening blue sky. "What do you propose?" he asked finally.

Peter turned toward Lamb and Larsson, both of whom gave him encouraging glances. "Epson ... In our future, we were told that you died in an accident much like this one. A sort of test gone wrong." Peter swallowed. "I don't see any reason why your coming with us would alter the timeline."

"To the year 2013?" Epson asked. His voice croaked once more. He spoke the words with disbelief.

Peter nodded. "You can see all that has come after you—a privilege, I assure you, that will enrich that incredible mind of yours. You can see how far we've come in the future, and you can enhance what you already know. We could use a man like you in the lab in 2013. You can make time travel more fluid."

Epson's eyes had darkened. "I don't know about messing around with this technology any more. It doesn't seem safe. Time travel shouldn't be touched. Perhaps Mandrake was right, in the beginning."

Peter nodded, understanding. "Then you can find a way to start over. But it's not safe for you in 1942. Mandrake will find you and kill you." Peter's mind ached, trying to find the appropriate way to convince Epson to come with them. For some reason, he'd grown attached to this old man. He wanted him to be safe. He didn't want another disastrous outcome from this terrible time-traveling adventure. He wanted to make sure Dr. Epson was safe. He felt accountable for him, in a way.

Together, the four men walked down the steps. Peter could sense that Dr. Epson had already begun to think about his future in 2013. "Do you eat differently?" he asked, spinning his head around with a strained expression on his face.

Peter nearly laughed, shaking his head. "I think you'll find that there will be something for you in 2013. Something good." He tried to remember how he'd felt when he was preparing to travel 70 years into the past. His mind hadn't been able to comprehend what the past would truly hold—what it would look like, in three-dimensional form. He assumed it was far worse to think about a future you couldn't comprehend, like Dr. Epson was doing now.

And truly, Peter didn't know what the future would hold for any of them, either. He knew the timeline had spun in many unexpected ways. He didn't know if his children would exist, if he would even meet Minnie—his wife—in this indeterminate future. He swallowed, hoping that he would still hold the memories of her in his mind. Her laugh, her smile. The way they'd planned their future together; the way he'd learned that one couldn't really plan the future at all. That it didn't work out that way.

Down in the lab, Dr. Epson began to adjust a few of the wires at the base of the time machine, his eyes focused and clear once more. Peter had been worried when he'd seemed so dispassionate, so far away. But now he had a goal in mind. He had to make this great beast work.

"I know I shouldn't ask, but how will they—and by they, I mean your people from the future—know we're coming through?" Epson asked.

"Luckily, the brain trust that formulated the plan for this mission has thought that through. The last thing I had to do before returning through the time machine was simply mail a letter—instructions for them to leave the light on for us," Peter explained. "I did so just before I came on base." He stopped there, not wanting to explain the reason for his final visit to his future home, which was still under construction.

Epson accepted Peter's explanation at face value before advancing to the next obstacle.

"The problem is this. We don't have a trigger on the outside to close the latch on our way out," Dr. Epson said, rising up from the floor. He tapped at his thighs, thoughtful.

Peter and the doctors from 2013 looked around the room: at the glinting test tubes, at the strange equipment. They had to find a way to latch the door from the inside. On their way in, Applegate and his crew had latched the door from the outside, allowing them to fly safely. But they didn't have anyone on this side of time to help out, anymore.

"We could set a timer," Dr. Epson suggested. He knelt back down to the wires and began yanking at something, articulating a different path for them. "The machine will need to know to latch itself and then send us through time, even while we're strapped in on the inside."

Peter shook his head. "We won't need to be strapped in. The route here was smooth. We didn't feel any bumps along the way." He searched the doctors' faces, and they both nodded, agreeing with him.

"Well," Dr. Epson said, running his fingers through his hair. He was the only one who hadn't successfully traveled through time in the very machine he'd built.

Peter hovered toward the side of the room, allowing his mind to roam free as the doctors manipulated the machine, making sure that they could safely escape their past. With all his heart, he wished Julie was with them. He wondered what she was doing right now. He pictured her kneading bread, for some reason, with little Marion in that sunny farmhouse, beginning a life together. He tried to imagine her stomach, wondering if it had grown bigger in the weeks since he'd left her alone.

Dr. Epson rushed toward him, speaking excitedly with his hands. Peter jostled from his reverie, hearing the words. "It's on a timer! Peter! We have to move. Come on!" Dr. Epson grabbed Peter's arm with incredible strength. He dragged him into the mouth of the time machine, followed by the other doctors.

"Everyone! Maintain contact with the platforms as we move! This—this is the essential, important factor of time travel! It allows the zipping to take place!" Dr. Epson called out to them.

They stood together, their hands on the walls and their feet on the platform. A great beeping sound was emanating in at them from the outside. Suddenly, the door shot closed. A whirring sound erupted beneath them, and the machine began to loop them through time, as it had all those months before.

Peter closed his eyes, feeling chaos erupt in his mind as they traveled. He felt so alone in these moments. He couldn't remember another time when he felt so terrified and yet so at peace: content with death, if it came for him.

CHAPTER 25

Peter was thrust against the wall as the whirring subsided. He blinked wildly into the light and peered toward Dr. Epson, whose face was creased in anticipation. They'd made it back to 2013. Peter breathed an earnest sigh of relief.

The door opened, then. The door was far less antiquated than the one through which they'd just entered; the lab outside seemed brand-new, whitewashed. An entirely different world.

A great crowd of laboratory staff stood outside, peering in at them. Peter wondered how much time had passed for them in the present—how much time had passed since he'd embarked on this adventure, almost certain he wouldn't see 2013 again. He took a step forward, and all the people outside began to clap. The clapping was nearly uproarious as the four men sauntered from the machine like war heroes—like men who had gone to the moon and back.

Applegate stood at the helm of the great crowd of engineers and scientists. To Peter's surprise, he looked virtually the same as he had before the mission began. How could that be? he wondered.

Applegate held his hand out and shook Peter's hand, a fierce expression taking shape on his face. "It's good to see you," he said—words Peter had been certain he would never hear from Applegate. "We heard the machine stirring and we all came running." He shook his head in disbelief. "Welcome to 2013."

Peter shook his hand gratefully, nodding. He felt his heart beat wildly in his chest. "Thank you, sir." Everything seemed almost exactly like he remembered it. The people were so modern compared to what he'd grown used to, their styles slightly different, even in their lab coats. The women wore their hair differently; the men wore different eyeglasses. So many strange alterations through time had brought them there, to this new forever.

As he stood there, he suddenly noted that Applegate's expression had altered. He reared back for a moment in fear as Dr. Epson came toward him, standing next to Peter. Dr. Epson placed his hand on Peter's shoulder. They'd been through the wringer together, certainly. They were a united front.

"Dr.—Dr. Epson," Applegate said, his voice uneven. "Welcome to 2013." His eyes were alarmed. "If you'll excuse us." He latched onto Peter's arm and led him away from the surrounding crowd. "What is he doing here?" he hissed.

Peter felt a rush of hatred for Applegate once more. God, he hated this man. He scowled back at Applegate with rage. Did he even fucking know what Peter had been through the past few months? "He had to come with us. It was life or death," he fired back.

"But this screws his timeline," Applegate said, smacking his hands together angrily. "Do you even know what you're messing with? This is *time*, Peter. It's not something to be taken lightly."

But Peter held up his hand. "Just hold on a minute ..." He swallowed, trying to think clearly. There was no way Applegate had known what he was truly asking Peter to do, all those months ago, when this had begun. Peter had to have patience with him. He had to explain the other side of the time machine, the way so many worlds had been created. "It was essential that he come with us. There were elements of the—of the entire process that you didn't anticipate. A man named Mandrake, for one." He swallowed. "The laboratory just exploded."

"The bomb," Applegate said, nodding. "I didn't imagine it

would happen while you were all still there."

"Right," Peter said. He felt himself begin to cool down. He could control his anger, bit by bit. "It was the very day that Epson was meant to disappear, anyway. In that botched lab experiment."

Silence hung between the two men like a cloud. They both considered this strange alteration in the timeline.

Peter realized what he was saying, then. There was no alteration in the timeline. History had simply fallen into line. The bomb had blown up in the precise area it was meant to, even in Peter's timeline. Epson had disappeared in the past on the exact day that he'd been meant to die in the botched experiment. But ... what did this mean for Peter's life? Could history repair itself that many times, over and over again?

"So. Actually, bringing him forward avoids contamination of the past," Applegate said, pounding his hand on the wall beside him lightly. "If he had remained in that timeline, things could have changed. We all might not be here, ultimately." Peter had never seen him look so surprised. He realized there was much of this mission that Applegate had left up to chance.

After a moment, Peter nodded. "He'll be an essential part of the team, I think. His mind is a mess of endless energy. Give him a chance. He doesn't—he doesn't have anyone back there. Not anymore."

Peter and Applegate turned back toward the time machine. The smoke had dissipated from the machine, taking away the smog-like feel of the room. In the distance, he saw the two doctors, Lamb and Larsson, as they pored through a binder of their findings from the past. Peter remembered his journal, then. He was grateful that he'd left it in his house, away from the prying eyes of Applegate and his crew. He knew that everything they'd brought with them was extremely classified. In order to return to his children, he had to continue to follow orders.

Dr. Epson was in the corner, removing his white coat. Beneath his coat, he was wearing his antiquated 1940s garb. His black pants rode high on his stomach, and his tie—not an attractive one, even for the 1940s—hung sadly below his belt. Peter's heart ached for him. He walked forward, toward the corner, and saw that Dr. Epson's eyes were red. Had he been crying?

"I'm sorry about all this," Peter said.

Dr. Epson shook his head. "No, no." He played with his tie. "It's all very exciting, truly. I can't believe I'm here." His eyes searched around him, taking in all the new equipment. "I can't even begin to comprehend what all of this stuff does."

Peter laughed, seeing a hint of excitement creep onto the other man's face. "We'll have to get you in touch with the lead scientist." Peter glanced around the lab, looking for a familiar face. There were few, but none that stood out. With all the personnel changes, Peter began to think about what else might have changed since he was last in 2013.

Applegate approached. "I'm sure you both have many questions, as do I."

"I was just explaining to Dr. Epson that we should introduce him to a few of your lead scientists, to help him begin his acclimation to an entire new timeline," Peter explained.

"Ah, yes. You're quite right, Peter. The person you'll want to speak with is Dr. Vanessa Crane." Applegate pointed to a woman standing across the lab. She stood confidently next to Doctors Lamb and Larsson as she jotted down notes on her digital tablet.

"Wait, she's a scientist?" Dr. Epson asked, his eyebrows furrowed.

Applegate laughed. "Of course. You'll find a great deal of women scientists here in the future."

The men walked toward Dr. Crane. She looked up, smiling at Dr. Epson. She stuck out a hand, and he shook it. "Dr. Epson. It's such a pleasure to meet you. You must know that I've studied nearly every one of your notes."

"My notes?" Dr. Epson said, shaking his head.

Dr. Crane adjusted her glasses. "Of course. Your notes from 1942. I have them with me all the time. I used them to fix the machine." She leafed through her pocket and brought them out.

They'd been laminated to seal the seventy-year-old paper.

Epson reached for them and brought the yellowing paper closer to his face. He shook his head, and when he spoke, his voice caught in his throat. " I was just looking at this paper not three hours ago." His shoulders slumped forward, dealing with the weight of this new knowledge. "I can't believe anyone looked at these silly drawings."

Dr. Crane nodded. "God, yes. They've been my Bible for the past three years. I did have a few questions about your side project—"

"You have those, as well?" Epson asked, his eyes wide.

Peter's heart jolted. Side project? Dr. Crane, this mysterious scientist, turned toward Epson, trying to block Peter from the conversation. "If you can come to my office now—we can peruse the papers?"

"Oh, yes. Right away. Peter? Mr. Applegate, do you mind?"

Before they had a chance to say anything, Epson was nodding passionately toward Dr. Crane, waving a swift good-bye to them. As they disappeared, Epson began walking quickly, speaking with his hands. Dr. Crane had trouble keeping up with him. They walked down the long hallway outside of the great laboratory—toward the very hall and stairwell that had been rebuilt nearly seventy years before, after the explosion that had nearly taken their lives.

Peter shook his head, uncertain of what to think. He needed Epson to grasp this new reality.

Beyond anything else, however, Peter wanted his life back.

CHAPTER 26

"Just a little bit of time before we can allow it, Peter," Applegate said.

"I need to see my kids, General," Peter said harshly. The crowd around them had dissipated and the time machine was being analyzed by a few lab-coated team members.

Peter waited for a response, feeling the anger rising in him. He felt he'd done his duty; he was tired and just wanted to go home.

Applegate shook his head. "I'm sorry, Peter. We have to debrief you first. The entire team, actually. Also ..." Applegate paused. "There is another matter."

"What is it?" Peter demanded. "Is it my family? Are my kids all right?"

"Oh, no. It's nothing like that. Your family is fine." Applegate dabbed a bead of sweat from his temple. "It's just a formality, really. We're going to have to quarantine you and the other members of your team for a few days. Three, tops."

"Why didn't you tell me this before?" Peter said.

"First off, it wasn't me who spoke with you in that alternate timeline, Peter. Frankly, this is the first time I've met you."

Peter nodded. He thought he understood. The Applegate he'd known before no longer existed. He only hoped that this new Applegate was less devious than his predecessor.

"All right. I guess that makes sense. But three days? Can't we just fill out the paperwork now, so I can go home? It's feels like it's been years since I've seen my kids."

"Unfortunately yes, Peter. It's only precautionary. We are dealing with something—this time travel business—for the first time. We want to be sure that we aren't exposing the world to something that we might have failed to identify properly," Applegate said, glancing at his watch. "Now, If you follow Randall here, he can show you down to the sleeping quarters."

"Hold up a minute. What exactly are you concerned about? Should we be worried? Do you think we brought back some kind of plague from '42?"

Applegate had already took several steps away from Peter. "Relax, Peter. Everything will be fine. Just follow Randall, and you'll be home before you know it."

"If you'd follow me, Mr. Cooper," Randall said, motioning forward.

Peter shook his head in disgust. "Lead the way."

They wound down the hall toward the stairwell. Peter couldn't help but feel pangs of fear as he remembered the explosion back in 1942. He followed his guide down the steps.

Despite the promise of a new and improved model, Peter still didn't trust Applegate, and he longed to be out of his grasp. He knew once he left this compound, their contract would be up. He wouldn't have to think about time travel or 1942 ever again. He could scrape this entire experience off his boots.

Randall led Peter down to the lower apartments, where he knew Stella and Benny had been living before they were murdered. He briefly wondered if they were alive and well in this timeline, but he couldn't think about that, not now. He was far too exhausted. He thanked Randall for the sheets and the toothbrush Randall had given him, then shut the bedroom door.

Thirty minutes later, Peter had showered and was lying on the bed, staring up at the ceiling, his thoughts whirling. Suddenly, a crushing realization hit him in the chest. Julie was dead. There was no feasible way that she was alive. She'd been thirty-eight when they'd arrived in 1942. That meant that she'd be hundred and nine years old in 2013.

He closed his eyes, trying to fall asleep. But all he could imagine was Julie's life, both before and after him. He could only imagine the men she had courted, the way she'd looked as she'd grown older. His heart ached for her. He wanted her beside him in bed, kissing him. Rubbing his back. For only a moment, he imagined what their child might look like. Seventy-one years old, by now. Seventy-one years old ...

Peter fell into a fitful sleep. He dreamed of the French countryside, of little Marion's face as she helped Julie milk the cow. He dreamed of the canals of Sete, and he imagined that couple on board the ship, headed back to the United States from France. He wondered what had happened to them, if they'd reached Boston. He wondered if they'd been happy, all those years ago.

When Peter woke up the next morning, he blinked into the sour light of his underground room. A knock at the door brought him fully awake. Perhaps it was Applegate's crony with some breakfast. He ran his fingers through his hair and opened it. He did, indeed, find Randall. He looked up at Peter nearly menacingly; his breath smelled of rotten eggs as he spoke. "Applegate is ready for your debriefing. You need to be ready in five minutes."

"What?" Peter said, rubbing his straggly morning beard. "Debriefing? God, what time is it?"

"That's right," Randall said authoritatively. "It's seven in the morning. Get dressed."

Peter breathed deeply, squelching his anger. He grabbed his pants from the chair and slid his legs into them, fastening the button at his belly. The pants were from the past, giving him an anachronistic look. His crotch was tight. He pulled at it for a moment, huffing. "Fine. Let's go," he said finally. The sooner they got through this, he thought, the better.

Randall led him back down the hall, toward the stairwell. Peter longed to pepper him with questions, but he didn't feel he had it in him. His very soul was fatigued. A small thought passed through him, then. He thought that, perhaps, he had finished his mission; he'd completed what they'd wanted from him. And now he knew too much. Maybe he'd be killed.

Peter drew his hands into fists as they passed by many security guards, all of whom were much too strong for him. If he tried to run away, there would be no hope of escaping them. He'd come all the way into this future only to meet his death.

Finally, Randall stopped at what Peter recognized to be Applegate's office. He held open the door and gestured for Peter to enter. Peter frowned. As he entered, he found that Applegate's desk had been pushed to the side. Only a table stood in the center. A pair of chairs were positioned on either side. The room reminded him so much of that German cell he'd been imprisoned in in France. Manstein flashed into his mind, and he shuddered.

Applegate turned from his desk, holding a cup of coffee. He gestured, offering the chair to Peter. "Please, Peter. Want a cup of coffee?"

Peter nodded. The aroma wafted toward him, making his mouth water. He sat at the table and heard the chair creak under him. "How long is this going to take?" Peter asked.

"Ah, Peter. You didn't think I'd let you just waltz out of here after all that, did you?" Applegate chuckled as he sat down on the other side of the table. He held a tape recorder in his hand and placed it between them. The tape was already whirring. "You don't mind if I record this session, do you?"

Peter shook his head, sipping at the coffee.

"You're going to have to speak into the recorder, Peter. Cooperate with me. The sooner we get through this, the better it is for you. You know that, of course."

"No. I don't mind if you record this," Peter said through his teeth.

"Good. Well, let's get started." Applegate sipped his coffee, peering at his notes. "Why don't we begin with the very first day."

"You mean the day that Mark killed my friend Stella in front of me?" Peter asked, his voice icy.

Applegate tapped at the recorder quickly, stopping it. He chuckled for a moment. "Peter. I have no idea what you're talking about. Is this Stella someone from 1942 or from your past 2013 existence?"

"My past. You said you wanted me to talk about the very beginning. I'm telling you what I remember," Peter retorted. He felt a bead of sweat slide down his face.

"Whatever happened before the actual mission is irrelevant," Applegate said. He cleared his throat and hit record once more, rewinding just a bit to delete the previous part. "All right. So. You're in the time machine. Now tell me what happened."

Peter allowed his mind to drift. He tried to calm his rushing heart. "We arrived in 1942. Julie, Dr. Lamb, Dr. Larsson, and I. We met with Dr. Epson, who believed us about our origin almost instantly. His assistant, one Michael Gallagher, disputed us. We soon learned that he was a mole."

"Dr. Epson had an informant? Just as my counterpart suspected," Applegate said, his voice serious.

"Yes. We were alerted to a secret society run by Asher Mandrake, who was very concerned with our mission. I was kidnapped and taken to their offices."

Applegate's eyes were wide. "Kidnapped?"

Peter sighed. "Yes. Kidnapped. But ultimately, at least in the beginning, Mandrake wanted the mission to succeed."

Applegate held up his finger once more. "You told him about the mission—"

Peter brought both hands to the desk. There was so much to go over. "You don't understand. We wouldn't have been able to go on with the mission, otherwise. We'd still be in 1942, in some jail cell, if we hadn't told him."

"Relax, Peter," Applegate said.

"I'll relax when you tell me when I can see my kids again," Peter said.

"Your family is fine," Applegate said. "Please. Continue your story."

Peter flared his nostrils and continued. He told the story

from the beginning, from the train ride across the country to New York, where he and Julie had taken the passports from the couple who, they found out later, had been eliminated.

Applegate nearly fell out of his chair at this news. "Eliminated?" he asked. He leaned toward Peter and tapped his fingers against the desk. "You may have in fact destroyed two entire timelines, Peter. We can't know how this will affect—"

Peter looked at him grimly. "No, we can't. But you've been living in this timeline forever, haven't you? And you're still here." Peter thought for a moment. "What about my family? Are they still here?"

"Peter," Applegate said, turning his head toward the door. He'd tired of this, Peter assumed. "I think that's enough for this session. Randall!"

Randall burst through the door. "Yes, sir."

"Please show Peter back to his room. Peter, you're to stay there until our session tomorrow."

"How long is this going to go on?" Peter asked.

"As long as it takes," Applegate said, raising an eyebrow toward the sky.

Peter followed Randall, feeling completely defeated. He began to wonder if he would ever get out of there; he knew he couldn't trust anything that Applegate said to him. He just needed to get through the debriefing.

The next day seemed to go on much like the first. Peter and Applegate argued; Applegate stopped the tape and reprimanded him with a sour word, with a rewind of the tape. "If you want to get out of here to see your family, Peter, you'll cooperate," he said, tapping his tongue against the top of his mouth again and again. "Never have I seen such lack of cooperation during a debriefing. We're here to help each other, Peter. Remember that."

———————✦———————

Five days later, Peter sat at the same desk. He hadn't been able to eat for days; he'd been tossing and turning every night. He needed to get out of there. His thoughts had begun to revolve in a sort of helter-skelter: Julie, his children, even Minnie. He'd begun to think that those memories were only illusions—that nothing in his life had really happened.

"Julie voluntarily stayed in Oradour-sur-Glane, then?" Applegate asked many hours later, tapping his pencil against his notebook.

The hum of the tape recorder had begun to grind into Peter's mind. He brought his fist forward with a sudden anger. "I already told you. She had to, to look after Marion. Just tell me if my kids exist here or not. Tell me if I even had kids to begin with. I don't know how this time travel shit works. I don't even know if I exist in this timeline. Suppose my parents never had me; suppose I was never married."

Applegate clucked his tongue against the roof of his mouth again, his eyes flashing. "What makes you question me, Peter?" he asked. He tapped at the tape recorder once more, stopping it.

Peter thought about that for a moment, frustrated. Applegate had lied to him at nearly every opportunity. He'd spied on him; he'd taken his friends and killed them. For all Peter knew, Applegate could have lied about everything. His children might never have been. Tori. Brett. Peter tried to picture their faces in his mind. He sputtered, looking for words. "We didn't exactly have a history of trust," he murmured.

Applegate rolled his head back a little. "History of trust?" he sneered. "So we had a deceitful relationship in your past, eh?"

Peter slammed his fist onto the desk, making the tape recorder bounce. "The hell with you," he said. "I've told you everything you need to know. I've completed your mission, and more. You failed to tell me some secret society was going to come after us and try to blow us up with a bomb. You didn't tell us that the war was going to break out in Oradour-sur-Glane the very moment we arrived. You didn't tell us anything."

"You knew the variables, Peter."

But Peter looked at him furiously.

"All right, Peter. I understand. I'm just as lost and confused as you are. You have to understand—I received an anonymous envelope some ten years ago, and all I could think of was that it was a joke. Then, as some of the things I'd read in it started to come true, I re-evaluated everything. I started to look into everything the other Harrison Applegate had sent. I looked into the entire team, and into Dr. Epson. You wouldn't believe how much I had to put on the line to pull this stunt off. In my own timeline, life seemed pretty great," Applegate said as he methodically tucked all of the documents and paperwork strewn across the table into a manila folder. "I suppose that life in your timeline was much different, and I respect that. I just had to make sure that everything you experienced in 1942 coincided with my, um—the other Applegate's notes on the mission. The mere fact that the mission was a success is sincerely incredible."

His eyes traced Peter's face. "I'm sorry for the lies I told you, in the past. I can't tell you if they were meant for your protection and for the benefit of the mission or not. I can, however, assure you that your children are fine. They were unaffected by the mission. I think you'll find, in fact, that they benefited from it."

Peter felt his face releasing its tension. A small tear dripped from his eye. He was exhausted, beyond anything else. He needed to see someone other than Applegate—someone who could assure him that everything that had been worth it, that all his sacrifices hadn't been for naught. "Let me see them," he whispered. His throat felt tight.

Applegate rapped his knuckles on the desk. The noise echoed through the room. Randall burst through the door, on command, and nodded curtly.

"Prepare the car, Randall," Applegate said. His eyes searched Peter's. "It's time."

CHAPTER 27

Applegate and Peter sat in the back of the black limousine as it traveled through the city. Peter cracked the window and breathed in deeply, closing his eyes. He was going home.

The car rolled on past Peter's old neighborhood. He turned his head quickly, toward Applegate. "I thought—"

"Not everything can stay the same, Peter," Applegate said. "You should keep that in mind. Change has a tendency to promote a butterfly effect, which we spoke of in greater detail during your training. Whatever you did in the past probably affected where you ultimately chose to live in this timeline."

"But," Peter began, his voice having lost its synchronicity with his thoughts. "What if ... I can't remember?"

"I'm not saying that it will be easy, but trust in yourself and I'm sure you'll do fine. Peter, consider your life before the mission, and how far you've come, how much you've grown, all because of what you experienced. Simply arriving at a house that is new to you should be a breeze," Applegate said, attempting to build Peter's confidence.

Peter nodded. As the car sped toward his new life, his new home, he thought back through all the moments of his transformation. All thanks to his journey through not one, but two linear shifts. Applegate was right—he did feel like a new man, full of confidence that hadn't been present in his previous life.

"And you mustn't tell them anything that might confuse them, Peter," Applegate continued. "As far as they know, your job kept you away from them for a mere four weeks. They've been waiting for your return, of course. A few things have changed. Tori has gone on her first date, for one." Applegate's eyes were amused. "I'm sure the boy was glad not to have you waiting at the front door."

Peter's heart ached. Before the mission he'd been constantly drinking, missing entire days with his children because he felt as if he were at the bottom of a deep well. Now, he shook with the understanding that he'd missed thirty days of their lives. Tori had begun dating? So much could alter in a child's life, so quickly. Time was so fleeting.

The limousine pulled up in front of a quiet brick home. The house was smaller than the one Peter and Minnie had purchased in his original timeline, but it was decent, with beautiful flowers out front. He wondered if he and Minnie had been happy here, in this timeline's past. He imagined himself poring through old photographs of the two of them, pictures of adventures they hadn't really had, the first time around. He knew it didn't matter that they didn't share memories anymore, of course. He knew she was gone.

Peter unbuckled his seat belt and thrust his hand toward Applegate. Applegate accepted it, and the men shook hands.

"It's been one hell of a ride," Peter said.

"I can't thank you enough for all you've done, Mr. Cooper," Applegate said. "Now, you'd better get going. I know Minnie's been preparing your favorite meal for your arrival. I had Randall call a few hours ago. She's anxious to see you."

Peter's chest constricted as the air whooshed from his lungs. His grip tightened around Applegate's hand. "Wha-what did you say?" he stammered.

Applegate's eyebrow rose. "I'm sorry, Peter. Is there a problem?" Applegate winked knowingly.

Peter released his grip on Applegate's hand and brought his

hands toward his chest. He opened his mouth to speak, but his breath wouldn't come.

Minnie? *Minnie?* Inside of this strange house?

"Peter?" Applegate said, trying to get his attention once more. "Peter. Remember. You mustn't say anything about ..." But Peter's mind was somewhere else. He was on his own, and Minnie was the only thing on his mind. She was alive!

Peter lurched toward the car door. He pushed against it, stepping out onto the sidewalk. He walked with his head high toward the house, still feeling Applegate's presence behind him. He felt like he was walking through another dimension. His head spun. The flowers gleamed up at him: purples, yellows, pinks. They were petunias—Minnie's favorite. He swallowed, trying to find words. What would he say to her, if she was truly there? What would he do?

He brought his hand forward and grasped the door handle. The door was unlocked, allowing him entrance into this new world—the world of this timeline's Peter. He stepped warily into the foyer, gazing at a portrait he knew well—one that had been hanging in his own home, back in his previous timeline. Peter, Minnie, Brett, and Tori—taken about ten years before. His children's faces gleamed at him, and blood rushed in his head. The picture was exactly the same—down to the bad sweater he'd picked for the session. He ran his fingers through his hair, neglecting to shut the door behind him.

He felt like he was a ghost as he crept through the house, into the living room. He heard a slight sizzling as he walked further toward the kitchen; the aroma of steak simmered through the house.

She was making his favorite meal.

Peter stood like a shadow in the doorway to the kitchen. The young woman he'd met so long ago beneath the cathedral steps—his beautiful Minnie—stood facing the kitchen stove. She was stirring something. A small apron covered her pretty skirt, and her hair was ruffled a bit in back—as if she'd just risen from a nap. He could hear the scraping of the spoon against the side of the saucepan. Peter leaned his head against the side of the doorway, feeling a growing weight in his chest. He couldn't breathe. He didn't want to alter the moment by intruding on it. He wanted to hold this moment forever in his heart. He wanted to watch her stir whatever was in the pan, watch her live this beautiful life—in this future she was never meant to have.

Minnie was whistling something, a melody triggered a memory in Peter's mind. Peter's heart ached for her. God, his beautiful wife was alive.

Suddenly, she turned her head. She spun around, leaning against the stove. She pressed her hand to her heart, gasping with laughter. "Peter! How long have you been standing there?" Her face was so happy, so vibrant. She looked just like she had the last time he had seen her, so many, many years before.

Peter started to cry. He rushed toward her and wrapped his arms around her, spun her in a circle. She tipped her head back with glee, laughing as he did it. He kissed her neck, the side of her face. The tears moistened her face, as well, and she looked at him with concern. "Peter. Peter, baby. Why are you crying?"

But Peter could only shake his head. He had gone all those years without her; he'd fallen to the bottom of the bottle and burst his way back up again. He'd had to travel back to 1942; he'd had to survive war. And in spite of all his fears, it hadn't been for nothing. He had his wife back. He had her in his arms.

"Peter. It's all right. You're home with me, now," Minnie told him, pressing her nose to his. She wrapped her arms around his neck and kissed him passionately. Their lips fit so perfectly. "We missed you around here," she said, winking.

"Minnie," Peter finally said. His throat cracked. He brought his hands to her cheeks. "God, my beautiful girl. What would I do without you?"

"Gosh. You must have had some trip, huh?" Minnie asked, rubbing at his back. She kissed him again, still looking at him with a confused expression on her face. "You know, a lot has changed around here since you've been gone."

"I can only imagine," Peter murmured, collapsing into the

chair at the kitchen table. He blinked around this mysterious kitchen—this place he'd never been in before. He grabbed his wife's waist again; he wanted to feel her, touch her. He brought her down on his lap. She gasped lightly, laughing. The laughter was infectious, making Peter's entire body relax. She wrapped her arms around him and kissed him again and again.

"I won't leave you again," Peter whispered, gazing into her eyes. "Please. Know that." He grasped her shoulders, looking at her intently. She had to know that he would protect her, that things would be different.

Suddenly, they both heard a door slam. "Mom! Someone left the door open!" The voice was Tori's. She came rushing through the foyer, her school backpack still strapped to her back. She dropped it, her eyes wide. "Dad! You're back!" She wrapped her arms around her mother and father.

Peter grabbed her head and pulled it toward him, fitting it neatly against his shoulder, like a puzzle piece. "Oh, Tori. God. I missed you so much."

"It's been too long, Dad," Tori murmured into his ear. "Please don't leave us for so long again."

She pulled back, blinking at him. "Plus. Mom's a wreck without you." She winked at her mother, who blushed.

"Come on, Tori. Give it a rest." Minnie laughed good-naturedly.

Peter couldn't believe what he was seeing. His wife had never been around their raucous teenager. He imagined the fights they'd had in his absence, and his heart nearly burst with happiness. They had a relationship! They knew each other, in this future. His child had a mother. This—this was the happiest day of his life.

Tori sat down across from him and began eating a granola bar, chattering about school. Minnie stood up, grazing her fingers across Peter's eyebrow, across his ear. They exchanged a look, and in that moment Peter felt a passion he thought had been lost a long time ago.

The door opened and crashed closed once more. Minnie

shook from her reverie and called out, "If I've told you once, Brett, I've told you a hundred times!" But her face shone with laughter, with happiness.

"Sorry, Mom." Brett shuffled into the room and dropped his backpack immediately. "Dad!" His familiar face burst into a smile. Peter stood and held his son close, feeling the strength and vitality in him.

Nearly overwhelmed, Peter peered around the small kitchen in the tiny home he would now call his own. His wife looked at him with gleaming, loving eyes; his daughter chattered on, her eyes turned toward him full of adoration and hope. His son was growing so strong, so certain in his movements. His family was complete. Peter realized that while he'd been waiting for them to be a part of his life once more, all this time, they'd simply been waiting for him to return to this life—to the timeline in which he truly belonged.

Peter was home.

EPILOGUE

Six weeks after Peter arrived home in his new timeline, he sat down at the desk in the small, cluttered study just down the hall from the bedroom he shared with Minnie. She'd left earlier that morning with the children for her job as a real estate agent. She dressed so precisely in her pencil skirt, her blazer. She had kissed him in the morning, asking him to sleep in. His protestations hadn't been enough to sway her. She'd hurried out the door, gathering books and lunch boxes and complaining kids along the way.

For the first several weeks after his return, Peter hadn't allowed himself a moment away from Minnie. He'd had so much to talk to her about. Just little things, really; nothing earnest, nothing important. He knew he couldn't talk to her about the mission; he couldn't share with her all he'd been through—all he'd experienced without her. But he'd grasped her hand continually, asking her questions about herself—little things he already remembered from some shadow of his past.

"Haven't we talked about this before?" Minnie had asked him one evening over beers out on the deck.

Peter had shrugged. "Maybe. But I want to hear it again."

But now, he was giving her space. He was assimilating into this life. He hadn't heard from Applegate at all, and he was beginning to believe everything had been some sort of treacherous dream. The memories portrayed for him in each of the photo albums Minnie kept so diligently seemed more like a reality he understood, that he remembered. Sure, in his old timeline, Minnie had died , but this timeline offered a Lake Tahoe camping trip in the past, during that very same weekend. He had the photos to prove it. Minnie stood next to him in the photos, her face gleaming. Brett had mud caked on his face, and Tori was rolling her eyes. God, what a weekend they'd had. Peter didn't like to think about the other weekend—the one from the now-nonexistent timeline. Not if he didn't have to.

Peter sat at the desk, thinking about his life—about the insane memories flitting through his mind. Now that he was safely home, he wanted to find a way to capture these memories before he lost them. He wanted to find a way to hone them, to understand them. Which was why he suddenly picked up a pen and a pad of paper and began writing small notes. Just little things, in the beginning.

"The streets of 1942 New York were humming with life as Julie and I reached the Empire State Building. I felt her lips on mine up there on the hundred-something floor, and I felt I could love her, even after all the troubles of my past. I felt like we were two souls searching for each other, uncertain of both our pasts and our futures."

But then, these words gave way to others. He began to think he could write an entire memoir and call it a novel. He could even publish it, if he wanted to. Perhaps people would scoff at it; they would question how World War II could have ever ended in 1945, especially given the existence of Operation Sledgehammer.

He tapped his pen against his lip, thinking about this world in a backwards sense. He'd been on the other side of the mirror. He was, in so many ways, like Alice. Trying to convince people that other realms existed was nearly impossible.

Before he knew it, several hours had gone by as he scratched on the pad of paper, searching for a way to recreate his experiences and give completion to his memories. He heard the door shut in the foyer, and he started for a moment, lost in thought.

"Hello?"

Peter heard Minnie's voice as she waltzed through the door. He sprang from his chair and rushed toward her. He grabbed her around the waist, lifting the grocery bag from her arms. "Hi, baby," he murmured. He caught her lips with his. "How was your day?"

Minnie bit her lip, studying him. "I sort of have something to tell you."

Peter's heart began to beat quickly. He studied her face. "What is it?" Her eyes were still bright, looking at him. They were in uncharted territory; their relationship and their life together could go anywhere.

"Well. There's this investment property. And I know I should have talked about it with you before I did it, but I've had my eye on it ever since you went on that work trip. And I—they told me I couldn't wait."

Peter's eyes widened. "You put an offer on a house?" he asked.

Minnie nodded, biting her lip once more. Her pretty dark hair swirled around her chin. "Are you mad?" she asked.

Peter laughed. "Of course not! This place is too small for our hectic lives now. Tell me about it!"

He walked through the foyer, toward the kitchen. He placed the bag on the counter, taking out the groceries as he spoke.

"Well. It's over on Glencoe Drive. I know we've always really liked that neighborhood—"

Peter spun around, shocked. Glencoe was his old house's street name. He looked for the right words to say. "Oh, that neighborhood," he said, nodding. "Pretty affluent."

Minnie brought her fingers toward her lips. "I know. I know. It's just—the business is going so well. And with your work. I just figured it was time for us to broaden our horizons a little bit." She rested her hands on his chest and rubbed at his shirt, massaging the muscles beneath suggestively. "It could be a good change of pace, you know?"

"Tell me about the house," he said, his eyes bright.

He listened as Minnie described the very home that they'd chosen together, all those years before, during his old timeline. How young she'd been, then. How beautiful she still was, now. History was repeating itself, just a few years late.

"You say it has a fireplace?" Peter asked.

Minnie brightened. "Oh, yes. It's this beautiful fireplace. I don't think it's been updated since the 40s, when they built the place. We might have to do some renovations, you know."

"Well. We'll certainly want to use the fireplace," he mused.

Peter and his wife brought their lips together, there in the sunlight of their small kitchen. His hopes lingered on the future they would forge together: a future in the home they'd been meant to share years and years before. And as Peter gave himself to this woman he loved more than life itself, his mind reached toward one small element of his plan he still hadn't forgotten.

His journal still lay at the base of the fireplace floor. Proof of his past. And strength for his future.

ABOUT THE AUTHOR

When not practicing architecture, Paul works on his writing. He lives in Littleton, Colorado, with his wife and daughter. To learn more about him and his books, visit www.Paul-Kohler.net

www.ingramcontent.com/pod-product-compliance
Lightning Source LLC
Chambersburg PA
CBHW020459260626
47156CB00006B/1789